THE SUNFLOWER GIRL

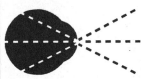

This Large Print Book carries the
Seal of Approval of N.A.V.H.

THE SUNFLOWER GIRL

ROSANNA CHIOFALO

THORNDIKE PRESS
A part of Gale, a Cengage Company

A Cengage Company

Farmington Hills, Mich • San Francisco • New York • Waterville, Maine
Meriden, Conn • Mason, Ohio • Chicago

Copyright © 2018 by Rosanna Chiofalo.
Thorndike Press, a part of Gale, a Cengage Company.

ALL RIGHTS RESERVED
Thorndike Press® Large Print Clean Reads.
The text of this Large Print edition is unabridged.
Other aspects of the book may vary from the original edition.
Set in 16 pt. Plantin.

LIBRARY OF CONGRESS CIP DATA ON FILE.
CATALOGUING IN PUBLICATION FOR THIS BOOK
IS AVAILABLE FROM THE LIBRARY OF CONGRESS

ISBN-13: 978-1-4328-5357-0 (hardcover)

Published in 2018 by arrangement with Kensington Books, an imprint
of Kensington Publishing Corp.

Printed in Mexico
1 2 3 4 5 6 7 22 21 20 19 18

AUTHOR'S NOTE

While I drew from historical facts for this novel, I also took creative license for the purpose of developing the story. For instance, I made up FAF — Florentines Against Fascism — the Resistance organization that Franco and Maria belonged to, but it was loosely based on the actual Italian Resistance movement called CLN — National Liberation Committee (*Comitato di Liberazione Nazionale*). The other Resistance organization I mention, GAP — *Gruppi di Azione Patriottica* — was an actual Resistance organization.

There were several books that were instrumental in my research for *The Sunflower Girl: Italy's Sorrow* by James Holland (Harper-Collins, 2008); *The Other Italy* by Maria de Blasio Wilhelm (Norton, 1988); and *Partisan Diary* by Ada Gobetti, translated and edited by Jomarie Alano (Oxford University Press, 2014). In addition, I got the idea of the birdcage that Maria places in the window of her apartment as a sign for Franco to let him know that there were no guards at their home making inquiries or standing guard outside from *Partisan Diary,* the published diary of the late Italian Resistance fighter Ada Gobetti. Ada's neighbor employed the use of placing a birdcage in his window to alert Ada if it was truly safe for her to return home.

Per mia madre, la mia migliore amica
e il mio eroe.
For my mother, my best friend
and my hero.

PROLOGUE:
THE SUNFLOWER GIRL

Siena, Italy, 1970

Dante was dreaming about her again.

She was running through the same field of sunflowers he had seen her in the last time she visited him in his dreams. Her long, chestnut brown hair bounced along her back, mimicking the motion of the sunflowers that swayed to and fro as she brushed past them. As she ran, she dropped roses in the most vivid hues behind her. Every few seconds, she looked over her shoulder to make sure Dante was following her. She would laugh and then turn away, running even faster. This time, Dante was sure he was finally going to catch up to her. But just when he was within reach, he would wake up startled.

The dream was always the same. Sometimes, a few of the details changed, like the dress she was wearing. She never seemed to wear the same color dress. This time, it had

9

been a vivid scarlet hue. It was almost too bright. The sunflower field and the roses were always present. He wondered why the flowers didn't change, only her dress, and, sometimes, she didn't run in her dreams, but walked ahead, always heading away from him. But though she walked, Dante could still never catch up to her.

As long as Dante could remember, he hadn't really cared for flowers and hadn't understood why people went crazy for them, especially when they were given as gifts since they didn't last long. But now he was seeing them in a whole new light and couldn't believe that as an artist he had never paid that much attention to them before. When he rode his bike to the small towns outside of Siena, he often passed sunflower fields, which were abundant throughout the Tuscan countryside. He could see the beauty in most flowers like roses, gardenias, or lilies, but he'd always thought sunflowers were ugly with their gangly height, pointy petals, and large dials. And yellow was his least favorite color. Their only feature he'd ever liked was the edible seeds. Every August, when he was a child, he and his friends would pull the ripe sunflower seeds and eat them. But now whenever he was riding his bicycle by the fields, he'd never had the urge to stop and take a few of the sunflower seeds.

Dante had begun dreaming about the mysterious woman six months ago. Shortly afterward, he decided that if he couldn't catch her in his dreams, then he would have to capture her in his paintings. Dante sat up in bed and let his eyes wander from painting to painting, each depicting the beautiful, almost ethereal woman. He was beginning to feel obsessed with her, but he wasn't worried. Obsession was good for an artist, and ever since he began painting *La Ragazza del Girasole — The Sunflower Girl —* his work was selling faster than he could produce it.

Although he felt his paintings of the sunflower girl were among his best, he'd only brought a few to Siena's Piazza del Campo, where he displayed and sold his paintings. He had attempted to take the entire collection with him on several occasions. After all, he needed to make money. But he'd always felt a strong pull urging him to leave the paintings behind, even though he had taken photographs of them so they wouldn't be completely erased from his memory once they were sold. She had become a constant companion to him in his shabby little loft apartment that sat above a bread shop, and he wasn't ready to completely let her go — at least not yet.

He was distracted from his thoughts by the aroma of bread baking. At least the aromas from the shop all day disguised some of the paint fumes he was always breathing. And the owner, Signora Fiorucci, who was also his landlady, gave him a large loaf of *ciabatta* every morning, convinced he would starve if she didn't do so. The old lady wasn't too far off in her suspicions. There were days when he would forget to eat, and, even when his stomach was growling furiously, he would ignore it when he was in the middle of his painting. His friends, most of whom were also aspiring artists, teased him all the time.

"Dante doesn't need a girlfriend. He has his sunflower girl," as his best friend Luca often loved to say.

"Why don't you give her a real name, Dante? Isn't it about time after all these months? Surely, you don't whisper *'ragazza del girasole'* as you make love to her." Paolo, a former art school classmate, snickered.

"All joking aside, why haven't you given her a name yet? She looks like a Maria Magdalena to me," Luca said.

"The former prostitute in the Bible?" Paolo asked, then broke into laughter.

"*Basta!* Enough!" Dante yelled. "You are both artists. Haven't you ever been touched by your own personal muse?"

Almost as soon as he was done uttering the words, he knew he'd set himself up for the next joke.

"Of course, we've been touched, but our muses are real — they are present here in the flesh," Paolo said, elbowing Luca, as they laughed once more.

"Forgive us, Dante. We are just having fun with you. Actually, we're jealous because ever since you started painting your special girl, your work has been selling like crazy, while Paolo and I are still lucky if we sell one of our paintings a week. If only we could have dreams that inspire us as much as yours do you."

Dante ran his hand through his long bangs, which always hung over his eyes. His hair was getting too long, but instead of wasting time — or the money — to get a haircut, he tied it back in a ponytail. Neglect had become commonplace in his life, whether it was his diet, his grooming, or replacing his wardrobe, which was beginning to resemble the tattered clothes the beggars in the piazza wore. His work was the only aspect of his life that he devoted himself completely to, and though he used

13

to function on only a few hours of sleep, he'd begun sleeping a full night, in hopes that his sunflower girl would visit him. For when he woke up after a night of dreaming about her, he would feel invigorated and inspired to begin a new painting.

"So getting back to my earlier question, Dante, why don't you give her a real name?" Luca asked.

Dante shrugged his shoulders. "Not every artist has given his female subjects Christian names. Why do I need to?"

"*Vero.* That is true, my friend. And calling her 'the sunflower girl' further adds to her mystique, no?" Paolo offered.

"I suppose, but that isn't why I haven't named her. It's just . . ." Dante's voice trailed off. They would think he was crazy if he told them his reasons.

"What?" Luca prodded.

"I don't know. It just doesn't feel right. That's all."

After that day, Dante had often thought to himself that perhaps it was time to name the woman in his paintings something else. But the reason he hadn't, the reason he was afraid to tell his friends, was that a part of him couldn't help feeling she was real and that she existed somewhere other than his dream world. It was crazy. He knew it. He

14

just couldn't bring himself to name her.

Sighing deeply, Dante pulled back the bed covers and got out of bed, stretching his aching back. Yesterday, he'd been hunched over all day as he painted his latest work. This one was much different from the others. He was going to paint a series in which each work would be one feature of the sunflower girl's face and body. He was starting with her eyes — the eyes that had captivated Dante as they teased and urged him to chase her through the field. The next painting would be her nose and lips. Then he would proceed to her body. He packed up three smaller paintings; each of these represented his muse in a different stage in life — child, adolescent, and young woman. He would try to sell these today.

Opening the door to his loft, he found Signora Fiorucci's daily loaf of *ciabatta,* wrapped in a clean dish towel, waiting for him.

He kissed the loaf. "God bless you, Signora Fiorucci," Dante whispered, smiling as he placed the bread in his satchel.

As he drove his shabby Fiat to the piazza, he passed a neighboring house with a small garden of sunflowers adjacent to the home. He shook his head. The flowers didn't look right at all and looked as if they had been plopped absentmindedly into this small plot. He noticed the seeds of the flowers looked ripe and realized they would be since it was now mid-August. For some reason, he decided to stop today and snip one of the sunflowers, making sure no one from the property was standing behind the windows witnessing his transgression. Getting back in his car, he rode down the road and pulled over to the curb. He stared at the sunflower as fragments of his recurrent dreams flashed through his mind. Perhaps on the way back to his apartment, he would snip more flowers and keep them in a vase with water in his room.

Once he arrived in the Piazza del Campo, he set up his easels and canvases. Sitting on the ground, he was waiting for the usual throng of people to make their way across the bridge when a woman came into his line of vision.

"Scusi, signore. Quanto costa?" A young man was asking Dante how much his painting of the sunflower girl depicted as an adolescent cost. But Dante ignored him.

His eyes followed the woman. Her hair was the same chestnut hue as that of the woman from his dreams. And her body. He swore the same perfect hourglass figure he'd admired in his dreams was now standing a mere few feet away from him. And then, the woman looked up, her gaze meeting Dante's. He froze. It *was* her. She offered a shy smile, then turned her attention back to the woman by her side — an older woman, perhaps her mother, no, maybe her grandmother. The older woman had her arm linked through the younger woman's arm as they walked slowly toward a flower vendor. He then noticed the younger woman carried a large straw basket in her free hand. When she and her companion reached the vendor, she took out a large bundle of roses — all in different colors. Dante almost gasped out loud. The details were just like those from his dreams. He began walking slowly toward her. He had to see her up close and be certain that she really was the same woman from his dreams.

The flower vendor paid the woman for her roses. Dante was now just a couple of feet away from her when suddenly he felt himself lifted and thrown forward. Hard objects hit him in the head and the body. Sitting up, he saw he was covered in apples. An old man was hurrying to pick up the apples that had fallen from his cart as he yelled to Dante, *"Scusi, signore!"*

Dante got to his feet and frantically looked to where his sunflower girl had stood with her grandmother, but she was gone. He strained his eyes to see if she was up ahead or perhaps had gone in the opposite direction, but the crowds were even denser that day than usual, making it more difficult for him to find her. He hurried over to the flower vendor.

"Where did those two women who were just here go? The younger one sold you all those roses." Dante pointed to the flowers that the vendor was now separating and tying with ribbons.

"How should I know?" He shrugged his shoulders before adding, "I guess they went back home." The man shook his head in annoyance and returned to organizing his bouquets.

"Do they always come here?"

"*Si*, their roses are the best I've ever laid eyes on. My customers snatch them up right away. Would you like to buy a few for a special woman?"

"So she grows roses?"

"She and her mother have a rose farm in the countryside."

"Which town?"

"I don't know. I'm a businessman. I don't have time for pleasantries."

"*That* woman was her mother?" Dante asked incredulously.

"*Si, si.* I know she looks quite a bit old to be her mother. I thought the same thing when I first met them. She must have had her when she was older."

"Are they always together?"

"Not always. Why all the questions?"

The vendor looked at him suspiciously. Dante pointed to one of the rose bouquets that the vendor had already tied with a ribbon.

"I'll take that one, the one with the red roses."

The vendor was pleased Dante was actually buying flowers and not merely wasting his time.

"What is the young woman's name?" Dante looked at his money, trying not to sound as if his life depended on learning her name.

"Ah! I see. You have a thing for Signorina Ferraro."

"No, no. I'm an artist and need models to pose for me. She has the right look. I would like to hire her."

The vendor arched his brow. "I see. Well, she is not that type of girl."

"No, no, you misunderstand me once again, *signore*! Of course, I can tell she is not that type of girl. She would be clothed. I don't paint nudes."

19

"Hmmm." The vendor still did not believe him and began busying himself with tying the rest of the roses Signorina Ferraro and her mother had sold him.

Dante took all of his *lire* out of his pocket. "How many roses can I buy?"

The vendor reached for the money, but Dante raised his hand in the air.

"But first, I need to know Signorina Ferraro's christened name."

"Anabella. Which color roses do you want?"

"You decide."

"*Va bene.* Has anyone ever told you that all of you artists are a strange lot?"

Dante ignored him. "Anabella. Anabella." He kept silently whispering her name. The beautiful name fit her perfectly. Now all he needed to do was find the woman from his dreams.

CHAPTER 1
ANABELLA

Pienza, Italy, 1950

Six-year-old Anabella Ferraro's world was filled with beauty. Wherever she looked, roses in every hue surrounded her. There were the softest shade of pink roses, creamy white roses, deep red roses, orange roses that resembled the copper sunsets over Tuscany, and her favorite of all — exquisitely vivid yellow roses. She giggled as she skipped among the rows of flowers on her mother's sprawling rose farm. Mamma always clipped a few just for Anabella, which she would hug to her chest as she carried them to the house, inhaling their sweet fragrance.

Only Anabella and Mamma lived in the house on the vast property they owned. Papà had been taken by the angels to heaven — the other paradise. Mamma had told Anabella that their beautiful home was their paradise on Earth, but there was

21

another paradise even more stunning, where Papà now lived. A place where Anabella could eat all her favorite foods like *pane con cioccolato, pasta Bolognese, zuccotto* cake, *nocciola* gelato, and *torrone.* It was a place where no one was ever in pain. A place where Anabella could run anywhere she wanted to, not just on the land that encompassed their property.

There were days when Anabella would be sad, wishing Papà were here, even though Mamma continually reminded her he was with her.

"Your papà is always with you, even though you cannot see him. He is always watching over you and protecting you. Remember that, Anabella."

But Anabella was confused. How could her father be with her and watching her if he wasn't here with them? She wanted to be able to hear his voice rather than imagining what he sounded like. And instead of merely seeing him in the old photographs Mamma kept on her dresser, Anabella wanted to be able to kiss his cheek and play with his eyeglasses. She wanted to be able to crawl into his lap and press her head up against his chest as his heartbeat lulled her to sleep, just as she did every night with Mamma.

Mamma assured Anabella that someday, the three of them would all be reunited in this other paradise. Sometimes, Anabella stared up at the sky and talked to Papà. She usually spoke to him about her favorite roses and what she was learning from Mamma. She also spoke to the roses when she was out in the gardens alone. She thought of them as her friends who played with her when her mother was too busy or when the workers on the farm had gone home for the day. She even had names for them. Only Cioccolato knew that she spoke to the roses. But that was all right. Cioccolato wouldn't tell anyone — for he was her chocolate Labrador retriever and her best friend, second to Mamma. Mamma didn't seem to mind though that Cioccolato was her other best friend.

Unlike the rest of the children in her village of Pienza, Anabella didn't attend school, even though it was just on the opposite side of the fence that hemmed in their rose farm. Mamma told her she could teach Anabella everything she needed to know. Anabella was content. After all, Mamma was her best friend in addition to her parent. And that was all she needed, as her mother always reminded her. Still, she couldn't help but be drawn to the school

23

yard as she was today. She put her face up against the wire diamond shapes that made up the fence and stared at the schoolchildren who were having their recess. The yard had a playground set, which is what captivated Anabella the most. The children screamed and pushed one another out of the way as they tried to reach the playground's slide and swings. Anabella wondered what it would be like to go down the shiny slide that always caused the children to squeal in delight and to fly high up into the air on the swings. Maybe she could get closer to Papà in the sky if she went on one of those swings.

Anabella had been so absorbed in her reverie that she hadn't noticed the boy who came over until she felt something hard hit her head. Startled, she looked up and saw the boy standing up on a small wooden box so he could reach over the fence and continue his assault of throwing pebbles and small rocks at Anabella. She covered her face as she cried out. Within seconds, her mother came running over.

"Cretino! Vai via!" Signora Ferraro insulted the boy as she yelled at him to go away.

The boy narrowed his eyes at her as if he were about to cry and then rejoined his classmates on the playground.

"*Vieni, mia bella figlia.* Come, my beautiful daughter. Neither that boy nor anyone else will bother you again."

Anabella let her mother lead her away by the hand. She snuck a sideways glance toward the playground. She could see the boy who had thrown the rocks at her was chasing another boy as they laughed. Anabella was now far away in his thoughts, and she wondered why he had decided to hurt her. Did he not like the way she looked? Or maybe he didn't like that she was staring at him and the other children?

After that day, Mamma didn't let Anabella play outside during the time that the school had their recess.

"You can go out later around four o'clock. It won't be too hot then, and the sun will still be out for a few hours," Mamma had told her.

Anabella was an overly obedient child and rarely, if ever, questioned her mother's judgment. Mamma knew best and was teaching her everything not just in their homeschool lessons, but also in the garden. Mamma also explained to Anabella what she would need to know as she grew older and became a big girl someday.

One afternoon, Signora Ferraro had an emergency in the gardens and had left Anabella alone to finish her lunch. Usually, Signora Ferraro ate lunch with Anabella and then caught up on a few chores before going out to the gardens to finish her work there. Anabella had no idea that her mother was afraid to leave her unattended during the hours when the school had their recess and when it was time for the children to go home.

Anabella was playing with Rosa, her favorite doll. She loved braiding her hair and coming up with new ways to make Rosa even more pretty than she already was. Mamma had given Anabella the doll for her sixth birthday this year. And ever since that day, they had been inseparable. An idea came to her. She had seen in one of her fairy-tale books an illustration of a princess with a beautiful wreath of roses on her head. Excited, Anabella ran outside, forgetting that her mother had forbidden her to go out until four o'clock. When she stepped outside, at first, she ignored the sounds coming from the school yard of the children laughing and screaming. She was absorbed in pulling the roses from the bushes that Mamma had planted here just for Anabella so she could enjoy them and take a few of the flowers for herself if she wanted.

She held the roses against her chest and

began to walk toward her house when something shiny caught her peripheral vision. She turned toward the school yard and saw a large dollhouse. Its metal exterior gleamed in the sunlight. And the house was painted bright red, just like the roses that Mamma grew and sold the most. Red must be a lot of people's favorite color, Anabella guessed. She gasped when she saw a little girl emerge from the door in the house. She had no idea the house was for little girls and not dolls like her Rosa. The girl held a doll. It had blond hair but did not look as beautiful as Anabella's Rosa. Another girl giggled as she entered the house, but instead of entering it through the door that the first girl had come out of, she went around to the back of the house. Anabella could see her walking through the house as she passed the windows. Anabella went up to the fence to get a better look at the dollhouse. Maybe Mamma could buy her one for her birthday next year. But that was still a long way off.

"Ciao. Come ti chiami?"

Anabella jumped, remembering what had happened the last time someone was standing on the other side of the fence. It was one of the young women she'd seen watching over the children when they had recess.

"Anabella." She glanced down at her

sandals, noticing her toes pushing out well past the soles. She wondered when Mamma would take her into town to buy a new pair. Her heart leaped at the thought for she always enjoyed any outing they took.

"What a beautiful name! My name is Signorina Ducati. I am one of the teachers at the school." She waited to see if Anabella would say something, but Anabella continued to look down at the ground. Signorina Ducati noticed Anabella was clutching a few roses to her chest. Something about the sight made her heart twist a little. The girl looked so forlorn — unlike her students who were full of energy and didn't seem to have a care in the world. Not that the child looked unhappy, but she sensed there was a certain unrest in her.

"Where do you go to school, Anabella?"

"Here."

Signorina Ducati frowned for a moment before realizing what the little girl meant.

"You don't go to school, do you? That is why you are home today?"

Anabella finally looked up. She pointed to the sprawling house that stood behind her, past the beautiful rose garden. "My school is in there. At home. Mamma teaches me."

Signorina Ducati nodded. She strained her head to see if Anabella's mother was anywhere in sight. She spotted her in one of the rose gardens, working alongside a few men.

"Would you like to come play with the other children, Anabella?"

Anabella glanced at the dollhouse. The girls who had been playing with it were now gone. She could explore it all on her own. She looked up at Signorina Ducati and nodded.

"We'll have to ask your mother first. Can you tell her to come here?"

Anabella ran off. She was going to get to play in the big dollhouse — and Rosa, too! She couldn't wait. She ran even faster. The sooner she found Mamma, the sooner she could explore all the wonderful things the school yard had. Maybe she could even go on the swings and fly high up in the air and talk to Papà.

CHAPTER 2
SIGNORA FERRARO

Pienza, 1950

Signora Ferraro was tending to a cluster of yellow roses that had been infested with thrips. Hopefully she could treat them effectively and she would not lose the flowers.

"Mamma! Mamma! The teacher wants to talk to you."

"*Calmati,* Anabella. What are you talking about? Is this another one of your imaginary friends?"

Anabella blushed. It was true she had made up a few friends, but she only spoke to them when she thought she was alone. Mamma must've heard her. She shook her head.

"Then, what are you talking about, my dear child?" Signora Ferraro regretted asking her daughter about her imaginary friends once she saw her cheeks turn as crimson as some of the roses she grew.

"The teacher from the school on the other

side of our fence. She came to talk to me and asked me if I wanted to go play. Her name is Signorina Ducati."

Signora Ferraro frowned. How dare that woman approach her daughter?

"Are you mad, Mamma?"

"No, no. That is all right. Let us go talk to Signorina Ducati."

Anabella smiled. She ran ahead. Signora Ferraro did her best to quicken her pace. Though she was only thirty-five years old, she was often sore from all the crouching and bending she did on the rose farm. She had a few workers employed on the farm, but she loved to do as much as she could herself. Tending to the roses had saved her life many years ago, and she felt the most at peace when she was caring for them.

The teacher was waiting on the other side of the fence, watching the schoolchildren. Anabella ran up to the fence and pointed to her mother. For a moment, Signora Ferraro cringed at what she must do, but she could not falter. As Anabella's mother, she knew what was best for Anabella.

"Buongiorno, signora," the teacher called out to Signora Ferraro as she made her way toward the fence. The teacher smiled. She was an attractive woman, but her hand did not display an engagement or wedding ring.

31

"Buongiorno." Signora Ferraro nodded her head in the teacher's direction. "How can I help you?"

"My name is Signorina Ducati. I am the head teacher at the school."

"Signora Ferraro."

"Piacere, signora. I'm sorry to call you away from your work. Your garden is breathtaking."

"Grazie." Signora Ferraro did not offer more, for she did not want to encourage the teacher with pleasantries.

Signorina Ducati cleared her throat. "I've noticed Anabella on a few occasions watching the children during recess, and I asked her if she wants to play with them."

"But she is not a student of your school, Signorina Ducati. I thank you, but that won't be necessary." Out of her peripheral vision, Signora Ferraro saw the smile Anabella had had a moment ago quickly turn into a huge pout, and her eyes widened as if asking why. Signora Ferraro's heart tightened, but no matter how much her daughter was hurting, she would not be swayed.

"It would be no trouble at all, Signora Ferraro, and it would do her good to be around other children her age. Anabella tells me that she doesn't attend school and that you teach her at home."

"*Si.*" Signora Ferraro couldn't resist a curt tone for she knew what was coming.

"The school is public as you know, so it wouldn't cost you any money to enroll Anabella. I'm sure you have your hands beyond full as it is with the farm."

"This is none of your concern, Signorina Ducati. Please excuse me for being direct, but my daughter's welfare is no one's business but my own. I can assure you she is receiving as good an education with me at home — if not better — as she would be in your school."

"Of course, Signora Ferraro. I meant no offense. Will you at least allow her to come play in the school yard?"

Signora Ferraro followed Signorina Ducati's gaze, which fell on Anabella, who was now holding on to the fence, her face pressed up against it as she observed the children playing on the playground set.

"*Grazie,* Signorina Ducati, but I cannot allow my daughter to be out of my sight."

"I, and the other teachers, would be watching her."

"Again, thank you for your kind offer, Signorina Ducati, but we really need to return to the house. It is time for Anabella's nap." She pried Anabella's hand from the fence. "*Vieni,* Anabella. It's time to sleep."

Anabella looked down at her sandals, disappointment clearly etched across her features.

"*Ciao,* Anabella," Signorina Ducati called out to her, but Anabella ignored her.

"Perhaps another day, Signora Ferraro?"

The teacher was quite persistent, she would give her that. But what Signorina Ducati didn't know was that Signora Ferraro was even more persistent, especially where her convictions and her daughter's welfare were concerned.

"*Buongiorno,* Signorina Ducati," was all she said.

Signora Ferraro held on to Anabella's hand tightly, lest she break free from her grip. But she did not have to worry. It was rare that Anabella rebelled. She had been an exceptionally obedient child, even as a toddler. Sadness began seeping into Signora Ferraro that she was causing her daughter pain, but it was for her own good. Everything Signora Ferraro had done since she first learned she was pregnant with Anabella had been in her best interest.

"I'm not sleepy, Mamma. Can I just go play in my room?" Anabella looked up at her mother with her big brown eyes that often made Signora Ferraro lose her resolve and give in to whatever her beautiful daugh-

34

ter wanted.

"You have to nap first, Anabella. How will you grow up to be a big girl if you don't rest? Ah? You can play after you sleep. I'll play with you, too."

Her daughter was not lonely. She had her, Cioccolato, and the workers on the farm, who had become an extended family to Anabella. True, Signora Ferraro knew they were not other children, but her daughter was content. Besides, on a few occasions she'd witnessed those children be absolutely wicked to one another, just like the day she found that boy throwing rocks at Anabella. They would be nothing more than a bad influence. She would not have her daughter corrupted by those unruly brats.

"I'm sorry, Anabella. I know you wanted to go to the school yard, but it's not safe. Those swings go up too high, and you can fall off of them and break your legs. How would you help Mamma in the gardens if that happened? Or run with Cioccolato? You have all you need in our home — Cioccolato, Mario, Carlo, and Chiara. And of course, our beautiful roses. The other children don't have all of this, and I feel very sorry for them."

Anabella's eyes roamed over toward the rose bushes that surrounded them on either side as they made their way back to their house. But what about other little people like her? Like the children in the school yard. It was true that Cioccolato, and Mario, Carlo, and Chiara — the farm workers — were also her friends, but ever since she began noticing the schoolchildren, she had wondered what it would be like to talk to them and play with them.

"I'm going to make your favorite cake today."

"Zuccotto?" Anabella's eyes glowed as she looked up at her mother.

"*Si!* You can help me after you have your nap. This way the *zuccotto* will be all ready after we have our supper tonight."

Signora Ferraro had hoped to distract her daughter by mentioning her favorite dessert, which was a cake with a dome shape that was said to be in honor of the dome that sat atop Florence's famous Duomo Cathedral, also known as the Basilica di Santa Maria del Fiore.

Signora Ferraro had told Anabella all about the Duomo and had promised her that, when she was older, she would take her to see it someday. But whenever Anabella would ask when they were going, Signora Ferraro would say, "You're not big enough yet." A fear gripped her when she thought about her former childhood home in Florence.

"I can't wait to see the Duomo someday! Soon, I will be a big girl and can go, right, Mamma?" Anabella looked up at her mother with the widest, most innocent eyes.

Signora Ferraro nodded, happy to see that the light that was almost always present in Anabella's eyes had returned after her earlier disappointment. Signora Ferraro stopped walking and embraced her daughter fiercely. No one could ever break their bond. Signora Ferraro was as sure of that as she was of the sun that rose every morning.

CHAPTER 3
DANTE

Siena, 1970

Dante was working feverishly. He needed to hurry before the sun set. He was standing to the left of the open window in his one-room apartment, and as he painted, his eyes darted back and forth to the sky outside. It was important that he get the lighting perfect.

Of course, the painting depicted Anabella. How good it felt to know the name of his muse! He had been in exceptionally good spirits since the day he saw Anabella at the piazza. Tomorrow would be a week since he saw her, but he felt as if it had been only yesterday, since he'd replayed the moment in his mind over and over. As soon as he had arrived home after seeing the mysterious woman from his dreams, he had begun a new painting of her — the same painting he was now working on. He wanted to finish it tonight. Dante was hoping Anabella

38

would come to the piazza again tomorrow so he could show her his latest painting.

Driving home that day, he had realized he had forgotten to ask the flower vendor how often Anabella and her mother came to the piazza to sell the roses. Dante sensed it wasn't every week since he had never seen them before. Dante wondered how he had missed them in the past. He'd been going to the piazza to sell his work for a few months. He supposed he had been pre-occupied, either talking to people who were interested in buying his paintings or, when it was slow, drawing the famous Tuscan landmarks. The visitors who came to the piazza loved seeing Dante and the other artists present at work. Dante never painted in the piazza as a few other artists did. It was a waste of time since the paintings would not dry in time for customers to take them home the same day. True, sometimes customers left a deposit and arranged to pick up the completed paintings at the artist's home, but many lost interest when they learned the painting needed days to finish drying. He also didn't like to have an audience while he did his more serious paintings. So he drew when he was in the piazza. Drawing also brought him more money than just his finished paintings. He mainly drew a few silly landscapes, and, if someone asked him to do a portrait, he obliged. Although he was good at drawing, painting was where his true passion lay.

His pulse quickened as he added the final brush stroke to his newest sunflower girl painting.

"Finalmente!" he uttered aloud to himself as he stood back and took in his latest creation.

The painting featured a dramatic sky in all its glorious colors — pink, orange, blue — as the sun was preparing to make its descent. Beneath the sky, in the background was Siena's Piazza del Campo, but rather than being filled with the usual flurry of people, the square was empty with the exception of Anabella, who stood in the forefront of the painting. She was stepping into the piazza, her back facing the viewer of the painting, and her head was turned so that she was looking over her shoulder. Her smile invited the observer to follow her, as did her right hand, which was raised and held one single red rose. A few of the flower's petals had fallen to the ground, leaving a trail in the woman's wake.

Dante was certain this was his best painting of her. How could it not be? For now she was more than just a shadowy figure from his dreams. She was real. From the blush in her cheeks to the light that flickered in her eyes and even the veins in her hand that held out the rose, there was no doubt that the woman in this painting was alive, whereas his earlier paintings had depicted her with a paler complexion and a more ethereal quality.

Satisfied with the finished product, he dipped his paintbrush into some black paint and signed his name in the lower right-hand corner of the canvas: *Galletti.*

Yawning, he went to wash his hands in the bathroom. It was only now that he noticed how his back ached from the long hours spent painting. His stomach grumbled, reminding him that he hadn't eaten since just before noon. Wiping his hands dry, he walked over to the small icebox in his room and pulled out the bowl of minestrone that Signora Fiorucci had given him earlier in the day. He heated it up in a small pan on the stove.

As he ate his soup, his thoughts wandered to his mother, who always cooked minestrone for him when the weather turned cold. Although Signora Fiorucci's minestrone was good, it still didn't measure up to his mother's. As Dante's gift was painting, his mother's was cooking. How he missed her cooking. Dante had shown a passion for drawing when he was as young as four years old. He loved drawing the birds and insects he saw in the yard of his grandmother's home, where he and his mother lived. Nonna Andreanna and his mother were the only family he'd had. He'd never met his grandfather, who had died of a stroke before Dante was born. The same went for his father, who had scorned his mother when she became pregnant at nineteen with his child. Wanting nothing to do with her, he quickly left town. So Dante had his mother's surname rather than his father's.

Dante had worked hard in high school to ensure he would receive a scholarship or else he wouldn't have been able to afford to go to art school in Florence — even with the money he had saved while working as a bricklayer's assistant. His mother cleaned the homes of wealthy elderly women, but her earnings were just enough to keep food on their table and to help Nonna Andreanna pay the bills. Then tragedy struck when Dante's mother died when he was in his final year of art school. She had been killed by a drunken motorist as she walked home from work one evening.

Instead of staying in Florence, like so

42

many other art students did once they completed their studies, Dante had returned to Siena to be near his grandmother. But within a year of his mother's death, Nonna Andreanna had passed away. After losing her only daughter, the grief was too much for her to bear. She ate less and less every day, even though Dante did all he could to get her to eat. She became so weak that he had no choice but to hospitalize her. Within days of arriving at the hospital, she died, leaving Dante truly alone in the world.

In the past three years since his mother had died, Dante hadn't been able to fill the deep void he'd felt — until he'd begun dreaming about Anabella. Whenever she had visited him in his dreams or had stared back at him from one of his paintings, he'd immediately felt comforted. And then on the day he'd first seen her, when their eyes had met, he'd felt as if the hole inside of him was beginning to close. He had acknowledged to himself that it was bizarre to feel this way about someone he'd only met in his dreams, but he couldn't ignore the strong instincts telling him this woman would be part of his destiny. Who knew? Maybe it was as his friends had said — she was merely a source of inspiration for his work. But now that he'd seen she existed in the living world, there was no doubt in his mind that he must meet her and learn more about his stunning muse.

He glanced at his watch, a gift from his mother and Nonna Andreanna when he had been accepted to art school. It was almost nine o'clock. Though it was too early for bed, he was absolutely exhausted, and, if he wanted to get to the piazza early and stay throughout the day, he needed to get a good night's rest. Pulling his shirt and trousers off, he collapsed on his bed, causing the loose headboard to shake. He hadn't wanted to keep his grandmother's house after she died. The memories were too painful to relive — even if they had been mostly happy ones. And his mother's and grandmother's ghosts would torment him, reminding him he no longer had the family he'd loved so much. So he had sold the house, relying on the money from its sale to help tide him over until he could begin to earn a more substantial living from his paintings. He rented the one-room apartment that made up his home. Although it was small, the almost constant aroma of fresh bread baking that entered his apartment from Signora Fiorucci's shop made the space feel more inviting and like home, reminding him of all the wonderful foods his mother and Nonna had cooked.

Soon Dante was fast asleep. He dreamt of his mother, standing in front of her stove, giving him a taste of what she was cooking. But as he was about to place his lips on the wooden spoon, the vision of his mother disappeared and was replaced with Anabella. He reached out to touch her, but she took a step back and another as he followed her. As always, he was chasing her in his dreams. He awoke with a start, and his heart raced furiously; his forehead had broken out into a sweat. He sighed deeply, running a hand over his face. This woman would be the death of him if he did not meet her soon.

Unable to sleep, Dante got up and did what he always did when insomnia took hold of him. He painted.

CHAPTER 4
ANABELLA

Pienza, 1954

Anabella was running through the maze of rose bushes that sprawled across her mother's property. Cioccolato was at her heels, barking and wagging his tail. Although she was now ten years old, she hadn't tired yet of playing this game of chase with her dog. The late July sun was especially scorching today as the temperature soared to 100 degrees. But Anabella didn't mind. Being outside was where she always longed to be — even on the days that it rained. She couldn't explain it, but she felt less alone when she was engaging with the natural world all around her, whether it was running through the stunning roses on the farm, climbing the trees that formed a protective fortress around the perimeters of the nursery, or riding in her mother's beat-up gray Fiat as Anabella stuck her head out the window to feel the breeze blowing through her hair and admire the beautiful Tuscan countryside.

As she ran, she saw in the distance Chiara carrying a huge straw basket. Chiara waved to her. Anabella waved back and quickened her pace. She was out of breath when she reached her.

"*Vai piano! Vai piano!* No need to rush, Anabella. I'm not going anywhere." Chiara laughed as she placed her hands on either side of Anabella's flushed cheeks and kissed her forehead.

"*Ciao,* Chiara. I was just happy to see you. What are you carrying in your basket?" Anabella strained her neck to peer inside the basket.

"I brought these for you. Sunflowers." Chiara took out a bunch of sunflowers that had been clipped so they could fit into her basket. Every day on her drive to the nursery, Chiara passed an immense field of sunflowers. Today, she had felt a compelling urge to stop and clip a bunch. She knew Anabella would love them.

"I didn't know you could take these." Anabella looked confused as she took one of the sunflowers from Chiara's grip and stared at it. They weren't as pretty as her roses, but there was something striking about the sunflowers. Perhaps it was their

47

bright yellow petals.

"Of course. I took them from a field that doesn't belong to anyone."

Anabella had seen sunflowers before, whenever she and Mamma drove into the village. She remembered being excited by the immense blanket of yellow that seemed to spread out forever in the horizon. Anabella had pointed at them and exclaimed, "Mamma, look how pretty!"

But her mother had screamed, "Don't pay attention to those horrid flowers!"

Anabella had been shocked by her mother's tone — for her mother had never yelled at her before. Tears had quickly slid down Anabella's face as she sobbed softly. And that had been another first for Anabella — Mamma not comforting her when she was upset. Instead, her mother's gaze remained fixed on the road ahead, but there was something in her eyes that terrified Anabella. After that day, she never mentioned the sunflowers again as they passed them on their way to town.

Chiara looked at Anabella, noticing her suddenly serious expression. "What's the matter? Don't you like them?"

"They're nice. *Grazie,* Chiara."

"You can keep them in a vase with water and place them on the windowsill of your room. Soon, you'll be able to eat the seeds. Have you ever had sunflower seeds?"

"You can eat the seeds?" Anabella was stunned. Her face twisted up in disgust. She couldn't imagine why anyone would want to eat any part of a flower, let alone its seeds.

Chiara laughed. "*Si!* That is another wonderful thing about sunflowers. These seeds will ripen, and then you can pull them off the flower's bulb and eat them. They taste very good; you'll see."

Cioccolato was sniffing the remaining flowers in Chiara's basket and began chewing on one of the petals.

"Ah! Cioccolato! These aren't for you to eat." Chiara laughed, gently admonishing him.

"He likes them, too!" Anabella smiled, petting Cioccolato's head.

"Come, Anabella, let's head back to the house. Your mother will be wondering where I am. We have a busy day in store for us."

Anabella linked her arm through Chiara's as they walked. When they approached the house, Chiara handed the basket of sunflowers to Anabella.

"These are all for me?"

"Of course. Remember what I told you: Keep them by the window, and, in a few weeks, be sure to try the seeds. But you'll have to make sure Cioccolato doesn't get to the flowers before the seeds ripen."

Anabella laughed. Chiara took her leave as she went around the house to find Signora Ferraro.

Once inside her room, Anabella cleared the space on her windowsill that had three vases filled with roses. Each of the rooms in her house always contained fresh-cut roses from their gardens. Anabella loved inhaling the flowers' sweet fragrance as she fell asleep at night. And when the weather began to change, bringing with it cool breezes in the early hours of dawn, the roses' fragrance greeted her in the morning. She took an empty porcelain pitcher she kept on her dresser and filled it with water. It was rather large and would have no problem holding all of the sunflowers Chiara had given her. She loved how the pitcher's turquoise color contrasted nicely with the yellow of the sunflowers.

After just a couple of days, Anabella noticed her sunflowers had dried up and wilted considerably. The seeds looked like they might be ready to pick. She got excited as she anticipated trying them. Anabella ran out of her room in search of Chiara, whom she asked to come to her room so Chiara could tell Anabella for certain if the seeds were ready to eat. But when she returned with Chiara they found her mother standing in front of her bedroom window. The porcelain pitcher holding the sunflowers was lying by Mamma's feet, shattered in pieces, and the sunflowers were crushed as if they had been stomped on. Their dried petals were torn apart, and the sunflowers' seeds were scattered all over the floor. A few had even landed on Anabella's bed.

"Is everything all right, Signora Ferraro?" Chiara asked.

Signora Ferraro turned around, landing her steel gaze first on Chiara, then on Anabella, who quickly lowered her eyes. Anabella's heart was pounding as she remembered the day in the car when her mother had screamed at her not to look at the sunflowers. But they were just flowers, just like their roses. What harm could there be in them?

"Why are these flowers here?" She looked from Anabella to Chiara as she pointed at the crushed flowers that lay strewn by her feet.

Anabella looked up at her mother, tears streaming down her face. But she could not open her mouth to speak. Chiara jumped in.

"I gave them to her, Signora Ferraro. I thought she would like them, especially now that their seeds can be eaten."

"You were sorely mistaken, Chiara. We don't like sunflowers. Do you see us growing any here on the farm?"

Chiara was momentarily stunned and perplexed. She couldn't understand why Signora Ferraro was so irate over her daughter having sunflowers. Chiara remained silent until Signora Ferraro repeated her question in a shout.

"I asked you, do you see any sunflowers on this property?"

"No, no, *signora*," Chiara said softly. She was angry at Signora Ferraro for destroying her daughter's flowers and for the way she was now acting, but she fought to keep her tone even, not wanting to escalate the situation and further upset Anabella. She then added, "*Mi dispiace,* Signora Ferraro. It will not happen again."

Signora Ferraro turned away from Chiara and Anabella, focusing her attention once more outside the window. Her expression quickly changed from angry to sad, and her eyes took on a faraway look. *How strange!* Chiara wondered why Signora Ferraro had such hatred for the sunflowers. Anabella, who still looked frightened, was staring at her mother, too.

"Let's go outside, Anabella." Chiara took

Anabella by the hand and led her away quietly; when they passed Signora Ferraro, Chiara said, "I'll ask one of the workers to come here and clean up the broken pitcher."

Signora Ferraro seemed to almost jump at the sound of Chiara's voice and said, "*Grazie.* I'm sorry I yelled at you, Chiara, but I cannot have those flowers anywhere near my child."

"I understand. I will see you in the gardens."

When Anabella stepped outside, she broke free of Chiara's grip and ran off.

"Anabella! Wait! Where are you going?" Chiara ran after her.

"Leave me alone! I want to be alone!" Anabella was crying, her tears clouding her vision. Cioccolato was napping against the trunk of a fig tree and quickly leapt up when he saw Anabella, racing to greet her. But Anabella pushed him hard with her hand, causing Cioccolato to whimper.

Chiara finally caught up to Anabella. She grabbed her by the arm. Anabella tried to push her away, but Chiara held on firmly.

"Let me go! Let me go! It's because of you that Mamma yelled at me. You and those stupid sunflowers. I hate them!"

"Shhh! Shhh!" Chiara held Anabella close to her chest, stroking her hair. "I'm sorry,

Anabella. I didn't know your mother hated them. I would never have given them to you had I known that." Chiara then remembered the grim expression that had passed over Anabella's face when she'd shown her the sunflowers. Had Anabella been aware that her mother despised them?

"You knew that she didn't like sunflowers, didn't you?" Chiara gently asked.

Anabella kept her head pressed against Chiara's chest. She nodded and began crying again.

"Why didn't you say anything?" Chiara asked in a gentle tone.

Anabella pulled away, rubbing at her eyes with the back of her hand. She shrugged her shoulders, but remained silent. Chiara decided to let her question go unanswered, especially since Anabella had finally calmed down, and Chiara didn't want to upset her more than she had already been today. Cioccolato walked over tentatively; concern filled his eyes. Slowly, he approached Anabella, his head lowered. When he reached her side, he nuzzled her hand with his wet nose. She wrapped her arm around his neck, and Cioccolato began licking her face, all too happy to be back in his mistress's good graces.

"I'm sorry I pushed you, Cioccolato. And

I'm sorry, Chiara."

"That's all right, Anabella. We all get mad from time to time, even your mother. That doesn't mean she loves you any less. Remember that."

Anabella thought for a moment before saying softly, "I'll try to remember."

"What do you say we go water the roses that haven't been watered yet? And then we can have lunch together?"

As Anabella and Chiara walked to the rose gardens that had not been watered today, they spotted Signora Ferraro coming from the house, holding a tray with glasses and a pitcher of water containing rose petals. Setting the tray on the table that sat on the front porch, she looked up in Anabella and Chiara's direction and waved, motioning for them to join her.

Once they reached Signora Ferraro, she said, "It's so hot today. I thought we could take a break and have some rose water." She smiled, but her voice cracked a little as she spoke.

"That's very thoughtful of you, *signora.* Thank you." Chiara placed her hand on the small of Anabella's back, prodding her forward. She was taking small steps toward her mother, still frightened by her mother's earlier outburst.

Mamma always kept a pitcher of water with rose petals in the refrigerator. Anabella had been drinking rose water since she was a little girl. "It's very good for you," Mamma had always said. She poured the water through a strainer so they wouldn't swallow the rose petals, but when Anabella was three years old, she had wanted to see what the roses tasted like and had eaten a few of the petals. They didn't make her sick like Mamma had warned. But they didn't taste as good as Anabella had thought they'd taste. Anabella was surprised. She thought roses were perfect — from their intricate shape to their breathtaking shades and intoxicating fragrance, and of course, their astounding beauty. They tasted good in the rose water, so it had only surprised her more that they didn't taste good once consumed. She thought about all of this now as she drank her glass of rose water. The roses weren't perfect as Mamma had always led her to believe. So if Mamma thought the sunflowers were bad, maybe she was wrong about them?

Later that night, Mamma tucked Anabella into bed. She read to her from her favorite book — a collection of fairy tales by Italo Calvino. When she was done, she kissed

Anabella on the forehead and whispered, "Mamma is sorry she was upset with you earlier. Are you still mad at me?"

Anabella had barely spoken to her mother since her mother's outburst in the morning. She shook her head and managed a small smile for her mother.

"*Brava!* You are the best daughter in the world. I am so blessed to have you. Now get some rest. *Buona notte.*"

"*Buona notte,* Mamma. *Ti voglio bene.*"

"I love you too, my dear daughter."

Mamma turned off the overhead light, but kept on the nightlight Anabella liked to have so she wouldn't be afraid of the dark. Anabella was tired, but she wasn't sleepy yet. She stretched her arms over her head, yawning. When she lowered her arms back down to her sides, she noticed something bounce off the bed onto the floor. She sat up and looked to see what had fallen. A sunflower seed! She quietly got out of bed and bent down to pick up the seed. But she froze when she saw there were numerous seeds under her bed. Whoever had cleaned her room earlier had failed to notice all the seeds that had fallen there. Her heart raced as she stared at the door. Quickly, with one hand she scooped up the seeds, and, with her other hand, she held up the hem of her nightgown so she could place the seeds inside. She then carefully walked over to her dresser and took a small china bowl that her mother placed chocolates in whenever it was Anabella's birthday or the Feast of the Epiphany. Anabella emptied the seeds into the bowl. She then placed the bowl in the back of one of the drawers in her dresser. After she shut the drawer, she waited for a few seconds, then opened it again. Reaching for the bowl, she took out one of the seeds and placed it in her mouth. She chewed on its shell until she reached the seed. Chiara had told her she was supposed to spit out the shell, but Anabella was too afraid her mother would find them if she threw them into the wastebasket in her room. So she swallowed the seed and the shell. Except for the slight scratchy feeling it made as it passed her throat, she didn't mind the shell. She ate a few more seeds. They were good — unlike the rose petals she had eaten that time. But she supposed if she tried eating the sunflower's petals, they probably wouldn't taste good either. Still, she wondered.

Returning the bowl to its hiding place, Anabella tiptoed back to her bed and climbed in. For the first time ever, she was keeping a secret from her mother. Mamma had always told her it was bad to keep secrets, but Anabella knew she could never tell her about the sunflower seeds.

CHAPTER 5
SIGNORA FERRARO

Pienza, 1954

Signora Ferraro kept her eyes fixed on the road in front of her. She was doing her best not to glance at the fields of sunflowers that blanketed the road on either side. How she hated this weekly hour-long drive north to Siena, but she sold many of her flowers to the vendors in the city's Piazza del Campo. She could not do without this large source of income, even though she also delivered her roses to flower shops in many of the smaller towns surrounding her home of Pienza. She had thought about having one of her workers make the deliveries to the flower vendors in the Piazza del Campo, but she didn't fully trust them to bring back all of the earnings. The workers had been loyal throughout the years, and for the most part she knew they were honorable. Still. She'd learned the hard way a long time ago to always keep her guard up.

Her thoughts drifted to the previous morning when she'd found the ceramic pitcher of sunflowers on the windowsill in Anabella's bedroom. At first she had thought she was losing her mind and had imagined seeing the pitcher there. But no, the image had been only too real. Reacting swiftly, she had stormed over to the pitcher and, with one stroke of her hand, knocked it over. Shards of porcelain had flown everywhere. And if that weren't bad enough, she had stomped on the flowers over and over again. Sobs had escaped her throat and tears swam fiercely down her cheeks as she closed her eyes, desperately struggling to keep at bay the dark thoughts that were threatening to break through.

When Chiara and Anabella had entered the room, she was no longer crying. At the sound of their voices, she had suddenly realized with horror what she'd done and that her daughter would be witnessing this bizarre scene. But she'd pushed her mortification aside, focusing instead on unleashing her anger at Chiara and Anabella. Though she later regretted her outburst, she knew they had to realize this could never happen again. Her sanity depended on it.

Signora Ferraro took a deep breath. Sadness suddenly filled her heart. She hadn't

61

always despised sunflowers. Signora Ferraro remembered a time when she had loved them as much as the other people who grew up in Tuscany. Suddenly, her mind flooded with happy memories — memories she hadn't thought about in a very long time. Her parents used to take her and her brother, Michele, to neighboring sunflower fields and let them run free when they were children. They would play hide-and-seek, their little bodies hiding behind the sunflowers that towered over them. Mamma used to clip sunflowers and fill her straw basket to take them home and place them in vases throughout the house. Papà loved them so much that he had decided to plant a sunflower garden behind their house. By the time Maria had reached her teens, the garden had grown quite large. How she had loved that garden! But that was another time, another life — one that seemed so far away now.

Her father's sunflower garden was where she'd met the love of her life — Franco Ferraro, Anabella's father. It had been in June 1943, at the height of World War II. Then, she was simply known as Maria Rossi, and she had been an entirely different person than the one she was now. That woman had died long ago. And whenever she saw old photographs of herself, it felt as if she were looking at a stranger.

She veered slightly to her left as a vehicle came dangerously close. Righting the car back into her lane, she ignored the angry wail blasting from the other driver's horn. Her hands were shaking as she pulled over to the side of the road. She took a few deep breaths, resting her forehead against the steering wheel. Once she felt calmer, she lifted her gaze. For a moment, she allowed herself to glance at the sunflowers that still surrounded her on either side of the road. Soon, her thoughts traveled back to her hometown of Florence, where every summer she walked through her father's sunflower garden.

CHAPTER 6
MARIA ROSSI

Florence, Italy, 1943

Maria was weaving in and out of the sunflowers in her father's garden. It was another exceptionally beautiful summer day in Florence. One almost forgot that there was a war going on and all wasn't right with the world.

The sun was at its highest in the sky on this sweltering June afternoon, but Maria didn't care. It was the only time of the day she could escape unnoticed, after their midday meal when the entire Rossi clan would be taking their siesta and would not notice her absence. She would rather be out in nature, alone with her thoughts, than idly sleeping. And while she loved her family, it was rare that she had some time alone in the house that she shared with Papà, her brother Michele, and his wife Enza.

Maria's mother had died ten years earlier of influenza. Since then the duties of the

64

household had fallen strictly to Maria until Michele had married and brought his wife to live with them in the second-story apartment of their home. Maria couldn't have asked for a better sister-in-law than Enza, who was kind and good-natured and helped with the chores. Sometimes, Maria thought Mamma had sent Enza to them, and she thanked her mother in heaven for doing so. It had been hard living in a household where Maria had been the only woman after her mother had died. Her views were rarely taken seriously whenever she participated in the political discussions her family had. She would get so angry, wondering why women had been cursed to have this inferior role in society. But naturally, she knew the answer. It had all started when that cursed Eve had tempted Adam with the apple all those years ago. Although Maria's father and brother contested her opinions vehemently, she still offered them and would continue doing so, if only for the fact that they seemed to irritate her family immensely, much to her pleasure.

At twenty-eight years old, Maria had accepted that she was considered an old maid and would probably never leave home. But she'd never been like her starry-eyed classmates and friends who could dream of nothing else besides finding a man to marry and having children. She enjoyed living with her close-knit family, and the thought of leaving them someday had never sat well with her. Although she adored seeing babies at the hips of other women, she was at peace with the fact that God had other plans for her and motherhood wasn't one of them.

Maria lowered herself to the ground and lay back in the garden, shielding her eyes from the sun by draping her arm over her forehead. Her father's sunflower garden took up most of the property that their house sat on. Sunflowers were the only flowers her father grew, even though Mamma had tried in vain to convince him to grow other flowers. He did grow tomatoes, zucchinis, and peppers, but where flowers were concerned, sunflowers were the only flower that mattered to him. Her father had always wished he'd been born in one of the Tuscan towns south of Florence that were known for their abundant fields of sunflowers. "Pienza! That's where I want to be born if I come back in another life," he would often say.

Maria laughed softly to herself as she thought about her Papà and how funny he could be. But lately, he hardly ever joked. And no one in her family had to ask why.

With the world at war and events growing worse in Italy, it was becoming nearly impossible to take joy in anything. Papà's sunflower garden continued to give Maria comfort and reminded her that there was still beauty left.

Closing her eyelids, she focused on the sounds and sensations that surrounded her — bees buzzing, birds chirping, the gentle breeze that swayed the sunflowers, the warm sun on her face. She was beginning to drowse when suddenly a noise caused her eyes to flash open. Had she been dreaming? She waited a second. There it was again. It sounded almost like a dragging sound followed by a soft grunt. Maria gasped. She wasn't here alone. Perhaps it was a child playing just the way she and Michele had often played in the sunflower garden when they were growing up. Still, she couldn't ignore the slight unease she felt in the pit of her stomach.

Slowly, she sat up and scanned the garden, trying to see if she could spot anyone. But the garden was vast, and, if someone was crouched low to the ground, she would never see him or her. Though she was nervous, she was also extremely curious. Before she could change her mind, she stood up, exposing herself fully. She was being silly. It was probably just a child. She'd always felt safe here and had no reason to begin feeling differently. This was and had been her home for her entire life.

Walking through the garden, she gazed down to see if she could spot anyone hiding. This was madness! She should head back home instead of playing detective. After about five minutes, Maria decided to do just that. Maybe it had been a child who was now lying still, not wanting to be found by her or any other adults who might be looking for him or her. Not taking any chances, she quickened her pace. But after a few steps she let out a soft yelp as a man suddenly came into view, rising up on his knees and blocking her path. He placed his index finger over his lips. Maria took a step back, her heart thrashing wildly against her chest. She glanced around, but no one else was in sight.

"Please, do not scream. I will not hurt you," he whispered just loud enough so she could hear him. "I have been hiding here for the past hour. I heard you walking through the fields, and I was afraid you were one of the police officers who are looking for me."

Maria was alarmed. This man was a fugitive? What had he done?

"Where are the police now?" Her eyes looked off into the distance, as she hoped the police were indeed nearby.

"No, I'm pretty sure I lost them before I reached your property, but one can never be too careful with the OVRA police skulking about everywhere." His eyes scanned the garden.

OVRA stood for the Organization for Vigilance and Repression of Anti-Fascism, the secret police that Mussolini had formed in 1927 to stop any anti-Fascist activity or sentiment. Maria could see fear in the man's eyes.

"May I ask what you did exactly?" Maria did her best to keep her voice even.

"*Mi dispiace.* They are looking for me because I publish an anti-Fascist newspaper. That is all." He gave her a soft smile. There was something almost boyish or naïve about him, even though she could tell he was in his thirties.

"*Mi chiamo* Franco." He held out his hand, which was bandaged.

Maria paused for a moment before taking his hand, giving it a light squeeze to avoid causing it further injury. "Maria."

"*Piacere.* My mother's name was Maria." He smiled, and their eyes locked.

Maria let go of his hand, immediately feeling self-conscious. Her face had probably broken out in the tiny white blisters she often got when she was out in the sun for too long, and her hair had come free from its bun. She ran a hand through it, but she knew it was no use to try to calm her curls, which had a mind of their own and often broke free of her attempts to tame them.

"What happened?" Maria gestured with a tilt of her chin to his bandaged hand.

"Ah! Trust me, you do not want to know. All I will say is that I was in jail last night, and they got a bit rough with me when I wouldn't tell them what they wanted to hear. Bastard Fascists! This morning, I was able to escape when the guard on duty opened the door to my cell to take a prisoner and forgot to lock it. Once I stepped outside, I was greeted by two guards who were returning to the jail. I managed to punch one of them and get away before the other guard came after me. Soon, there were a dozen soldiers chasing me. But all is well now." Franco gave Maria a reassuring smile.

"Surely they could not have kept you for long just for publishing a newspaper that goes against our government?"

"Ah, they have not only been jailing people who oppose Mussolini and his regime, but they have also been exiling many anti-Fascists to remote Mediterranean islands. And of course, others have even been sentenced to death." He glanced nervously over his shoulder.

"Of course. I don't know what I was thinking with my earlier comment. I have heard of the horrible things that have been going on." She'd made a fool of herself with her earlier naïve statement. Her cheeks reddened. Hoping to cover her embarrassment, she said, "Don't worry. I won't tell anyone I saw you."

"May I ask why you are out alone? I assume this is your property and that is your house, but this garden is enormous, and as you saw it's quite easy for someone to hide here. It's not safe for any woman or even man."

Maria was surprised he had included "man" in his sentence. Everyone always noted how a place wasn't safe for women. One rarely, if ever, heard the reference made for men.

"*Sì,* this is my home. It is absurd that I should not feel safe here. Besides, I am not voicing any anti-Fascist opinion." She gave a soft laugh before adding, "But thank you for your words of caution."

"Ah! They cannot be trusted to leave alone people who support the regime.

Promise me you will always have someone by your side when you are out in your garden. I know you feel it's safe because it is your home, but these days one cannot exercise enough caution. Surely your husband can spend time with you." He glanced at her left hand.

"I am not married. My father, brother, and sister-in-law live with me at the house. I do not need to have a babysitter shadowing my every move." She could not hide from her voice the irritation she felt and added, "If I decide to stop spending time alone in my garden, it will be *my* decision. But thank you for your warning."

"Ah. I see I have wounded your pride, *signorina.*"

"No, you have not wounded my pride, but I do not take orders from men so easily. I have grown up with a very opinionated father and brother, and, after my mother died, I was the only female in my household until my brother wed and brought his wife to live with us. It would've been easy to have my voice drowned out since I was outnumbered until recently in my family. So I have become accustomed to challenging my father and my brother whenever I can and making my own choices."

A subtle, surprised expression came over

Franco's features as he studied her.

"Very well. But again I must emphasize that these are dangerous times, and things might get even worse, as I'm sure you realize. Just promise me you will be extremely cautious — no matter what you decide to do." He held her gaze, and Maria saw how serious he was.

"I promise. Thank you again for your concern."

He nodded before adding, "I must go. But first let me escort you back to your front door."

"That won't be necessary, but thank you."

"I insist. It will make me feel better to see that you have entered your house safely." Franco smiled. He had a warm smile, which completely melted Maria's resolve.

"How about you wait here while you watch me go to my house? If my father sees you, he might call the police since you are trespassing."

"Is he a Fascist?"

"No, but you are committing a crime by being on our property uninvited. So if you don't want to return to jail, I suggest you wait here and then leave as quickly as possible."

"Of course. I'm sorry, Maria. It was a pleasure meeting you. *Grazie molto.*"

"Buongiorno." Maria slightly bowed her head before taking her leave.

As she walked toward her house, she could feel his eyes on her. Once more her cheeks flushed, and she was grateful he could not see her face this time. She was a grown woman in her late twenties, not a silly teenager. What would he think seeing her blush over the littlest thing? Then again, why should she care what this stranger thought of her? Every so often Maria would glance over her shoulder. Franco remained in the same spot as he waited for Maria to reach her door. Though he watched her, she noticed he would also look from side to side quickly, ensuring the police hadn't returned.

When she reached her house, she turned around and waved. He waved back, but still waited. She shook her head in exasperation. He did mean it when he'd said he wanted to make sure she got into her house safely. Maria stepped inside. She could hear Enza singing softly to herself. Enza always sang whenever she was in the kitchen. Soon the sound of the espresso pot percolating reached Maria's ears. Papà and Michele would be getting up from their siesta any minute now. She walked over to the window that looked out onto the sunflower garden and stood to the side lest Franco see her staring at him. But he was already gone from where he'd been standing. Perhaps he had gotten back down on the ground and was crawling his way off the property. Maria had to place her hand over her mouth to stifle a giggle.

Her gaze went over to the sunflowers. The sun was getting lower in the sky. Although she knew it was absurd to feel afraid in the garden she'd played in since she was a child, Franco had managed to instill some fear in her — and curiosity. She wondered where he was from. Was he also from Florence or from one of the neighboring towns? What had been the catalyst for him to start his anti-Fascist newspaper? He had an intellectual look with his glasses and his serious gaze. He looked like a man who pondered a lot.

As Maria made her way to the kitchen, she sent out a silent prayer for Franco, asking God to keep him safe.

CHAPTER 7
DANTE

Siena, 1970

Dante was setting up his easel as he did every Wednesday morning at Siena's famed Medici Fortress, the site of a weekly outdoor market that boasted a dizzying number of long tables and trucks that displayed everything from housewares, clothing, jewelry, scarves, shoes, and bags to plants, produce, meat, cheese, and other items. Many tourists visited the market, hoping to find inexpensive goods to take back home. It was an ideal place for Dante to sketch and attract tourists who wanted a unique piece of artwork to bring back home. But tourists weren't his only customers here. Many of Siena's wealthy residents came by regularly to purchase Dante's larger canvases to adorn their villas.

It had been a couple of weeks since Dante had seen Anabella, and he was beginning to lose hope that he would ever see her again.

He had gone to the Piazza del Campo every day of the week except Sundays and Wednesdays. On Sundays, he and everyone else in Italy attended church, and most shops remained closed for the day. And on Wednesdays, he came to the market at the Medici Fortress. Perhaps that was why he hadn't seen her again? Maybe she and her mother had gone to the Piazza del Campo on the Wednesdays when he was here. Yes! Why hadn't he thought of that before?! If he didn't see her the rest of this week, he would change his routine next week and go to the Piazza del Campo on Wednesday as well.

Feeling a bit more hopeful, he decided to stray from the drawings of landscapes that he normally did when he worked at the Piazza del Campo or at the Medici Fortress market. He began a sketch of Anabella. It was the first time he would be drawing her instead of painting her. The sketch's background was the bustling market and in the forefront was his sunflower girl. Her back was toward the viewer as she stood at one of the merchants' tables. An open leather handbag, which hung around her wrist, contained a bouquet of sunflowers. A few of the flowers' petals were strewn by her feet. Only her profile was visible to the viewer as she stared at an antique mirror that hung in the vendor's tent on a shelf. The other half of her profile was visible in the mirror. Her eyes looked very sad. Her long chocolate-brown curls framed her face and hung over her shoulders, which were exposed in the silky sundress she wore.

"What a stunning work!" A portly man stood over Dante, who was now adding a few final touches to the sketch.

"Grazie."

"She looks so pensive and sad. Is she not happy with what she sees in the mirror? I cannot see how that is the case with her perfect classical features. *È molto bella!*" The man leaned in closer and peered intensely at Anabella.

Dante couldn't help feeling a stirring of jealousy. He knew it was crazy to feel this way, but he couldn't help it. He had become protective of his sunflower girl, perhaps even more so now that he knew she was very alive and present in the real world.

"Please, be careful. I need to get a new easel. This one is not stable," Dante pleaded with the man, hoping he wouldn't notice the easel was actually stable. But the man simply nodded and took a step back.

"I must have this drawing. How much?" He whipped out a fat billfold and began separating his *lire.*

Dante paused. Although he still had in his possession several sunflower girl paintings, it was becoming even harder for him to sell any of them. Maybe when he saw Anabella again, he could sell more of them. He knew he needed to let go of this obsession that had taken hold of him. And his landscape drawings hadn't been selling as much in the past few weeks, which he wasn't surprised by, since they hadn't been the best of his work. He blamed it on his recent distractions — at least where the landscape pieces were concerned. But when he painted Anabella, his work still shone.

Returning his thoughts to the waiting customer, he swallowed hard before replying, "How much would you like to pay for it?"

The man looked surprised. "Please, my son. Don't devalue your work. You are a very talented artist. Surely you must know your worth. As you can see, I have the money and am willing to pay handsomely for it."

How could Dante tell him he did not want to place a price on his sunflower girl? While he'd quoted rates for the paintings of Anabella that he had sold, that had been before he'd seen her in person. Now, he felt as if he knew her and as if he would be selling *her.* But he needed the money.

"I trust you, *signore.* Please just pay me whatever you think is fair. I am more than happy to sell you the drawing since I can tell you are a lover of art and will appreciate my work for a long time to come."

The man seemed pleased with Franco's compliment. Shrugging his shoulders, he said, "Very well." He took out what looked like most of the *lire* in his billfold and handed them over to Franco without counting them.

"Aren't you going to count it?"

"I know how much money I had when I left home, and I have yet to purchase anything today. Please take the money. No more arguing."

Before Dante could refuse again, the man placed the money in Dante's shirt pocket. Then the man lifted the drawing from the easel and hoisted it under his arm. Dante cringed, wondering if the man would perspire all over his beautiful sketch.

"Buongiorno." The man quickly walked away as if he'd heard Dante's thoughts and was afraid he would change his mind about selling.

Sighing, Dante decided to call it a day and began packing up his easel and art supplies.

As he bent down to put his drawing pencils in his satchel, he saw, out of his peripheral vision, a woman with long, dark, curly hair. He whipped his head to the right. Anabella!

Though he couldn't see her face, he would have known that glorious crown of hair and figure anywhere. Slinging his satchel over his shoulder and leaving his easel behind, he ran after her. She was alone and hurrying toward the back of the market. Dare he shout her name, even though they had yet to formally meet? He didn't want her to think he was stalking her.

A large group of tourists suddenly appeared and were heading in the same direction as Anabella. Damn them! They completely obliterated her from his view. He roughly pushed his way through the crowd, much to the dismay of the tourists, who glared at him. But once he made it to the front, he saw Anabella was gone.

Out of breath, he walked over to a wall covered in ivy that was set several feet back from the vendors' tables. He squatted, leaning his back and head against the wall as he waited for his heart rate to return to normal. Closing his eyes, he exhaled deeply. Just as in his dreams, he was now chasing his sunflower girl in his waking life. Would he ever catch up to Anabella Ferraro and actually talk to her? Or would he be doomed to chase her forever?

CHAPTER 8
ANABELLA

Pienza, 1961

Anabella could hear the church bells chiming in the distance. It was Easter Sunday, and she and her mother were dressed in their finest. Anabella wore a belted chiffon dress with three-quarter-length sleeves. The shopgirl had called the color of the dress pale lemon. That was what Anabella loved the most about the dress — that it wasn't simply called yellow. *Lemon* made it sound more alluring and tempting — just like the many wonderful lemon desserts Mamma made. And it wasn't a glaring yellow or a yellow tinged with orange like the color of the sunflowers that her mother hated so much.

As Anabella stepped out of the car, she pulled on her white lace gloves, which Mamma had crocheted for her. Though there was a light breeze and a chill in the air, she decided to leave her cardigan

83

sweater in the car. She wanted to show off her dress. It was the prettiest dress she had ever worn, and the first dress Mamma had bought for her instead of sewing it herself. Anabella was now seventeen, and her mother had finally relented to her pleas to buy her Easter dress in the shop in town. Every Sunday, when they attended Mass, Anabella had noticed the other teenage girls and their dresses that reflected the latest styles. Though she knew several of the girls' dresses had been sewn by their mothers as well, theirs were always stylish, exhibiting voluminous skirts and fitted bodices that fully accentuated the figure and drew attention to the waist and bosom. In contrast, Anabella's were all shirtwaist dresses that had been the rage in the forties. Though older women like her mother often still wore them, Anabella rarely saw them on the younger girls her age, especially at church. For the past two years, the other girls in Pienza had begun dressing in these stylish dresses, but Mamma had told her that, at fourteen and fifteen, they were too young to be dressed like women.

"They are still children, after all! What are their mothers thinking?" And for emphasis, Mamma followed these words with a disapproving *tsk, tsk.* Anabella had always liked the dresses and clothes Mamma made for her. But ever since she'd begun to look at the fashion magazines Chiara had secretly given her once she turned seventeen, Anabella had longed to have one of the glamorous-looking dresses she'd seen on the models in the glossies as well as on the village girls.

Anabella blushed as she remembered their visit to the boutique in town last weekend. When she and Mamma had stepped into the shop, Anabella had felt shy and awkward. Her mother had wasted no time in taking charge as she flipped through dresses on the racks, oblivious to the choices that Eloisa, the shopgirl, was making. Anabella had merely stood to the side, glancing at the dresses as if she were afraid to touch them. But, oh, how she longed to! They were so beautiful. She'd never owned any clothing that was even remotely this extravagant.

Eloisa had looked to be in her late teens, a mere year or two older than Anabella, but she exuded maturity and sophistication. She'd reminded Anabella of the confident models in the magazines that Chiara had given her. Eloisa had been very kind to Anabella and had taken her under her wing as she measured her, praising her with compliments while Mamma had continued perusing the dress racks.

"You have the perfect hourglass figure. Many girls would die to look like you," Eloisa said, much to Anabella's embarrassment. "No one has ever told you this, have they? It is nothing to be ashamed of. You should be proud. Someday, you will drive a special young man crazy," Eloisa said in a hushed tone, winking at Anabella and smiling.

"Grazie," Anabella managed to murmur in a tiny voice, keeping her gaze fixed on her sandals — a habit she hadn't outgrown since she was a little girl, whenever someone said something to make her feel self-conscious.

"So, you have not chosen any dresses yet."

"My mamma is still looking."

"Si, but what do *you* want to try on? After all, you will be the one wearing the dress, not your mother." Eloisa frowned, casting a glance in Signora Ferraro's direction.

"It is all right. I've always liked the clothes that Mamma has sewn for me."

But Eloisa hadn't missed Anabella's furtive glances every so often to two of the mannequins in the shop's display window. One was wearing a lovely lemon-colored belted chiffon dress, and the other was in a violet dress with a full bubble skirt and organdy sash around the waist.

"Did you see the dresses in the window? I think they would look perfect on you."

Anabella's eyes immediately lit up as she turned her head once more to the window. She looked at Eloisa, almost fearful, and then back at the dresses in the window, before letting her gaze rest on her mother, who had a few dresses draped over her arm.

"Let me go get them." Eloisa hurried off just as Anabella was about to stop her.

Her pulse raced in anticipation of trying on the dresses that she'd been drawn to.

"Anabella, I have a few dresses I think would suit you," Mamma called out as she made her way over to Anabella. Both of her arms were covered in dresses.

The dutiful daughter that Anabella was, she tried on all of the dresses Mamma had selected without one word of complaint. Never known to break from tradition, Mamma had chosen mostly shirtwaist dresses with the exception of a couple of staid-looking embroidered suits. A few of the shirtwaist dresses were nice, but Anabella didn't feel her heart leap as it had when she'd first seen her favorite dresses in the window. Naturally, Mamma's displeasure was etched across her features as Eloisa brought the dresses over.

"You need to make up your mind, Anabella. We've already been gone from the farm for an hour. I can't waste all day in here," Mamma said in an irritated tone, glancing at her wristwatch.

"But she hasn't tried these dresses on yet," Eloisa protested as she helped Anabella out of the last shirtwaist dress she'd tried on.

"I don't think those are quite right," Mamma replied as she hung her favorite dresses on an empty clothes rack. She hadn't even asked Anabella which were her favorites.

"Well, we won't know unless she tries them on first. Besides, Anabella told me earlier when I took her measurements that she loved these dresses the moment she spotted them in the display window."

Mamma looked over her shoulder at Anabella, surprise etched over her features. "*È vero*, Anabella?"

Without meeting her mother's gaze, she nodded.

"Why didn't you tell me?"

Anabella shrugged her shoulders.

"*Va bene*. Let's see how they look." Mamma sighed as if she knew this would be a waste of time.

Eloisa first helped Anabella slip on the violet dress. The violet contrasted nicely with Anabella's long chocolate-brown hair, which Eloisa had taken and draped over one of her shoulders.

"Look how gorgeous your hair looks against the violet. This suits your coloring very well, and it fits you perfectly! No alterations are needed."

Mamma came over and lifted the hem of the dress, inspecting the stitching, before saying, "This skirt seems a bit frivolous, no? We are attending church, not going to a wedding, after all."

"But it will be Easter. People do get more dressed up for such an important holiday. You want Anabella to look her best, *signora,* no?"

Signora Ferraro didn't respond as she continued scrutinizing the dress. "I don't agree with your assessment that the dress doesn't need any alterations. It is too tight in the bust and will need to be let out."

"But that is how the dress is supposed to fit — snug in the bust to accentuate it."

Signora Ferraro's brows quickly knitted in anger. "My daughter's bust does not need to be on full display before the whole congregation of Pienza."

"I did not mean any offense, *signora.* I was just stating that these dresses are sewn to fit this way."

"We don't have to get this dress, Mamma," Anabella said in a soft voice, much to Eloisa's dismay.

"Do you like the dress, Anabella?" Eloisa hoped the girl would not cower once more to her mother. She'd seen this before with other mothers who came in with their daughters, but never to the extreme that she was witnessing now with Signora Ferraro and Anabella.

"It is nice." Anabella looked at herself admiringly in the full-length mirror.

"Don't forget you still have the lemon dress to try on. You can decide which dress *you* like the best after seeing how that one fits."

Eloisa's emphasis on "you" was not lost on Signora Ferraro. She crossed her arms. Who did this young woman think she was, challenging her tastes? She was after all Anabella's mother and would know better than anyone what her daughter liked. But Signora Ferraro remained silent. Anabella would come to her own conclusion that these last two dresses were not right for her. They always agreed on everything. Why should that change now?

Anabella stepped into the lemon chiffon dress. She shivered with excitement as she felt the whisper-light chiffon against her skin. She waited to look up in the mirror as Eloisa zippered the dress to the top. When Anabella did finally glance up and saw her image in the mirror, she couldn't help but let out a small gasp.

"*Dio mio!* You look absolutely breathtaking in this dress. It's as if it were made just for you." Eloisa clasped her hands in excitement.

Anabella smiled as she turned around, taking in the view of the dress from the back. She felt . . . the words were escaping her . . . grown-up? Yes, the dress made her feel and look like a woman. She liked what she saw. None of the dresses Mamma had chosen had this effect on her. Anabella truly felt transformed in this dress, almost like Cinderella. She glanced at her mother, who was staring at her, but her mother's face was unreadable. Anabella's elated spirits quickly plummeted, as she knew her mother would not approve.

"Signora Ferraro? What do you think?" Eloisa held her breath as she waited for Signora Ferraro's response. Like Anabella, Eloisa held little hope that the stubborn woman would agree to this dress.

"It is beautiful. I cannot deny that, even if this one also seems too tight in the bosom."

"It's not too tight, Mamma. I can still take

a deep breath in it." Anabella inhaled deeply as she puffed out her chest.

Eloisa's and Signora Ferraro's gazes met as they realized it had gone over Anabella's head why her mother didn't want attention to be drawn to her bust. But Signora Ferraro wasn't surprised. Her daughter was innocent, and that was how she intended her to remain, unlike many of the corrupted girls she'd seen in town.

"I don't know if this is the dress." Signora Ferraro turned around and walked over to a rack of dresses, resting her hands on top of it as her gaze grew distant.

"Is this the dress you want, Anabella?" Eloisa asked, knowing the answer.

"I do like it very much, but Mamma is paying for the dress. I must defer to her wishes."

Signora Ferraro closed her eyes for a second. She couldn't have asked for a more wonderful, obedient, and respectful child than Anabella. Rarely did she question her mother's judgment. She'd seen how her daughter's eyes had lit up the moment she saw herself in the dress. Signora Ferraro had almost fainted when she saw her — for in that moment, she saw a flash of herself when she was her daughter's age. But unlike Anabella, Signora Ferraro had exuded an overly confident demeanor when she was a teenager. She had been far more mature than her daughter was. She'd been accustomed to having to assert her own identity among the all-male household of her family. And later, when she'd met Anabella's father and had begun a new life, her assertiveness and independence had increased. But if she'd only known then what she knew now. As she'd learned painfully, being a fighter and daring to challenge others had only proven to have dire consequences.

She sighed. This was merely a dress. What harm could it do? She did want her daughter to be happy, even if it didn't always appear that way, especially when she needed to exercise discipline.

Walking back to Anabella's side, she said, "This is the dress. Let's buy it."

"Oh, Mamma! You like it, too?"

"Si."

Anabella threw her arms around her mother, hugging her tightly. Tears came to Signora Ferraro's eyes, but she quickly blinked them back.

"Va bene, va bene. We must be on our way, so hurry and change back into your clothes while I pay Eloisa. We've taken up enough of her time."

"No worries, *signora.* I am only too happy to have helped you and Anabella. You made the right decision. She will be the best-dressed girl in church on Easter!"

Anabella smiled as she remembered Eloisa's prediction. She was shaken out of her thoughts by the voice of her mother.

"Where is your cardigan?" Signora Ferraro narrowed her gaze, letting it rest on her daughter's bosom.

Anabella knew her mother was still thinking the dress was too tight in her bust. She crossed her arms to hide her chest. "I was warm in the car. I'm sure it'll be warm in church as it always is, so I don't need it." She kept her gaze fixed straight ahead, praying her mother would not make her go back to the car to get her sweater. But Mamma didn't utter a word.

"*Buona* Pasqua, Signora Ferraro, Anabella!"

Anabella turned to see who was greeting them. It was Signora Mazzeo and her two daughters, Domenica and Concetta. Anabella's stomach grew queasy. She had never felt comfortable around the sisters when she and her mother ran into them. Though they were always polite, she sensed they were quietly assessing her. And sure enough, the moment they reached Anabella and her mother, their eyes scanned Anabella from head to foot.

"*Buona* Pasqua, Signora Mazzeo, Domenica, Concetta," Signora Ferraro greeted them.

Anabella hoped her mother would quicken her step as she often did when she ran into the villagers before they could engage her in small talk or inquisitive questions about their life on the farm. But sometimes, she was forced to talk to them at greater length, especially if they were customers of the farm.

"Anabella, you look lovely!" Signora Mazzeo said, turning to her daughters. "Doesn't she look beautiful?"

Domenica and Concetta remained silent.

"I wasn't sure about the dress, but Anabella had her heart set on it. I'm afraid it might be too fancy for church." Signora Ferraro's voice shook, just a tiny bit.

It was enough for Anabella to notice, though she didn't think Signora Mazzeo or her daughters had detected the nervousness in her mother's voice. Anabella was surprised, for her mother never came across as nervous about anything. Was she worried about what they thought? Anabella had always heard her mother profess that she didn't care what anyone thought of them.

"Nonsense! It is Easter, after all. The dress looks similar to the dresses Domenica and Concetta wore to Easter Mass last year."

"*Si,* these dresses were very popular *then,*" Domenica, the older of the sisters, said.

Anabella thought her comment was odd, since she'd seen the dresses featured in the magazines Chiara had been bringing her. But then she noticed their dresses. The dresses had a straighter fit. Gone were the voluminous skirts, and the waists were slightly relaxed. Domenica's dress was a striking cornflower-blue color and featured a belt made out of the same fabric as the dress that was tied in an elaborate bow centered on her waist. Concetta's dress was a pale green color and sported a similar belt, but her bow wasn't as elaborate as Domenica's, and it rested on the side of her waist.

Anabella looked over to where more villagers were making their way to the church. She noticed a few women were also wearing dresses with full skirts. She relaxed, but then she realized they were older, closer to her mother's age. The teenagers, on the other hand, were wearing fitted dresses that were similar to Domenica's and Concetta's.

"Did you make this dress, Signora Ferraro?" Concetta asked. Her lips spread into a slight smirk.

"No, I did not. Anabella and I went to —"

"La Donna Fiorentina?" Domenica and Concetta echoed as they interrupted her.

"*Si*. How did you know?" Signora Ferraro looked mildly irritated. Her daughter would never so rudely interrupt her elders.

"They are the only shop that is still carrying older styles. The other two dress shops in town are beginning to carry more dresses from Rome and Milan. We bought our dresses at La Moda d'Oggi. Mamma thinks La Donna Fiorentina is having financial problems, and they cannot afford to update their selection with the newest dresses that are coming from the big cities," Domenica offered.

Signora Ferraro looked at Signora Mazzeo, who nodded. Her voice lowered to a whisper as she drew in closer and said, "The husband has a gambling problem. *Povera* Rita."

Rita and her husband, Salvatore Garofalo, were the owners of La Donna Fiorentina and the parents of Eloisa, the shopgirl who had helped Anabella. Signora Ferraro detested gossip and refused to be a part of it.

"We should be on our way. Mass is about to start. *Buona* Pasqua, Signora Mazzeo." Signora Ferraro didn't bother addressing

Domenica and Concetta.

As Anabella and her mother made their way up the steps to the church, Anabella sensed the Mazzeo sisters' eyes boring into her back. She glanced over her shoulder, and sure enough, they were staring at her. But their gazes were fixed on her dress, and they hadn't noticed her turn around. She heard them whispering, but could not make out what they were saying among the throngs of parishioners talking excitedly and hurrying to get inside before Mass started. But once they entered the church and the crowds thinned a bit, she was able to hear Concetta whisper, "She needs to do something with her hair. We're not in the Renaissance era anymore."

Domenica giggled.

Anabella felt a blush rising up her neck and spreading to her face. Pools of sweat quickly formed under her arms and beneath her bosom. Mamma had been right. She shouldn't have bought this dress. Still, it was more contemporary than the shirtwaist dresses Mamma would've preferred she wore. If Domenica and Concetta thought her hair was outdated, surely they would think the same of the dresses her mother loved so much that harkened back to the forties. She ran a hand over her hair as tears stung her eyes. Everyone at the farm had always told her how beautiful her hair was. Even the shopgirl Eloisa had marveled at it. True, long hair wasn't in fashion now, as she'd seen in the magazines. But she had always liked her hair, and besides, she didn't think Mamma would approve of her getting a short hairstyle. It was a miracle, after all, that Mamma had not only relented and bought Anabella's dress this year for Easter, but also that she had let her pick the lemon dress.

As she and her mother found a seat in the very first row in church, Anabella scanned the crowd. Again, she could not spot any of the young women wearing a dress with a full skirt like hers. A few sported two-piece ensembles. A flash of pink caught her peripheral vision. She turned and saw Graziella Montana enter the row of pews to the right. Graziella was the daughter of the local butcher. For some reason, she was alone. Anabella wondered why her parents had not accompanied her to Mass, especially on such an important holy day. Her dress had a pleated full skirt, and, like Anabella, Graziella still wore her hair long, but hers was always pinned up into a bun. Graziella had beautiful blond hair and dazzling green eyes. But all anyone seemed to notice was that she was overweight.

Instead of feeling comforted that she wasn't the only girl in church to have a voluminous skirt, Anabella felt worse. A few times when Mamma and she went into town to buy their meat at Graziella's father's meat shop, Signora Montana had told them that her daughter was mercilessly teased in school. Anabella had felt bad for the girl and couldn't understand why the children made fun of her simply because she was overweight. But then she had remembered the incident when she was a child and the boy from the school yard next door had thrown rocks at her for no reason. What had the boy seen in Anabella that he didn't like? She wasn't overweight like Graziella. Maybe he had thought she was ugly? Or maybe he'd sensed she was different from him and the rest of the kids since she wasn't in school like them?

Graziella turned toward Anabella and smiled warmly when she saw her. Anabella froze and quickly looked away. Instead of feeling compassion for Graziella as she always had, she was mortified to be wearing a similar style dress to hers. Domenica and Concetta were seated in the pew behind Anabella. She didn't want to draw any more attention to herself than she already had.

Anabella tried to shut out the thoughts entering her mind, but it was no use. She knew she shouldn't feel this way toward Graziella. Hadn't Mamma always taught her to be kind to others and show compassion above all? Guilt washed over her. She turned back toward Graziella to try to catch her attention so she could say hi, but Graziella's face was now buried behind the pages of one of the prayer books that the church placed in every pew. Anabella could tell that instead of reading Graziella was using the book to shield her face.

"Mamma, would it be all right if I invited Graziella to sit with us? She's alone."

Signora Ferraro tilted her head and looked to where Graziella was sitting. "Why didn't Signore and Signora Montana come to church today?" She frowned. "Of course, ask the poor girl to join us."

Anabella stood up, and, as she did so, she noticed Domenica and Concetta look up. Willing herself to forget about them, she walked over to Graziella.

"*Ciao,* Graziella."

Graziella looked up, surprise etched across her features. But, instead of returning Anabella's greeting, she glanced down into her lap, where her prayer book now lay.

"I'm sorry I didn't say hi to you before. I

was upset about something. Mamma and I would like to know if you want to sit with us. There's still room in the pew, but we had better hurry up. The priest is about to make his procession down the aisle."

Anabella saw the altar boys and lectors lining up in front of Father D'Onofrio, who caught Anabella's gaze and smiled. She returned his smile, but quickly glanced away. Though she'd known Father D'Onofrio since she was a little girl, she still felt shy around him — and even a little fearful. Something about his demeanor had always instilled fear in her, even though he had never uttered a cross word to her.

"It's all right. You don't have to ask me just because your mother made you." Graziella shot Anabella an angry look.

Anabella was stunned for a moment. It was rare she was the receiver of anyone's scorn. But she knew Graziella had every right to be mad at her for the way she'd ignored her earlier.

"It was my idea to invite you, not Mamma's. Please, Graziella. Don't stay mad at me." Anabella reached out and placed her hand on Graziella's arm.

"All right, but you must tell me what upset you so much that you couldn't even return my smile."

"Fair enough. I'll tell you after Mass. Now let's go before Father D'Onofrio kicks us both out."

Graziella softly giggled as she picked up her pocketbook, which looked like a child's pocketbook and only served to emphasize her larger size. As they entered the pew and took their place alongside Signora Ferraro, Anabella saw Domenica and Concetta staring at them with an expression of disdain. They really were the meanest people Anabella had ever encountered. Then again, Anabella didn't come into contact with many people. She wondered if there were many more people out there like the Mazzeo sisters. If so, she was relieved to rarely venture outside of her rose farm. Except for the time when Mamma had been mad at Chiara for giving Anabella the sunflowers, she'd always witnessed her mother and the other workers treating one another with respect and kindness. Maybe that was why Mamma didn't have friends outside of the farm and why when she ran into the villagers she kept the conversations to a minimum. Mamma knew how mean people could be. Anabella would have to ask her mother about this sometime.

Later that evening when Anabella was alone in her bedroom, she walked over to her night table and picked up the most recent magazine Chiara had given her. She must have missed seeing the newer style of dresses that the other young women were wearing in church. But as she quickly flipped the pages, scanning each of the photos, she couldn't find any of the newer dresses. But when she closed the magazine, her eyes zeroed in on its issue date. March, 1960. The magazine was now more than a year old. She had always just assumed the magazines were new. No wonder she hadn't known that her A-line, full-skirted dress was going out of style. Eloisa must've known. Now that Anabella thought more about it, she remembered Eloisa had been wearing a fitted two-piece suit. But Anabella wasn't mad at her. After all, as Signora Mazzeo and her daughters had pointed out, La Donna Fiorentina was not carrying the latest fashions from Milan and Rome. So it wasn't as if Eloisa could've suggested Anabella buy one of the newer style of dresses.

Anabella picked up her hair and twisted it into a bun, securing it with a clip. She then pulled out a few strands in the front and tried to shape her hair to look like one of the styles the models in the magazine and the Mazzeo sisters sported. She didn't recognize the face staring back at her. No, the style was not for her — even if it was in vogue. Releasing her hair, she took one last look at herself in the dress before reaching behind to undo the zipper. Sadness slowly seeped in at the thought that she would have to remove what had now become her favorite garment. If only she could wear it every week. Though it had hurt at first to hear Domenica and Concetta say her dress was no longer in fashion, Anabella still loved it. The dress had made her feel for the first time like a grown woman. And for that reason alone, she knew it was a very special dress.

CHAPTER 9
DANTE

Siena, 1970

Dante had been working feverishly since the weekend, creating several smaller-scale paintings so he would have more to sell at the piazza this week. He'd thought of not making Anabella the subject in these paintings so that it would be less painful for him to part with them, but when he had tried to do so, he just found himself staring off into space and struggling to put paint to canvas. So once again Anabella was the star of his works, which he now had on display at Piazza del Campo. He had even done a few drawings of her last night so that he wouldn't have to wait for the paint to dry and would have more to sell.

It was nearing ten o'clock in the morning, and, though the market had only been open for an hour, Dante had already sold five of his works. He noticed several of the other artists glaring at him, no doubt envious that

106

he was selling more than they were. There were even people who had no intention of buying his art, but still stopped to ask Dante about the beautiful girl on his canvases. And when he'd been honest and told them she was a woman from his dreams, but omitted that she was also very much real, people were even more intrigued, causing a few to change their minds and buy one of the pieces.

Finally the crowds had dissipated, giving Dante a chance to take a short break. He sat on his folding chair and took out the *panino* of prosciutto and provolone that he had made in the morning. He had been too busy to give much thought to the fact that he'd had to part with more of his beloved works of Anabella. But he needed to make a living, and while he still wished he could hang on to every painting and drawing of her, it was beginning to become easier to sell the pieces. He had enjoyed hearing the comments from his buyers and even those who didn't purchase any work. Everyone seemed to be intrigued by the woman in the paintings and had complimented his technique.

Dante was startled out of his thoughts by what sounded like a little cry. He turned around and froze. Anabella was standing mere feet away from him. Her gaze was fixed on his paintings. A large straw bag was slung around her shoulder. It was gaping open with the numerous bouquets of roses it held. Her hair was plaited in one braid that hung over her left shoulder, giving her the appearance of a dairy maid and showing her perfect classical features to full effect — her unblemished olive complexion, her almond-shaped brown eyes, and her full, sensuous lips. He froze the image in his mind, having already decided his next painting would depict her exactly as she looked in this moment.

Anabella took a few steps forward, leaning in to get a better view of the paintings. Dante was too intrigued by her beauty to notice that she seemed alarmed. Her hand came over her mouth as she went from painting to painting and drawing to drawing, carefully studying each one. Finally, she lowered her hand and pointed to one of the paintings. Her eyebrows were knit furiously as she glared at Dante.

"Who are you? Why does this woman look so much like me?"

Dante's eyes widened in surprise at her accusatory tone. He looked at her and then to his paintings. It then dawned on him that she, or any other woman, would be disturbed by the paintings and drawings since they'd never met.

"Please, *signorina,* let me introduce myself. My name is Dante Galletti. You probably don't remember, but we did see each other briefly, here at the Piazza del Campo earlier in the summer."

Anabella looked at him, and after a moment he could detect a brief flicker in her eyes. She *did* remember seeing him before.

"You decided to paint a woman whom you only saw briefly, and in every one of your works? Have you been following me since that day?"

Dante could not help but laugh. "No, no! I lost sight of you quickly that day. I was actually on my way to come talk to you when one of the fruit vendors crashed into me with his cart, causing me to fall. When I got up, you were already gone."

"Why were you coming to talk to me?"

Confusion was etched across her features. He could tell she didn't believe him. How was he to answer her question without sounding absolutely mad or like a pervert? How could he tell her he had been dreaming about her?

"If I tell you, Signorina Ferraro, you will think I'm crazy or worse."

"How do you know my name? You have

been following me! I don't know who you are and why you have decided to paint me, but I warn you to stay away from me!" Anabella's voice rose sharply before she turned around and stormed off.

"Wait! Please! Let me explain!" Dante ran after her, not caring that he was leaving his works unattended.

Anabella walked hurriedly away and soon was weaving through the crowds, which were denser now. He saw she kept glancing over her shoulder, and, once she cleared the throng of people she was pushing her way through, she broke into a run. He couldn't lose her again, especially now that she was thinking the worst about him. He ran after her, all the while shouting, "Anabella! Anabella!"

A boy on a bicycle came careening out of nowhere and almost crashed into her. She stumbled wildly forward, falling onto her knees, and sending her straw bag of roses flying into the air. The boy on the bicycle also fell. Besides a few scrapes on his knees, he was unharmed, but he seemed to be more concerned about his bicycle. After inspecting it to make sure it hadn't been damaged, he waved his hands in Anabella's face.

"*Stupida!* Watch where you're going!"

Anabella seemed to shrink at the boy's words, looking down and blushing profusely.

Dante caught up to them and wasted no time in scolding the boy. "*Cretino!* Is this the way you treat a young lady? You could've killed her riding your bicycle like a lunatic! Apologize to her at once!"

The boy blanched and looked afraid of Dante, who was staring at him menacingly.

"*Mi dispiace, signorina.*"

"If I ever see you act that way again toward another woman, I will pummel you. Do you hear me?" Dante lowered his head so that he was at the boy's eye level. The boy swallowed hard, giving a slight nod before getting on his bicycle and pedaling quickly away.

"Are you all right?" Dante bent down next to Anabella.

"*Si.* I was just startled."

"Let me help you back up." Dante offered his hand. Anabella looked at it warily, before placing her hand in his.

"*Grazie.*"

Dante began picking up the roses that were now strewn all over the ground.

"Ah! My flowers! I won't be able to sell them now. Mamma will be so upset."

"They're not all ruined. We can tie the ones that came free from the bouquets back together again, or you can sell them as single roses to couples. Many young men can't afford to buy a whole bouquet."

"We don't sell to the people walking through the piazza, just to the flower vendors."

"You're losing out on money, then. I guess you never thought of that?"

Anabella shook her head. "Mamma handles the business of our farm. We own a rose nursery in Pienza and . . ." Her voice trailed off.

"And?" Dante asked.

"Nothing. I've said too much already. It's bad enough you know my name, and you still haven't explained why I am in all of your artwork."

"All right. It is time I confess, but before I do so, please don't be mad at me. Give me a chance to explain."

"I suppose I must, now that you have helped me collect my roses and have even given me a solution for selling the roses that we can't put back into bouquets."

"And, don't forget, I came to your defense with that little scoundrel!" Dante laughed.

"I'm sorry. *Grazie.* But you did not need to yell at him. He was just a boy."

"True, but how is he to learn the proper way to treat a lady if someone doesn't

112

discipline him? My mamma brought me up to always respect a woman and treat her well. But who knows? Maybe he is an orphan and doesn't have anyone to instill manners in him."

Anabella gave a slight smile, the first she had given him. *"Vero."*

"What was I saying a moment ago? Ah! My confession." He gave her a nervous smile.

"Go ahead. I promise I won't get upset." But instead of returning his smile to reassure him, she was staring at him intensely, obviously still not trusting him.

"I actually already know that you and your mother own a rose nursery, but I didn't know it was in Pienza."

Anabella's face twisted in anger, and she was about to say something before Dante held up his hands.

"I can explain. Remember I said that?"

She paused, nodded her head, and crossed her arms before saying, *"Va bene.* Go on. Explain."

"The day I saw you at the piazza, back in June, I was curious to know more about you, so I went over to the flower vendor whom you and your mother had sold your roses to. He was the one who told me your name, and he also told me about your rose farm."

"I see. But that still doesn't explain why you have decided to paint me. Have you seen me at the piazza every week since you first saw me and stalked me? Watching me while I was unaware so you could paint me?"

"No, no! I haven't seen you since that day — until now, of course. I admit, I was hoping to see you and looked for you when I came here every week, but I have not seen you. We must've missed each other. I alternate selling my work here and at the Medici Fortress. You were probably at the Piazza del Campo on the days I was at the Medici Fortress. But I am perplexed as to why I had never seen you before that first day in June if you and your mother come here regularly to sell your flowers."

"The piazza is usually very busy. It would be easy to miss each other. We don't come every week."

Dante nodded thoughtfully. At least her face had relaxed, and she didn't look as angry anymore. But he knew she was still waiting for him to explain why she was the subject of his paintings.

"Would you mind if I helped you sell your roses today? It would be quicker that way, and it's the least I can do since I feel I am the one to blame for your running off and almost crashing into that bicyclist."

"*Grazie.* But that won't be necessary. I will just tell Mamma that the boy knocked me down and I lost a few of the roses. She will understand."

"But you said earlier she would be upset."

"At first, but she won't be mad at me. She'll probably be angry that the boy was careless and ran into me. Mamma hardly ever gets cross with me."

Dante didn't know how true her statement was since Anabella's eyes grew distant for a moment.

"Please. Let me help you sell the roses. As I said earlier, you can make more money that way. You can then still tell your mother about the boy crashing into you with his bike and how you got the ingenious idea of selling the loose roses to couples and other people who might like to have a rose but cannot afford a bouquet."

"I don't know. I don't think I would feel comfortable approaching strangers. The flower vendors have known me since I was a little girl. It is different with them."

Anabella looked nervous. He noticed she had a habit of staring down at her sandals every so often. There was a certain shyness about her, although she didn't seem overly uncomfortable talking to him — even though she was angry. Perhaps her curiosity over the paintings had made her forget her shyness.

"Well, I can do all the talking. This way you can see how it's done and how easy it is."

Anabella sighed. "All right. It would be a shame to waste the roses, and it is getting late. Mamma will be expecting me for lunch and will be worried if I get home late. She often accompanies me, but did not feel well today."

After Dante helped Anabella tie whatever roses they could put back into bouquets and collect the ones they would sell loosely, they returned to the center of the piazza. He breathed a sigh of relief when he saw that all of his paintings were still where he had left them.

"Ah! I forgot about your paintings. Someone could have stolen them. Please, don't worry about me. Return to your stall. I will just sell the few bouquets I have to the flower vendors."

"Wait. Don't go anywhere. I will just ask one of the other artists to keep an eye on my paintings."

"But won't you lose money? What if

customers come by and want to buy a painting?"

"That is all right. I have made quite a bit of money this morning. If I don't sell any other paintings for today, I'll still be ahead."

"How many paintings did you sell?"

"Five."

"They were all of me?"

"They were."

"People liked them that much?" Anabella looked surprised.

"Of course. You are a very beautiful woman. Even people who have not bought any paintings have asked me about you. They are intrigued."

Anabella blushed.

Dante ran over to one of the other artists and asked him to keep an eye on his work. The artist seemed annoyed, but agreed anyway.

Twenty minutes later, Dante and Anabella had sold all of the loose roses. He accompanied her to the flower vendors and waited while she sold her bouquets.

When she was done, she walked over to Dante and smiled without reservations this time.

"Thank you again so much. You are a very good salesman, but I suppose that makes sense since you have to sell your paintings. I

117

don't know if I would ever have the courage to approach people and ask them if they want to buy a rose for their sweetheart."

"You will some day. It just takes some practice. If you want, I can help you sell more roses the next time you come."

"I don't know. I still don't think Mamma will be too keen on that idea, and, as I said earlier, she usually accompanies me when we come to sell our roses. But thank you." Anabella glanced at her watch. "I should be going, and I don't want to take you away from your work any more than I already have today."

"You cannot go until I tell you why I have been painting you."

Anabella looked surprised.

"You thought I would not bring it up."

She shrugged her shoulders. "I just wanted to make sure you weren't following me. But I can see you are a good person. I'm sure you have painted other people before, some of whom you might've seen only once. It was silly of me to have become so upset. I'm sorry."

"No, please, don't apologize. You were right to wonder why all of my paintings are of you and to be concerned that perhaps I was a creep."

Anabella laughed. "I didn't say that."

118

"But you were thinking it, which is all right. Most other women would have thought that as well."

"Let us just say we are good now. You helped me with my sales. And as you said, you have been selling a lot of your paintings of me, so we are even."

"Remember when I told you that you would think I was crazy if I told you why I was painting you?"

"*Si,* but it is okay, Dante. Really. You do not need to explain it to me. After all, we just met today. You don't owe a stranger any explanations, and it is your work. You can paint whomever you want to."

"But that is where you are wrong, Anabella. We have met, and I don't mean seeing each other on that afternoon back in June."

Anabella knitted her brows in confusion.

"I met you already in my dreams."

Her mouth dropped open as she took in what he said, before saying, "You are not playing with me?"

"No. I am being completely honest with you. That is why I wanted to talk to you when I first saw you at the piazza. I couldn't believe that the woman I had been dreaming about for a few months was actually real. I was curious to know your name and know more about you."

119

Anabella was silent for a few seconds before saying, "I'm not quite sure what to say. This is very odd."

Dante laughed. "I agree."

"Well, I really need to be going. Mamma will be worried. It was nice to meet you."

Dante took her hand. He wanted to place a soft kiss on the back of it, but knew that would be too forward of him, especially after making his admission that he'd been dreaming about her. She would surely think then that he was a creep. He placed his other hand on top of hers and merely said, "I am so happy to have finally met you — in person, this time. I'm sorry if I frightened you when you saw my paintings."

"Grazie. Buongiorno."

Dante knew it was time to let go of her hand, but he held on to it for a moment longer as their eyes met. He didn't want her to leave. His heart was pounding. Although she'd told him that she came to the piazza regularly to sell her flowers, he was still terrified of never seeing her again — and losing her forever.

"Arrivederci, Anabella. I hope to see you next time you are here." Reluctantly, he let go of her hand and watched her as she walked away, hoping she wasn't walking out of his life when he had only just met her.

When he returned to his stall, he took a seat on his folding chair. Suddenly, a fatigue washed over him. Although he had planned to stay at the piazza till sundown, he packed his belongings and began to leave. The artist whose stall was next to Dante's called out to him.

"You're leaving already? What's gotten into you, Dante? You disappear for over an hour, and then you come back and leave. Ah! That's right. You aren't starving like the rest of us artists with all the paintings of that girl that you've been selling."

Dante ignored him as he continued making his way out of the piazza. He knew what he was feeling at the moment had nothing to do with fatigue — at least the physical kind. His heart was aching — for without any doubt he had fallen victim to love at first sight. He'd known it that day back in June when he saw Anabella at the piazza. But if there were any doubts that he was in love, they had been put to rest today after seeing his muse and spending time with her. She was beyond beautiful, but she possessed gentleness and an innocence that drew him in even further. He smiled as he remembered how she had come to the defense of the boy on the bicycle, even though he had not deserved it after the way he'd insulted her. And then when she had told Dante that he didn't owe her an explanation for why he had chosen to paint her.

"Somehow, I will find a way to win your heart, Anabella," Dante vowed aloud.

CHAPTER 10
SIGNORA FERRARO

Pienza, 1970

Signora Ferraro was on her knees, tending to her white rose garden. The clusters of white roses reminded her of the scoops of vanilla gelato her father would buy her as a child. Her heart ached for a moment as she remembered her father.

Visitors to the farm were always surprised to learn that the white roses were Signora Ferraro's favorite.

"But they're so simple. How can you not prefer one of the brighter hues that you grow — like the vivid crimson or fuchsia roses, or the fiery orange and yellow blooms?" they would often ask.

"Their simplicity is the very reason why I love them so much. They have a subtle, quiet beauty that says they don't need any additional adornment to show that they are just as special as the colored roses. The

123

white roses are pure, not tainted with anything."

Her answer would often seem to satisfy
their curiosity as well as give them a new-
found appreciation for the white roses. What
Signora Ferraro didn't tell them was that
she also loved these flowers because they
represented new beginnings, but, more
important, they were a token of remem-
brance.

In addition to being used in weddings,
white roses were popular in funeral arrangements, especially when the deceased was a
young woman or a child. Although Signora
Ferraro mainly sold flowers to neighboring
florists and other vendors in Pienza and its
surrounding towns, sometimes the villagers
came directly to her farm and asked Signora
Ferraro if she would arrange the flowers for
their special occasions. And when the
request was for a funeral, she always took
care of the order herself, even though
Chiara was just as adept as she at creating
stunning arrangements.

But the white roses she chose for weddings and funerals did not come from the
garden she was tending to today. For this
was her private garden, forbidden to everyone including Anabella. The garden was the
first she had planted after she bought the

property — even before she knew she would turn all of the acres into a rose nursery. Every year, her private white rose garden grew. Signora Ferraro loved planting the seeds and watching the plants grow and then bloom. She never grew tired of them. Her need to continue growing and having the satisfaction of watching the flowers come to life was what had given birth to the idea of owning a rose farm.

Her customers and the villagers always praised her roses. So it came as a shock to Signora Ferraro one day when she was in town, purchasing a few food staples at the local market, to overhear two women gossiping about her and accusing her of being crazy for growing so many roses.

"There is Signora Ferraro," one of the women whispered, although her hushed tones were carried clearly to Signora Ferraro.

"You mean the crazy flower lady. Everyone in Pienza knows there is something not right with her. Every year, that rose farm grows."

"Well, maybe she is just greedy. After all, she is not the first business owner to be guilty of continually expanding."

"No, that is not it. Look at how she barely talks to any of the villagers, and, when she does, it is as if she doesn't trust them. There is a certain wild, almost paranoid look in her eyes. And then you just have to look at Anabella to know her mother is crazy."

Signora Ferraro's hand tightened on the loaf of *ciabatta* bread she was holding. How dare they talk about her daughter? She was about to turn around and reproach them. But then the rest of their conversation reached her, causing her to remain fixed in place.

"That poor girl. She is what now, twenty-six? It's well beyond time for her to marry and start a life and a family of her own. Instead, Signora Ferraro has her cloistered on that farm as if she is a nun. She might as well send the girl to a convent. Maybe you are right that Signora Ferraro is greedy — not just with her need to make more money on the rose farm, but also in keeping her daughter to herself. What a selfish woman. I don't think that girl has ever had a friend."

"*Povera ragazza.* Poor girl," the other woman whispered.

The two women were distracted by another villager who had come over to greet them, and soon Signora Ferraro was forgotten about as they began gossiping about another neighbor.

Signora Ferraro slowly made her way to

the cashier. Her legs felt like deadweight, and an overwhelming fatigue quickly washed over her. She was tempted to just leave the market, but she needed the groceries to prepare dinner.

"*Buongiorno,* Signora Ferraro! *Come sta?*" Carlo Battali warmly greeted her. He was the son of Vittorio Battali, the market's owner.

She merely nodded, still feeling too drained from overhearing the cruel words that had been spoken about her.

"Are you all right, *signora?* Would you like a glass of water?" Carlo looked at her with concern.

She almost cried at the young man's kindness, before managing to utter, "*No, grazie.* I just have a headache. I will be fine."

Signora Ferraro waited as Carlo rang up her items on the register. Although he was done in a few minutes, the time passed too slowly for her. Every few seconds, she glanced over to the gossiping women, hoping they wouldn't come over to the cashier while she was still standing there. She had never met these women, but she wasn't surprised they knew of her because of the rose farm. Pienza had been growing, and there were new people who moved here every year. It wasn't as it had been when she first came to Pienza years ago, when it had been easy to know most, if not all, of the villagers. And she'd always known people gossiped. These women must've learned all about her from the older residents.

After she paid Carlo and he packed her bags, he said, "I will carry these groceries to your car for you, Signora Ferraro. Though you say you are fine, I can clearly see you are not."

Before Signora Ferraro could protest, he had walked away with her bags. She followed him, casting a final glance in the direction of the ugly women who had gossiped about her. But they didn't notice her, as they were still talking animatedly among themselves.

Thanking Carlo, Signora Ferraro drove away from the market. But she did not go far. She pulled over on a quiet road. Her heart pounded violently against her chest as she gasped for air. Stepping out of the car, she walked to the passenger side so oncoming motorists wouldn't see her and then sank to her knees as she bent forward, trying to force her breathing to slow down. Closing her eyes, she thought about Franco's smile — his wonderful, gentle smile that had always disarmed her and managed to comfort her even when she had been afraid or distraught. Soon, her breathing returned to normal. She stood up and placed her hands on her lower back, which always ached from the long hours she spent crouched while gardening.

Pacing to and fro, she took in slow, deep breaths and tilted her chin slightly upward to the sky as she let the breeze cool her face. She'd sweated profusely during her panic attack. It had been years since she'd suffered from one, though sometimes in her sleep her nightmares led her to believe she was having another attack. Sometimes she was surprised that after twenty-six years, she was still having the same nightmares. While they had grown less frequent, she knew she would probably always have them until she died. She remembered there had been times when she had screamed in her sleep, forcing Anabella as a little girl to run into her bedroom, crying and pleading with Signora Ferraro to wake up. But the screaming had subsided by the time Anabella was a teenager. Signora Ferraro supposed she had gotten too old to muster the energy to scream anymore. And Anabella had learned early on not to pester her mother with questions when she had her nightmares. On a few occasions, Anabella crawled into Signora Ferraro's bed, nestling close to her until they both fell asleep. If she could have, she would have had her daughter sleep with her every night to ward off the bad dreams, but she did make Anabella return to her bed on certain nights. Despite what the two villagers had said, she had not been that selfish — or crazy. If she had been, she would've insisted that Anabella sleep with her every night.

Still. She replayed the women's words in her head: *Maybe you are right that Signora Ferraro is greedy — not just with her need to make more money on the rose farm, but also in keeping her daughter to herself. What a selfish woman. I don't think that girl has ever had a friend.*

Had she been that selfish? Anabella had always seemed like a happy child, running around the farm, having free rein on the massive property. And she had companions. Chiara, the other workers, and of course, Cioccolato. A handful of times, she had even let Anabella invite Graziella Montana over. But after her father died of a heart attack, Graziella and her mother were forced to move in with an uncle who lived in Genoa. Signora Montana was unable to handle running the butcher shop on her own and had sold it. Signora Ferraro hadn't understood that. After all, if she had managed to run her large farm, why couldn't Signora Montana handle a little butcher shop? But she knew she should not judge. As she had learned in her own life, everyone had his or her cross to bear and was struggling to do his or her best.

The gossiping women at the market were just jealous of her — jealous of her success with the farm, jealous that she did not have to worry about money as so many of the other villagers had to, perhaps even jealous that she could do as she pleased without having to run everything by a husband. But if Signora Ferraro could change any of the circumstances in her life, she would change the fact that she was a widow. When Franco had been alive, Signora Ferraro had never minded consulting with him on decisions, and once they married, Franco had granted her all the freedom she desired. He had always respected her intellect and her fierce independence. She'd known she was very lucky — for that was not the norm in most marriages in her time and even today.

Stupida! *What is the matter with you? Why didn't you give those women a piece of your mind? How could you have let them get away with talking about you and Anabella like that?* She silently scolded herself, shaking her head. The young woman she had been twenty-six years ago would never have let anyone get away with mistreating her or those she loved. What had become of that woman? Rarely did Signora Ferraro look at herself in the mirror. She brushed her hair without even checking to ensure every strand was in place. And she never bothered examining herself in her clothes to see how they fit. Besides, most of her clothes were her everyday sundresses and shirtwaist dresses or the dungarees she wore when the weather cooled and she was working out-doors on the farm. Even on Sundays when she wore a nicer dress to attend church, she didn't bother looking at herself. But some-times she could not resist the temptation to see how time had been treating her. And from what she saw in the mirror, it had not been kind to her. The woman who stared back was unrecognizable from the vibrant, beautiful woman she had been in the prime of her youth.

Returning to her car, Signora Ferraro got inside, but instead of starting the ignition, she lay down across the seats and closed her eyes. She was not ready to return home just yet. Though her panic attack had subsided, she was still feeling weary. Soon, she drifted off to sleep and, dreaming, returned to one of the happiest — and most terrifying — times in her life.

CHAPTER 11
MARIA ROSSI

Florence, 1943

Maria was up early, making her way through the outdoor market, where she purchased her family's produce and other grocery staples. She loved waking up early and arriving at the market as soon as it opened, before the crowds descended upon it. As she walked by the vendors' tables, she hummed softly to herself. She stopped at Filomena's table. Filomena always had the best, most fresh produce at the market, and Maria loved chatting with her.

"Buongiorno, Filomena. *Come stai oggi?"*

"Ciao, Maria. *Bene, bene, grazie.* I hope you are doing well today." Filomena smiled.

"Si. We must be grateful for whatever blessings we have, at least for now." Maria's face clouded for a moment, before she realized that she should've kept the conversation light. Ever since the war had begun everyone was on edge as they constantly

wondered if things would get worse and when it would end.

Filomena sighed. "I know. As we've learned, things can change in an instant. But it is out of our control. All we can do is pray."

Maria nodded. Her thoughts turned to the man she had met in the sunflower field two weeks ago. Since then, she'd wondered several times if he'd been captured again and had remembered what he'd told her about people being sent to remote Mediterranean islands or worse. A shiver traveled down her spine. She hoped he was safe.

"So, what can I interest you in today? Look how beautiful my eggplants and zucchini are. I think they might be the largest crop I've grown yet. It's your lucky day if you ask me." Filomena laughed as she gestured toward the vegetables.

"Ah, *si*! They are gorgeous. I'll make a ratatouille. I wasn't sure what to make for dinner today, but now that I see how ripe the eggplants and zucchini are, they'll be perfect for that dish."

In addition to the eggplants and zucchini, Maria took a pound of plum tomatoes. She paid Filomena and wished her a good day before she took her leave. As she was placing her produce into her large straw tote bag, she noticed a paper folded in half inside. She frowned. The bag had been empty when she took it out of her closet this morning. All she had placed in it was her wallet. Taking the paper out, she unfolded it and gasped softly when she saw it was none other than an anti-Fascist leaflet written by FAF — Florentines Against Fascism. How did this end up in her bag? Quickly, she glanced over her shoulder to see if anyone was looking at her or if any police were present. But all she saw were ordinary people going about their day, engrossed in picking out their fruits and vegetables. She was about to crumple the leaflet and find a discreet way of discarding it, when curiosity took a hold of her, and she decided to continue reading it.

My fellow Florentines, we must continue to RESIST our Fascist regime. Many of our fellow *paesani* continue to be imprisoned unjustly. FAF needs all the help we can get. Please consider joining our efforts. If you have already fallen victim to the forces that currently hold us imprisoned in our own motherland, you do not need to stand idly by. Come RESIST with us. Come fight for justice and for a free Italy. For those who have been fortunate enough not to experience personally yet the evils of Fascism, I still implore you to join us. It is only a matter of time before you, too, will be affected. Things are only becoming more dire in our country as the war rages on around the world. Soon no one will be immune to the havoc the Fascists have laid in their wake and will continue to mete out. RESIST, my fellow Florentines — for it is our only chance for salvation.

The rest of the leaflet then went into detail about recent incidents that had happened in and around Florence. A couple had been arrested, falsely accused of writing anti-Fascist literature. Both the man and woman had been imprisoned and tortured. To the surprise of the couple, they were released, but not before being told, "Go home and show your neighbors your beaten faces. Warn them that this and much worse will happen if they, too, speak out against Fascism." But as the couple left the prison, the husband had been shot in the back. Another incident described two old men, minding their own business playing bocce at a park just outside of town. The men were accused of being spies for FAF and were also imprisoned. Their families had not been able to visit them in prison, and no one knew of their fate.

There were other incidents, but Maria stopped reading. A seething anger began growing inside of her. How dare they kill and imprison innocent people? But as the man in her father's sunflower garden and this leaflet had warned, no one was truly immune. For years as Mussolini grew ever more powerful, scores of young men had been rounded up and asked to profess their allegiance to Mussolini or risk being punished.

Although her father had confessed behind closed doors that he hated Mussolini and thought he was the devil incarnate, her father had refused to attend meetings that were held in secret to try to retaliate against the Fascist regime. And even with more and more of their neighbors joining the fight, he had not wanted to become involved. Maria didn't blame him. He was growing older, and her father had always had more of a pacifist nature. But her brother Michele was another story. Unbeknownst to their father, Michele had recently begun attending anti-Fascist meetings, but she wasn't sure of the name of the group. Could it be Franco's group, FAF? She'd overheard Michele talking about the meetings to Enza, but when she'd stepped into the room, he had quickly ended the discussion. Later, Maria had tried asking Enza about it, but Enza had changed the subject. Maria had felt a little hurt that neither Michele nor Enza had taken her into their confidences. Though she later realized that they were probably just trying to protect her, the rejection had still stung.

So it had been easier for Maria to try to pretend that what was happening in her country was not really happening. But deep down, there was a part of her that feared someday the horrors she'd heard about would infiltrate her world.

She crumpled the leaflet and discreetly threw it on the ground by a sack of potatoes leaning against a vendor's table. Maria walked away, but only managed to take a few steps before she heard someone call out to her. Her heart raced, but then she realized she had nothing to fear since only her family or friends would know her name. Turning around, she didn't recognize the man standing before her. He was wearing a gray fedora hat with a black band around its brim and dark sunglasses. He smiled and removed his sunglasses. She was stunned to see Franco, the man she had found hiding in Papà's sunflower garden.

"I think you dropped something." Franco

139

stepped forward and placed in her palm the leaflet she had discarded a moment ago. He closed his hand over hers. The gesture felt strangely intimate.

She swallowed hard before looking around nervously to see if anyone was watching them.

"*Grazie,* but I do not need the leaflet anymore."

"Are you sure? You didn't finish reading it." Franco gave her a half smile.

Maria opened her mouth, about to ask him how he knew she hadn't read the entire leaflet, but instead said, "You were watching me."

"You catch on quickly. Smart as well as beautiful." Franco's gaze traveled the length of her body, causing Maria's face to flush. "I also noticed you looked moved by what you read."

"So now you are a mind reader in addition to a stalker." Maria crossed her arms in front of her chest, but the action only caused Franco to rest his gaze on her bosom. She did her best to remain composed and willed herself silently not to blush again.

When he looked back up into her face, he said, "You should attend our next meeting. We're having one tomorrow night at seven o'clock. Many other women will also be present. We can really use all the help we can get." Franco took a pen out of the satchel bag he wore across his body and quickly scribbled on the back of the leaflet she had discarded earlier. "Here's the address." He handed the leaflet back to Maria.

She paused for a moment before taking it. Franco gestured with his head to the opposite side of the market in the direction of a young woman who looked to be no more than eighteen years old. She was walking slowly, casually peering at the produce on the vendors' tables. But as she leaned in to get a better look, she discreetly dropped a leaflet into the basket of an unsuspecting shopper.

"So that was who dropped the leaflet into my bag. She's quite good. I had no idea."

"Actually, it was me. By the way, I love the perfume you are wearing." This time, Franco's lips broke into a wide grin.

He was having fun with her. Although she didn't quite know why she was pleased that he had noticed her perfume, she was also becoming irritated by his smugness.

"I see my earlier assessment of your being a stalker was correct." She glanced at her wristwatch. "If you'll excuse me, I need to be going. I am glad you are safe and well. *Buongiorno.*"

Maria walked away before he could return her good-bye. She quickened her step, but it was no use. In seconds, Franco was by her side again.

"That is good to know that you were worried for my safety, *signorina*. I was also worried about your safety — so much so, that I returned to your property the next day to make sure that you weren't walking through the sunflower garden alone again." Instead of smiling arrogantly this time, he merely stared at her with concern evident in his eyes.

Maria was taken aback, but then realized his ploy. "You did not return to my house. Do you take me for a fool?"

"Of course not! I told you earlier you are smart, and I meant it. But I sensed when we met that you don't frighten easily. That was why I thought you might not heed my words of caution."

Again, she was taken aback. She had never met anyone so observant before.

"Thank you for your concern. You are right. It takes a lot to frighten me."

"But you should be afraid. As I mentioned when I first met you, these are very uncertain times."

Maria nodded. "Yes, yes, I do realize that."

"I must admit, even though I was relieved you weren't out alone again in your father's garden, out of fear for your safety, a part of me was disappointed because I wanted to see you again. So you can imagine how pleased I am to have run into you today."

Maria looked over to the young woman whom Franco had pointed out. She was still dropping leaflets into shoppers' bags.

"I know you must be on your way. Will you come to the meeting tomorrow night?"

Maria paused for a moment before responding. "I cannot make any promises, and I must give it more thought. This is not a matter that can be decided at a second's notice."

"Naturally, I understand. I hope to see you there. If not, I'm sure our paths will cross again. *Arrivederci*, Maria." He took her hand and softly kissed it before taking his leave.

Maria watched him as he headed in the direction of the young woman who was helping him. Once he reached her, Maria noticed how their heads came close together as they engaged in what looked like an intense discussion.

Throughout her walk home, Maria could not stop thinking about Franco. He had managed to amaze her with his insight into her mind and feelings. There was no way she would attend their meeting. It was too dangerous, and if Papà found out, he'd never let her out of his sight again. But she had to admit she was curious. Maybe she should tell her brother about the meeting? But no, he would only tell her to steer clear. Although she was Michele's senior by five years, he often acted like he was the older sibling, and he'd always been very protective of her. He would then want to know how she had met Franco, and she could never tell Michele that while everyone was taking his or her siesta, she was walking alone in the sunflower garden. For Franco wasn't the first one to have warned her recently against taking walks alone through the garden.

Well, she had several hours to decide if she would attend the meeting tomorrow night. Franco had managed to intrigue her. She wondered if his work with FAF involved more dangerous activities, other than his writing and publishing his anti-Fascist newspaper. There was something innocent about him although she knew that was ridiculous. She could tell he was at least a few years older than her, which would make him in his early to mid-thirties. Naturally, he was an experienced man. But he seemed . . . good. That was the only way she could put it. Even with his smug comments, she could tell he had morals, especially after he admitted he'd gone back to the sunflower garden to ensure she was not there. He'd risked getting caught again to make certain she was safe. There was no doubt he was also very courageous for standing up for his ideals and speaking out against the opposition, knowing he was risking imprisonment and perhaps worse. For all of these reasons, Maria knew he was a conscientious person. But she also knew that when it came to revolution and fighting for what you believed in, even the good were forced to commit acts that might go against their moral code.

CHAPTER 12
ANABELLA

Siena, 1970

As Anabella grew up, she learned from her mother everything about roses and growing them. Their farm had expanded when the school next door was sold, and Signora Ferraro bought the adjacent property. Though Anabella loved the rose farm, recently she'd begun to feel restless. She often wondered what else there was outside of their sheltered world. Her only foray beyond their small village was when she and Mamma went into Siena to sell their roses to the flower vendors who lined the Piazza del Campo. Anabella always tried to take in as many of the sights and sounds as she could. She stared at the people, especially the college students who hung out in the piazza, and wondered what it was like to live in such a bustling city. But what fascinated her the most were the young couples she saw. They seemed to be everywhere in Siena, and they were always locked in embraces and kissing. Many of the couples looked younger than her, still in their teens. Recently, it had dawned on Anabella that she was twenty-six years old and had yet to be kissed by a boy.

Mamma had not been feeling well lately, complaining of being more tired than usual, so she hadn't been accompanying Anabella to Siena.

"You are a grown woman now after all. You don't need your mamma by your side every waking minute." Mamma had said this in a playful manner.

Sometimes Anabella wondered if it were really her mother who needed her more than the other way around. When Anabella was a child, Mamma had repeatedly said that Anabella needed her in order to learn and thrive. But Anabella had always sensed that her mother needed her just as much, if not more.

In the month since she had first talked to Dante, she'd visited him at the Piazza del Campo. Anabella had tried to resist walking over to where Dante sold his drawings and paintings, knowing Mamma wouldn't approve. But her curiosity had been too overwhelming. She'd wanted to see if he had created more works of her, which he had.

When she looked at the drawings, and especially the paintings, which felt so life-like, Anabella felt almost as if she were seeing herself in a mirror, mainly because Dante had captured her likeness so well. But the Anabella in his creations was much different from the real one who greeted her each morning in the mirror when she washed her face and brushed her hair. For when she looked at the woman in Dante's works, it was as if she were seeing facets of herself that were only just now beginning to reveal themselves, whereas the Anabella she saw in the mirror had nothing new to reveal; it was the same Anabella.

There was something alluring about the woman in Dante's works. She seemed from another world, and there was this knowing look in her eyes and even her smile — a confidence Anabella herself had never seen or felt. She'd never believed she was insecure. But just as soon as this thought popped into her head, Anabella remembered that Easter Sunday when she was a teenager and had felt uncomfortable after the Mazzeo sisters pointed out that her dress was no longer in fashion.

She liked the Anabella that Dante depicted. Part of her wanted to take one of the paintings home with her, although she could never be so presumptuous and ask Dante if she could, especially since she knew he needed them to make a living. She could purchase one, but how would she explain the painting to Mamma? Mamma would think Dante was a creep, and Anabella wouldn't blame her, since she'd wondered the same thing about him when she first saw she'd been the subject of his works.

Each week when she visited him, Dante asked her if he could take her to a nearby café for an espresso, but she'd always declined. Today, however, she was going to accept — that is, if he asked her again. Her heart began to pound against her chest as she contemplated the possibility that he might not ask her. After all, she had said no every time he asked. Surely, he would soon get tired of asking.

Anabella had taken extra care with her appearance that morning. She'd brushed her hair to the side so that it draped over her right shoulder and across her right bosom. She had secured it with two jeweled combs that Mamma had given her for her birthday. And she'd dabbed a few drops of perfume on her wrists and neck — something she only did when she attended church with Mamma. She had prayed her mother wouldn't notice the fragrance as she walked by her, before she left the house. But Mamma had been at the kitchen table, reading the newspaper, and had briefly looked up to say good-bye before returning to her paper.

As Anabella entered the Piazza del Campo, she felt even more nervous. Part of her wanted to rush over to Dante and see if he would ask her to go to the café. She could not take the anticipation any longer. But she knew that would seem strange, since she only went to visit him after she sold her roses. Besides, she wanted to be done with work so that she would not have to worry about unloading the flowers. So she made her rounds quickly to the different vendors.

"Anabella, sei bellissima oggi!" Many of the vendors complimented her appearance. Her cheeks colored, but she was glad they had noticed, for if they thought she looked beautiful, hopefully Dante would as well.

She saved two of the pink roses from the last bunch she sold. Breaking off most of their stems, she tucked the roses into her hair combs. Before heading over to Dante, she walked over to the table of a merchant who sold mirrors, brushes, and perfumes in crystal bottles. Pretending she was interested in one of the handheld mirrors, she quickly took a look to ensure she had placed the roses perfectly in her hair. She smiled shyly at the old lady selling the wares and placed the mirror back down on the table before she took her leave. She could hear the old lady curse at her under her breath for not buying anything. Anabella giggled softly to herself. She was beginning to feel like the Anabella from Dante's drawings and paintings — daring rather than her usual shy, meek self.

As she made her way toward Dante, she saw he was sketching a little boy who sat on a stool. The boy's father kept reprimanding him to stop fidgeting. Dante worked quickly. Anabella waited, not wanting to disturb him. After he was done with his sketch and the boy's father paid him, she walked over. His back was turned to her as he was putting his money away.

"*Ciao,* Dante." Anabella's voice sounded shaky to her. She hoped Dante didn't hear how nervous she was.

He looked up, his face immediately beaming when he saw her. "Anabella! *Che bella sorpresa!*" He smiled, instantly easing some of her nerves.

"It isn't really a surprise since I have been stopping by every week for the past month now." She laughed softly.

Dante looked pleased that she had made a joke. Usually, he did most of the joking — and even talking — when she visited him.

"That is correct, but you are here earlier than you normally are."

"I was able to sell my flowers quickly today."

Something flickered in Dante's eyes. Did he realize she had rushed so she could see him sooner? She felt her cheeks warm. Bending over quickly so he wouldn't notice, she pretended to look at one of his drawings of Florence's Ponte Vecchio.

"I like how you are wearing your hair today. You should wear it like that more often."

Anabella looked up. He was staring at her intensely.

"*Grazie.*" She didn't meet his eyes as she stood up and glanced over to where a puppy was chasing a pigeon.

"Do you have to go home soon?" Dante's voice sounded guarded.

Her heart leaped. He was about to ask her to go to the café again.

"No. Since I am finished with work early today, I have time. Besides, Mamma has been taking longer naps since she hasn't been feeling well. She won't notice if I arrive home later."

Dante raised his eyebrows. She thought she could detect a hint of a smile forming at the corners of his lips. "I see. I hope she is not too ill?"

"I don't think so. She has been more tired than usual lately. I keep telling her she needs to let the workers do more of her work. But she is stubborn. Thank you for asking."

"Well, we should not let the day be wasted. How about we finally go get that espresso at Café San Lucca?"

"I would like that." Anabella smiled, and this time she didn't pull her gaze away from Dante's. She could detect a faint blush spreading across his cheeks. Was he just as nervous as she was?

"I will just be five minutes as I pack my paintings and drawings and take them to my car, which is parked just outside of the piazza's entrance."

"That is fine. Please, take your time."

Dante whistled. It sounded familiar to Anabella and like one of the operas her mother played on their record player, but she wasn't quite sure which one. She was about to ask him when he said, "I painted a new work of you this past week."

"You did?" She didn't know why she sounded surprised. He'd had at least one, if not more, new works of her every week she'd visited, although she hadn't noticed any on display today.

"*Sì.* I didn't bring it because I am still working on it. It's my largest painting of you yet."

Anabella nodded. She wanted to ask him what it looked like, but she refrained.

"Don't worry. You will see it soon enough." Dante laughed.

Anabella was taken aback that he'd been able to read her thoughts. "How did you know I was thinking about what it looked like?"

"Your face showed disappointment when I said I didn't bring it with me today."

A few minutes later, they were seated at Café San Lucca. In addition to espresso, Dante had bought almond and hazelnut biscotti for them.

Anabella glanced at her surroundings and at the café's patrons. She had never been in a café before. Everyone was talking animatedly, laughing, or gesticulating feverishly with their hands. The café's walls were decorated with gilded wallpaper. And the aromas of freshly brewed espresso and just-baked pastries were heavenly. She stared at a young woman whose ankle was interlocked with the ankle of the man she was with. Their chairs were pulled so close together that she could have just sat in his lap. The woman smiled and batted her eyelashes at the man as he whispered in her ear. She noticed Anabella staring at them, and she frowned in her direction.

Anabella didn't realize why she seemed angry with her. She was just admiring how pretty the girl was and had been curious about how close she was to the young man she was with.

"Are you all right?" Dante lowered his head so that his gaze met Anabella's.

She glanced once more to the young couple before returning her attention to Dante.

"*Si.* That woman looked at me as if she were angry."

"Ah! Yes, those two. They should keep their business behind closed doors instead of forcing the rest of us to watch them. She probably thinks you're after her man."

"Why would she think that?" Anabella's eyes widened.

Dante laughed and placed his hand over Anabella's. "I was just kidding. But then again, women can be very jealous, especially when they think they've found their Prince Charming — although I'm not so sure that man could be anyone's ideal Prince Charming."

"I suppose she was also mad because I was staring at them. I didn't mean to. I was just curious."

Dante looked at her thoughtfully. "It is all right. We all get curious, and what better place to stare at people than in a café? You just have to learn to be a bit more discreet, that's all. I am always staring at people. It's research for my art."

"Research?"

"How can I capture emotions in my portraits if I don't study people in everyday life and see how they act in their environments? I am always observing and registering everything I see in my mind." Dante pointed to his head.

"Is that what you did when you dreamed about me? You made yourself remember your dreams and what I looked like in them so that you could paint me accurately?"

"*Si.*"

Anabella took a sip of her espresso. It was much stronger than the espresso Mamma made.

"The espresso is very good, but I think my mamma's biscotti are much better." Anabella took a bite out of her *biscotto.*

Dante laughed. "You are so honest."

Anabella stopped chewing, suddenly feeling self-conscious. "I'm sorry."

156

"No, no. There is nothing wrong with that. Your candidness is so refreshing. People often put on a façade, rather than being their genuine selves. But with you, everything I see is what I get. I do not have to wonder if what you are saying is really how you think and feel. I like that. It's a compliment."

"I see. *Grazie,* then. I don't think I thanked you for my espresso and biscotti. *Grazie molto.*"

"*È niente.* It's my pleasure. I'm just glad you didn't have to pay for biscotti that you are not crazy about."

"No. They are good. They're just not as good as Mamma's."

"Perhaps some time I can taste your mamma's biscotti. She must be an excellent cook and baker. My mother was." Dante's eyes grew somber.

"Is your mother still alive?"

"No. She and my grandmother were my only relatives. My grandmother died shortly after my mother. The grief over losing her daughter was too much for her."

"How did your mother die? Was she ill?"

Dante shook his head. "She was coming home late from work one night and was struck by a drunk motorist. The pig drove off. The police never found out who it was."

"I'm so sorry. And what about your father? When did he die?"

"I don't know if he's alive or dead. He left my mother after he found out she was pregnant with me. She was only nineteen."

"So you are like me. I have never known my father either, but in my case, he died during the war when I was a baby."

"I am sorry, Anabella."

"We all have our crosses to bear in life. That is what Mamma always says."

"How true that is."

"I like it here. Thank you for taking me."

"I am happy you are enjoying yourself. Do you have any favorite cafés you like to go to either here in Siena or where you live in Pienza? I imagine there must be a small village with shops and cafés there."

"No. This is my first time in a café."

"Really?" Dante raised his eyebrows. "You have never been to a café? How can you live in Italy and have never gone to one?"

Anabella looked down. She didn't think it was that big of a deal. She doubted many of her neighbors or the other farmers in Pienza went to cafés or regularly dined in restaurants. Anabella had gone to a restaurant once, when she turned sixteen. But her mother had seemed uncomfortable the entire time they were there. Chiara had joined them and had talked with Anabella for the duration of the evening while Mamma merely looked at the people around her and said little.

"We work a lot at the rose farm. The farmers in Pienza would rather eat their own food and drink their own espresso than pay double at a café or restaurant."

"Maybe next time we can go to a restaurant."

"I have been to a restaurant, but only once."

Dante looked sad, but remained silent.

"I should probably be going." Anabella's voice sounded wistful. She was having a good time and was not ready to leave.

"You don't sound so sure." Dante smiled.

"This has been nice."

"Before you leave, I want to show you something. Can you spare ten more minutes?"

Anabella glanced at her watch. Mamma would be waking up soon from her nap. Anabella could tell her there had been an accident and that had delayed her. She had never lied to Mamma, but it was a small lie. She would pray to God tonight and ask Him to forgive her.

"All right."

As they left the café, Anabella could feel

Dante's eyes on her. Was she making a mistake? Spending all this time alone with him? She'd never been alone in the company of a man before. Doubt began to seep into her mind, but, as if reading her thoughts, Dante gave her a reassuring smile and said, "I hope you know you can feel comfortable, and safe, with me. I would never do anything to disrespect you."

Immediately, she felt better. Again, there was something about Dante that made it easier for her to trust him.

"We could walk to the place I want to show you, but it would be quicker if we drove, just a five-minute drive. Are you all right with that?"

"*Si.* That is fine."

Dante's car looked quite old and as if it had seen its fair share of accidents, with multiple dents and scratches.

"Are you sure it's safe for me to get in the car with you?" Anabella asked, unable to hide her grin.

Dante looked at her, surprised, and then followed her gaze to his beat-up car.

"Ah! I bought the car this way. It's used. Unfortunately, it's the only car I could afford, but I can assure you the motor and the rest of its parts are in excellent working condition, and I am a very careful driver, especially after how my mother died."

Anabella immediately regretted her joke. "I'm sorry."

"No, no! Has anyone ever told you that you apologize too much? I know you were only joking, and I love it that you seem more comfortable around me today. Please do not hold back."

"I suppose I do apologize a lot, but it is how Mamma taught me — to always be polite and considerate toward others."

"And she taught you well, but there are occasions when you don't need to apologize, especially when you are just being your true self."

Anabella nodded, though she wasn't exactly quite sure what Dante meant.

As he promised, they reached their destination within five minutes. She had been lost in her thoughts and had not noticed the landscape before her until Dante stopped the car. When she looked out her passenger window, she gasped. "Oh, my! What a vast field."

An enormous field of sunflowers spread out before her. Although she was accustomed to seeing sunflower fields on her weekly drives to Siena, she had never seen one so large. The sunflowers swayed to and fro every time the soft breeze that was present today blew by. She got out of the car and walked ahead of Dante. When she was a child and had first seen a sunflower field from Mamma's car, she had wondered what it would be like to run, or even simply just walk, through the rows of sunflowers. But her mother's angry reactions to sunflowers had made Anabella repress the yearning to walk among them. Now, here she was, free to do as she pleased and finally close enough to touch the beautiful, large flowers. She quickened her step as she walked among the flowers, holding her hands out to feel their stems. She stopped and stared up at an especially large sunflower, before reaching her hands up to gently pull it toward her face. She inhaled deeply, taking in the flower's scent. While it wasn't as fragrant as the roses on her farm, the sunflower still had a subtly pleasing scent. She then noticed a group of sunflowers whose seeds had ripened. She rushed over to them and broke a few seeds free from one of the flowers. She popped some of the seeds into her mouth and chewed on them, and, as she had done when she'd first eaten the seeds in her room, she swallowed the shells instead of spitting them out. Anabella then realized Dante was not by her side. She had been so excited to see the beautiful sunflowers and to walk through them that she had left him behind. How rude must he think she was? She turned around and was startled to realize he had been right behind her the entire time. But he was sketching feverishly.

"What are you doing?"

"Don't mind me. Please, go back to enjoying the sunflower seeds." Dante smiled before returning his attention to his sketch.

Anabella then realized he was drawing her. She felt self-conscious, so, instead of eating the rest of the seeds she held, she let them drop from her hand as she turned her back toward Dante and walked a few feet ahead. Closing her eyes, she enjoyed the feeling of the sun's warmth on her face. When she opened her eyes again, Dante was standing in front of her. His face was mere inches away. Anabella opened her mouth to ask him if everything was all right, but before she could utter a word, he placed his hands gently on either side of her face and leaned in closer, placing a soft kiss on her mouth. She was stunned — and afraid. But almost as soon as the fear entered her heart, he stepped back.

"I'm sorry, Anabella. I don't know what came over me." Dante ran his hand through his hair as he looked off to the side. His face was flushed.

Anabella remained silent. Her heart was racing, and her stomach felt funny. And then the strangest thought entered her mind. She wanted him to kiss her again. Though she had felt afraid as soon as he'd placed his lips on hers, the fear was now entirely gone, leaving in its wake a longing to be close to Dante again. But she was too embarrassed to tell him her thoughts.

A few more seconds elapsed before Dante broke the silence.

"Would you like to see what I was sketching?"

Anabella nodded. She followed him back to the spot where he'd been drawing. He picked up his sketchbook from the ground. The breeze had flipped the cover of the book closed. As he riffled through the book to reach the page he'd been drawing on, Anabella stared at him. He was handsome. She'd never really noticed how handsome he was before. All she'd known was that there was something about him that had intrigued her. And it was more than just the bizarre fact that this man she'd never met before had dreamed about her and had then decided to make her the subject of his drawings and paintings.

"I was working quickly, so I still need to touch up a few aspects of it." Dante held up the sketch.

She was speechless. In the short amount of time he'd had to draw the picture, he had not only captured the scene with Anabella walking through the sunflowers, but he'd also managed to depict the emotions she was feeling as she strolled through the field. Her head was tilted up as she looked at the sunflowers, awe evident in her face, and a soft smile danced along her lips. There was a glow in her face, and her eyes were wide-open, as if some new knowledge was being imparted upon her.

"I have a name for it already. I've called it *Anabella's Awakening.*"

"My awakening?"

"Yes. I saw something inside of you light up as you first took in the field of sunflowers and then as you walked through them. It was as if you were seeing them for the first time, although I know that's not the case since you can't avoid seeing sunflowers here in Tuscany. It was similar to how you looked in the café when you were taking everything in. But this time it was heightened."

"You could see all of that?" Anabella's voice came out in a whisper as she tried to fight back tears. She didn't know why she was close to crying. Perhaps it was because this man, whom she had only met recently, seemed to possess the ability to see right into her soul. Not even Mamma, who was the person she was closest to, had ever been able to truly know Anabella's thoughts or feelings.

"Yes. And after the little you told me about yourself today, I sensed there is a lot about the world you have yet to experience. I am only too happy I brought you here today, if only for the reason that I was able to see the joy it brought you. Though you seem content for the most part, Anabella, I cannot help but detect that there is also a certain sadness in you. Am I right?"

Anabella was overcome. She looked down at her feet, a habit she had not managed to break from her childhood, whenever she was feeling shy or self-conscious. But this time she looked down to try to shield her eyes, which were quickly filling with tears, from Dante's line of vision. She tried to blink the tears back, but it was no use. Dante lifted her chin gently, forcing her to look directly at him.

"Don't be embarrassed. You are the most beautiful woman I have ever met, and I would like to know everything about you — what makes you happy, what makes you laugh, even what makes you cry."

"I don't know what to say, Dante. I've never met anyone quite like you. Then again, I don't know many people other than my mother and the workers on our farm."

Dante laughed. "There is again that frankness that I love about you."

Anabella laughed, wiping the tears from her face.

"This might be too forward of me, Anabella, but I guess after I had the audacity to kiss you earlier, this will probably pale in comparison. But I was wondering if you would pose for me?"

"Pose for you?"

"As I draw or paint you, like I did today."

"But you haven't needed me to pose for you when you created your other works."

"Yes, but now that I know you and can see you in the flesh rather than just in my dreams, I can bring more life into my paintings. I can see in your face the emotions you are feeling while I work. And it would give us an opportunity to become more acquainted with each other. But if you do not feel comfortable or if you do not wish to become better friends with me, that is all right." Now it was Dante's turn to look down.

"I would like to become your friend."

"Really?"

Anabella nodded as she gave Dante a shy smile.

"Is that a yes then to my request that you pose for me?"

"It might be hard since I only have so much time when I come to the piazza, and I don't know if Mamma will be feeling better soon and will want to accompany me again. But if you can work quickly as you did today, we can try to fit it in."

Dante knitted his brows as he crossed his arms around his chest and paced back and forth for a few moments before responding. "I have an idea. How about if I helped you sell your flowers as soon as you arrive at the piazza? This way, you will be done with your work earlier, and you will have more time to pose for me."

"But what about the sale of your paintings and drawings?"

"I can do that on the days of the week when I'm not with you."

"Are you sure?"

"*Cento per cento!* Besides, if these paintings come out even better than the ones I have already done of you, you might make me a rich man!"

"So I am a means to your making money?" Anabella frowned as she raised her eyebrow and did her best not to laugh.

Dante picked up her hands and placed a kiss on them. "Please, don't ever say that. As I mentioned earlier, I would never do anything to make you feel uncomfortable or disrespect you. I suppose that was a tasteless joke I made. Please forgive me." He held her hands to his heart as he said this.

Anabella could feel his heart beating, and she swallowed hard. Even if she had been angry, how could she not forgive him? "There is nothing to forgive. I, too, was joking."

After Dante dropped Anabella off by her parked car, they made plans to meet near the flower vendors' tables next week. He held open her car door as she stepped inside.

"*Ciao,* Anabella. I look forward to seeing you next week."

"*Ciao.*"

Dante waved as she drove away. She returned the wave and smiled. She sighed deeply as she thought about what she had just done. Was she out of her mind? Agreeing to pose for Dante? Even though he'd agreed to work with the amount of time she had before she was forced to return to the rose nursery, she couldn't help feeling a sense of trepidation. Still, she could not deny that she wanted to keep seeing Dante.

And she longed to feel again the freedom and elation she had felt today when she was in the café with him and in the sunflower field. She also was curious to see what other works of art he would create of her. But most of all, she wanted him to kiss her again.

CHAPTER 13
DANTE

Siena, 1970

Dante was painting feverishly. He only had so much time before Anabella would need to return home. Sweat beaded his forehead, and he continually wiped it on the back of his arm. But he didn't mind. He could honestly say he'd never been happier in his life. And now that he could paint his muse as she stood before him, he was even more inspired.

Anabella was sitting in the same field of sunflowers Dante had taken her to the previous week. He had instructed her to sit with her legs bent to the side. Her right arm lay draped over her right thigh, and her hand lightly grasped her calf. Fortunately, she had worn a dress today. Then again, Dante had never seen Anabella in slacks. He wanted her bare leg to show in the painting. As if reading his mind, Anabella had kicked off her sandals. He was going to have her sit upright, but then she lowered down onto her left arm. She pushed her gloriously long hair over one of her shoulders. He noticed two of the buttons in the long line of buttons that trailed along the back of her body had come undone. Dante was about to tell her to button them, but then he saw how perfect she looked — the relaxed position of her body, how her hair hung casually down her back, her bare feet. It was only natural that her dress wouldn't be buttoned all the way to the top.

Then suddenly, in that moment, he felt an overwhelming stirring of desire, similar to last week when he had abandoned all reason and kissed her. But he'd promised Anabella he wouldn't take advantage of her or disrespect her in any way. And Dante intended to honor his word — no matter how much it would be killing him.

An hour later, his heart raced as his painting took shape before him.

"How is it coming along?" Anabella asked. Her back faced him as she kept her head tilted upward toward the sunflowers as if she were listening to the flowers talking to her.

"I am almost done. I know you must be tired. Just a few more minutes, I promise."

"That is all right. Just please keep track of

the time. I don't want to get home late."

"You won't. Are you sure you've never modeled for anyone before? I am still amazed at how you positioned yourself perfectly, even better than how I had intended to place you. And your patience is quite remarkable. I'm sorry I was only able to give you two short breaks."

"That's all right. Knowing you will paint a beautiful piece of art is worth my being a little uncomfortable." Anabella looked over her shoulder, smiling at Dante.

He froze the moment in his mind. For he would have to capture her from this angle another time.

"I have really enjoyed being here with you today. *Grazie,* Dante." She turned to face the sunflowers again.

Dante's hand froze midair just as he was about to paint another stroke. He felt a pleasant, warm sensation spreading throughout him. He placed his paintbrush down on his easel and walked over to Anabella.

Anabella started for a moment when she realized he was standing near her.

"Is everything all right?" Her eyes opened wide.

"*Si.* I just wanted to tell you that I have also enjoyed being with you today." Dante's eyes grew heavy as he continued to look into her eyes.

Anabella swallowed and glanced back up at the sunflowers. "We'd better hurry up. Surely, it must be time soon for me to go."

But Dante remained standing beside her. He then squatted down to his knees so he would be closer to her on the ground. Pushing back a curl that was dangling along Anabella's cheek, he tucked it behind her ear. As he did so, he let his finger gently graze her earlobe. He could see the slight shiver Anabella gave, but she remained silent. Dante then let the back of his hand lightly stroke her cheek as he whispered, "You are the most beautiful woman I have ever laid eyes on."

Anabella turned her head, meeting his gaze. Her eyes then rested on his lips. It was too much for Dante. He lowered his head and softly kissed her. He waited a moment to see if she would push him away. When she didn't, he placed another kiss on her lips and waited again, and then kissed her for a second longer this time. After the next pause, she kissed him back. He let his knees come fully down on the ground as he placed his hands on either side of her face, deepening the kiss. Anabella rested her hands against his chest. His heart was beating frantically now, and his breathing was coming in short rasps. He wrapped his arms around her back, hugging her fiercely to him. Breaking the kiss after what seemed like an eternity but must've been no more than a couple of minutes, he stroked her hair as he inhaled deeply her fragrance. She smelled like roses, which shouldn't have come as a surprise to him being that she worked on a rose farm, but still.

He laughed softly. "How is it that you smell like roses?"

Anabella pulled back. "Why do you find that funny?"

"Naturally, you are surrounded by roses, but I wouldn't think their fragrance would rub off on you. But what do I know? I am just an artist who is locked in his own world of make-believe."

Anabella smiled. "Well, you are correct. I make my own rose perfume out of the roses' petals."

"It's beautiful. Don't ever stop wearing it. Promise me."

She looked down, blushing slightly.

"I hope I did not make you feel uncomfortable by kissing you again. What you must think of me after I promised you that I wouldn't disrespect you. But I cannot hide my feelings any longer, Anabella. Surely, you must have realized after I first kissed you last week that I am very fond of you, so fond of you that I would like us to be much more than friends."

Anabella shook her head. Dante froze. She didn't feel the same way as him. Then why did she let him kiss her? And he was still holding her.

"No, you did not make me feel uncomfortable. It is my turn to be forward now. I was hoping you would kiss me again today." She smiled shyly at him before lowering her gaze again.

Relief washed over Dante. He sighed deeply before resting his head against hers.

"You gave me a scare there for a second when you shook your head. I thought you were going to tell me you don't feel the same way about me."

They remained locked in each other's embraces for a few more minutes before Dante said, "I suppose I must ask your mother for her permission to let me court you."

At the mention of her mother's name, Anabella pulled back sharply.

"What time is it?" She picked up his arm and glanced at his wristwatch. "It is nearly one! Mamma will be worried. I must go."

Dante stood up and quickly packed his

art supplies. He had borrowed the truck of a friend so he could safely transport his painting of Anabella, giving it enough room so the paint could continue to dry while propping it carefully so the vehicle's movements wouldn't wreck his work. This was crazy. He couldn't continue to paint Anabella outdoors like this. If he got into an accident or even had to slam on his brakes suddenly, his work would be ruined in an instant. But they were also approaching autumn, and, soon, it would be too cold for them to work outdoors. He knew it would still be premature to invite Anabella to his apartment where he could paint her indoors. He would have to figure something out. Of course, this could all come to an abrupt halt if Signora Ferraro found out and forbade her daughter to see him. From the little Anabella had told him about her mother and her upbringing, Signora Ferraro had sheltered her daughter, more so than the average parent. But he was prepared to win Signora Ferraro over. For he couldn't imagine life without Anabella any longer.

As he drove Anabella to her parked car, he kept stealing side glances in her direction. Deep wrinkles furrowed her forehead, and her brows were knitted together like two swords clashing in battle.

"Anabella, are you afraid that your mother will be upset with you for coming home late?"

"*Si*. But don't worry."

Dante was moved. Although she stood a good chance of getting in trouble because of him, she was still concerned about his feelings.

"I'm sorry, Anabella. I should have been more careful. It won't happen again."

"Does that mean you won't kiss me again?" Anabella looked at him, smiling in the most sensual way.

He felt his knees go weak, and he had to quickly return his attention to the road before he got them both killed. Although, upon first impression, Anabella seemed shy and meek, which she was no doubt, there was also a daring side to her that was coming out more and more each time he saw her. He wondered where she got this from, especially given the sheltered life she'd had. Perhaps her late father had been confident this way, unafraid to speak his mind and take chances. While he had only seen Signora Ferraro once, he couldn't imagine her as an assertive woman. And this life she had created on the farm for herself and her daughter only further convinced Dante that Signora Ferraro was a person who had

taken few chances in her life and had always
played it safe.

CHAPTER 14
SIGNORA FERRARO

Pienza, 1970

Signora Ferraro was standing at her stove, making manicotti — Anabella's favorite dish. Though she often made manicotti for special occasions like Anabella's birthday or on certain holidays, sometimes she surprised her daughter by making them out of the blue. She picked up her cast-iron skillet and swirled the manicotti batter so that it filled the pan's diameter. Her thoughts turned to Anabella.

Lately, Anabella's attention seemed to be elsewhere, and her enthusiasm for her work on the rose farm seemed to be diminishing. In fact, Signora Ferraro had noticed that Anabella was losing interest in the activities that had always given her so much pleasure like her cooking. Since she was twelve years old, Anabella had taken an interest in cooking. But lately, she seemed only too glad to let her mother do more of the cooking. And when Signora Ferraro asked Anabella to cook if she wasn't feeling well or had an especially tiring day on the farm, Anabella's heart didn't seem to be in it. Then there was her increasing forgetfulness. Anabella's attention to detail had always been flawless, but recently, she'd forgotten to add ingredients to a few of her dishes or she'd overseasoned the food.

Signora Ferraro was worried about her daughter. But when she asked her if everything was fine, Anabella always nodded. Even their conversations had become strained. Whereas in the past, Anabella had always shared stories with her mother about her day on the farm with Chiara and the other workers or what she might have witnessed on her weekly visits to the Piazza del Campo, now she just said nothing much had happened. Signora Ferraro had always heard that children became this way when they were teenagers, but thankfully, Anabella had never gone through that phase. But she was now twenty-six years old, too late to be going through a moody, rebellious adolescent period. Then again, she knew her daughter had always been a bit immature for her age and unlike most of her peers. She supposed she was to blame, having homeschooled her and not providing more social interaction for her. But whenever Signora Ferraro encountered the other young women from the village at church or when she went grocery shopping, they seemed haughty. She'd even witnessed a few of them talking back to their mothers. No, she did not regret how she had raised her daughter. For Anabella had become a thoughtful, respectable young woman.

Suddenly, Signora Ferraro felt a constriction in her chest. She pressed her hand to her heart. It was nothing. She knew that. Signora Ferraro had suffered panic attacks since the war. They only happened occasionally now. She waited a few moments, closing her eyes and willing her heart rate to slow down. After a couple of minutes, the attack subsided. She looked down at the manicotti shell she'd been cooking. It was burning. Turning off the gas, she walked over to the kitchen table where she had left her glass of rose water. She gulped the water down quickly. When she was done, she wet a dish towel and dabbed her flushed face with it. Sighing deeply, she sank heavily into one of the kitchen table chairs.

Had she done right by Anabella? Though she'd begun asking herself this question more as Anabella had become an adult, she'd always defended herself as she'd done in her thoughts a moment ago. But lately, her doubts were beginning to cloud her confidence. Most of the other young women in Pienza had already married or were engaged. Soon, they would be starting their own families. But Signora Ferraro couldn't imagine her life without Anabella. She was her world. What would she do without her? And who would protect Anabella? Naturally if she married, her husband would take on that role. But a mother's fierce loyalty and protection overshadowed anyone else's. Signora Ferraro wasn't foolish enough to think she would be here forever. And what would become of her daughter then, alone on this large farm?

The church held dances for single people in town. Perhaps she should take Anabella. Yes, that was what she would do. She would take her next Saturday. Signora Ferraro's mind leapt forward to what life would be like once her daughter married and left her. What if Anabella's husband found work far away and took her daughter away from her? What if he didn't treat her well? Signora Ferraro's heart began racing again. No, it would be better for her daughter never to marry — for this way, she would be spared the heartache she herself had experienced with Franco. While she had been very happy with him, what later followed was not worth the short bliss they'd shared.

She was startled out of her thoughts by the sound of the screen door opening. Signora Ferraro looked up at the clock that hung above the kitchen's entryway. Two o'clock? That couldn't be right. She frowned. Why was Anabella coming home so late? She then realized she'd been lost in her thoughts for too long, and the manicotti should have been in the oven by now. Anabella would be starving.

"*Ciao,* Mamma." Anabella entered the kitchen. Her gaze avoided her mother's and instead rested on the empty kitchen table. "Are you not feeling well? Is that why lunch isn't ready yet?" She then turned her back as she made her way over to the china cabinet and took plates out.

Signora Ferraro knitted her brows as she watched her daughter set the table. Anabella didn't even seem to notice that she had not answered her question. What was going on with her daughter? If she hadn't known better, Signora Ferraro would have been convinced Anabella was hiding something from her. But Signora Ferraro had often explained to her the importance of not keeping secrets from her mother.

"Why are you getting home so late?"

Anabella finally glanced at her. Fear flickered in her eyes for a brief moment.

"Ah! I'm sorry, Mamma. There was an accident. The traffic delay was horrible."

Anabella noticed the burnt manicotti shell sitting in the skillet. She picked it up with a spatula and tossed it in the garbage.

"Is everything all right, Mamma? You're never late with lunch."

"And you've never been late coming home from the piazza before." Signora Ferraro crossed her arms over her chest.

Anabella looked up at her, not missing the cross tone in her mother's voice. She blushed as she returned her attention to the manicotti shell.

"I'm sorry, Mamma. As I said, there was an accident. It could not be avoided. I see you made my favorite! I cannot wait to have them. I'm famished." Her voice shook slightly as she said this.

They remained silent for the duration it took to finish preparing the manicotti shells and placing them in the oven.

"Mamma, I'm going to take a quick shower while the manicotti cook." Anabella left the kitchen without waiting for her mother's response.

Forty minutes later, as they ate lunch, Signora Ferraro was having a difficult time

185

enjoying her meal. She kept thinking about Anabella's strange behavior for the past few weeks. And today seemed to be the oddest. It was time she got to the bottom of what was going on with her daughter.

"Anabella, I want to talk to you about something that has been troubling me." Signora Ferraro placed her fork down and took a sip of water before continuing. Anabella continued eating.

"Please, look at me. You have barely looked at me since you came home, and you haven't said much. Is something wrong? You know you can tell your mamma anything."

"No, Mamma, I'm fine."

"But you have been so quiet lately and withdrawn. And your thoughts seem to be elsewhere. Are you not feeling well?" Signora Ferraro's voice had a slight tremor as she asked this. "That is it, isn't it? You are sick and are not telling me." Signora Ferraro rose out of her seat and rushed over to Anabella's side, feeling her forehead with the back of her hand.

"Please, Mamma!" Anabella's voice rose sharply as she pushed her mother's hand away. "I am not sick. Do I look like I am dying?"

Signora Ferraro froze. Never had her daughter raised her voice to her. And the expression on her face right now. She was looking at her with disdain.

"I . . . I am sorry. I was just worried. You haven't seemed yourself lately." Signora Ferraro returned to her seat. She resumed eating her manicotti, but she could barely chew as she fought back the tears that were threatening to break through.

"I'm sorry, Mamma. I didn't mean to talk to you like that just now. Really. I am fine. Please don't be upset with me." She looked at her mother and gave her a small smile.

Signora Ferraro felt relieved.

"What can I say? A mother is always worried. I have been feeling better. Maybe next week I can come with you to the Piazza del Campo. You've probably just been tired from the extra work you've been doing with my being under the weather lately."

Anabella's eyes quickly shot up.

"You know, Mamma, I can manage on my own. As you've seen, I have been selling all of the flowers. And it would probably be best if you reserved your energy. Perhaps I can permanently handle selling to the flower vendors at the piazza."

Suspicion began seeping into Signora Ferraro's mind. Her daughter was keeping something from her. But it was apparent she was not going to get it out of her — at least for today.

"*Si,* you have been doing a wonderful job. And you know how much I appreciate all you do for me." A thought then entered Signora Ferraro's mind.

"Anabella, I was thinking, while I was cooking. How about I escort you next Saturday to church? I don't know if you are aware that they have a dance for people your age every weekend."

Surprise etched across Anabella's features.

"Oh, I don't know, Mamma. You know how shy I can be, and besides I am content with my friends here on the farm — even if they are not my own age."

"I can buy a new dress for you."

"That is all right, Mamma. Besides, I don't know how to dance."

"I believe it said in the church bulletin there is a dance instructor on hand to help beginners. I could even practice with you here at home. I used to be a good dancer."

"You?"

"I was young once, too." Signora Ferraro felt embarrassed. She knew she had let herself go over the years, not that she cared. But for some reason having her daughter scrutinize her now made her extremely uncomfortable.

"Did you dance with Papà?"

"Of course. We used to dance at a club we belonged to."

"A club? What kind of club was it?"

Signora Ferraro bit her lip. She'd said more than she should have. "Oh, just a church social club, with events much like the social functions of our church here in the village. It was fun as I'm sure the dances at our church are. You would probably enjoy the dances. So, we will go next week."

"Mamma, *grazie,* but I really do not want to go." Anabella stood up and cleared the dishes from the table.

Signora Ferraro watched her daughter as she stood at the sink washing the dishes. Maybe she was being paranoid. Why would Anabella want to go to the dance at the church when she had barely interacted with her peers over the years? Yes, that was it. She was shy. Of course she would be terrified of going to church and having to meet new people. And as Anabella had mentioned, she didn't know how to dance — yet another reason for her to be afraid.

Still. Signora Ferraro remembered last year when Anabella had expressed an interest in joining the church choir. It was innocent enough, but Signora Ferraro had told her they were too busy at the farm. She couldn't spare Anabella for the weekly choir

189

rehearsals. Regret filled her when she thought of the small lie she had told her daughter. The truth had been she didn't want Anabella meeting new people — people who could either take her daughter away from her or hurt her. She had allowed her daughter to become friends with Graziella when she was younger, but that was different. Graziella had been shunned at school because of her weight. There had been no chance that she would lead her daughter astray. Graziella had been even shyer than Anabella, and her parents had been quite strict with her — more so than Signora Ferraro ever was.

Signora Ferraro didn't want to entertain the thought, but once it had entered her mind, she could not let it go. Had her daughter met someone? A young man? Is that why she wanted to continue going to the Piazza del Campo alone? Is that why she was late today? Anger began coursing through her. She was ready to demand that Anabella tell her the truth. But what if she were wrong? She couldn't hurt her daughter that way. Then, she remembered how Anabella had spoken to her earlier. Her heart cringed. Anabella was so much more to her than her daughter. She was a companion and a friend. That was why it had been even more disturbing these last few weeks that she hadn't engaged in much conversation. Signora Ferraro missed their talks. But now, none of the subjects Signora Ferraro brought up seemed to hold interest any longer for Anabella. She would merely nod her head politely in assent. Signora Ferraro had wondered at times if her daughter was even listening to her.

She hated not trusting her daughter, but her instincts were telling her more and more that Anabella was seeing a man behind her back. After all, she, too, had once been a young woman who had lied to her family for love.

CHAPTER 15
MARIA ROSSI

Florence, 1943

Maria and her family were enjoying *panini* made with fried eggs and potatoes for their evening supper. But she was merely taking small bites from her sandwich. Maria and her sister-in-law took turns cooking dinner on different days of the week. Whoever didn't cook was in charge of washing the dishes. But many times they just decided to cook side by side and help each other out. Enza had become like a sister to Maria, and she enjoyed her company.

"What is the matter with you, Maria? Usually you are the first one to finish eating, but you've barely eaten your *panino,*" Papà bellowed in his boisterous voice.

"I'm really not hungry. I'm still full from the lasagna we had for lunch." She patted her stomach before continuing, "I don't even know why I bothered with the *panino.*" Maria smiled, looking in Enza's direction.

She hoped none of them had heard the slight tremor in her voice.

"My wife is the best cook — no offense to you, Maria." Michele winked at Maria before leaning over and planting a kiss on Enza's cheek.

"Ah! You are a very good cook, Enza, but I still miss some of my wife's dishes." Papà's eyes filled with tears, which he quickly blinked back before taking a bite out of his egg sandwich.

Silence followed as they all remembered Signora Rossi. Maria missed her mother and thought about her every day. Suddenly, an intense sorrow filled her, making it even harder for her to finish eating. But it was her nerves that were truly to blame for taking her appetite away.

"I think I am done. If you'll all excuse me, I'm going to take a bicycle ride."

Maria avoided glancing in Enza's direction and prayed fervently that she didn't offer to accompany her. They often rode their bikes or took a *passeggiata* in the evening after supper.

"*Si,* Enza and I are going to take a walk and enjoy this weather. Before we know it, autumn will be here and the gloomy rain and cold that come with it," Michele said as his eyes met Enza's.

Maria sensed they were exchanging a silent message with each other. She breathed a sigh of relief. She just had to hurry and leave home before them so they wouldn't see where she was headed.

"Maria, don't worry about cleaning up. I'll do it. Go enjoy yourself." Enza patted Maria's arm as she stood up and began clearing the dishes from the table.

"*Grazie*, Enza."

A few minutes later, Maria was applying lipstick in her bedroom. With one final look in the mirror, she grabbed her purse on the bed and was about to leave her room when she noticed her perfume bottle on her dresser. Remembering Franco's compliment about her perfume, she hurried over to the dresser and sprayed a few pumps on her neck and wrists.

Once on her bicycle, Maria pedaled quickly until she was certain there was no way Michele or Enza could see her in the distance. They had been about to leave the house as she had gotten on her bike. Glancing at her wristwatch, she saw she still had plenty of time before the meeting started. She could feel her heart racing, and, once she arrived at the address Franco had written on the back of the leaflet, her stomach did somersaults.

"Calm down, Maria. It is just a meeting, nothing more. You are not attending an assassination plot or getting ready to detonate a bomb," she softly said aloud to herself. Then, realizing her foolishness, she glanced over her shoulder to make sure no one was standing nearby and had heard her.

The address Franco had given her belonged to an old, abandoned church. She wished Franco had told her this, for how was she to enter when the doors were all bolted? A moment later, she saw a woman scurry by, glancing side to side, as she quickly made her way down the dark alleyway that ran beside the church. Was she also attending the meeting? Maria left her bike perched against a lamppost and hurried her step as she followed the woman who looked to be in her forties.

The alleyway led to a small yard. The woman was on the opposite side of the yard, lifting what looked to be a large bush from the ground. But then Maria saw the bush was being used simply as a ruse to cover a basement door. As the woman pulled open the door, she noticed Maria. Her eyes widened in fear.

"Don't worry. I am here for the meeting, too." Maria smiled reassuringly as she glanced down the alleyway to make sure no one had followed them.

"You could have said something instead of standing there like a phantom!" The woman's brows knitted furiously. "Hurry!" She gestured with her hand for Maria to enter the basement first.

Maria carefully stepped down the basement steps. When she reached the bottom, she waited for the woman, who seemed to be struggling to prop the bush in place with one hand while closing the door with the other. She then joined Maria at the foot of the stairs.

"There is no way you were able to completely cover the door. What if someone sees it?" Maria immediately began regretting her decision to come here.

"It will soon be pitch-black outside. It'll be good enough. Besides, once the meeting starts, one of our members stands guard outside and comes around to the back to make sure the bush completely covers the door. What is your name? I don't believe I've seen you here before."

"Maria. Maria Rossi." She held out her hand. The woman gripped it with an iron-like strength that momentarily startled her. She'd never had a woman shake her hand so firmly.

"Ninetta. We don't exchange last names

here. It's for the better. But don't worry. I've already forgotten yours." The woman smiled before turning her back to Maria and knocking on another door that led to the interior of the church's basement. She knocked three times, then waited a few seconds before knocking twice. The knocks were done slowly, and sounded more like loud thumps than a quick succession of knocks.

Franco opened the door. Maria's heart beat hard against her chest when she saw him.

"Ninetta. *Ciao!* Ah!" He stopped when he saw Maria. Though he had invited her, she could tell he was surprised she'd come.

"This is Maria. I met her outside," Ninetta offered before walking ahead and joining a small crowd that was gathered at a folding table.

"*Si,* we've met," Franco said, smiling as he held out his hand to Maria. "Please, come in. I am so happy you decided to come."

Maria began to shake his hand, but Franco instead pulled her close to him. A soft gasp escaped from Maria. Franco looked into her eyes, his expression growing somber. But then, just as quickly, he cleared his throat and said, "Go on inside and make yourself

197

comfortable. There is espresso on the table. I'll be there in a moment." He dropped her hand and made his way to a door on the opposite side of the basement and stepped out.

She walked over to the crowd at the table. "*Ciao!* Welcome!"

Everyone welcomed her and introduced himself or herself. Immediately, she felt comfortable.

A young man who looked to be in his early twenties went behind the table and clapped his hands. "*Silenzio, per favore!* We are about to commence our meeting."

Everyone took his or her seat on the folding chairs that were lined up in front of a makeshift podium, forming a semicircle. Maria sat next to Ninetta.

"My name is Alfredo, for those of you who are new. I welcome you here tonight, and thank you for attending. I believe this is the largest gathering we've had so far. Ah! And a few latecomers."

The group of six people who entered from the door Franco had disappeared through earlier paused after Alfredo's comment.

"*Vieni! Vieni!*" He motioned with his hand for them to come in before adding, "I was just joking. The more the merrier. I'm afraid we've run out of chairs. I hope you don't mind standing."

The group walked to the side of the room. Franco followed behind them. His gaze searched the room until it landed on Maria. He winked and smiled. Maria felt herself warming all over. She nodded in his direction, but refrained from smiling.

Alfredo resumed talking, telling the audience that FAF could use help from everyone in attendance. In addition to writers for their newspaper and leaflets, they needed couriers who could discreetly deliver the papers and leaflets to people around the city. They also needed administrative help in the office in the abandoned church. Then the next statement he made caused a flurry of whispers across the room.

"We know that everyone realizes this work is risky, and there is the chance of being jailed or worse if one is discovered working here in the office or delivering our literature, but we need to remind everyone of that, especially the newcomers. While we need all of the help we can get, we do not want to mislead you. So if there are those of you who feel this might not be right for you, you may leave. Again, no judgments from us. We appreciate your coming here."

He waited. Maria glanced around the room. Others were doing the same. Then, one young woman stood up and quickly made her way out. A couple stood up a moment later and also exited.

Hearing Alfredo remind them of the risks this work entailed heightened Maria's anxiety. She thought about taking her opportunity to leave once the other attendees had left, but she remained frozen. It was silly, but she felt Franco's eyes on her, even though he stood to the back of the room. Why should she care what he thought? He was practically a stranger to her. But then the answer came to her. She didn't want him to think she was a coward. Not after he had told her that day at the market that he sensed she didn't frighten easily, and she'd told him she didn't. But again, she shouldn't care about the impression she made on him if she left. All she had to do was get up, walk to the exit, and never return here again. What were the odds she would run into him again? That was a mere fluke the day she'd seen him at the market.

But just as she was about to stand up, Alfredo announced, "Now I am going to give the floor to my comrade Franco, who will tell you more about FAF and our history, how we got started and so on."

Franco made his way to the front of the room. Alfredo slapped Franco on the back as he passed him.

Maria observed Franco's features while he spoke. His complexion was a medium olive tone that offset his deep brown eyes. They reminded her of the espresso beans Papà ground every morning. His hair was a rich sable shade, and his bangs, which needed a trim, hung over his right eye, giving him a dangerous allure. But his black horn-rimmed eyeglasses softened his features and made him look very intelligent. Maria wondered what he looked like without them. For if he was this handsome with the glasses, she could only imagine how much more attractive he looked without them. She blushed as she saw Franco glance in her direction for a moment before he continued what he was saying. Had he been able to tell she was scrutinizing him?

She felt her knees go weak, but once she heard Franco remind people again that this was risky work and they needed to exert the highest level of secrecy and caution, she forgot about the way Franco was making her feel whenever he looked at her, and her nervousness from earlier returned. What was she getting herself into? She didn't belong here. Standing up, she excused herself as she made her way past the members. Avoiding Franco's gaze, she quickly exited via the basement door she had come in from. She was relieved to hear he was still talking.

Pushing open the exterior basement door, she struggled to push the bush out of the way. Once outside, she took a deep breath and lowered the basement door, but she felt someone pushing it back open.

"Maria, it's me, Franco."

She frowned. He must've quickly ended his speech. She stood back, away from the basement door so he could fully open it. Once he exited, he closed the door and laid the bush back in place.

"That was a short speech you gave." Maria crossed her arms over her chest. Though it was a mild night, she was shivering.

"I'll join them in a little while. Would you like to take a walk with me?"

She was about to politely refuse, but something in Franco's face kept her from doing so.

"All right," she said softly.

They walked in silence for a few feet before Franco spoke.

"It was very brave of you to come here tonight. I take it your family doesn't know?"

Maria kept her gaze to the ground, though she could feel he was looking at her.

"No, they don't."

"Naturally, they wouldn't approve."

"My papà would be very upset. He doesn't even know —" She caught herself before saying more.

"He doesn't even know what?"

"Nothing." Maria shook her head.

"You can tell me, Maria. If there's anyone who can keep a secret, it's an anti-Fascist after all."

Maria laughed.

They walked a few more steps before Franco stopped. Maria had no choice but to look at him now.

"It's natural to be afraid to work with us, and, as you heard earlier, Alfredo and I didn't mince words. It is risky work — even just doing administrative work for FAF. I don't blame you for being afraid."

"I'm not afraid," Maria lied. Again, his words from that day at the market came back to her: *You don't frighten easily.*

"I wouldn't think less of you, Maria. I was afraid when I decided to write and publish my first anti-Fascist article. I was afraid the first time I was brought in for questioning and later when I was jailed. And I still get afraid from time to time. That won't change."

"But you seem so . . ." Maria searched for the right word.

"Brave? Daring? I have to exude confidence at all times for if I, one of FAF's leaders, show anything less, how can I expect my comrades to take the risk of working with us? We're all afraid, Maria. We wouldn't be human if we weren't."

Maria nodded.

"Let me ask you, do you like the idea that we have not been truly free for a long time, and, each day, we are losing more of our liberties? Does it ever trouble you to know that innocent men have been rounded up and arrested, many of whom were not even involved in any anti-Fascist rhetoric or activity?"

"Of course. It enrages me at times, especially after I read the leaflet you dropped into my shopping basket."

"I know. I saw the anger in your face. That's good. You should be mad. We all should be very mad, but not everyone is. And that is dangerous as well, Maria."

"How so?"

"Citizens who become indifferent or numb to changes in their government only see too late the dangers. Citizens who accept whatever their government dictates to them and who never question the regime's authority or decisions might as well be committing suicide. Slowly, their rights are taken away until, when they open their eyes and realize what's happening, it is too late."

Maria shivered, but this time it wasn't because she was cold. It was as if Franco were directly talking about her. Again, it was as if he'd read her mind and had seen how she tried so hard to pretend everything was really all right in their country and that it would not affect her. Her thoughts then turned to her brother and Enza. They were not asleep like she was and had decided to join one of the underground anti-Fascist movements. If they were brave enough to do so, then why wasn't she?

She turned her back toward Franco and remained silent for a moment before asking him, "Do you know Michele Ferraro?"

"No. Ferraro? Is he a relative of yours?"

"He's my brother." She paused for a second. "That is what I almost said earlier. My father doesn't even know that my brother Michele is attending the meetings of an underground anti-Fascist group. I wasn't sure if perhaps it was FAF. Please, don't tell anyone."

Franco took Maria's hand in his and gave it a light squeeze. "I told you earlier, you can trust me. Don't worry. Maybe my path will cross with your brother's at some point. My group has recently begun combining our efforts with those of a couple of the other organizations."

"Michele doesn't even know that I know. I overheard him and his wife talking about it one day. I think she might be involved in some small way, too, although I can't see how Michele would ever allow Enza to be placed in danger like that."

"Maybe it wasn't his decision. Maybe your sister-in-law insisted on being a part of it."

"I had never thought of that."

"Maria, I sense you are curious about our work and are tempted to contribute, but your fear is holding you back. I am not going to talk you into doing this. It must be your own decision. As you heard for yourself, we do not pressure anyone and are fully candid with everyone about the risks. But if you do decide to join FAF, I can promise you I will do my utmost to keep you safe. How about if you helped with some of the duties involving the newspaper? Maybe even write a few articles. You can do that from the safety of your home. You don't need to come to our office if that makes you feel unsafe."

"You would let me do that?"

"Of course. If you really want to contribute, I'd do that for you. Ninetta, the woman you walked in with, writes a few articles at home. She has to do it at night while her husband is sleeping. He doesn't know she is helping us. During the day, when she can, she helps distribute the newspaper and collects donations from the villagers and drops them off at the office."

"I do like to write. Maybe I could do an article here and there, from home, if that's really all right with you?"

Franco smiled. "Of course it is."

"But how would I deliver my articles to you? I would have to come to the office."

"We could meet at the market or even at a café. Would that make you feel more comfortable?"

"*Si,* that would. *Grazie.*"

"Does that mean you will help?"

Trepidation was still giving Maria pause. She thought about how brave Franco and the other FAF members were. Shame suddenly filled her for being afraid. It would feel good to know she was doing her part — even in a small way. What harm could come from helping Franco with the newspaper?

"Yes, count me in." She smiled.

Franco laughed and hugged her. Maria froze. But he didn't seem to notice her reaction. Pulling away, he placed his hands on either side of her arms and said, "I know you will be a great asset to us. And if at any time you change your mind for any reason, you can quit. Again, I don't want you to feel coerced. Will you promise to let me know if anything makes you feel uncomfortable?"

"Okay. I promise."

"I should be returning to the meeting. They're going to think I was captured again." He laughed, but when he saw Maria's frown, he said, "Sorry. That was not funny."

"I should get going too before my father worries."

Franco walked with Maria back to where she had left her bicycle. They exchanged phone numbers, and Franco promised to be in touch sometime during the week so he could give her a writing assignment.

"Before I leave, Maria, I have a question. Do you like to dance?"

Maria looked up at him in surprise. "*Si*, but it's been years since I last danced with everything that's been going on."

"We hold a weekly dance at FAF's headquarters, here at the abandoned church. There is a room in the back of the basement that we turn into a mini dance hall. We have the dance every Saturday night. Would you like to come?"

She was tempted, but again, she didn't

even know if she was going to work for FAF for long. While it was just a dance, it was still being held at their office. What if the secret police stormed the office and she was arrested?

Again, Franco seemed to read her thoughts. "I know you're probably thinking you don't feel safe here, especially since you just said you would feel more comfortable writing for the newspaper at home. I'm sorry. I shouldn't have asked. I just thought it would be nice to dance with you." He looked at her sheepishly, before averting his gaze.

She was touched. "Let me give it more thought. If I decide to come, you'll see me there."

"All right. Will you have problems getting away? Will your . . ." Franco's voice trailed off.

"Will my father let me go? Is that what you were about to ask me?"

Franco was staring at his shoes as if he felt self-conscious or was slightly embarrassed. This image was in sharp contrast to that of the man she'd seen earlier at the podium. For there, he had exuded the utmost confidence.

He looked up, shrugged his shoulders, and gave her a half smile. "That wasn't the question I was about to ask, but *would* your father allow you to go?"

"It wouldn't be up to my father. I am twenty-eight years old, a grown woman; even though I still live under his roof, I am not his mule."

Franco laughed, holding up his hands. "I didn't mean it that way. Many fathers are strict with their daughters, no matter their age, and especially if they still live under their roofs and are unmarried. I see your father is an educated man who respects the women in his life."

Maria was taken aback by his comment, but it was true. Papà had always treated her more like an equal, and although they often hadn't agreed when they discussed politics, he never made her feel like her opinion was worth any less than his.

"So if your question wasn't about whether my father would give me permission to go to the dance, then what was it?"

Again, Franco glanced at his shoes. Taking a deep breath, he stared up at the sky.

"I was going to ask if your boyfriend would allow it."

"My boyfriend? What makes you so sure I have a boyfriend?" She couldn't help letting a smirk spread across her features. It was mean of her to mislead him and let him think she might have a boyfriend, but she couldn't help herself. There was something very appealing about him when he was nervous as he was now, acting much like a young schoolboy with a crush on his teacher.

"How could a beautiful woman like you not be taken?" He looked directly into her eyes.

Maria swallowed hard, but forced herself not to look away.

"Well, what would it matter if I had a boyfriend? Surely he would be welcome to escort me to the dance, wouldn't he?" She opened her eyes innocently.

Franco's face reddened, and immediately, she regretted being so cruel.

"Oh, of course, he would be welcome! I-I . . ." He stammered as he searched for the right words. "I just wouldn't have wanted you to get the wrong idea and then feel uncomfortable and possibly not want to continue working with me." He avoided Maria's gaze and looked back down at his shoes. He was absolutely adorable when he did this.

"And what would the wrong idea have been?"

Franco finally looked up at her. His face was still as red as the cherry tomatoes her father grew in their backyard. She was truly mean putting him through this. What was the matter with her? Here he was, admitting to her that he didn't want her to feel uncomfortable if she had to turn him down, and in contrast, she was taking pleasure in making him squirm.

"Forget I said anything. I'm not making any sense tonight."

"So does that mean I can forget your invitation to the dance?"

"No, you're more than welcome to come with your boyfriend, of course."

Maria had to place her hand over her mouth before a giggle escaped. Forcing herself to remain serious, she lowered her hand and said in a steady voice, "I'll come to the dance, but only on one condition."

Franco looked up at her, surprised.

"I'll only come if you dance the first dance with me . . . and maybe a few more. This might come as a surprise to you, but I can be shy." Maria smiled seductively at him.

"Shy? No, I would have never thought that about you, but if you insist, of course I will dance the first dance with you and however many other dances you'd like. That is if your boyfriend doesn't get upset." He returned her smile, and, in that moment, she could tell that he knew she didn't have a boyfriend. His face had visibly relaxed.

"Well, I should let you get going. So hopefully I will see you at the dance, and in the meantime we'll talk on the phone about your first newspaper article."

"Va bene."

"Buona notte, Maria." Franco waved before hurrying off in the direction of the church's secret entrance.

"Buona notte," Maria called out after him. He turned around once to look over his shoulder and smiled. Maria returned the smile. He held her gaze for a moment longer before turning back around and disappearing down the church's alley.

As Maria pedaled her bike home, she wondered what it would be like to see Franco and spend more time with him. She felt happy at the thought that she would be seeing him regularly. She smiled and began to hum softly to herself. Yes, she would attend the dance this week. She had made up her mind before leaving Franco, but she didn't dare tell him that. For it was good to leave him in suspense. And the thought that he would be thinking about her all this week as he wondered whether or not she would go to the dance left her with a glow. Her thoughts then turned to FAF. A thrill ran through her as she contemplated the work she would do for the organization, and in that moment, she felt something she'd never felt before — a sense of purpose.

CHAPTER 16
DANTE

Siena, 1970

Dante was deep in sleep when the sound of his telephone ringing woke him up. He glanced at his watch on his night table. Nine a.m. While it wasn't terribly early to be receiving a phone call, he'd gone to bed late the night before. It was probably his annoying friends, asking him if he wanted to join them for an espresso at the café in town.

"Ahhh!!!" He groaned as he sat all the way up in bed and reached for his phone.

"*Pronto!* Who is waking me up?" he growled into the phone.

"Dante? I'm — I'm sorry. I will call you back later."

"Anabella? No, wait! Don't hang up!"

"It's all right. I will call you later. I'm sorry for having disturbed you."

"You could never disturb me. I thought you were my annoying friends, waking me up to take pleasure in doing so. Please. I'm

215

happy to hear your voice. Is everything all right?"

Dante looked at his watch again to make sure he had seen the time correctly. Why was she calling him so early?

"*Sí*. Well, no. I was wondering if we could meet somewhere today. I can't talk long on the phone. Mamma might walk by any minute."

Dante's pulse raced at the thought that he would be seeing her again so soon after their last meeting. He would not have to wait until next week.

"Of course. Do you want to meet at the piazza?"

"No. Somewhere quiet."

"The café?" Although as soon as he'd uttered the words, he realized the café, which was always bustling with customers, was not the quietest place either.

"I guess that will have to do, but can we meet out front and then just take a walk somewhere?"

Dante frowned. It was as if Anabella was afraid of someone seeing them. And her voice, which had a hushed tone as if she were whispering, shook slightly.

"All right. That's fine. But I must say you are worrying me."

"I'm sorry. I don't mean to distress you.

It is probably just me overreacting, but I do need to talk to you. It can't wait until next week when I come to the piazza."

"*Va bene.* What time works for you?"

"Can you meet me in an hour? And please, don't be late. I don't have much time."

"I'll be there at ten."

"*Grazie.* I'll see you then."

Before he could say good-bye, she had hung up the phone.

Dante got out of bed and took a quick shower. Then, he hurriedly dressed and left his apartment. He was about to walk to his car when he realized it would be better to take his bicycle. It was Friday, and the traffic tended to be much heavier than midweek when he normally drove into town.

As he pedaled, he noticed a few of the sunflowers in the fields were starting to wilt. Soon, their petals would be all shriveled up. He needed to paint one last portrait of Anabella with the sunflowers while many were still alive. Once more, he looked at the flowers that were beginning to die. With their dried-up petals and stalks, the sunflowers almost resembled scarecrows. But he still saw some beauty in them. After all, it was another phase of life. The wheels in his mind began turning as he wondered if he could depict Anabella in this stark landscape, but manage to bring beauty to it, even though the flowers were no longer alive. Nothing came to him at the moment. It was difficult for him to imagine a painting in which all of the elements weren't as vibrant as his stunning Anabella. For now, he stored the idea away. The inspiration would come to him later.

Thoughts of what Anabella had to talk to him about diverted his attention away from the sunflowers. He had given his phone number to Anabella the last time he'd seen her in the hopes that if she could ever manage to get away during a time other than their weekly meetings at the piazza, she would call him. When she had called this morning, he'd been surprised that she had used the number so quickly. His elation over thinking that she wanted to see him and couldn't wait until next week was quickly dimmed when he realized there was something important she needed to tell him. His heart suddenly sank as he wondered if she was going to say she could no longer see him.

Pedaling even more feverishly, he reached the café ten minutes ahead of schedule. His shirt was sticking to him, and he immediately regretted riding his bike like a madman. He took a few deep breaths, trying to do his best to calm down, but he couldn't help stealing glances at his watch every few seconds.

Dante didn't have to wait long, for he saw Anabella pull up in her car five minutes later. He waited patiently for her to park. He wondered who had taught her to drive — perhaps her mother. Or was it one of the workers on the farm? Did Signora Ferraro employ any young male workers? Jealousy suddenly coursed through him as he contemplated another man staring at her or working closely by her side. He quickly shook the thought out of his head. What was happening to him? This girl was surely going to send him to an asylum. No other girl he'd been with before had had this effect on him, not even his first love. But now that he compared his feelings for Anabella to his feelings for his first girlfriend, he realized what he'd had with that girl was far from true love.

Anabella got out of her car and came over to Dante. She looked from side to side and again over her shoulder once she reached him.

"*Ciao,* Anabella. Are you sure you don't want to get an espresso? It doesn't look crowded inside yet. It should be quiet enough for us to talk."

Anabella adamantly shook her head without even glancing into the café. "No, let's take a walk. Maybe we can go to the sunflower field where you've been painting me?"

"That's a bit of a walk. I don't mind, but you said you couldn't stay for long."

"I was able to buy more time. I told Mamma I was going grocery shopping, and fortunately, she added a few extra items to my list, so it'll take me longer to complete my errand. Besides, she knows the market gets busy on Fridays, and I often get home later."

"Let's go then." Dante took hold of Anabella's hand.

She glanced at him questioningly for a moment. It was the first time he had held her hand. He felt an overwhelming need to comfort her. She looked nervous. Or was he the one who needed to feel comforted? He still wondered if she was going to tell him she couldn't continue to meet him.

Neither spoke as they walked. Dante waited patiently for Anabella to begin, but he was ready to erupt. He took a few sighs, willing himself in vain to remain calm. Finally, Anabella broke the silence.

"I'm sorry if I alarmed you on the phone. I was just so nervous that Mamma would

overhear me or pick up the phone in the kitchen to make a call. She would be shocked to hear me on the other line. I never have a need to make phone calls. And then if she'd heard your voice . . ." Anabella's voice trailed off.

"That is all right. I understand. Was she very mad at you for coming home late on Wednesday? She didn't . . . she didn't hit you or anything like that, did she?"

Anabella's eyes widened in surprise. "Of course not! My mother has never laid a hand on me."

"I'm sorry. I meant no disrespect. Naturally, I don't know your mother. Please do not take offense. I just know many parents still choose to discipline their children this way. Although you are a grown woman, and it would be quite ridiculous, even if she had hit you as a child, for her to continue to do so now that you are in your twenties."

Anabella laughed softly. "That is true."

It felt good to see her laugh.

"Mamma did ask me why I was returning home late, but I told her there was an accident on the road. She seemed to believe me. Besides, she was late, too."

"Did she go somewhere that day as well?"

"No. I meant she was late with preparing lunch. She is always very punctual with lunch, but when I arrived home, she still hadn't placed the manicotti she was making in the oven. It was odd. She didn't seem herself. So I was able to turn the attention back on her and ask her why lunch was late."

"That was clever of you." Dante gave Anabella's hand a slight squeeze. She blushed slightly and smiled. He wanted to kiss her, but refrained since she had something important to tell him.

"The reason I wanted to see you is that Mamma told me she might resume coming with me to the piazza every week."

Dante stopped walking. He let go of Anabella's hand and ran it through his bangs that were always dangling in his line of vision. He then closed his eyes, pressing his fingers to them. It was coming. He knew it.

"Are you all right, Dante?" Anabella brought her face closer to his.

"You can no longer meet me. That is what you have come to tell me, isn't it?"

"No . . . Well, yes, sort of." Anabella turned away from Dante, crossing her arms as she paced back and forth. The walk to the sunflower field was forgotten in both of their minds as they stood in the middle of a quiet street. A stray dog passed them and sniffed Anabella's leg. She stroked the dog's head and bent over as she spoke a few soothing words. The dog perked up its ears and licked her wrist.

"I wish I had some food to give it. Poor thing." Anabella looked around on the sidewalk as if hoping a piece of food would suddenly materialize.

"Wait here."

Before Anabella could ask Dante where he was going, he had broken into a jog. She returned her attention to the dog, who was now sitting by her.

A few minutes later, Dante came back, out of breath from running. He held a white bag, which she saw was from the café they usually frequented. Reaching inside the bag, he took out a brioche roll. Breaking off a small piece, he fed it to the dog. He then broke off more small pieces from the rest of the brioche and placed them on the ground, by the dog's feet.

"That was so sweet of you!" Anabella's eyes shone as she looked at Dante.

"Eh!" He shrugged his shoulders. "It was nothing. The truth is I was hungry since I haven't eaten breakfast yet." He smiled and took out a *biscotto* and held the bag toward Anabella. "I got something for you, too."

She looked inside the bag. "Almond cake!" She had told him the last time they were at the café that the cake was her favorite. "You remembered. *Grazie.*"

"*Prego.* So you see I didn't go back to the café for the dog. It was selfishness on my part and to quiet my growling stomach." He smiled sheepishly.

"I don't believe that." Anabella swatted his arm playfully.

They resumed walking toward the sunflower field. The dog followed them.

"It looks like you won't have the privacy you were hoping for." Dante tilted his head in the dog's direction.

Anabella laughed. "No. I suppose that was the harm in feeding him. He won't let us out of his sight now."

"Maybe you can take him back to the rose farm with you. I'm sure you can always use a good working dog."

"I already have a dog. Mamma would probably not take too kindly to my bringing home a stray dog that could carry illness, as she would say. When I was a little girl, I pleaded with her for us to take home a stray cat I saw by the side of the road when we were driving back from Siena. But no matter how much I begged, she kept saying, 'We don't know what illness the creature carries. Cioccolato would get mad at you anyway.'"

"Cioccolato?"

"That was my dog when I was a child. We now have Bruno, his son. We bred Cioccolato since he was such a good work dog on the farm."

"Ah. I see. Surely, Bruno would enjoy the companionship of another dog."

"Why don't you take him? You live alone. You must get lonely." Anabella smiled shyly.

"True, I do get lonely, especially when you're not around." Dante's eyes grew heavy as he stared into Anabella's eyes. Their gazes met for a few seconds before Anabella looked away.

"I have enjoyed being your model and seeing the paintings and drawings you have created of me. If I could find a way to do it on another day, other than Wednesdays when Mamma comes with me to sell the roses, then I could continue our work. But I have no idea what excuse I can offer to her so she doesn't get suspicious."

Relief washed over Dante as he heard Anabella say she wanted to keep seeing him. Surely, they could figure something out.

"Can you say you're going grocery shopping as you did today?"

"But that would give us even less time. And I'm supposed to be shopping closer to where I live in Pienza. I will already have to race to buy my groceries today and get home at a reasonable hour." She looked at her watch and stopped walking. "You were right. This walk is too far. I won't make it back in time after I go shopping. I don't know what I was thinking."

"That you wanted to spend more time with me?" Dante placed his index finger beneath her chin, tilting it slightly upward so she would be forced to meet his gaze. He lowered his lips toward hers and kissed her softly. But soon their kiss deepened. They continued kissing until the sound of a car horn beeping loudly forced them to pull apart.

"Forza!" The man behind the wheel of a Volvo stared at them, holding his fist up in the air.

"Idiot!" Dante yelled at him, but the car had sped up and was soon out of their sight.

"Let me walk you back to your car. I don't want you to be late." Dante took Anabella's hand again. Every few seconds he lifted it to his lips, placing a kiss on the back of it.

"It is all right if you no longer want to see me, Dante. I would understand."

"What? Are you crazy?"

"It's too much trouble. This was all a bad idea." Anabella let go of his hand, even though Dante tried to hold on to hers. "I'm sorry, Dante."

"Stop." Dante grabbed Anabella's arm, forcing her to stop walking. "You do want to see me. I can tell when I kiss you. I know you feel just as strongly for me as I do for you."

Anabella looked down, but Dante lowered his head, forcing their eyes to meet.

"I do like you, Dante. And if it were all up to me, I would keep seeing you. I like spending time with you."

"It should be all up to you. Your mother is scaring you. Anabella, you are a grown woman. You can make your own decisions now."

Fear filled her face. "What will I do if she gets mad? I have nowhere else to go but the farm."

"Surely your mother would not throw you out of your home?"

Anabella shrugged her shoulders.

"You said she has never hit you. I can't imagine she would be so cruel as to kick you out."

"Mamma is the sweetest person I know — at least with me. But that doesn't mean she has never been angry or become upset with me. She relies on me a lot, and she is getting older. I don't know if I could ever leave her."

"Haven't you dreamed of marrying and having children someday like every other young girl has?"

"No, not really." Anabella's voice sounded very small as she said this.

Dante's heart reached out to her. Of course she had never had the same dreams that other young girls possessed. In this moment, he realized that her mother had never encouraged her to have a life beyond the rose nursery. Anabella's mother had probably never talked to her about setting goals for the future. For why should she when she planned on having her daughter live out the rest of her days on the farm, keeping her company and tending only to her needs? Anger coursed through him as he thought about Signora Ferraro's extreme selfishness.

"I know this is going to sound crazy, but please hear me out before you refuse. What if I were to come by your house and meet your mother? I would let her know that I only have the most honorable of intentions toward you. I would ask her if I could court you, just like the old days. This way, we wouldn't have to sneak around and come up with elaborate plans for seeing each other."

Anabella quickly shook her head. "I don't think it would work."

228

"But isn't it worth a shot? What do we have to lose? She'll say no, and then we can still meet secretly — although yes, it will be harder. But all that matters is that we both want to be together. We can make it work."

"I cannot share your optimism, Dante. Mamma would probably never let me out of her sight again."

Dante could see that happening. He sighed deeply.

"I should get going."

Dante nodded. "Will you do me a favor? Can you try to call to let me know if you will be able to meet next week? That is, of course, if your mother isn't accompanying you. I think we should still try to see each other until we can decide how best to deal with this situation with your mother. I don't think we should give up right away. Besides, it would be nice to hear your voice more than just once a week." He smiled.

"All right. I should be able to call you once Mamma goes to sleep. She goes to bed quite early since she begins working shortly after dawn."

"In the meantime, I'll keep thinking of ways we can continue to meet without arousing your mother's suspicion. But Anabella, the day will come when you will have to let your mother know about me, whether you like it or not. I know you need time, and I won't pressure you."

"Yes, I do need time. You have to understand, this is all new to me." She took a deep breath. "Who knows? Maybe I am underestimating Mamma. Maybe she will come to adore you as I have."

"You adore me?"

Anabella smiled, her cheeks burning up. "*Ciao,* Dante." She reached up on her toes and kissed him on the lips before running off to her car.

He waited until she pulled away from the curb.

As he pedaled his bike back home, his mind raced with possible ways he could continue to meet Anabella — or rather possible lies she could offer to her mother. He hated the deceit of it all. That was why he had also suggested meeting with Signora Ferraro. But Anabella was too afraid and not ready to tell her mother about him yet.

Please, God, don't take her away from me, he silently prayed.

When Dante passed the sunflower field and saw again the flowers that were beginning to die, his spirits plummeted even more deeply — for he couldn't help seeing it as an omen of what was to come.

CHAPTER 17
ANABELLA

Siena, 1970

Anabella was leaning against the open window, staring out into the sunflower field. She wore a long, flowing sundress. A warm breeze came through the window, causing the hem of her dress to lift, revealing her tanned calves. One of the straps on her dress dangled seductively off her shoulder. Her hair was casually tossed over her left shoulder, and her chocolate-brown ringlets swirled in every direction. Dante had placed two roses in her right hand and instructed her to hold them down by her side. At her feet, rose petals lay strewn across the floor.

While Dante painted Anabella, she shivered slightly as she thought about Dante's gaze on her. At times, she felt he had stopped painting and was merely staring at her intensely. She smiled to herself, reveling in the feeling that he was observing her. Her stomach fluttered. She swallowed hard as

231

she contemplated that she had not only had the courage to go to Dante's apartment, but that she was now standing in his bedroom, a few feet away from his bed. If Mamma only knew. Anabella's pulse raced in fear. She had never been alone with a man before in his home. What was she doing? Still, it hadn't been difficult for her to say yes when Dante asked her if she would go to his home and let him paint her there. She had only paused for a moment before agreeing. The truth was she wanted to be with him as much as possible, and each time they met, the feeling only grew. Being here alone with him intensified her feelings for him. She tried not to think about the fact that she was in his bedroom. Thus far, Dante had shown her the utmost respect, and she trusted him.

Though Anabella had led a sheltered life on the rose farm, she was not completely ignorant of the ways of the world — or of what happened between a man and a woman once they got married. When she'd begun puberty at thirteen years old, Chiara had taken her aside to explain to her that she was now officially a woman. Anabella remembered her words as if it had just been yesterday. . . .

"I am sorry that I am the one to be having

this conversation with you, Anabella. It really should've been your mother. But it is hard for her to talk about such subjects. Do not be upset with her, and please don't let her know I am having this discussion with you. You are like a daughter to me, and I feel it is important to educate you. Someday you will need to know all about what I am telling you."

Chiara had spoken to Anabella gently as she explained how babies were brought into the world. At first, Anabella had been afraid when she learned the details, but Chiara had assured her she would be fine, and she would grow to love a special man someday. But at thirteen, Anabella couldn't imagine leaving Mamma to go live with a man she hardly knew — even if he were her husband. As Anabella grew older and became more curious whenever she saw couples kissing and embracing in town or at the Piazza del Campo, she had wondered what that felt like, but not enough to want it for herself — until now.

Though she desired Dante and knew he desired her just as much, she would not make love to him until they were married. That is, if he ever asked her. Lately, she'd begun wondering what life would be like if Dante proposed and they married. She thought about the home they would share.

She closed her eyes. It was crazy for her to have such thoughts so soon. She'd only met him a couple of months before, and neither had expressed their love for the other yet.

In addition to the magazines Chiara had given Anabella when she was a teenager, she had also given her novels. Anabella's favorites were the novels by Jane Austen. In these books, she'd seen how women were courted by men and how the couples professed their love for each other before they married. As with their secret conversation when Anabella was thirteen, Chiara had asked Anabella to keep the magazines and books hidden. Anabella didn't understand why the magazines would upset her mother so much. After all, hadn't her mother once fallen in love with her father? But Anabella knew Chiara was right, and so she'd never breathed a word to her mother about her hidden magazines and books.

"Let's take a break, Anabella," Dante said, interrupting her thoughts.

Anabella leaned away from the window, noticing her elbows were beginning to get sore from having rested on the windowsill for so long. She didn't mind. The little bit of discomfort she felt when she posed for Dante was worth it. She still marveled at his talent and how he could create such stunning works of art.

Dante turned his easel so that the painting was facing the wall and away from Anabella's inquisitive stare.

"I don't understand why you can never let me see the works while they are in progress." Her voice conveyed her slight annoyance.

"It wouldn't be the same if you saw the paintings for the first time before they are completed. I want you to see and feel every sensation I am trying to convey in my art, and how can that be possible if you are seeing a half-finished piece? Ah?" He walked over to Anabella and wrapped his arms around her waist as he placed a soft kiss on her lips. He then held her tightly against him.

He softly rubbed the small of her back, sending little ripples of pleasure throughout Anabella. She pulled away slightly so she could look up into his eyes. As she lifted her chin up and parted her lips, Dante took the cue and kissed her. His hands left her waist and came up to cup either side of her face. She heard a soft groan escape his lips. Then, abruptly, he pulled away.

"What's the matter?"

"Nothing. We should step outside and get some air. It's stuffy in here."

Anabella saw his gaze momentarily land

on his bed. When Dante saw she'd noticed, his face turned as red as the roses she'd been holding. She took a deep breath, understanding suddenly why he'd ended their kiss and his need to leave the apartment.

Once they were outside, they walked over to the field. Anabella sat down on the ground. She was beginning to feel more and more at home whenever she was in the sunflower fields, almost as much as she'd felt on the rose farm. Lately, she'd begun losing interest in the work on the farm. She knew her mother had noticed. Anabella didn't know why she'd begun feeling this way. She looked at the sunflowers. They were beautiful. Yes, they looked dramatically different from the roses she'd been surrounded by her entire life, but that didn't mean they were less beautiful. They were different. After all, there were many other flowers besides roses that were equally as stunning. But Mamma had always talked about the roses as if they were the only flowers that mattered. And her hatred for the sunflowers was perplexing. One night last week, Anabella had almost asked her mother why she hated sunflowers so much. But the memory from that day, when Anabella was a child and had witnessed her mother's outrage over the sunflowers in her room, was enough to keep her from asking.

"Where are you?" Dante knelt down beside Anabella and tucked a few strands of hair that were covering her face behind her ear.

She held on to his wrist and stroked his arm. It was now easy for her to show him affection, unlike when they'd first met.

"I was just thinking how much my mother hates sunflowers."

"Really? How can you live in Tuscany and hate sunflowers? They're everywhere."

"It is odd when you look at it that way. I have no idea why she hates them so much. But I can't even mention them to her or have them in the house. I still remember the two times that happened when I was a child and how angry my mother was. It was the angriest I've ever seen her."

"You don't really know a lot about your mother, do you?"

Anabella's face grew sad as she shook her head.

"Does she ever talk about your father?"

"Very little. I know that they loved each other very much, and she was devastated when he died. I used to ask more questions when I was a child, but then I would see how sad it made her, so I learned to stop asking."

"I can understand that from when my mother died." Dante's face looked pensive.

Anabella leaned back so that she was now lying on the ground. Dante joined her. He turned on his side to face her.

"I have something important to ask you." His voice had a slight tremor.

She turned to face him. "Please, Dante, don't be afraid. I hope you know you can tell me anything." Anabella reached out and placed her hand on his cheek.

He cupped his own hand over hers as she sighed deeply.

"Will you let me come to your home so I can finally meet your mother and ask for her blessing to court you?"

Anabella pulled her hand away from his face and rested her head back on the ground as she looked up at the sky. The sun was playing hide-and-seek with the clouds. She wished she could hide behind one of the clouds right now.

Since that morning when Anabella had told Dante they would have to figure out a way to continue seeing each other, they had met in secret. The two of them had plotted different scenarios to give to Signora Ferraro so she wouldn't question Anabella's

238

whereabouts or if she came home later than expected. But it was getting harder to come up with more lies. She always felt a stab of guilt after she'd lied to Mamma, and there were times she had told herself it would be the last time and she would just come clean with her. But every time Anabella tried to work up the courage to do so, the fear of her mother's reaction would consume her. There had even been occasions when Anabella had considered ending it with Dante, but the thought of never seeing him again hurt too badly. Though she hated deceiving her mother, she hated more the idea of not being with Dante.

"Anabella, I love you."

She turned her head toward Dante. Her heart leapt at finally hearing him say he loved her.

"I have since I first laid eyes on you at the piazza." He laughed. "I think I might've even fallen in love with you after I began dreaming about you. It's crazy. I know. But I can't deny you've had me under your spell since then, and once I found out that you were real and I came to know you, I only loved you even more."

"I love you too."

Dante looked at her questioningly. "You do? Really? You don't have to say that out of fear of hurting my feelings or because you feel pressure to repeat it because I've said it."

She reached out and placed her index finger on his lips. "Shhh! Haven't you been able to tell that I feel the same way? You said it yourself when we met outside the café a few weeks ago, that you could tell I wanted to be with you. That was absolutely correct. I've never felt this way, and you are the first man in my life. But I don't care about meeting anyone else. I want to be with you."

Dante took her hand away from his mouth. He propped himself up on his elbow and lowered his head, kissing Anabella. She wrapped her arms around his head and whispered, "Take me back to your room."

A soft growl slipped from Dante's lips, and he kissed her more deeply. Anabella reached her hands inside the opening of his button-down shirt. His skin was very warm. She breathed in his scent. Dante placed his hand over hers and pulled it off his chest. He stopped kissing her and sighed.

Anabella frowned. "Don't you want to be with me — that way?"

"Of course I do. But I promised myself and you that I would never take advantage of you. I love you too much."

"But I am giving you my permission. You are not taking advantage of me. We love each other. What harm can there be?"

"You know what could possibly happen once we cross that road, Anabella? What if you became pregnant? How would you ever explain that to your mother? No, it must be right. We haven't even told your mother about us. I am content just being with you and holding you and kissing you. I can wait."

"The waiting is beginning to kill me." Anabella surprised herself with this admission as much as she could see it surprised Dante. Though initially she had thought she wanted to wait until she married — that is, if she and Dante ever married — her feelings had quickly changed; she wanted to feel closer to him in every possible way.

He laughed. "Patience. We have all the time in the world. Let us just savor each moment."

Anabella snuggled closer to him as he took her in his arms. They lay silently for a few minutes.

"So you never answered my question. Are you ready to take me home to your mother?"

Anabella exhaled deeply. It was time she stopped being a coward. "Let's do it. We will deal with whatever consequences might arise. All that matters is that we love each other."

As Dante hugged her, she silently prayed she was making the right decision. But the queasy feeling in her stomach was all but guaranteeing the meeting with her mother would not go smoothly at all.

CHAPTER 18
SIGNORA FERRARO

Pienza, 1970

Signora Ferraro was walking through one of her rose gardens, inspecting each of the roses. She couldn't believe they were in mid-August, and soon summer would be over. The roses remained in bloom from May until well into autumn here in Italy. When the roses began to die, Signora Ferraro felt her spirits sink, and her mood remained low throughout the winter and early spring months until the roses returned.

Though she had a large greenhouse on the property where she also grew roses so that she could continue to sell them during the winter months, it wasn't the same for her as seeing the flowers that grew in the gardens. She didn't know how to explain it. But at least she could continue to nurture and admire the roses that grew in the greenhouse. Not seeing roses at all would've been quite devastating for her.

243

She was so engrossed in inspecting the roses that she hadn't noticed the two figures approaching her until she heard "Mamma" in a voice so soft she could've sworn she'd imagined it. When she looked up, she was startled not only to see Anabella standing nearby, but also a young man. Perhaps he was a new customer. Sometimes the customers came to her farm, especially if they had large orders they were looking to fill.

"Anabella, you gave me a slight start. You could've announced yourself."

Signora Ferraro saw the young man frown slightly at her comment. She then noticed Anabella was staring at her sandals, a childhood habit she had never outgrown. She also saw her daughter looked pale.

"*Buongiorno.* I am Signora Ferraro." She quickly wiped her hands on her gardening apron and offered one to the man in greeting. He looked surprised, but stepped forward and shook her hand.

"*Piacere, signora.* It is a pleasure to finally meet you." He glanced nervously at Anabella and waited, as if he were hoping she would say something.

"Are you here to view our gardens? Where did you hear about us? I can assure you that you won't be disappointed with our roses.

I'm sorry. I don't believe you gave me your name."

"Dante. Dante Galletti. And no, I'm afraid I am not here to view your gardens or buy any roses — although they are beyond gorgeous. You have a stunning property."

"*Grazie.* So how may I help you?"

Once more he glanced at Anabella. Signora Ferraro knew her daughter was beautiful. This was not the first time she'd noticed a young man eying her. Ever since Anabella had turned sixteen, Signora Ferraro had seen how men stared at her whenever she and Anabella were in town or at the piazza. And now that Anabella was in her mid-twenties, she seemed to be at the pinnacle of her beauty. When Signora Ferraro had first noticed all the attention her daughter received from men whenever they were out in public, she had felt nervous. But there was nothing she could've done about it. She couldn't deny that her daughter had quickly become a stunning woman. Still, Signora Ferraro hadn't wanted to think about the day that Anabella would leave her. Even though she was twenty-six years old, Anabella had yet to express an interest in any young man and never talked about marrying someday. While Signora Ferraro realized this was the course many young women took, she didn't believe that marriage had to be an absolute rule for everyone to follow. After all, for a time when she was in her twenties, she hadn't thought she would get married. But then she'd met Franco, and her whole world had changed. Sometimes she still wondered how her life would have turned out if she'd never met and fallen in love with him. Then regret would fill her for having such thoughts. It was just that Signora Ferraro couldn't help wondering if she would've been spared much of the pain she'd suffered if she had never met him. But then Anabella wouldn't have existed, and she could not imagine her daughter being absent from her life.

"Mamma, Dante is a friend of mine." Anabella finally spoke.

As realization slowly sank into Signora Ferraro, she looked from Anabella to Dante.

"*Da vero?* Really? For how long?"

Anabella blushed deeply as she stammered, "A f-f-few weeks."

"Few weeks?" Signora Ferraro all but yelled out her response.

Her pulse quickened and her head throbbed as she began to feel a headache coming on. Signora Ferraro's mind raced as she remembered how strangely Anabella had been acting recently. And then there were all the times she'd come home late from the piazza or even whenever she ran out to run an errand. Although Signora Ferraro had been suspicious and had resumed accompanying her daughter to sell the roses to the flower vendors at the Piazza del Campo, she hadn't noticed anything out of the ordinary during their visits. There was no handsome young man whom Anabella was stealing glances at. No one seemed to be taking an extra-special interest in her daughter other than a few passersby who had stared at her for a few moments. But again, Signora Ferraro was accustomed to people noticing her daughter's beauty. Then recently, Anabella had begun to seem more like herself again at home. So Signora Ferraro had stopped going with her to the piazza. She'd felt foolish for doubting Anabella in the first place. Anabella would never lie to her or betray her in any way. She had finally resolved that in her mind. Now she saw she'd been very wrong. Tears came to her eyes, but she quickly blinked them back.

"Signora Ferraro, can we please go sit somewhere and talk?"

The young man seemed to be silently pleading with his eyes. Maybe he was just a friend and nothing more.

"We can talk here. Whatever you have to

tell me won't be different if we sit down."

Her clipped tone seemed to take the young man aback, but he merely nodded.

"*Va bene*. As you wish. Your daughter and I met at the Piazza del Campo. We have become friends, and I have come here today to ask you if you will . . ." — he cleared his throat before continuing — ". . . if you will allow me to court her."

Signora Ferraro's heart dropped to the pit of her stomach. It was just as she'd feared. So they had been secretly seeing each other behind her back whenever she hadn't gone with Anabella to the piazza. And of course whenever Anabella was out doing her errands and returning home late. She shook her head as her gaze landed on Anabella, whose eyes quickly averted from her mother's disapproving stare.

"Is what this young man says true, Anabella?"

Anabella nodded, but continued to look down at her sandals.

"Look at me, Anabella!" Signora Ferraro's voice rose, causing her daughter to immediately shoot her head up. Tears quickly filled Anabella's eyes.

"Why didn't you tell me? Do you remember what I told you when you were a little girl? Do you?"

"*Si,* Mamma. You told me I was never to lie to you. I'm sorry. I didn't mean to hurt you."

"You are hurting yourself, my dear child, whenever you lie to me or deceive me in any way. Remember that."

"Signora Ferraro, please. Do not be upset with Anabella. We do not mean to disrespect you. That is why I have come here today. We want to do right by you, and we regret that we didn't tell you sooner that we have been seeing each other."

"You should have thought about respecting me when you first had the audacity to approach my daughter. I know she would never have approached you first. It is not in her nature. If you really wanted to do the right thing, you would have come here immediately after you met her rather than waiting several months to introduce yourself and express your interest in my daughter. Instead, you snuck around like nothing more than a snake!"

"Mamma, please, don't say that! Dante is a kind person!" Anabella's voice went up a few octaves, eliciting shocked looks from both Signora Ferraro and Dante.

Signora Ferraro could not believe her daughter was raising her voice to her own mother and for what? For this fool standing beside her?

"Anabella, do not speak to me like that!"

"*Signora,* please. I will come here if that is what you want so you can get to know me better. And I promise not to see Anabella any longer without your consent. We care about each other very much. I have nothing but the most honorable intentions toward her."

Signora Ferraro's lips were pursed tightly together. She waited a few moments to collect herself before her rage boiled completely out of control. Taking a deep breath, she said in a firm voice, "Signore Galletti, please leave my home. I do not give you my consent to see my daughter, and if you go against my wishes, I will have you arrested."

"But Anabella is a grown woman. She can do as she pleases and see whomever she wants. There is no crime in that."

"You are not welcome here. If you do not leave immediately, I will have you arrested for trespassing. Now, please leave." Signora Ferraro pointed to the driveway.

Dante narrowed his gaze in her direction and looked as if he were about to say something, but thought better of it.

"*Ciao,* Anabella. I am sorry for having gotten you in trouble. You were right. I should have listened to you." He waited for a moment to get a response from Anabella, but she merely stood with her arms crossed against her chest. Tears slid down her face. Finally, he turned around and walked off of the property. His head hung low, but when he reached the gate that led to the farm's entrance, he looked at Anabella one last time.

"Anabella, let us go inside. We need to talk." Signora Ferraro stormed off toward their house, not looking to see if her daughter followed her.

Once they were indoors, Signora Ferraro poured a glass of rose water for herself. She took a sip, but it did little to calm her nerves. She went to the pantry closet and took out a bottle of grappa. She rarely drank grappa, but at one time in her life, it had helped her greatly. Her hand shook as she poured the grappa about a quarter of the way up her glass. With a quick toss, she downed the liquor, closing her eyes as she let its sting soothe her nerves. When she opened her eyes, Anabella was looking at her with surprise etched all over her features.

"Anabella, sit down." Signora Ferraro gestured toward the kitchen table. Anabella pulled out one of the chairs and sat down.

She kept her gaze averted from her mother's.

"From now on, you are only to go out with me. Is that understood?"

Anabella nodded.

"No one else is to accompany you. Not even Chiara."

"Chiara didn't know," Anabella said in a very low voice.

"Hmmm. It would not be the first time she has gone against my wishes." Signora Ferraro thought back to the time Chiara had given sunflowers to her daughter. In all fairness, Chiara had not known about Signora Ferraro's aversion to sunflowers, but still. And then there were the magazines. Signora Ferraro had found them under Anabella's bed when she was a teenager. She had had a few words with Chiara and asked her never to give her daughter anything without her consent. She'd never said anything to Anabella, and she had returned the magazines to their hiding place. It was no use taking them away from her since Anabella had already read them. After Signora Ferraro had seen the magazines, she had understood why her daughter had wanted the fitted, more stylish dress that year for Easter. She could not have her daughter corrupted by outside influences.

"Also, going forward, we will no longer sell our roses at the Piazza del Campo."

"But Mamma, we will lose out on quite a bit of money." Anabella finally looked up at her mother.

Signora Ferraro held up her hand to silence her daughter.

"We will be fine. As you know, that is not our only source of income. I cannot encourage that young man, and it won't do either of you good to see each other even if I am present. You are to forget he even exists."

"Mamma, what is the harm in us getting to know each other? Don't you want me to get married someday and start my own family?"

Signora Ferraro froze. So Anabella did want to leave her. The admission was too much for her. She felt her legs go weak, but she refused to sit down and show her daughter how hurt she was feeling right now.

"Anabella, he is not the right man for you. That is all I will say on this subject. I repeat my wishes that you are to go out only with me by your side. Now go upstairs to your room. I will call you when dinner is ready."

Anabella stood up. Anger was etched all over her features, but she didn't utter a word as she turned around and left the kitchen.

As soon as she was gone, Signora Ferraro poured more grappa into her glass and gulped it down. She then sat down on one of the kitchen table chairs. Anabella's angry face haunted her. Never had she seen her daughter look at her in such a way. Even when she was a toddler, she'd never been upset with her mother. She had been such a happy baby and child — the model child. Signora Ferraro had always counted herself lucky that Anabella had never gone through a rebellious stage as so many other children did once they reached adolescence. Signora Ferraro thought she had escaped all of that now that her daughter was in her mid-twenties. Then again, Anabella had seemed to mature more slowly than the other girls in Pienza. So it should've come as no surprise to her that Anabella was reaching this stage later in her life.

She buried her face in her hands and began sobbing. "My daughter. My daughter," she mumbled over and over to herself. Although she had forbidden Anabella to leave the house without her and to see Dante Galletti again, she knew deep down she had already begun to lose her child.

CHAPTER 19
ANABELLA

Pienza, 1970

Anabella was walking purposefully, taking long strides and holding her hands clenched in fists by her sides. Tears stung her eyes and her breathing was coming in rapid, short bursts. When she was satisfied she had gone far enough from her house, she stopped, glancing over her shoulder to make sure no one, especially her mother, had followed her. She paced to and fro. Anger surged through her, but she was doing her best to contain it.

Oh, how she wanted to scream, but she was afraid someone might hear her. Clutching at the collar of her blouse, she undid the three little buttons. Her skin felt hot as if she had a fever. It was no use. No matter how many deep breaths she tried to take, she could not calm down. And her rage was only increasing.

How dare her mother treat Dante so terribly! Anabella was mortified at her mamma's rude behavior. True, Mamma was angry at them for going behind her back, but that was no excuse for treating Dante the way she had. She could have at least been civil. But what had Anabella expected? She knew her mother would be upset when she met Dante and learned that Anabella and Dante wanted to see each other. Naturally, most parents would be upset to find out their daughter had been secretly seeing a man they'd never met. She couldn't necessarily blame her for that. What angered Anabella was that she sensed her mother was angry because Anabella had for once exerted independence and not consulted her or asked for her permission to do something she wanted.

Lately, ever since she'd begun seeing Dante, Anabella had reflected more on her childhood and her life on the rose farm. She'd realized just how much her mother had sheltered her. Mamma just wanted Anabella to obey her every command and agree with her on everything. It was rare that Anabella had a say in choosing something she wanted. Like on that Easter when Mamma had finally relented and let Anabella choose the lemon-colored dress she had fallen in love with.

The image of Mamma's face after Anabella had asked her if she wanted her to
marry came back to her. She had looked
horrified. And in that moment, Anabella
knew her mother's answer. She didn't want
her to marry — not ever. She could also tell
her mother had never even considered it for
her daughter. Although her mamma had
said in response that Dante wasn't the right
man for her, Anabella knew those were just
words. In Mamma's eyes, no man would
ever be right for her daughter. And why
would Mamma want her to marry? That
would mean Anabella would have to leave
the farm, and then Mamma would not be
able to control her.

Anabella's pulse beat even faster at this
last thought. Her head was throbbing as she
felt a headache coming on. She ran, hoping
she could tire herself enough to distract her
from the overwhelming anger she felt. When
she thought she could run no farther, she
stopped and dropped to her knees. Her
chest was heaving hard. She closed her eyes
and waited for her heartbeat to slow down.
It was peaceful out here as it usually was.
Anabella opened her eyes. An ocean of
white roses greeted her.

She hadn't realized she'd run all the way
to Mamma's favorite rose garden. Ever

since she was little, Anabella had known this garden was off-limits to her and everyone else who worked at the nursery. It was Mamma's private garden. Anabella had always thought her mother loved it so much because it was the first garden she had planted when she moved to Pienza. But she was surprised to learn when she grew older that her mother had never harvested the roses from this garden and sold them.

One time when Anabella was seven, she had pulled one of the white roses and tucked it behind her ear as she'd seen Chiara often do. But instead of Mamma's white roses, Chiara would take one of the colored roses. While Anabella had her pick of any of the multicolored roses on the farm, for some reason the white ones intrigued her the most. Perhaps because they were forbidden. What harm could one do? There were so many anyway.

An hour later, when Anabella returned home after playing outside, she had forgotten about the rose tucked behind her ear. When her mother saw it, she asked Anabella where she had found the rose. Anabella smiled and said, "From your favorite garden, Mamma. Doesn't it look nice?"

Her mother bent over and pulled the rose out from behind Anabella's ear.

"Do you remember I told you a long time ago that these roses were never to be touched? They are sacred."

Though her mother had not screamed, Anabella could tell she was upset with her. Tears filled her eyes as she said in a tiny voice, "I'm sorry, Mamma. I just wanted to see what they were like. I've never held one of the white roses in my hand before."

"Well, now that you have and your curiosity has been satisfied, you can forget about them. I will not punish you this time, but if I find out you pulled more roses from my garden, you will be punished, Anabella. Do you understand?"

Anabella had nodded, and while she'd wanted to ask her mother what *sacred* meant, she'd been too afraid. Eventually, when she had learned the meaning of the word, she often pondered why her mother had described her white roses as sacred. Did she just mean they were special to her?

Anabella walked over to Mamma's garden, which was enclosed by a white picket fence. Each year when the garden grew larger than the previous year, her mother would extend the fence. Anabella paused before entering. There were so many white roses that they seemed to form one massive white cloud. None of the other gardens contained solely one color. She couldn't see now why the white roses had held so much allure for her when she was a little girl. They seemed boring and lacking in splendor, unlike the colored roses. No wonder her mother loved the white roses so much. She was a woman who never deviated from her simple tastes and routines, just like the plain shirtwaist dresses she still wore and the simple bun she always pulled her hair into and how on certain days of the week they always ate the same meal. Mondays was *pasta e fagioli* and some meat dish, which surprisingly did vary from week to week. Tuesdays they ate whatever leftovers they had from the previous day. Wednesdays was *pollo alla cacciatore.* Thursdays was some pasta dish, and Fridays was a fish dish. The weekends were the only days when Mamma cooked a different dish from week to week. She often saved her more elaborate dishes, such as risotto or manicotti, for the weekends.

As Anabella stepped into the garden, tears slid down her face. She would never see Dante again — all because of her mother's selfishness. She would never leave home or this rose farm. Her life would continue to be the same monotonous routine that her mother's life had become. She would probably start wearing the same clothes decade after decade and keep the precise daily schedule her mother had kept all these years. And of course, she would have nothing more to do with her life than tend to the roses.

Anabella looked at the white roses and, for the first time in her life, she didn't think they were beautiful. Even the more colorful roses and her favorite — yellow roses — she now saw in an ugly light. This rose farm that had once been paradise to her and the roses that had even been like her playmates when she was a lonely little girl were now nothing more than her prison — a prison her mother never wanted to free her from.

Before Anabella knew what she was doing, she was pulling her mother's beloved white roses free from their bushes, throwing them to the ground, and stomping on them. She ignored the thorns that scratched her hands and arms. When she was done, none of the roses remained on the bushes. Anabella's anger finally abated. But instead of feeling better, a deep sadness took hold. Her mother would be devastated when she saw the garden. Anabella had never hurt her mother, but already today she had done so several times. First, when she acknowledged that she'd been seeing Dante behind her mother's back. Then, when she admitted she wanted to get married someday. And now she had destroyed something her mother loved so much.

Slowly, she stood up and made her way back to the house. Her thoughts drifted to Dante. She would never see him again, and she would never see how his last painting of her had come out. Who knew? Maybe Dante would destroy his paintings and drawings of her, just as she had destroyed her mother's garden. For why would he want a reminder of what he couldn't have? At least she had no physical reminders of Dante. But how would she ever erase the wonderful memories of their time together?

CHAPTER 20
MARIA ROSSI

Florence, 1943

As Maria turned off from the Piazza del Duomo onto a quiet alleyway, she was startled by the sound of the bells clanging from the Campanile. Naturally, because of where she was headed, she was especially jumpy. Then again, most Florentines were uneasy these days. Quickening her steps, she soon was at FAF's office at the abandoned church. Glancing over her shoulder to ensure no one had followed her, she parked her bicycle and then hurried to the back of the church and down its basement stairs. She actually felt safer whenever she descended to the underground office. If only she could remain underground until the war was over.

As Maria stepped into FAF's office, she was surprised at its transformation into a makeshift dance hall. She marveled at the decorations. Though upon closer inspection, one could see they were a bit tattered, they still gave a festive air to the room. Streams of ribbons in the colors of the Italian flag hung from the ceiling. Plastic flowers were placed in small vases on the two folding tables that were lined up against the walls. The folding chairs that normally filled the space of the room for when FAF had their meetings had been placed instead on either side of the folding tables. There weren't many refreshments, which wasn't surprising with the rationing. Someone had made *taralli*. There was also an unopened box of *panettone* on the table. Maria noticed that many of the men had brought a bottle of wine or liquor.

Maria had arrived ten minutes late, thinking most of the members would have already arrived at the dance. But she saw half of the members weren't there yet. It was now half past seven, and though a few stragglers were still arriving, Franco had yet to show up. She began wondering if perhaps he wouldn't be here tonight, but surely he would have told her — unless it had slipped his mind that she was going. No. He didn't seem like the absentminded type.

As the clock ticked closer to eight, she began worrying. What if something had happened to him? What if he'd been captured again? She crossed her arms and slowly paced the room. No one seemed to notice her. People were quickly pairing up and walking toward the dance floor.

For a moment, one could almost forget that the world was at war. It was just another ordinary Saturday night, when young men and women were enjoying one another's company. Maria might have been able to forget if just for the duration of the dance, but Franco's absence only reminded her of the realities they now lived with.

She was completely lost in thought and had not noticed someone was standing next to her right until she heard, *"Vino?"*

Franco held out a small glass of wine. Maria caught her breath, not only because she was relieved to see he was all right, but also because he looked incredibly handsome. He wasn't wearing his glasses. The navy suit he wore made him look distinguished. He was the only man present wearing a suit. Everyone else just wore button-down shirts and trousers. A few had worn ties, but that was it. It then dawned on Maria that Franco had gone out of his way to look his best for her.

"Or maybe you'd like something stronger? Whiskey?" Franco smiled, looking amused.

Maria then realized she had never answered his first question. Her cheeks burned, but she cleared her throat and did her best to appear relaxed.

"No, wine is fine. *Grazie.* I was just distracted." She took the glass of wine from Franco and turned her face slightly away as she took a sip. How could she have said she was distracted? No doubt he'd noticed she had been staring at him.

"You look beautiful, Maria." Franco's gaze traveled the length of Maria's body.

She had borrowed a dress from Enza. It was a deep midnight blue with cap sleeves. The bodice was ruched and fitted, and the skirt hit slightly above her knee. Maria was a good two inches taller than Enza, so whereas the dress would've fallen below her sister-in-law's knee, on her it rode higher. Franco had noticed this as well since his eyes lingered on her legs. Though she had several dresses she could've worn, she had wanted to wear something she'd never worn before. And with the war going on, she couldn't ask Papà for money just to buy a new dress. They didn't know when they might need to tap into the money they were saving.

"Thank you, Franco. You look handsome. I like your suit."

He smiled. "*Grazie.* I suppose I overdressed, but I thought why not?" He took a sip of wine, clearing his throat before saying, "So you said you were distracted earlier. Is everything all right?"

Maria nodded. "I'm fine." She smiled to reassure him, but didn't meet his gaze.

"Tell me. Please." Franco reached out and placed his hand on her arm.

"It's nothing, really. I just tend to get anxious sometimes before there's any cause to do so."

"Are you nervous about being here?"

"No." She walked over to the table and took a *tarallo,* nibbling on it. "These are very good. You should have one."

"Please, Maria, don't change the subject. Why were you feeling anxious?"

Maria sighed. He wasn't going to let her off the hook.

"I was just a little worried when I saw you weren't here. I thought perhaps you had been captured again."

Franco's face grew somber. "I'm sorry if I worried you, Maria. And I'm sorry I was late. I was detained by a phone call. That's why I didn't arrive earlier."

"It's all right. You don't owe me an explanation. It's just, with what we're doing, it's only natural that I would be concerned."

"Of course. Thank you for your concern.

267

That means a lot to me." He reached out and pushed a strand of hair that had escaped from Maria's bun. She had worn her hair in a low bun. When she'd looked at herself in the mirror earlier that evening, she had decided to take the ivory silk flower that was pinned on her dress and tuck it into the side of her bun. Maria looked into Franco's eyes. Her heart stopped as he stared back at her. Part of her wanted to look away, but she didn't. She parted her lips slightly and tilted her head to the side, smiling at Franco.

"Have you danced yet?"

"No."

"Then, let's go. We've already wasted an hour — all my fault of course for arriving late."

"Well, you weren't the only latecomer. The dancing only started about half an hour ago, so you didn't miss much."

"Good! *Andiamo!*"

Franco grabbed her hand and rushed to the dance floor. A song with an upbeat tempo was playing. Maria did her best to keep up with Franco, but she didn't have to worry. He expertly led her through the movements and twirled her several times. They laughed after each twirl, and every time their eyes met, she felt waves ripple through her stomach.

After dancing to four songs in a row, they took a break. Franco held her hand as they made their way to the refreshments table. Maria noticed the other members were looking at them and smiling.

"I think after all that dancing you need a shot of whiskey. Will you join me?"

Maria hesitated, but then thought *why not.* She nodded.

"Ready? *Uno, due, tre!*" Franco clinked her glass before quickly downing the whiskey.

Maria did the same, doing her best not to scrunch up her face. Though the whiskey tasted horrible, the warming sensation she felt as it went down her throat made her feel relaxed.

"It's nice that you have this dance every week."

"It is. But I don't know how much longer we'll be able to do this. I'd like to as long as we can because it helps keep morale up. But things are getting more intense." Franco's attention seemed to drift elsewhere.

Maria waited until he was ready to resume the conversation. She realized her bun was coming undone.

"Will you excuse me, Franco? I need to fix my hair."

"Of course. But you might want to just

leave it loose. It'll get messed up again after I twirl you some more on the dance floor." He smirked and winked.

"I think I have had enough dancing for one night." Maria did her best to keep her face serious, but Franco shook his head, knowing she was teasing him.

As she made her way to the restroom, she noticed a few of the couples were sitting on the steps that led to the main floor of the church. They were locked in embraces and kissing. Maria quickly walked past them and went into the bathroom. While she knew it was a party, it felt wrong to be kissing, and maybe even drinking and dancing, in a church. Though they were in the basement, which didn't have any religious ornaments, and though the church was no longer actively being used, she couldn't help feeling a little guilty. But she also couldn't deny how good it had felt to forget about the war for a few hours and lose herself in dancing. It had felt good to pretend that everything was fine and normal.

She took out the pins holding her bun in place and shook out her hair. Franco's words came back to her about leaving her hair loose. She always kept her hair up in a bun or pulled back in a long braid. Most of the other women present at the dance wore their hair on the short side as was now the style, or like her, they kept it pulled back. Franco had dared to stand out by wearing a suit. So why shouldn't she. Her hair reached to the middle of her back. She brought it forward and draped it over her shoulders. The bun she had worn it in had done little to relax her curls. She took a few shorter tendrils that framed her face and wrapped her index finger around them, increasing the curl. Then she took the silk rose that had been in her bun and tucked it into the front of her dress, creating a little cleavage. She smiled at herself in the mirror.

Her eyes scanned the room as she walked back out to the dance floor until she saw Franco in a heated exchange with one of the other men. She slowly walked toward them until she was close enough to eavesdrop without making it obvious she was doing so.

"We cannot wait any longer, Franco. We must act now or we'll regret it."

"I refuse to discuss this any more. We can't just rush into this decision."

"You are making a mistake."

"So be it, if it is. But how do you know that it won't be a mistake to go ahead sooner than we'd planned?" Franco shook his head, disgust plainly evident in his features. He noticed Maria standing nearby. Turning to the man, he said, "We'll discuss this more later."

He walked over to Maria. "I see you took my advice with your hair. I didn't realize you had curly hair."

"I always wear it up."

"You should wear it this way more. Are you ready for another dance?"

A waltz was playing. Maria had only danced the waltz with her father and brother when they had attended relatives' weddings. Though she had been courted by other young men in her village when she was a teenager and in her early twenties, she had never gone to a dance hall with them.

Without waiting for her response, Franco took Maria's hand and led her to the dance floor. The closeness of their bodies in this dance made Maria catch her breath as she let her eyes meet Franco's and he smiled. She returned his smile, but then looked away, pretending to be absorbed in the music and dance. Her thoughts drifted to those other young men who had courted her when she was younger. They had all been polite and handsome enough, but she hadn't had the interest to continue seeing any of them beyond more than a couple of dates. She didn't know why, and sometimes it troubled her that she could be so difficult. For many of her friends had married the first men they dated. Now, as she danced with Franco, excitement coursed through her, and she felt almost giddy. She'd never felt this way before. Who knew? Maybe if she had had the chance to dance with the other young men who had courted her and to be in such close proximity to them, she might've felt the same sensations. But deep down she knew that wasn't true. Hadn't Mamma always told her when she was growing up that she would know without a doubt when she had found the right man? Mamma had told her she would feel it in her body. Perhaps this was what Mamma meant — feeling her stomach flutter, her pulse race, and the elation that she was experiencing right now.

When things hadn't worked out with those other men and as she got older, Maria had just accepted that marriage wasn't in the cards for her. And she'd been all right with that. She loved living with her family and enjoyed their companionship. She didn't need to be married to feel fulfilled.

"Maria, how about we get some fresh air out in the yard?" Franco's voice purred close to her ear, sending a shiver down her neck and throughout her body.

"Is it safe for us to be out there?"

"It'll be fine. Come on."

Maria followed Franco as he made his way to the basement stairs that led to the yard.

Once outside, he took out a pack of cigarettes, holding the pack to Maria.

"I don't smoke."

Franco nodded, then lit his cigarette, taking a deep drag. They remained silent for a few minutes before he spoke.

"You're unlike most of the women I know. I notice you seem at ease just being quiet and in your thoughts, even when you're in the company of someone. I like that."

"Oh, I can talk, especially when I'm having a debate with my father and brother." Maria laughed softly.

"I'm sure you can."

"I do think a lot. I guess you can say I'm a thinker."

"So am I."

"May I ask what you and that man were arguing about earlier? I'm sorry if I'm being nosy. It's just that I couldn't help sensing something is terribly wrong."

Franco didn't miss the nervous lilt in Maria's voice. He looked at her somberly for a moment before throwing his cigarette on the ground and stubbing it out with his foot.

"The less you know about certain operations, the better."

"You don't trust me." Maria stated it rather than asking.

"It's not that. It's for your safety."

"As you told me before, none of what we do is safe — even my writing the articles or coming to FAF's office."

"And that is true, but this is much worse."

Maria didn't say anything. She paced around the perimeter of the yard. Anger was beginning to seep through her. Just when she had thought that Franco was different from most other men and saw her more as an equal, he'd now convinced her otherwise. Those were just words — words he'd hoped would gain him favor with her and perhaps make her like him more. For she had no doubt after the other night, and especially after dancing with him tonight, that he was attracted to her.

"Please don't be mad, Maria."

She looked at him, surprised. Once again, his perception amazed her. Then again, she was certain her face must be pinched with anger.

"I don't want to be treated like a delicate woman. In fact, Franco, I've been giving more thought to what else I could do for FAF besides write for the newspaper and distribute it." She waited before continuing, trying to gauge Franco's reaction. But he remained silent as he watched her.

Swallowing hard, she said, "I was thinking I could deliver messages to the men out in the field. It would be easier for a woman to distract the soldiers."

Franco's complexion suddenly paled. His lips pressed together so tightly she could see the skin puckering around them. And his eyes. They were filled with intense anger. He took a step toward her. Maria took one back.

"Is that what you want? To distract the soldiers?"

Maria walked back toward him until her face was mere inches away from his. "I can see you are thinking the worst about me. It is true. I am a woman, and some say a pretty one. While I'd rather use my intellect, I might as well also use my assets as a woman if it means I can help the cause. In fact, I don't need your permission. I will do as I please."

Maria turned around to leave, but Franco gripped her arm tightly and spun her around so fast that she almost lost her balance. She was about to hurl an insult at him, but just as she was opening her mouth to do so, Franco's lips came down on hers. He kissed her greedily, causing a soft moan to escape from Maria. Her anger from a second ago was quickly forgotten, as all she could think about was the feel of his lips pressed against hers. He wrapped his arms around her, pressing her up against his chest.

The sound of cats fighting nearby caused them to stop. Maria pulled away, doing her best to catch her breath. Franco ran his hand through his hair, and then loosened his tie, unbuttoning the top of his shirt. Maria's eyes darted to the exposed skin, and she felt her knees go weak. She then noticed Franco was looking at her chest. She glanced down and saw the silk rose had fallen to the ground and her dress had shifted a bit, causing more of her cleavage to show. Bending down, she picked up the silk rose and discreetly adjusted her dress, inserting the flower back where it had been.

"Do you like white roses?"

Franco spoke so softly she wasn't sure she'd heard him. "Excuse me?"

He pointed to the silk rose in her dress. "Are white roses your favorite?"

Maria shrugged. "Not really. I love all flowers."

"The white rose suited your complexion when you wore it in your hair and even the way you're wearing it now, against your chest." His gaze once more returned to her bosom.

She blushed.

"I'm sorry I was so forward. I guess you can say you got the better of me in more ways than one." He softly smiled.

"Did you really think I would do something horrible with the soldiers?" Maria crossed her arms, staring at him defiantly.

"No, no. Of course not. I'm sorry for giving you that impression. Just the thought of you anywhere near those soldiers and of your flirting with them sent me into a fury. You have to understand, Maria, these aren't naïve schoolboys whom you can flirt with and then go off on your way."

"I know. I am not that disingenuous. I just meant that the soldiers tend to examine the men more."

"But what about what you said about being an attractive woman who might as well use all of her assets?"

"I meant that a pretty woman could sneak messages or even ammunitions past a soldier more easily than a man could. I didn't mean to imply I would grant them any favors." She blushed as she said this. "But I apologize as well. From your viewpoint, I can see how that must've sounded to you."

"It is all right. I don't want you to take

278

such risks. I can deal with your writing for the newspaper. But I can't stand the thought of your doing anything more dangerous that could place you in harm's way. I'm sure it must be obvious that I have feelings for you, Maria."

"But it is my decision, Franco. You even said that yourself, and that day at the outdoor market, you were encouraging me to get involved. And you seemed so pleased that I did decide to help."

"I confess. My intentions weren't all honorable and for our cause. I wanted to see you again and get to know you better. I'm sorry, Maria. Perhaps I should've never asked you to write for the newspaper. And now you are saying you want to do more dangerous work. I can't allow it. How would I ever live with myself if something happened to you?"

"As I said, Franco, it is my decision. If you try to forbid me from getting more involved, I'll just do it on my own. In fact, I can volunteer at *Gruppi di Azione Patriottica.*"

"GAP? You cannot be serious. You are bluffing me."

"Yes, GAP. I'm sure you've heard of them. And I am not bluffing." Maria stared at him squarely in the eyes.

He looked away and took another cigarette out, quickly lighting it. He took a few drags and paced back and forth around the yard. Shaking his head, he sighed deeply. "I suppose I'd rather have you working with us. That way I can keep an eye on you at least and do my best to keep you safe."

"You don't need to do that, Franco. I can take care of myself."

"I'm beginning to see that, and I don't doubt it. But I would rest easier if you were here. Please, stay with us." He walked slowly over to her and took her hand, drawing her to him. He kissed her again, but this time it was gentler. The smell of his cigarette drifted up to her, making her feel slightly dizzy.

She pulled back and said, "All right. But please don't make assumptions like you did earlier or else I will be out the door. Remember that." She lifted her index finger and waved it in his face, but she couldn't resist smiling.

Franco took her finger and crossed his heart with it. "I promise." He then brought her finger to his lips, planting a kiss.

After he released her finger, Maria asked, "So what will my first mission be?"

"I guess we can start with your delivering messages to the men in the field and other supplies such as food, bandages. Let's take it slow. There is a lot you still need to learn about how we operate. It is imperative not just for your safety, but for the safety of everyone involved."

"Va bene."

"Let's head back inside. We shouldn't be talking about these matters out in the open." His eyes scanned the yard, and then he walked over to the driveway, ensuring no one was present.

Maria followed him back down the basement steps. She couldn't help wondering if she was out of her mind, offering to take on more dangerous work. But what she had said about considering getting more involved was the truth. There was no backing out now, not after the way she had to convince Franco. Although if she did tell him she had a change of heart, she knew he would only be too pleased to not let her go through with becoming a courier.

The music had stopped, and the members were getting ready to leave. Maria was saddened for a moment that she wouldn't get to have one more dance with Franco. She would definitely come to the dance next Saturday. She smiled as she remembered Franco's kiss. Had he just given in to a restrained moment of lust and nothing more? Or was he beginning to have feelings for her? Maria could no longer deny that she was falling quickly for the most intriguing man she'd ever met. And for some reason that realization frightened her just as much as the dangerous work she would soon be undertaking.

CHAPTER 21
DANTE

Florence, 1970

Dante was walking through the Piazza del Duomo in Florence. As always, whenever he came to the beautiful city, he marveled at all the architectural genius surrounding him. His favorite was the Duomo atop the stunning Cathedral. The famous Duomo could be seen throughout the city, and he never tired of taking a few moments to stare up at the incredible dome. Crossing his arms, he let his gaze then wander to the ornate details of the cathedral. He remembered the first time he came to Florence for art school and how much he had admired the pink, green, and white Tuscan marble tiles that formed the cathedral's exterior. Anabella would no doubt be in awe if she were here with him. At the thought of her, Dante's heart filled with an abysmal sadness — a sadness so great it could fill the interior of the massive Duomo.

While it felt good to be gone from Siena and have this weekend break from his work that he was allowing himself, the trip had done little to lift his spirits. Two weeks had passed since Anabella had taken him to meet her mother. What a fool he'd been! He kept mentally chiding himself for not heeding Anabella's warnings about Signora Ferraro. To think he had actually thought he could sway the bitter woman into accepting him and giving her blessing for him to continue seeing her daughter. He supposed love was to blame for his lack of reasoning. The famous proverb about love being blind was so true. If he had just listened to Anabella and continued seeing her in secret, he wouldn't be suffering now. But what good would have come out of that? Eventually, they would have been caught. And how could he go on indefinitely without making more of a commitment to Anabella?

He had stayed away from the rose farm for a week after Signora Ferraro forbade him to see Anabella. Finally, he could stand it no more. He'd woken up at the crack of dawn and had driven to Pienza. Like an intruder, he had staked the property from all angles until he was able to find a tall fence that separated the property from the back road. The fence was covered in ivy, which allowed him to remain hidden, but still be able to view the rose gardens.

For three consecutive mornings, he made the hour-long drive and waited at the fence for a glimpse of Anabella. It wasn't until he made the drive on the second day that it dawned on him just how hard it had been for Anabella to make the long commute into Siena, sell her roses to the vendors, visit with Dante, and then make it back in time to Pienza at a reasonable hour that wouldn't cause her mother to be suspicious. She did care for him — why else would she have gone to such painstaking trouble for him? He felt selfish for not having realized all this before and for pressuring her to take him home to her mother.

On the third morning, he had finally spotted Anabella. She was working in the field with a woman who looked to be a good ten years older than her. Although the woman was smiling and talking animatedly to Anabella, he could see she merely nodded her head occasionally and didn't engage in much of the conversation. Dark circles as large as silver dollars were under her eyes, which looked as sad as Dante felt. Their time apart from each other was affecting her greatly as well. He wanted to climb over the tall fence, run to her side, and take her with him. Although the image was certainly romantic, he still had enough sense in him to know such an action would only get him arrested, and further ruin his chances of ever being with the woman he loved. So he had merely watched her, memorizing every nuance of how she looked, how she moved, the way the sun hit her face. And when he had returned home, he committed the memories to canvas.

He called the new painting *Anabella Alone,* depicting her on the rose farm, but with none of the workers surrounding her. She was on her knees working the soil, but instead of vibrant roses blooming from their stems, all of the roses were wilted. He had exaggerated the dark circles he'd seen under her eyes, and he had painted her hair so that it was pulled up into a disheveled bun, loose strands dangling haphazardly down her neck and partially obscuring her face. Her sad, worn expression came through vividly, and her face conveyed a deep sense of despair. The work was the darkest one he'd created. Still, he felt it captured Anabella more than the ones that showcased her beauty or her innocent, childlike personality. For now, he felt as if he truly understood her and knew her soul.

Seeing her working on the rose farm had

given him a view into her innermost thoughts. As he watched her that day, he spoke to her silently in his head. He reminded her of the times they had spent together . . . of the day in the sunflower field when she had run free through the flowers . . . how they laughed while they hurried to sell her roses to the vendors so that they would have more time together . . . the first time he brought her to his apartment . . . and he reminded her of their intimate moments, their kisses and embraces. At one point, she had looked up from the roses she was tending to, and stared at the fence. He wanted to pull the ivy farther apart and let her see he was there. He wanted her to know he hadn't given up on her. But for some reason, he hadn't.

Part of him reasoned that he needed to let her go for her own good, and that was why he hadn't revealed himself. But another part of him refused to believe that they were better off without each other. No. There was a reason God had introduced Anabella to him in his dreams and later in his waking life. It was not mere coincidence. They were meant to be part of each other's destiny. After meeting Anabella, he hadn't been the same again. And he knew he would never love another woman the way he loved her.

The bells coming from the famed Campanile shook him out of his thoughts. He watched the clanging bells in the tower. This was such a beautiful city. How he wished Anabella could see it. The sounds of the bells soothed him. A thought then came to him. It was risky, but what did he have to lose at this point? All he knew was that he couldn't continue to wait and do nothing.

CHAPTER 22
MARIA ROSSI

Florence, 1943

As Maria left her house and walked her bicycle to the street, she noticed a slight chill to the air. It was September, and she could feel summer was beginning to give way to fall, even though the new season's arrival wouldn't be for another week. But the seasons were not all that was changing. A week ago, Italy had signed an armistice with the Allied forces. Initially, the announcement had led everyone to think the war was over. Italian soldiers immediately shed their uniforms and returned home in civilian clothes. But within two days of the armistice, the Germans attacked Rome, forcing the Eternal City to surrender. Before the armistice, German forces had already been present in central and northern Italy, but now even more soldiers occupied the cities.

Mussolini had been deposed the last week

in July. Franco and the other members of FAF had rejoiced, believing that the tide was truly turning in their favor. But the celebration was short-lived when six weeks later the armistice was signed and the German occupation soon followed. Spirits quickly plummeted as everyone realized that Italy still had a long way to go to achieve freedom. Once the shock that Florence was now under German rule had subsided, Franco and FAF wasted no time in shifting their focus to driving out the Nazis. Franco gave impassioned speeches, which reenergized the other members and gave them hope once again.

Maria and Franco had become romantically involved shortly after the first dance she'd attended at FAF's headquarters. She'd never been so happy. Franco surprised her often with flowers and notes, many of which contained verses from Shakespeare's love sonnets. And Maria had begun baking more at home so she could take some of her sweets to him. As they worked side by side, he became her mentor as well, guiding her as she wrote her articles for FAF's newspaper and pamphlets. They brainstormed ideas for the pieces as well. Franco appreciated her intellect, and, in response, Maria wanted to impress him by giving him her best work. Gone was her earlier fear about writing the articles at the headquarters. For she longed to spend as much time as she could with Franco and, when she didn't find him in his apartment, she always went to the office in search of him. Yes, it had been a whirlwind of a summer between the recent current events and her burgeoning romance with Franco.

As Maria pedaled her bike through the streets of Florence, she held on to the bike's handlebars with her right hand, and with her free hand she threw newspaper bundles in front of the houses she passed. So far she had not spotted any German soldiers along her ride. With every newspaper she threw, she felt a rush of adrenaline, knowing she was helping in FAF's efforts to rid her country of Nazi and Fascist rule. She felt a sense of fulfillment like she'd never known before.

Vittorio Lanza, the senior editor of Florence's local newspaper, *La Toscana,* had recently joined FAF and agreed to enclose the Resistance newspapers within the pages of their paper. The newspapers were distributed in this fashion twice a week. Ever since Maria had come on board to help in writing the articles, FAF was able to produce an issue three times a week. Immediately, she had thrown herself into the work, often staying up late at night to complete writing the newspaper and other literature they distributed. Then, whenever she had free time and could get away from home, she would take her bike and distribute FAF's newspapers. But it was becoming more difficult to evade her family's suspicion. Enza had been the first one to question Maria as to where she was going. Then, it was Michele. Though he didn't accuse her of lying whenever she used the excuse that she was meeting friends, he gave her a warning and had said, *"The deeper you enmesh yourself, the more there is no turning back."*

His words resonated with Maria, and she often thought of them when she was out distributing the newspapers. Though she had become less afraid and more emboldened, at times her mind still strayed to the fact that what they were doing was very dangerous. But she knew there was no quitting now — for she believed too much in the Resistance, and she could not let the organization or Franco down. But more important, she couldn't let her fellow Florentines and her country down.

"Halt!"

Maria had been so lost in her thoughts that she hadn't seen the German soldier who was holding his hand up and blocking her path a few feet ahead. She came to an abrupt stop. Her heart dropped to her stomach.

"Guten Tag, Herr." As she wished the soldier good morning, she did her best to smile and not show her fear. Franco had taught her a few key German phrases so that if she ran into any soldiers she could immediately ingratiate herself by showing she knew some of their language.

"May I see your newspaper, *Fräulein?*"

Maria swallowed hard before handing the newspaper over. Her mind raced as she thought of ways to extricate herself from this situation. Then, a thought came to her. Before letting go of the newspaper, she lightly brushed her fingers along the soldier's hand. He looked up, slightly startled. She deepened her smile.

"It is a beautiful afternoon. Will you be taking a break soon?"

Maria's voice sounded foreign to her as she flirted with the soldier. Thankfully, he was young, probably in his early twenties. Though she was twenty-eight, she was often told she looked much younger.

"Nein. I won't be off until late tonight." He frowned as his eyes scanned Maria from head to toe.

Maria silently thanked God. She didn't know what she would do if he asked her to have espresso with him at one of the cafés. It had become commonplace for Italian women to entertain the German soldiers. A few of the women did it out of fear when approached by the Nazis. But others solicited the soldiers, hoping they could gain special favor with them and receive more ration cards.

He returned his attention to the newspaper as he flipped through a few pages. Sweat began forming along her hairline, and she was grateful she'd worn a scarf over her head. The seconds seemed to tick by painfully slow as she waited for him to finish inspecting the newspaper. Since FAF's own newspaper was much smaller than *La Toscana,* Vittorio had stapled it toward the back so that it wouldn't easily fall out in such a situation as the one Maria was now finding herself in. Maria hoped that the soldier's inspection would be brief, and he wouldn't peruse the paper to the end. Her heart beat rapidly, and her chest felt constricted, making it harder for her to breathe normally.

"That is too bad. I would have liked to share an espresso with you." She hoped the slight tremor she heard in her voice wasn't apparent to the soldier.

He glanced up and finally smiled. "You are too kind. Do you normally travel this route to deliver your newspapers?"

Maria nodded, tilting her head slightly as she met his gaze.

"Perhaps next time. I will keep my eyes open for you. Enjoy the rest of your day, *Fräulein. Ciao!*" He handed the newspaper back to Maria. This time he held her hand for a moment before completely relinquishing the paper.

"Ciao." She waited until he walked away before pedaling away.

It wasn't until she reached the corner of the very long street that she realized how fast she'd been pedaling. Glancing over her shoulder, she was relieved to see the soldier was nowhere in sight. She still had a few more newspapers to deliver, but her nerves were too jolted. She quickly made her way to FAF's office. Her heart wouldn't stop pounding.

Jumping off her bike, she let it fall to the ground as she ran down the alleyway of the abandoned church. Removing the bush that concealed the basement door, she lifted the door, but had to put all of her weight into it. Her arms were shaking badly. Before closing the door, she propped the bush as best she could over it. Running down the steps, she miscalculated the last step and fell to the ground. Her head banged against the door that led to the office's interior. Standing up, she rubbed her forehead as she knocked on the door in the code that was used. She waited for a few seconds, but no one answered. She tried once more. Finally, she heard footsteps coming to the door. Franco opened it.

"Maria, what's the matter?" Franco's eyes widened in alarm when he saw her.

Her scarf had fallen off her head, and strands of her hair clung to her cheeks. When she reached up to straighten her hair, she felt something warm and sticky on her forehead. She pulled her hand away and saw there was some blood.

"I didn't see the last step and fell."

"It's not just your disheveled appearance and the cut on your head. You are as pale as a sheet." Franco then noticed she was carrying the tote with several newspapers in it. "Were you stopped?"

Maria nodded.

"Come in, come in." He put his arm around her shoulders as he guided her into the office.

Maria hoped he didn't notice how badly she was shaking. She didn't want him to think she was a coward. Tears began filling her eyes, but she forced them back. Once she and Franco entered the office, she was relieved to find no one else was around. It was bad enough Franco was seeing her like this. If the others saw her in this state they might think she was too fragile to do the work. The admiration she'd received from the partisans had given her a sense of fulfillment and the feeling that she was making a valuable contribution.

Franco pulled the chair out from his desk. "Sit down. I'll get you a drink."

"Grazie," Maria managed to say in little more than a whisper. She closed her eyes and took a deep breath, willing her nerves to calm down.

Untying her scarf with one hand, she used her free hand to reach into her purse and take out her compact. After inspecting the cut on her head in the mirror, she saw it was nothing more than a scratch, and it had already stopped bleeding. She was about to use her scarf to wipe the blood that had smeared onto her face when Franco returned.

"Wait. Don't ruin your scarf." He knelt down by her side and dabbed at her cut with a wet kitchen towel. He then gently cleaned the blood and dirt off her face.

Maria could feel his breath on her, and the warmth of it immediately comforted her.

When he was done, his eyes met hers. "Better?"

She smiled. "*Grazie.* I'm sorry to have frightened you. I am fine."

"Here. Drink this." He handed her a shot glass filled to the brim with liquor.

Maria took a sip. It was grappa. She had never cared for it though Papà and Michele drank it. But now she greedily swallowed it, letting it burn her throat. Franco reached over to his desk where he had placed the bottle of grappa and filled her glass once more. She hesitated for a moment as she pondered returning home in an inebriated state, but right now all she cared about was regaining control of her nerves. Before she could change her mind, she downed the second glass of grappa as well.

Franco laughed. "I see you like your liquor."

She blushed. "Actually, I hate grappa. I've never had more than a sip here and there."

Franco looked at her thoughtfully as he patted her hand. "You never had a need for it like you did today. That is when most of us learn to enjoy our liquor for the first time. Are you now feeling better?"

"*Si, si.* I'm sorry, Franco, but I didn't finish distributing the rest of the newspapers. I'll do so before I return home."

"Don't worry about it. I can deliver them. You should go home and get some rest. But please, tell me what happened first."

"I was stopped by a German soldier. Naturally, he wanted to see one of the newspapers. But thank God, he didn't find our newspaper."

"Did he . . ." Franco paused before continuing. "Did . . . Is that all he did? Look through the newspaper?" Franco's eyes filled with worry as his gaze shifted to Maria's clothes.

She glanced down at her shirtwaist dress and noticed the top button of her dress was undone. It must've opened when she fell. She reached up and quickly fastened the button.

"Of course all he did was examine the newspaper." Her cheeks burned as she remembered how she'd flirted with him. She saw Franco still looking questioningly at her. He didn't believe her. "My dress must've opened up when I fell down the basement stairs."

"I'm sorry, Maria. I didn't mean to offend you with my questioning, but I had to ask. They're capable of anything."

She nodded.

"Maybe you shouldn't deliver the news-papers anymore. We have other people who can do that. Just focus on writing the arti-cles."

Maria quickly shook her head. "No. I want to continue. Please don't let what happened today worry you. I will be fine. I handled it, didn't I?"

She regretted her words as soon she'd ut-tered them. Franco looked at her once more questioningly, but thankfully dropped the subject.

"We'll talk about this more tomorrow. You need to go home and get some rest. I will accompany you."

"You don't have a bicycle."

"I'll ride your bike, and you can ride behind me. Your hands are still shaking. I wouldn't want you getting into an accident. Don't try to say no. I insist."

He stood up and grabbed his wallet and keys from the top drawer of the desk. Maria followed him out of the office. Once they stepped outside, he placed his arm around her shoulders again. She felt safe with him. If only he could be by her side when she was delivering the newspapers, she would never worry.

Franco held Maria's bike as he waited for her to get on. When he got on, she placed her hands on either side of his waist.

"Wrap your arms fully around my waist. I wouldn't want you to fall again." He said it in a teasing manner.

After a few minutes of riding, she felt herself finally relaxing enough to rest the side of her face against his back. She closed her eyes and felt the warmth from Franco's body and the breeze blowing through her hair.

"It's a nice evening." Franco finally broke the silence that had ensued from the moment they left FAF's office.

"*Si*, it is."

"These days it can be hard to try to take pleasure in small delights such as these. There is so much to worry about. But we should be taking every possible moment to appreciate nature and the few good things we still have in our lives like each other." Franco's voice sounded sad.

Maria hesitated for a moment before asking him her next question, but it was one she'd wanted to ask him ever since the Italian armistice had been signed and FAF had redirected its focus to ousting the Germans from Florence.

"Are you now involved in the more dangerous aspects of the Resistance?"

Though they'd been dating for almost two

months now, she felt much closer to him than she ever had. Perhaps it was because of his seeing her afraid earlier and in a vulnerable state. And his caring attitude toward her afterward had made Maria feel like she could ask him anything.

Franco didn't answer immediately. She waited, wondering if he would. His continued silence only convinced her he was already doing dangerous work. But then he said, "Not yet. But that will change at some point. You have to remember, Maria, whether one of our members is planting an explosive or writing and publishing our newspapers, the work is all dangerous. And as you know, I have already been arrested, and others have been tortured, exiled, or even killed. That was when we were fighting against the Fascists, but it is a whole other story with the Nazis, as I'm sure you're aware."

Maria swallowed hard. After the atrocities the Nazis had committed against the Jews across Europe, she didn't want to think what could happen to Franco or any of them if they were caught. This was all so crazy! Was she really living in this world and risking not only her life, but also the lives of her family? Or had she been dreaming these past few months as she became involved with FAF and dug herself deeper into its trenches? While she knew there was no going back — it just wasn't a choice for her anymore — she still at times, like now, questioned the sanity of it all. But she didn't want to remain passive any longer, the way she'd been before she met Franco.

"Franco, I know you told me before that you are afraid at times, but has your fear increased ever since the Germans occupied Florence and now that the work at FAF has become more dangerous than ever?"

Franco was silent for a few seconds, and Maria knew he was thinking how best to answer her so that he didn't frighten her. He'd told her one night when they had gone for a *passeggiata* along the Ponte Vecchio that he would never lie to her, and that he believed in honesty always — except of course when dealing with the enemy. So she knew that, while he was now trying to find a way to answer her in a manner that wouldn't scare her, he would not lie to her.

"We can't let fear stop us, Maria. Too much is at stake. If we ever hope to see a free Italy again, we cannot let fear consume us. Instead of seeing my Resistance work as a choice, I see it as a requirement. This is what I must do. I must go forward or else I would never be able to live with myself, knowing I hadn't done all I could to stop the Germans. I wish I could tell you not to be afraid and not to worry about me — or even yourself — but I cannot. All I can assure you of is that we are doing the right thing. I feel that more so than ever. However, as I have told you before, if you decided to stop working with us, I would understand and would never think differently of you. I want you in my life — whether you are part of FAF or not. And, if anything, I have become more afraid because I'm worried about your getting hurt and losing you. In fact, I would be immensely relieved if you did decide to quit."

"I'm touched, Franco. But I am proud of my country and of being Italian. I don't want us to continue living under German rule. I sense things will get worse with them here in Florence now. How could I live with myself if I quit now and did nothing while the man I love is risking his life to keep me safe and protect the future of Italy?"

"You love me?" Franco stopped pedaling, placing his feet on the ground as he looked at her over his shoulder.

Maria had been so wrapped up in what she was saying that she hadn't realized she'd told him she loved him. For a second, she felt embarrassed, but then she quickly pushed the feeling away. It was true, so why should she pretend that she hadn't said it? If Franco didn't feel the same way about her, that wouldn't invalidate her love for him. So she looked him directly in the eyes and said, "*Si. Ti voglio bene molto,* Franco."

He got off the bike and took Maria's hand, helping her off the bicycle, and led her under a tree. She leaned back against the tree as Franco took her face in both of his hands and kissed her. It was the most rapturous kiss they'd ever shared, even though they had already made love a few weeks ago.

Franco stopped kissing her and stroked her cheeks with his thumbs. He looked at her, and she could see desire filling his eyes. But then his eyes glistened. She was stunned as she saw a tear slide down his face.

"I love you very much, Maria Rossi. I know there will never be another woman for me. I want to keep telling you over and over again how much I love you. I knew I loved you from the moment I saw you walking through the sunflower garden."

"And I will never love another man as I love you. I've never met anyone as brave as you, Franco, and I know I never will meet anyone braver."

He shook his head. "I should have told

you sooner that I loved you, but I was afraid of becoming even closer to you and afraid of being separated from you if I got arrested again or . . ." He averted his gaze, shutting his eyes tightly.

Maria wrapped her arms around his waist and held him fiercely. Neither said anything as they held each other. Finally, she pulled away and looked at her watch.

"I need to get home before everyone gets worried."

Franco nodded his head and kissed her one more time softly. He wrapped his arm around her shoulders as they walked over to the bike. He helped her on, and as they rode the rest of the way back to her house, her brother's words came back to her: *The deeper you enmesh yourself, the more there is no turning back.* Clearly, there was no turning back for Franco — or for herself. They had both just resolved that even more. And now that they had expressed their love to each other, there was no way Maria was going to leave Franco's side in his fight against the Germans. For if they only had a short time together, she wanted to be with him as much as possible.

Soon, they were approaching her house, but Maria wasn't ready to say good-bye just yet.

"Let's walk the rest of the way."

Franco glanced at her over his shoulder, surprise etched across his features, but he shrugged and said, *"Va bene."*

He walked her bike up the steep incline of the long street Maria's house was located on. Maria crossed her arms. How she wished things were different and that the world wasn't at war. If only Franco weren't escorting her home because he was worried for her safety. She wished instead that their only worries were about what they would eat for dinner at one of the *trattorie* and if her family would approve of Franco.

"I probably should have let you drop me off farther back to avoid questions, but that's okay. You can be the friend I've been telling them I've been going to see."

"Maybe I can meet your family someday — when you feel ready of course. I would love to meet your father. He sounds like someone I would get along with."

"I've thought that already as well."

Franco met Maria's gaze. She waited. Was he, too, thinking that he didn't want to part from her tonight? If only they could spend the entire night together.

"I'll wait until you step inside. *Buona notte.*"

"*Buona notte,* Franco. Thank you for

escorting me home — oh, and for the grappa." She smiled.

He stepped forward and whispered in her ear, "I love you."

"I love you, too," she whispered back. She kissed him on the lips and didn't care anymore if someone from her family was witnessing them from behind the window.

She pulled away and began walking to her front door.

"Maria?"

She stopped walking and turned around. "*Si?*"

"I'm sorry you had to go through what you went through today with that soldier. Again, if you change your mind about distributing the newspapers, I wouldn't think less of you and neither would the others. I know I must be sounding like a parrot, but I really don't want anything happening to you."

"Thank you for saying that, Franco. The feeling is mutual. I don't want anything happening to you either. Promise me you'll be careful, especially when you begin the more dangerous work."

Their eyes locked for a few seconds before Franco said, "I promise."

She waved again and walked to her front door. She could feel his eyes on her back up until she stepped inside, but she didn't look at him again. Tears were now sliding down her face. The weight of all that had transpired today was too much for her. And the thought of something happening to Franco terrified her even more now that they had professed their love for each other. She walked over to the windows in her living room and peeked behind the sheer chiffon curtains. Franco wheeled her bicycle to the side of her house and perched it there. She realized she had forgotten to take the bike from him. He looked toward her house one last time. She stood to the side so he wouldn't see she was spying on him. But she couldn't help feeling as if he was looking right at her. He then walked away, whistling to himself as he placed his hands in the pockets of his trousers. She waited until she could no longer hear his whistling, and then she went up to her bedroom.

The deeper you enmesh yourself, the more there is no turning back.

Once again, Michele's words haunted her as she lay in bed. She couldn't help thinking they applied not only to her Resistance work, but to her feelings for Franco as well.

CHAPTER 23
ANABELLA

Pienza, 1970

Anabella was sitting at her desk in her bedroom. She hadn't sat at the desk since she was in high school. But it was no use lying in bed, waiting for sleep to overtake her. She had slept, at best, only a few hours each night since Mamma had forbidden her to see Dante again. Though only a couple of weeks had passed, to Anabella, it felt like months since she'd seen Dante. If only she could forget him and stop feeling this excruciating pain in her heart whenever she thought about him.

Chiara had given Anabella a journal yesterday, telling her to use it to express her emotions. The day after the disastrous meeting between Dante and Mamma, Anabella had collapsed into Chiara's arms when they were out tending to the roses.

"I hate her! I hate her! She's taken away from me the one person who has made me the happiest I've ever been." Anabella was inconsolable as Chiara stroked her hair and back.

"You don't hate your mamma. She is just doing what she thinks is best for you. That has always been her intention where you are concerned."

Anabella furiously shook her head. "You know that's not true. She is also thinking about herself. Mamma has never wanted me to have a life outside of the rose farm." Anabella's face twisted in disgust as she gestured toward the roses. "I used to think I was the luckiest person, living here surrounded by these beautiful gardens, but that was Mamma brainwashing me. She merely created a pretty prison for me, hoping I would never be curious about the world outside of our home. She wants me all to herself and always has. I see that so clearly now, Chiara. That is why she homeschooled me and didn't let me interact with the children in town. Why she never encouraged me to take up a profession other than gardening or encouraged me to get married and have my own family. The only time she mentioned taking me somewhere to meet other people my age was a few weeks ago when she was getting suspicious as to why I'd lost interest in the farm and why my visits to Siena were taking longer than usual. She suggested I attend the dances the church holds every week." Anabella laughed. "Again, her motivation wasn't to help me meet other people, but rather it was to control me and ensure I wasn't straying too far from her."

Chiara's eyes met Anabella's. She remained silent. Anabella knew Chiara agreed with her, but she was a good person and would not speak badly of her employer.

"You must compose yourself, Anabella. Falling apart will do no one any good. Your mother just needs some time to get used to the fact that you are now a grown woman and can make your own decisions. You do know that, don't you?" Chiara tilted Anabella's chin up so that their gazes met again.

"How can I make my own decisions? I have no skills to find work outside of here, thanks to Mamma. She provides for me."

"Maybe you just need to have a talk with her. Not now. Wait until she's had some time to calm down. Your mother is a good woman despite her having sheltered you so much. And if you really want to find work outside of the farm, it's not too late. You can go to school, learn a trade. You are still so young and have your entire life ahead of you."

"I don't know, Chiara. It all feels so hopeless. But I will think more about what you've said."

As Anabella's thoughts returned to the present, she tapped her pen against her journal. She decided to write to Dante so she could tell him fully how she felt about him and how much she missed him.

Dear Dante,

I wanted to tell you again, if only just on paper, I love you. These past couple of weeks that we've been apart have only reaffirmed my feelings for you. It has been sheer torture not seeing you . . . not posing for you and seeing the wonderful paintings you create . . . not being in your arms. Is this really the end?

We should have waited before talking to my mother. Still, after her reaction that day, I don't see how she would have ever given us her blessing. Have you forgotten about me already, Dante? Was I just a passing fancy? Do you still dream about me at night? Or has another woman entered your dreams, making you forget all about me? Do you feel foolish for having ever loved me — a naïve woman who has seen so little of the world?

I've wanted to call you, to hear your voice again. But I'm too afraid of Mamma finding out. I feel her eyes on me more now, and I can barely stand being in the same room with her. My anger toward her seems to grow each day. The meals we share are excruciating. I can barely swallow my food. Although she has tried to make conversation with me, I refuse to engage with her. I have never been so upset with Mamma, and this hurts me greatly, too. Why can't I have all of the people I love in my life?

I will never forget you, Dante. But I understand if you have chosen to move on without me.

Love,
Anabella

She reread the letter three times. Each time, she felt an overwhelming urge to rip the page out and mail the letter to Dante. Why should she keep it hidden in her journal? She could give the letter to Chiara and ask her to mail it for her.

A light beaming from outside of Anabella's window startled her. The light flashed a few times through her window. She stood up and walked over to the window, staying to the side so she wouldn't be seen. Her heart raced as she noticed the outline of a figure down below aiming what looked to be a flashlight at her window. Was it a thief? She had to warn Mamma. But just as she was about to hurry away from the window, the light flickered on the figure's face.

Anabella gasped as her hand flew to her mouth. She pressed her face up against the glass to be sure. It *was* Dante!

She opened her window. He smiled at her and waved, holding his index finger up against his lips.

She smiled back, but was terrified. If Bruno was outside he would start barking once he noticed Dante's presence. She couldn't remember if she had let Bruno in before she went to bed. Some nights, he preferred to sleep on their porch.

"Stay where you are. I'll come out. I don't want my dog to see you if he is outside," she whispered as loudly as possible, hoping it wasn't loud enough to reach her mother's bedroom, which was down the hall.

Putting her robe on, she remained barefoot as she quietly tiptoed down to the first floor. She breathed a sigh of relief when she saw Bruno was deep in sleep in his basket by the fireplace. Her heart was racing as she made her way to the door that led out to the back of the house.

315

Dante had turned the flashlight off and was pacing back and forth. When he saw Anabella, he walked quickly to her.

"Anabella," he whispered before taking her in his arms. "I've missed you so much."

She closed her eyes, taking comfort in being in Dante's arms again as she hugged him back tightly. They remained like that for a few moments before Anabella pulled back.

"I can't stay out here too long in case Mamma wakes."

"I know. I'm sorry. I don't mean to give you any more trouble than I already have, but I had to see you."

"No, I'm glad you came. I wanted to call you, but was too afraid."

"I sensed that. So you are happy to see me?"

"Of course. I even wrote a letter to you, just a few moments before I noticed your flashlight beaming through my window. But I wasn't sure if I was going to have Chiara mail it for me."

"Why not?"

Anabella shrugged her shoulders. "I was afraid you had already forgotten about me and . . ." Her voice trailed off.

Dante lifted the tip of her chin with his

hand, forcing her to look into his eyes. "And what?"

"And met someone else." Anabella lowered her face as she blushed. She was grateful it was dark and he couldn't see the flush in her cheeks.

"Are you crazy? I told you I loved you. I've never loved anyone the way I love you. How could I just forget you like that? Have I come across as a reckless scoundrel to you? Do you think this was just some game for me?" Dante sounded hurt.

"No, of course not. You have been the utmost gentleman with me." She smiled.

Dante's face relaxed. "How I've missed seeing your smile."

"You took a chance coming here, and what were you thinking flashing that light in my window? You didn't know which was my bedroom. You could've flashed it in my mother's bedroom."

"I did know which was your bedroom."

Anabella frowned.

"I've come by a few times early in the morning. I was watching through a clearing in the ivy that covers the fence to the back of the rose gardens. You must think I'm a creep, but you have to understand, Anabella, I was going crazy not seeing you. Part of me hoped I could get your attention and talk to you, but when I did see you, I was terrified of creating more problems between you and your mother. Guilt has wracked me that I didn't listen to you when you warned me that it was too soon to meet your mother. I'm sorry."

Anabella reached up and placed her hand on Dante's cheek. "Don't be sorry. I gave in after all and brought you here. Besides, eventually I would have had to tell her about us. We couldn't keep sneaking around. She would have had the same reaction even if I brought you months later. Mamma has always been afraid of losing me. I see that clearly now. She has always acted as if everything she does is in my best interests, but it's only in her best interests."

"You don't truly believe that. Your mother does love you, and she has provided for you all these years and on her own. That was not easy. I know from my own experience with my mother having to raise me alone, although it was a bit easier for her because she had my grandmother to help her. But your mother had no one. I'm sure your mother has her reasons for sheltering you so much."

"You are too kind, Dante. Most other people would be mad at her for how she treated you when you first met her."

"Naturally, I was upset that she didn't give us a chance and that she immediately asked me to stop seeing you. But I don't hate her. How could I? After all, she raised you into the beautiful, caring woman you are. And you must give her credit as well."

"I suppose." Anabella nodded somberly.

"Is there somewhere we can go, away from the house, just for a few minutes so we don't have to whisper?"

Anabella glanced up nervously at the second-story windows.

"All right, but again, we mustn't be too long."

"Is your mother a light sleeper?"

"No, but still, we must be careful."

She took Dante by the hand and led him away from the house. Soon they were walking through the rose gardens with only the moonlight and a few lights that were posted along the property. Dante inhaled deeply the sweet perfume of the roses. This was an idyllic place. He could see why Anabella had loved growing up here. But he sensed that, now that she had discovered more of a world outside the farm, she was becoming weary of her home. Sadness filled him for a moment. He didn't want her to have bad memories of her childhood sanctuary or of her mother. But he could hear the disdain in Anabella's voice when she had spoken about her mother's selfishness. Time was what Signora Ferraro needed. He didn't know her, but surely she could not be mad at her daughter forever. Anabella was her only relative. No wonder she had protected her so fiercely and was so fearful of Anabella's having more of her own life. It was very clear now to him that Signora Ferraro was deeply terrified of losing her only child. Guilt began to gnaw at him, giving him doubts as to his motives for coming here tonight. But he saw how happy Anabella was to see him, and she, too, had expressed to him how she'd missed him. How could he deny himself her love? And was it fair for Anabella to deny herself a chance at happiness and love all because of her mother?

Anabella stopped in front of a pagoda. A semicircular bench was housed inside of it, and a rose trellis wove throughout the wooden structure.

"We can talk here." She stepped inside the pagoda and sat on the bench. Dante joined her.

"This is nice."

"Chiara suggested it to my mother a couple of years ago. We are getting more requests from the locals who get married and want to have their photographs taken on the rose farm. Chiara thought this would be a nice addition and would encourage more of our buyers who purchase their wedding flowers from us to also have their photos taken here. We charge them a small fee for doing so if they have also purchased their roses here. But we also get couples who do not buy our flowers for their wedding, yet want to use the property for photos. We charge them more than the customers who buy our flowers. Chiara has a good head for business."

"That is smart. You are close to her despite the age difference."

"You can tell?"

"I observed the two of you when I was spying through the fence. You seem more like a pair of close confidantes rather than colleagues."

"You know I sort of felt as if I was being watched on one of those mornings. If only I had known you were on the other side of the fence."

"Believe me, it was killing me, not letting my presence be known to you, as was the thought of having you so close but not being able to kiss or touch you. I knew I couldn't act impulsively and needed to figure out first what to do about our situation. That is why I am here."

Dante stood up. He paused for a moment before dropping to his knee and taking Anabella's hand. Before Anabella could ask him what he was doing, she felt something cold being slipped onto her finger. It felt like a ring. Had he bought her a gift? They were farther away from where the lights shone on the property and were more cloaked in darkness now.

"Anabella, will you marry me?"

She gasped as it finally dawned on her why he had slipped a ring onto her finger. How naïve was she? She had read books and seen old movies in which men proposed to the women they loved by getting down on their knees. It was just that she was shocked. Perhaps because she had never thought marriage would be part of her life or that she would even meet someone whom she would fall in love with. Tears came to her eyes as she realized once again how much she'd been sheltered and how she had never imagined a life outside of her home and away from her mother. She became so overcome with her emotions that her tears turned into sobs.

"Please, Anabella. Stop crying. It is all right if you are not ready. We can take our time."

She shook her head, doing her best to

compose herself. Through her tears, she managed to choke out, "I do want to marry you."

Dante dropped her hand and sighed deeply. He looked off to the side as he took a deep breath.

"Are you sure?" His voice cracked, and Anabella wondered if he were also about to cry.

"*Si*. I'm sorry I reacted the way I did. It's just I was stunned. Never in my dreams did I think I would meet someone like you and that I would have the chance to get married. You see, Dante, I never really have made dreams for myself."

"I know. I sensed that from what you said during one of our early conversations. But you can dream now — all you want. In fact, I want to show you more of what is out there beyond Pienza and even Siena. Come with me to Florence. An art dealer has expressed interest in my work — actually, my paintings and drawings of you — and he is going to give me an exhibit in one of the galleries in Florence. We can get married in Florence — or even in Venice. It's just a few hours away by train."

Anabella was overcome once again. She'd always wanted to go to Florence, her mother's birthplace. How many times had she asked Mamma as she was growing up when they could visit? She'd wanted to see the house Mamma had grown up in and the church where her parents had married. When Anabella was a child, Mamma had promised they would go someday. But as the years went by, Anabella picked up that her mother truly had no desire to return to Florence. Her mother's eyes would grow distant, and sometimes they would even fill with tears. By the time Anabella reached thirteen, she had stopped asking her. If only Mamma had told her more about her life before she'd had her. Anabella knew how much her mother had loved her father and how hard it was for her to lose him, but she sensed there was more. And why did she hardly ever talk about her family — her father and brother? One time, Anabella had expressed all of this to Chiara and told her how she wished her mother could be more open. But Chiara had said, "Many people changed after the war, and, even if there were good memories before things became so bad, they have chosen to erase them all. It might be best for her that she doesn't think at all about that time."

Anabella sighed as she remembered Chiara's words. How she wished Chiara could be with her right now to advise her. She returned her attention to Dante, who was looking at her as if he were trying to read her thoughts.

"I know I am asking a lot of you, Anabella. If you need more time, we can wait. I can go to Florence for the exhibit and come back for you when you are ready."

"Are you planning on moving to Florence permanently?"

"No, but I still would like to take you. It is such a beautiful city and has always been an inspiration to me. In fact, I studied art there. I want to introduce you to Florence."

"My mother is from Florence."

"She is?"

Anabella nodded. "My father was from there too. But my mother left after he died and the war was over."

"She has never taken you there?"

"No. I often asked as a child. I was curious to see where she had grown up. But it never happened."

"Does she still have relatives in Florence?"

"No."

"Were they all killed in the war?"

"Her mother died before the war. She was ill. And her father must've died from old age. I'm not sure how her brother died. I never thought to ask. He must have been ill. I seem to remember my uncle was married."

"So she never even told you how they died? You just assumed."

Anabella nodded. Hearing Dante's surprise emphasized to her even more how strange it was that she knew so little about her relatives.

Dante stood up and sat next to Anabella on the bench. He rubbed his knee. It was only then Anabella realized how long he'd been crouched down on his knee. She leaned into him and held the hand with her ring up to her face.

"From what I can see, it's pretty."

Dante laughed. "When we walk back toward the house and have more light, you can inspect it more. If you don't like it, please don't be afraid to tell me. We can go exchange it together when we are in Florence."

"That is where you bought it? When did you go?"

"I took a long weekend trip there not long after I met your mother. My head was a mess, and I needed a break from work. Once I knew I wanted to propose to you, I bought the ring and took the first bus back to Siena."

"I'm sure I will love the ring when I see it

326

in the light." She looked up at Dante.

He brought his face closer to hers and kissed her. It was a long, deep kiss, and he let himself become completely wrapped up in it, not caring anymore that he needed to hurry before Signora Ferraro woke up and noticed Anabella was gone. He didn't care if that happened. Anabella had told him she would marry him. That was all that mattered.

When they finally broke the kiss, Anabella asked, "When do we leave for Florence?"

"So you are ready for all of this to happen? You don't want to take some time?"

"No. I have waited too long for my life to begin. And it has been miserable not being able to see you, and dealing with the tension at home between Mamma and me. I am ready. I can't continue to live my days being afraid of her and obeying her every command. Those days are over. I have been a coward for too long."

"You are not a coward. Don't be so hard on yourself, Anabella."

They were quiet for a few moments.

"I will wait for you once we return to the house so you can pack your clothes."

"I can't just leave tonight, Dante. Even though I am mad at Mamma, I can't just disappear. As I said, I have been a coward for too long. I will tell her I am marrying you and going to Florence with you."

"But what if she keeps you from leaving?"

"She can't. I am a grown woman. She will have to call the police, and surely they will tell her there is nothing she can do." Anabella's voice sounded timid.

"Are you sure you can do this?"

"I must. I don't want to hurt her, but I can't bear not being with you, Dante. I'll assure her that we'll be back once your exhibit is over. I'll still come to the farm to help her."

"But you won't be able to come every day. I need the car to drive to the piazza to sell my work. We can come once or twice a week."

Anabella was silent.

Dante continued. "Your mother has Chiara and the other workers on the farm to help her. And she's been relinquishing more work to them."

"She's only taken a small step back. She still likes to be very involved on the farm."

"How about if you wrote a letter to your mother? This way it won't be like you have vanished into thin air, and you can give her time to absorb the shock of your leaving and avoid the outburst she would have if you were to tell her in person."

"That is still being a coward. And I can't do that to her. I need to face her. Don't worry. I will be leaving with you tomorrow."

Dante sighed. "All right. I can see your mind is made up."

"It is. All I know is that I want to be your wife, Dante. And no one can stop me from being with you. I should return to the house. It's getting quite late, and I'll need to pack as well as get some sleep, although with all the excitement you have given me tonight, I doubt I will be able to." Anabella smiled.

Dante kissed her once more before they made their way back to the house. They walked slowly through the rose garden. Dante stopped and plucked a rose from one of the bushes and tucked it behind Anabella's ear, pushing her hair back.

"I'm surprised your mother didn't name you Rosa, given that she loves roses so much and they are as beautiful as you. She was right in adding 'bella' to your name, however."

"There are other beautiful flowers. In fact, sunflowers have now become my favorite flower because they remind me of how you first saw me — in your dreams, running through a sunflower field. And of the times we met and you painted me with them."

"That is true. But I failed to tell you that when I had that same dream about you, there were always roses present. You were holding them and dropping them behind you as you ran away."

Anabella could not help but see the irony in this — for she was now turning her back on the rose farm and her mother. Her pulse raced as she contemplated whether she was truly ready to leave the only home she'd ever known. But more important, would she be able to leave her mamma behind?

CHAPTER 24
SIGNORA FERRARO

Pienza, 1970

Signora Ferraro was on her knees, working feverishly as she planted white roses in the garden to replace the ones Anabella had so violently pulled. Her heart still ached when she remembered first seeing the destroyed garden. Anabella had confessed immediately when she returned to the house. Signora Ferraro had never seen her daughter look so terrified. She had wanted to yell at her, but she was too hurt to do so. For it was the first time Anabella had intentionally set out to cause her pain. True, Signora Ferraro had been hurt when she'd learned that Anabella was seeing that young man. But that was different. She knew Anabella hadn't done that to hurt her. But this . . . this was done viciously, out of spite. And Anabella had known how much Signora Ferraro loved that garden. How many times had she warned her daughter as a child not to enter

331

the garden and told her that the roses were sacred?

Not until next year would new white roses grow on the bushes. So she went to a different garden on the farm and clipped white roses from amongst those she harvested and sold to clients. She knew it was a poor substitute for the roses that grew on the bushes, but it was better than having a barren garden. Naturally, when the roses died, the bushes would remain bare until the following spring. But they still had several weeks to remain in bloom. Anabella had cut short the time Signora Ferraro would have to admire the roses, and she just couldn't have that. There were times when she contemplated growing the roses in her greenhouse. The other roses she grew in the greenhouse often bloomed as much as three times a year. This way she always had a steady supply for her vendors. But if she grew her special white roses indoors, she would not have the same pleasure each spring of seeing the buds form on the bushes and watching them flower. And they would lose their symbolic significance. For it was important that these roses grew every year — new life to replace the ones that had died.

Signora Ferraro was completely absorbed

332

in her work when she heard Anabella call out to her.

"Mamma."

Her voice sounded strained as if something were wrong. Signora Ferraro looked up. Her daughter's face was as white as the roses, and her eyes were filled with worry.

"What is it, my child? Are you not feeling well?"

Anabella glanced over her shoulder, and it was only then that Signora Ferraro noticed the young man Anabella had had the audacity to bring to the house two weeks earlier. Signora Ferraro frowned. His complexion matched Anabella's. At least he had the sense to remain a few feet behind her. When he saw Signora Ferraro glaring at him, he turned around and walked farther away, giving them even more space.

"You've been out here for so long, and it's very hot today," Anabella said in a wan voice. Her eyes remained fixed on the roses Signora Ferraro had planted.

Signora Ferraro remained silent.

"I'm sorry, Mamma."

"There is no use in apologizing. What has been done is done." Signora Ferraro could hear the clipped tone in her voice. Now it was her turn to cause her daughter pain. She resumed her work, ignoring Anabella.

Her heart began to beat a little quicker.

"Can we go talk somewhere? Please, Mamma."

"You can say what you need to here. Besides, he's too far to hear us, but I'm sure he already knows what you are about to tell me." Signora Ferraro's voice shook as she resisted the urge to guess what Anabella was going to say.

"Mamma, Dante has asked me to marry him."

Signora Ferraro stopped working. "I see." She felt a cold sweat begin to break out on her forehead, even though it was a sweltering summer day. Lowering her head and pretending she was examining the hole she had dug to plant the rose that was in her hand, she did her best to keep her face shielded from her daughter. She would not let Anabella see how much her words had affected her.

"I've accepted, Mamma. I know you don't approve of Dante, but he is a good man, and he did try to get your blessing that day. We can be a happy family . . . together, if you will only give him a chance."

"We *were* a happy family — you and I. But I see now that wasn't enough."

"No, Mamma, that's not true."

"Please, Anabella, don't lie. I raised you

better than that."

"I have been happy with you on the farm, but I am a grown woman now. There is so much more to see and experience than what is here in Pienza."

Signora Ferraro continued gardening. How she wanted to place her hands over her ears and block Anabella's words from reaching them. With each word Anabella uttered, Signora Ferraro felt another blow hit her heart.

"Please, Mamma, will you just stop working and look at me?"

But Signora Ferraro continued to ignore her. What did it matter anyway? Her daughter had made up her mind. Anabella was going to leave her and marry this man she'd only known for a few months. Suddenly, fear gripped her. Would he treat her child well? She looked over to where he stood. Though he appeared a few years older than Anabella, he too still retained an innocent demeanor in his face. Signora Ferraro had seen firsthand what evil looked like during the war. The faces of the Nazi soldiers who had occupied Florence had oozed with evil. But not all of them had looked that way. The younger soldiers who were mere boys had looked innocent. While a few of them had not been involved in the more atrocious acts committed, others had been corrupted and had become as evil as their superiors. But it wasn't just the Nazis whose faces showed their evil souls. A few of her fellow Florentines had had the same look. They were the ones who had turned their backs on their country and people and had gotten into bed with the devil.

Dante's eyes locked with Signora Ferraro's, and, as if reading her thoughts, he came over.

"Signora Ferraro, I know you do not approve of me, but I wanted to assure you that I love your daughter very much, and I swear I will always protect her."

Tears filled Signora Ferraro's eyes. She looked away. Pain radiated throughout her body. She was getting too old to be dealt such a blow as this.

From her peripheral vision, she saw Anabella turn toward Dante and shake her head. For a moment, hope filled Signora Ferraro that her daughter would not abandon her. She heard Anabella whisper, "I can't."

Signora Ferraro now looked directly at them. Dante placed his hand on Anabella's shoulder. Anabella leaned into him as tears swam fiercely down her face. Signora Ferraro waited patiently for her daughter to compose herself. Finally, Anabella wiped her tears with the back of her hand and took a few steps toward her mother.

"Mamma, we are going to Florence for a few weeks, but we'll be back. I would like to get married here in the rose garden. I would like for you to be a part of our special day. In fact, Dante and I are planning on living nearby once we are more settled."

Signora Ferraro could not hide the disappointment that filled her face. Anger began to seep into her and replace the enormous pain she was feeling. It was better to feel angry than to feel the pain her daughter was inflicting on her.

"You might as well get married in Florence. We are too busy here on the farm to have a wedding."

Anabella looked crestfallen, but Signora Ferraro fought the guilt that threatened to take hold.

"Please, Mamma, don't do this. We want you to be a part of our life. I can still work on the farm."

"What happened to wanting to see the world outside of Pienza, ah?" Signora Ferraro waved her hand dismissively at her daughter, and disgust etched her features. "*Vai,* Anabella. *Vai.* We do not need you here, and I certainly do not need an ungrateful daughter. I can manage on my own."

Once more, she resumed her gardening. Her hands worked quickly, mounding the soil around the roses' stems as she planted them. The sun was now beating down on her, and her throat felt parched. It was getting too late for her to be out here. Besides, it was time for lunch. Suddenly the vision of her eating alone every day appeared before her. A wild look entered her eyes as she looked at Anabella, silently pleading with her not to leave. But Anabella was staring down at her feet. Signora Ferraro's heart ached as she remembered in that instant her innocent, beautiful daughter as a little girl. If only Signora Ferraro could've frozen time, Anabella would have remained her loyal, sweet daughter.

She could not stand this torture anymore. Why didn't they just leave already? "*Vai,* Anabella. Don't worry about me. I will be fine. Just, please, go."

Anabella broke free from Dante's embrace and crouched down beside her mother as she hugged her. But Signora Ferraro stiffened. Her eyes looked off into the distance.

Once more, Dante placed his hand on Anabella's shoulder. "Come, Anabella," he whispered.

Anabella waited a moment before standing up. She then walked away. Signora Ferraro breathed a soft sigh of relief. Finally, they were leaving. She had one more rose left to plant. Instead of using her gardening hoe, she used her hands to dig the hole. As she dug deeper and deeper, her hands worked at a feverish pace. The hole she was digging was much larger than what the rose needed, but she continued pushing deeper into the soil with her hands. Signora Ferraro could feel Anabella getting farther away. She didn't need to look at her to know this, for she felt a certain energy leaving her body, much like the energy she had felt as Anabella was being born. But that energy had filled her body, consuming her with elation she'd never experienced before. Now, it was as if she were dying. She stared at the large hole she had dug. If only she could bury herself in it.

When she could no longer feel Anabella's presence, she finally stood up and gazed into the distance. She dropped the last rose she was holding to the ground, forgetting she still needed to plant it, and slowly made her way to the house. Once again, someone she loved had left her behind.

CHAPTER 25
MARIA ROSSI

Florence, 1943

Maria was pedaling her bike as fast as she could, anxious to make her way back home. She wouldn't let herself relax until she knew she had made it back without anyone following her. Home was the only place where she truly felt safe these days. She had just returned from delivering ammunitions to a few of the partisans who were staked out in the hills, not too far from where her house was located. Her heart hadn't stopped racing from the time she left FAF's headquarters, where she had picked up the ammunitions, to when she met the partisans and handed over her package.

The mission was the most dangerous she'd undertaken since she'd joined the movement in July. She couldn't believe how quickly the past four months had gone and that it was now November. In just four months, her world had changed dramatically. If only the war would go by as quickly.

While Franco had let her deliver food, first-aid kits, and other supplies directly to the partisans, he was still reluctant to let her do anything more dangerous. Initially, he'd even been reluctant to let her deliver the basic staples, insisting that it was too dangerous, since if she were seen with the partisans, she could be killed on the spot. She'd had to remind him that that could happen even if she were caught delivering the newspapers or if the Nazis found out that she was the author of most of FAF's literature. When she'd overheard a conversation between Franco and another of the members about needing to deliver ammunitions, she had volunteered to do so. But he'd adamantly refused. So she'd gone behind his back and convinced one of the other senior members that she wanted to deliver ammunitions to the partisans out in the field. Not all of FAF's members were aware that she and Franco had become romantically involved. Surely if they'd known, they would have never allowed her to participate. Of course, there was the very real chance they would tell Franco she was the one who had delivered the latest package of ammunitions, but she would deal with Franco if and when that happened.

341

Though Maria had completed her mission and she didn't think anyone had followed her, she was still terrified. Her arms wouldn't stop shaking, making it hard for her at times to keep her bicycle straight.

"It'll get easier," she said aloud to herself, needing the reassurance of hearing her voice.

A part of her felt sad that she couldn't share with Franco the success of her mission. Maybe she should tell him even if it meant he would be furious? Her need to have Franco be proud of her was great. Whenever he complimented her on the articles she wrote for the newspaper, she basked in his words of praise. And their shared work in the Resistance was only making their bond and love for each other grow stronger. How she wanted to bring him home and introduce him to her family. But Franco had gently told her that would not be possible until the war was over. It was too perilous for her family. His words came back to her as she remembered their conversation.

"I struggle every day with having you be involved, Maria, so there is no way I could also jeopardize your family. Maybe you should consider taking a break from your participation. In fact, maybe we should stop seeing each other until this is all over. I don't think I could go on living if something happened to you."

"Franco, I told you already that if you forbid me from participating, I'll just go to GAP. I'm committed now to the effort. This is my country, too. I wouldn't be able to live with myself if I just gave up on Italy. I was pretending before I met you. Pretending everything was fine, even though of course I knew it wasn't. I can't pretend anymore. I love you for wanting to protect me, Franco, and I love you even more for always encouraging my intellect and my self-expression. Well, this is who I am now. You wouldn't want me to deny that, would you? Or love me less for it?"

Franco had pulled her toward him. As he'd held her, he had whispered in her ear, "I could never love you less. In fact, I've never loved anyone the way I love you."

They had been in her father's sunflower garden, and it had been an especially warm day in August. There was a corner of the garden that was set back quite a distance from the house and where the sunflowers and grass were extra tall and dense. Her family rarely came out to this part of the garden, and now that her father was getting older, he often didn't feel well enough to do

343

the gardening himself, leaving it to Maria or Michele. But the garden was so large that she and her brother mainly tended to the flowers that were more in view of the house. Franco had led Maria here so they could remain hidden as they talked. They both had known they were taking a chance of being seen so near Maria's house. But Franco had insisted on accompanying her this far. He'd wanted to make sure she reached home safely. They had finished working on the latest issue of the newspaper at the office. It was only three o'clock in the afternoon, but lately, he'd wanted to escort her home whenever he could. Sometimes she felt guilty that she was the cause of his worry. Was she being selfish by refusing to quit FAF, even though she knew how he felt about her involvement? But she worried about his safety, too, and she knew he would never give up the cause — even for her. And that was all right. Maria didn't need him to make such a sacrifice. She was confident in his love for her.

"I feel the same way, Franco, and I know I'll never love anyone like this again."

"Even if I don't make it?"

Maria had pulled sharply away from Franco. "Stop it! Don't say that, do you hear me? Don't even think it!"

"Shhh . . . shhh." Pulling her to him once more, Franco had stroked her hair. "I'm sorry I upset you. But we have to be realistic. As you said, the time for pretending is over."

Tears had fallen down Maria's face. Every day she had to fight to keep the thoughts of what could go wrong from driving her mad with worry.

"Maria, promise me that if something does happen, you won't let it keep you from living your life fully. I want you to be happy. I want you to love again."

She remembered how she'd shaken her head furiously, burying her face in his shoulder. "Didn't you hear me before? I can never love anyone like this again."

"Naturally, it will be different, but you can still love."

"What if I don't make it? I suppose you could then love another woman?" Maria had placed her hands on Franco's chest as she looked up into his eyes, which filled with tears, much to her surprise.

"I told you. If something happened to you, I couldn't go on living."

"So how can you expect me to love another man? I am devoted to you, Franco, and no one can change that."

Franco then had kissed her. Without

345

breaking the kiss, he'd taken Maria's hands and crouched to the ground, leading her down beside him. They'd embraced and lain back among the sunflowers as they made love. Though they'd only recently fallen in love, both felt as if they'd known each other for a lifetime. Maria hadn't wanted to wait to express her love to him, and she'd known she wanted him to be the one she would give her virginity to.

How it killed her not to be able to tell her family of her love for Franco. Only a few of the most trusted FAF members knew they were dating. That is, if you could call their meetings dates when they were forced to just spend time together at the office and lately at Franco's little apartment above a barbershop. But she didn't care that they couldn't go to dance halls or eat at restaurants or do the many things couples did when they dated. She cherished any time they spent together, even when they were in the presence of the other members. That was how much she loved him. She would do anything for him.

After they'd made love, they had lain together for what seemed like hours, but probably was no more than an hour at most. Her family was most likely wondering where she was. But in that moment, she hadn't cared. For she'd decided that the time for lies was over. She would tell her family the truth about her involvement with FAF — and she would tell them about Franco. Maria didn't want to hide her love from them anymore. If they could not meet him yet, they would at least know about him. True, they would be frightened for her and caution her against continuing with FAF. But they couldn't stop her. This was her life now.

The sharp cry of a bird flying overhead startled Maria, returning her to the present, as her bike briefly swerved to the left. Righting the bike, she smiled as she remembered once more the lovemaking she had shared with Franco that day. She noticed her heart rate had slowed down, and she wasn't feeling as anxious anymore.

Her house was beginning to come into view. The sunflowers were all gone now from Papà's garden. How bare and lifeless it looked. She missed them. The sky had clouded and darkened considerably from an hour ago. She'd be making it home in time before the rain came. It was almost eleven o'clock in the morning. Guilt seeped into her as she thought about what she was putting her father through. True to her vow that day in the sunflower garden after she'd made love to Franco, she had told Papà,

Michele, and Enza about her involvement with the FAF and Franco. Once more her thoughts traveled to that day.

"You lied to us," Papà had said in a hushed voice.

Maria had cringed, regretting how deeply she'd hurt her father.

"I'm sorry, Papà. Please know, it is the only time I've lied to you. I was just trying to protect you — all of you." Her gaze had traveled to Enza, who smiled softly.

Maria had then realized that Enza had already known she was involved. But Enza had only questioned her once and had merely asked, "Is there someone you've met?" But Maria had been too scared to even tell her about Franco. She now wished she had. For at times, she'd felt alone, not being able to share her secret about her work with FAF and not being able to confide in anyone about the wonderful man she'd fallen in love with. When Maria had shaken her head, Enza had looked hurt. Maria had been foolish for not telling her sister-in-law. If anyone would've understood, it would've been Enza. After all, Maria was almost certain Enza had been working with her brother in his own efforts in the Resistance. Maria supposed she was too afraid of her brother. And his glare in her direction now, upon learning of her involvement with FAF and Franco, had only proven she'd been right to fear him.

"How dare this Franco put you in harm's way! I'll kill him!"

"Michele, stop! How can you of all people say that?" Enza had grabbed Michele's arm, forcing him to look at her. He'd looked away, his face reddening.

"It is all right, Maria. You aren't the only one who's been keeping secrets. Papà, Michele and I have also been helping with the Resistance, and we were even attending secret anti-Fascist clubs before the German occupation. Like Maria, we only lied to protect you. Please forgive us."

Papà's eyes had widened. Maria had felt a pang of hurt when she'd seen his expression. The sadness his face had conveyed a moment ago had quickly turned to anger.

"What has gotten into all of you? Do you want to be imprisoned or, worse, killed? You know what those savages are capable of? I will not let my family endanger themselves!" Papà had raised his hand in the air, waving it for a few seconds before letting it drop to his side as he hung his head low, looking defeated.

"See what the two of you have done!" Michele shouted, startling Maria. He then had turned his back toward them and placed both hands on the table, curling them up into fists. Maria had seen how white his knuckles were turning.

"Michele, we should be united. And you should be proud of your sister that she is willing to be brave and selfless enough to help with the cause." Enza had stood up and had walked over to Michele, placing her hand on his shoulder. After a moment, he'd turned to Enza, taking her hand in his and placing a kiss on it.

He'd nodded before saying, "I'm sorry, my angel. Of course as always you are right. And I know I was being a hypocrite for saying this man whom Maria loves has put her in harm's way when I've done the same to you."

Wanting to give them privacy, Maria had walked to the other side of the kitchen and had stared out the window. She remembered thinking how hard it must have been for Michele to let his wife participate in his Resistance work, just as it had been difficult for Franco to give his consent to Maria and let her continue with FAF. She had never thought about that before, even though she knew Michele was involved with the Resistance. Although he'd never breathed a word about it to her, she'd overheard a conversation between him and Enza. And she could tell when he and Enza were lying before they left the house to go on whatever mission they were heading out to.

"Maria, I'm sorry. Just like Papà, I am worried about your safety. Now I have to worry about the two most important women in my life being hurt."

"It is all right, Michele. I understand. Franco feels the same way about my being involved and has asked me several times to quit. But I refuse to."

"Stubborn as always, I see." Michele had laughed.

Papà had remained silent. Maria had gone to his side and placed her arm around his shoulders.

"We don't wish to hurt you, Papà, and we know we are giving you great reason to worry, but you must see that things are only getting more dire in our country. We can't stand idly by and do nothing."

Papà had reached up and patted Maria's hand. "You are good children and truly have good hearts. I have been blessed to have you. I know I cannot keep you from doing what you feel is right. A father will always want to protect his children — and no cause, not even one as noble as the one you are both fighting for, is worth the loss of his kin. But I understand this is what you must do. I suppose I have been a coward for not doing something even if I am just an old man. I have heard of a few of the other elderly villagers hiding former Italian soldiers on their property and even going to the partisans' hideouts to deliver whatever food they can spare from their farms — of course food that the Nazis haven't requisitioned yet. Before we know it, we'll all die anyway from starvation. I suppose, if we're going to die, it might as well be for fighting for our country. Believe me, I have thought every night about what's going on in Italy, and I fear for your future as well as for the future of any children you might have. But I was too afraid to talk before and voice my own fear and anger over what's been going on. I was too afraid that Michele would get involved. I never dreamed, Maria, that you were also in danger of doing so."

"Why? Because I'm a woman?" Maria's voice had risen sharply.

"*Si.* I'm sorry, my dear daughter, but a woman should not be putting herself in such dangerous circumstances. You, too, Enza. I know how strong-willed both of you are, especially you, Maria, but Michele was right before. How could this man you love let you continue this dangerous work? And,

Michele, I would've never dreamed you would do the same with your own wife. I would never have let your mother do so, even if it meant that I had to shackle her to keep her from going out."

"Trust me, Papà, the thought has crossed my mind several times," Michele had said in a teasing voice.

Maria smiled as she remembered how Enza had playfully tugged Michele's earlobe before they'd all erupted into laughter, even Papà. They'd allowed themselves the brief moment of levity before growing somber once more.

Michele continued. "Maria, I'd like to meet Franco. Actually, I have heard about him and the work that FAF is doing. Although our organization isn't as big as FAF, we have been quite instrumental as well. I think it is time our group banded with yours. We can use all the help we can get, and perhaps they can benefit from some of the strategies we've employed."

"Franco mentioned as well that he wanted to meet you and learn more about what your group was doing, but he was waiting until I had told you about my involvement, since he knew I was hesitant to do so."

"So you knew all along?" Enza had asked.

"I overheard Michele talking on the phone

353

once, and it was quite obvious the way the two of you would make excuses when you had to leave the house together. I also noticed the shared glances you'd give each other."

"I suppose I shouldn't be surprised since I suspected there was something going on with you, too, Maria — and more than just a handsome man whom you were rushing off to meet."

Maria had blushed.

"You are brave, Maria, not only for the work you are doing with FAF, but for telling us the truth. I've been a coward all along by not confiding in my family. But I must say, if you hadn't come clean, I don't think I ever would have. I am a firm believer that the less your loved ones know, the safer it is for them. But we cannot worry about that now." Michele's eyes had darkened when he'd said this. And as Maria remembered his words from that day, she felt herself go cold.

Rain came pouring down as Maria got off her bike and made her way through the barren sunflower garden. As she'd become accustomed to doing, she looked from side to side and over her shoulder every few seconds, making sure no German soldiers were in sight. She always feared one day she would see again the soldier who had stopped her and had engaged in conversation when she'd been delivering newspapers. As she walked through the empty sunflower garden, she looked over to the spot where she and Franco had first made love. While the sunflowers had been especially dense in this area and they'd been fully concealed, they were still mad to have made love there. But neither of them had been thinking clearly that day. All that had mattered was their love for each other. And the thoughts they had voiced that day about possibly losing each other had lowered their guards even more.

Maria was drenched by the time she reached her house. Taking her sandals off, she placed her keys in the lock only to discover that the door was already unlocked. They hadn't kept their door unlocked in quite a while now. Maybe Michele or Enza had forgotten to lock it when they had returned home? As Maria stepped inside, she noticed how quiet the house was. Maybe her brother and Enza weren't home tonight.

"Papà, I'm home!" Maria called out, making her way to the bathroom.

She stepped out of her wet clothes and put on her bathrobe, which she kept hanging on the back of the door. As she shook the water out of her hair with a towel, she walked over to the kitchen. When she reached it, she stopped in her tracks. There was no food on the table for their supper, but the refrigerator door was open. She then noticed the jars of fruit that she and Enza had canned lay broken on the floor. Her heart raced as she broke out in a cold sweat. She stood very still as she waited to see if her senses picked up on anything. Nothing. It was deathly quiet.

Walking to the kitchen counter, she did her best to quietly open the utensils drawer. She took out the largest knife they owned and gripped the handle with both of her hands as she slowly left the kitchen. Before entering each room, she peered in, holding the knife in front of her chest. But no one lay in wait. Her eyes scanned the rooms to see if anything was amiss. Her father's bookshelf came into view. All of the books were gone from the shelves and lay open on the floor.

Dio, aiutami, she silently asked God to help her. *Please, don't . . .* She couldn't finish the sentence in her head. She was too afraid it would then surely come true.

Maria climbed the staircase that led to the bedrooms. She reached her father's bedroom first. Taking her left hand off the knife's handle, she gripped the doorknob. Waiting a moment to brace herself for whatever would greet her on the other side of the door, she took a deep breath and swung it open. Nothing. The bed was still neatly made. The framed photos of her mother and the rest of her family still stood on Papà's night table and dresser. This room had been left undisturbed.

Maria's room was next to Papà's. The door was wide-open. Already she knew something was wrong, since she always kept her bedroom door shut. When she reached the threshold, she almost cried out. The room had all but been destroyed. Feathers from her pillows, which had been torn open, still floated in the air. Her bed had been stripped, and the mattress looked as if someone had ripped it open with a knife. Even the wallpaper had been stripped, exposing the pink-painted walls, from her childhood, beneath. The drawers of her desk had been pulled out, and their contents had been dumped on the floor. Forgetting to keep her guard up, she rushed over to her dresser and pulled it a few feet away from the wall. She loosened two of the floorboards and was relieved when she saw her articles and recent issues of FAF's newspapers still remained in their hiding place.

She sat for a few moments on the floor. Did they know about her? Is that why her room had been destroyed, but her father's had been left alone? Still, wouldn't they have destroyed his room as well to make sure they'd covered all their bases? But then she remembered Enza and Michele's room. She stood up and made her way over. Though she still kept the knife raised, she was almost certain that whomever had been in her house was no longer there.

Her brother and sister-in-law's room had also been destroyed. When she stepped into the room, her foot slid, causing Maria to lose her balance and drop the knife. She gripped the bed's foot post. When she glanced down to see why the floor was slippery, she almost screamed. Blood streaked the floor. Maria's eyes widened. She began searching the room — underneath the bed, in Enza's wardrobe closet. She didn't know whether to be relieved or alarmed when she didn't discover any trace of her family. Picking the knife up from the floor, she then went into the bathroom, but like her father's room, it hadn't been disturbed.

Maria made her way back out to the corridor and then noticed droplets of blood leading from Enza and Michele's bedroom to the staircase. How could she not have noticed them earlier? Then again, the home's interior was quite dim since she hadn't turned the lights on, and, with the clouds gathering outside, there was no sunlight pouring through the windows. She followed the trail as it led her to the front door. She then remembered that she'd found the front door unlocked when she came home. As Maria stepped outside, she saw there were splatters of blood there too. She pressed her hand to her forehead. Once again she questioned herself. How had she missed all these signs? Her thoughts had been too consumed with her own life. Whatever had happened to her family, it had to be because of her and her involvement with FAF. Franco had been right. Why hadn't she listened to him and quit?

A movement in her peripheral vision caught her attention. Someone in the Salamone home next door was standing behind the window. Though the curtains were drawn, she could still make out a silhouette behind them. Felice Salamone, a widower, lived there. He was in his sixties, and his wife had died of cancer a decade before. They'd had no children. Besides the usual pleasantries whenever she or her family saw him, he kept to himself. Papà said Signore

Salamone had never been the same again after his wife died, but Maria remembered that when she was a little girl and Signora Salamone was still alive, he had seemed distant then as well. Signora Salamone on the other hand had always been warm and had even been friends with Maria's mother.

Had Signore Salamone seen something? She glanced at the knife still in her hand. Part of her didn't want to let it go, as she was still too afraid, but she couldn't show up on Signore Salamone's doorstep bearing a weapon. Her shirtdress had pockets just deep enough to hold the knife. The blade still protruded from the top of the pocket after she slid the knife inside. She placed her arm over the pocket, doing her best to try to keep it relaxed as she walked over to Signore Salamone's house.

She knocked loudly three times, but he didn't answer the door.

"Signore Salamone, it's your neighbor Maria Rossi. Please. I know you're inside. I saw you behind your window. I just want a quick word with you."

She waited. But still nothing. Anger began seeping through her. How dare he ignore her? Now she was certain he'd seen something and didn't want to be involved.

Glancing over her shoulder to ensure no

one was near, she shouted, "Signore Salamone, I know you saw the Germans enter my house! It is only a matter of time before they come here and enter your house, too!"

Within a couple of seconds, the door flew open. "What are you doing? Get inside before someone hears you, you stupid girl!"

Maria stepped into the unlit foyer. She wanted to correct him and tell him that she was far from a girl, but that was the least of her worries at the moment.

Signore Salamone shut the door and locked it. Three bolts fastened the door. He waited for a few moments as he peered behind the curtain that covered the door's window. This time he kept his body to the side so he wouldn't be detected.

Maria crossed her arms, bracing herself, for she knew she was in for a battle to get Signore Salamone to talk.

He came to her and shook his hands in her face. "Are you trying to get me killed? Both of us killed for that matter? Has all sense gone out of you? I know you're young, but you can't be that devoid of your senses!"

"I'm sorry, Signore Salamone. I was desperate, and I knew you'd open the door once I shouted those things. Don't worry. I made sure no one was present."

"You think they're always going to show

themselves?"

"Please, Signore Salamone, I need to know what you saw. My house is in a shambles, and there was blood in my brother and his wife's room. I know they've taken them somewhere. Please. I won't tell anyone what you tell me."

Signore Salamone ran a hand over his bald head. His eyes met hers for a moment before he looked away. Sighing deeply, he nodded his head before saying, "I saw two German soldiers leading them away from the house."

Though she wasn't surprised and had come to this deduction on her own, hearing confirmation of it almost brought Maria to her knees.

"They knocked on the door. I'm surprised they still exhibited that small courtesy instead of storming in. Once they were inside, I could hear the sounds of glass shattering. I heard your father raise his voice at them and then . . ."

"And then what?" Maria stood a couple of inches away from Signore Salamone's face, forcing him to look at her.

"Your father cried out in pain. Then, I heard Michele arguing with them. More sounds of glass and things being knocked over. It seemed to go on forever. I didn't know what to do. Believe me, I wanted to help, but what could I, an old man, do? What could anyone do? We're all powerless against them."

"So you saw all of them being led from the house?" Maria secretly hoped that perhaps one of her family members had gotten away and was hiding somewhere until it was safe to return home — though she knew the likelihood of that was slim.

"*Sì.* Your father was holding his forehead. Blood was running down his face and clothes. His white shirt was so covered in blood, I thought for a moment he'd been shot, but I didn't hear any gunfire. They must've butted his head with one of their guns. One of Michele's eyes was swollen. His nose was bleeding. And Enza . . ."

Maria grabbed Signore Salamone's arm. "And Enza?"

"She didn't look hurt, but her dress was torn open; her chemise was exposed." Signore Salamone averted his gaze, looking off to the side.

Maria's eyes widened. "You don't think they . . ."

"I don't know, Signorina Rossi. I never heard her scream or anything. They might've just ripped her dress to get your brother to calm down. He sounded as if he was giving

363

them a fight. I'm surprised they didn't just . . ." Again, his voice trailed off, but Maria didn't need to ask what he was about to say.

"I have to go find them."

"Don't, *signorina*! It's too dangerous. They might take you as well."

"I have to do something! They're my family."

She brushed past Signore Salamone as she began to undo the bolts on his door. He came over and finished unlocking the door for her.

"Please, Signorina Rossi, be careful. I will keep you and your family in my prayers. Perhaps it was all a misunderstanding, and they will be freed."

Maria and Signore Salamone exchanged a knowing glance. As Maria left Signore Salamone's house, she couldn't help but ponder why people felt it was necessary to offer false words of hope in such situations where none seemed to truly exist.

CHAPTER 26
ANABELLA

Florence, 1970

The Arno River beneath Florence's famed Ponte Vecchio swayed gently beneath the canoe Anabella and Dante were riding in. Anabella was leaning back against Dante's chest. Though it was a beautiful autumn day, Anabella's spirits remained low. Dante had been quiet for some time now. Anabella glanced up and saw he was sleeping. The oarsman masterfully steered the canoe and thankfully had not engaged them in conversation. She was even glad that Dante had fallen asleep so she could freely listen to her thoughts and let her mind wander to wherever it wanted. But ever since they'd left Pienza two months ago, she could not stop thinking about her mother.

What was supposed to be a short trip that would last a week, or two at most, was turning out to have no certain end since a gallery owner had offered Dante an exhibition.

His paintings of Anabella were selling well, and word had soon spread throughout Florence of his talent, bringing more invitations to exhibit his work at several galleries around the city. Anabella was overjoyed for Dante even if part of her was anxious to return home to try to mend her relationship with Mamma. But she couldn't ask Dante to leave now as he was making a name for himself and making so much money that would help them in their future together.

While she was having a wonderful time with Dante and was in awe of all that she was seeing and experiencing in Florence, which was more beautiful than she'd ever imagined, Mamma continued to haunt her thoughts. Anabella couldn't help but note the strange irony that here she was the happiest she'd ever been, but she was also extremely sad. And, as such, she couldn't help feeling that this trip was marred. No matter how much Dante tried to distract her and no matter how many new places they visited, Anabella could not forget the pain in her mother's eyes when she'd broken the news to her that she would be leaving with Dante. Although Anabella called Chiara regularly to make sure Mamma was all right, she could not stop worrying about her. There were even moments she'd been tempted to cut her trip short and return home alone. Dante could meet up with her back in Pienza when his exhibits came to a close. But as soon as she imagined being at the rose farm and under her mother's watchful eye, a sense of suffocation would begin to take hold, and she'd remember how lonely she had been growing up with just her mother, her dog, and the farm workers as her companions. Naturally, she knew the time would come when she would have to go back home and face her mother. If only she could let herself stop feeling guilty about Mamma for the duration of their trip. But she also felt guilty about Dante. For she could tell he sensed she wasn't fully enjoying herself and that her mother still weighed heavily on her mind.

But it wasn't just Mamma that occupied her thoughts. There were times all of the sights, sounds, and the throngs of people in Florence overwhelmed Anabella, giving her a slight constriction in her chest, making it hard for her to take a deep breath. Part of her was mad about feeling this way. She was finally out in the world and learning so much, but she was afraid. It was crazy to feel this way. She knew this. But she couldn't explain why fear filled her at times. And then there were the days Dante had left her alone in the apartment they had rented. Since his paintings were rapidly selling, he had had to paint additional works, so they needed a more permanent residence than the hotel they'd been staying at when they first arrived in the city. He'd encouraged Anabella to go out and take strolls instead of just waiting for him to return. The first day he left her alone, she went out onto the balcony of their hotel room. But the anxiety began creeping in, and she felt paralyzed every time she thought about leaving the room. The second time he left her, she forced herself to go out, but she only made it to the corner of their street before turning around.

It was all right. She could still enjoy being in Florence from her apartment terrace and not feel as if she was cooped up indoors for the hours it took Dante to return. When Dante had come back from his outings and asked her how she had enjoyed her day and where she had gone, she'd been tempted to lie and tell him she'd had a good time. But she had never been dishonest with him and couldn't bear to be so now. So she'd had to tell him about her anxiety.

"I've pushed you too far, too soon. I'm sorry, Anabella. We can return home."

"No, no. I am enjoying myself, but I'd

rather not go anywhere alone — at least for now. I just need to get my feet wet and slowly get used to such a large city."

Dante had nodded his head. "I thought you would've been fine since you do go to Siena regularly to sell your flowers. But Florence is bigger. I should've thought of that."

Anabella had walked toward Dante and had placed her hand on his arm. "Don't be so hard on yourself. You have been nothing but wonderful to me. I am the one who is the problem. If only Mamma hadn't sheltered me so much all of my life, things would be different now. It will just take time."

Dante had taken her hand and had brought it to his lips, kissing it before holding it to his heart. "Of course, it will take time. Don't worry. Before you know it, you will be walking through these streets as if you've always lived here, and you won't want me escorting you."

Anabella had laughed. "Are you saying I'll get tired of you? If so, you should know that will never happen."

Dante's eyes had filled with tears. He'd hugged her fiercely to him. "And I will never tire of you, my dear Anabella."

Anabella wiped the tear that had slid

down her face as she remembered that afternoon. She was so lucky to have found Dante. What was the matter with her? Here she was in one of the most gorgeous and romantic cities in the world, and she was brooding. She was no longer a child and needed to move forward and finally live her life. And if that meant leaving Mamma and her childhood home behind, then so be it. Besides, her mother had treated her horribly. Though Anabella forgave her, for she knew Mamma had lashed out at her because she'd been hurt, she also couldn't help feeling a little angry. Hadn't Mamma thought about how much she was hurting Anabella, turning her only child away and refusing to even give her a proper farewell? Wasn't she, as a mother, supposed to be completely selfless and only have her daughter's best interests at heart? Then again, Anabella supposed her mother could be having the very same thoughts about her, wondering how her daughter could have betrayed her and hurt her, especially since Mamma was all alone with no one to look after her. Sighing deeply, Anabella sat up, causing Dante to stir in his sleep.

The oarsman called out over his shoulder. "We are almost at the dock, *signore*."

Dante opened his eyes, squinting as the

high afternoon sun flashed in his face. He sat up and rubbed his eyes, yawning. "Did I sleep for most of the boat ride, Anabella?"

She smiled. "I'm afraid so."

"Ah! I'm sorry, my love. We'll take another tomorrow, and I promise I'll stay awake."

"It's all right. It was lovely just relaxing and resting."

"Are you saying it was lovely not hearing my chatter?"

"Of course not. But you need your rest as well. Between showing me the sights of Florence and working, it's no wonder you're exhausted."

"I should've just kept this trip about us instead of also juggling work."

"You need the money, Dante. Please, don't feel like you have to entertain me every second of the day."

Dante looked pensive for a moment, before nodding. "The money I am earning here will help us so that, after we get married, we can live somewhere spacious and more comfortable than my little loft apartment. I am doing this as much for you as for me, Anabella. Once we are settled financially, we can then take a true vacation during which I do nothing but spend all of my time paying attention to you and treating you like a queen."

"You are too sweet. But I do not need to be treated like a queen to be happy. All I need is your love." She leaned over and kissed him softly on the lips.

Sometimes Anabella was still surprised by how comfortable she now felt with Dante, especially with expressing her love for him. She no longer waited for him to initiate a kiss or an embrace. And she'd quickly gotten over the fact that they were not only sharing a home but also a bed, even though they were not married yet. But they had not made love. Dante had not even attempted to do so, which, on one hand, relieved Anabella, since she was terrified of what it would be like. But, on the other hand, she couldn't help feeling a bit insecure, wondering if he was not very attracted to her. He'd told her he wanted to wait until they were married. And Anabella had told him she wanted to as well. Lately, she'd begun wondering what the big deal was, since they were already living like husband and wife. Maybe she would broach the subject with Dante tonight. Her heart began to race. No. It was too soon. She still was not ready.

Dante had asked her, when they were on the train heading toward Florence, if she was ready to get married there since her mother had not given them her blessing and they could not wed at the rose farm like Anabella had wanted. But Anabella had said she needed time to think about it. Secretly, she was still hoping her mother would have a change of heart. Anabella would return to Pienza, and Mamma would realize how much she'd missed her and how much she'd hurt her. Mamma would welcome her with open arms and tell her she would get the farm ready for her wedding. They would then discuss which roses she would carry in her bouquet and of course her dress. Would Mamma tell her she could wear her wedding dress? Anabella desperately hoped so.

The boat hit the dock with a loud thud that shook Anabella out of her thoughts. Dante disembarked first and then held his hand out to help Anabella off the boat.

They linked arms as they walked over the Ponte Vecchio. The sun was getting lower in the sky as evening got under way. Every so often, Dante would lean over and kiss Anabella on the cheek, causing her to giggle. She loved it when he acted like a silly schoolboy who had fallen in love for the first time. They leaned against the wall of the bridge and looked out at the Arno River. Dante whistled softly, but soon his whistling was drowned out by the sounds of an accordion. Dante recognized the tune and changed his whistle to match its notes.

Anabella laughed. "You're quite talented."

"And you thought all I could do was paint and draw." He smirked as he said this.

"It's so beautiful here." Anabella leaned her head on Dante's shoulder.

"You know the Ponte Vecchio was the only bridge that the Germans didn't blow up when they retreated from Florence during World War II?"

"No, I didn't know that. I can't imagine it not being here."

"I agree, and being here with you, Anabella, makes it all the more magical."

Anabella looked up at Dante and smiled. He leaned down and softly kissed her lips. The music grew louder. She looked up and saw the accordion player coming closer to the bridge. A small group gathered around him to listen. Anabella closed her eyes, enjoying the music and thinking of nothing else but being here with Dante. Every day, she felt her love for him grow, and the thought of ever being apart from him pained her deeply, even more than the pain of her separation from Mamma.

A thought entered her mind. She waited for a few minutes, wanting to be sure before she spoke. The rose garden flashed before her eyes. Did she really want to get married there even if Mamma did forgive her and accept that she was going to marry Dante? After all, Anabella was making a new life for herself. She still loved the rose farm, even though she had begun to feel suffocated there and had yearned to explore what was beyond its confines. No. It did not feel right. And she knew deep down, contrary to her earlier fantasy, that Mamma would not welcome her with open arms once she returned to Pienza. Her mother was too set in her ways, and there was something else. The look Anabella had seen in her mother's face and eyes. It was as if Anabella no longer existed for her once she'd announced she was leaving with Dante. After all, hadn't Mamma refused to hug her back or even look at her before she left home? And Mamma hadn't written back to Anabella, who had sent at least a dozen letters in the two months since she'd gone to Florence.

It was now or never. She needed to fully leave her childhood behind. She turned around so that she was facing Dante.

"Can we go somewhere quiet?"

Dante smiled. "I was just thinking the same thing. I know exactly the place."

He took her by the hand and led her toward the end of the Ponte Vecchio, at the south bank of the river. They entered the

Piazza Santa Felicita and were soon strolling along a beautiful street called the Costa San Giorgio. Then, Anabella saw signs pointing to the Bardini Museum and Garden. Gorgeous flowers in every hue lined either side of the garden's walkways, some of which also contained bubbling fountains.

"This is breathtaking, Dante!"

"I knew you would love it." Dante smiled.

They walked over to a wrought-iron street bench. Dante sat down and motioned for Anabella to sit on his lap. She draped her arm around his shoulders and took in the charming neighborhood. Dante drew small circles on her back. The action was making her sleepy as she fully relaxed against him.

"You've looked rather pensive today, Anabella."

He placed a kiss on her head and then began running his fingers through her hair, which she wore completely down today. She loved it when he did this. The sensation sent strange feelings throughout her body. Is this what it would feel like when they finally made love?

"I thought you would be used to that." Anabella looked into his eyes, smiling playfully to let him know he didn't need to worry.

"I don't know. It seems more so today."

He shrugged his shoulders, but there was still worry evident in his eyes as he looked off into the distance.

Anabella brought her mouth close to his ear and whispered, "Look at me."

He met her gaze.

"I've just been thinking all day how lucky I am to have met you and how much I love you. And I have something to tell you."

Dante's eyes flickered for a moment. But there was still fear in them.

"I want to get married here in Florence — and as soon as possible. I don't want to wait any longer to become your wife. And I don't want to wait any longer to make love to you."

Dante opened his mouth to speak, but nothing came out. His eyes then grew heavy as he continued staring into Anabella's eyes. She leaned forward and kissed him. It was the most sensuous kiss they had ever shared. She could feel his heart beating against her chest, and she pressed even closer to him, wanting to feel his warmth and more of the sensations that were now flooding her body. Much to her disappointment, Dante finally broke the kiss.

"Are you sure? What about the rose farm and wanting your mother to be present?"

"I'm sure. Although I would still love it if

my mother were at my wedding, I know things will most likely not be different with her once we return home. You are my life now."

Dante's voice choked as he said, "I love you so much, Anabella. I promise you won't regret this. And I promise we *will* be very happy."

They embraced again and sat on the bench as they laughed and spoke about where they should hold their wedding ceremony and how they should celebrate afterward. For the first time since they'd arrived in Florence, Mamma was far from Anabella's thoughts.

CHAPTER 27
MARIA ROSSI

Florence, 1943

Please God, let them be all right, Maria silently prayed over and over as she rode her bicycle to the police precinct to inquire about her family. Approaching Via Camillo Cavour, she noticed a large crowd was gathered in front of the Palazzo Medici. A strange feeling came over her, and she steered her bike toward the crowd. They were standing in front of the entrance to the courtyard of the palace. Much of the crowd was standing inside the courtyard. She could make out German soldiers gathered out front. A few of the bystanders looked pale. A woman let out a soft cry and began to walk away, but a soldier nudged her back with the butt of his machine gun, forcing her to remain.

Maria stepped off her bike and pushed it closer to the crowd.

"What has happened?" she whispered to

379

an old man.

The old man glanced first in the direction of the soldiers before answering, "Lynchings."

Maria felt herself go cold. She swallowed hard before asking, "Have they been hanged already?"

"*Si, signorina.* But they won't let us go. We have been ordered to watch. People who tried to leave were forced back. They said we needed to see what happens to traitors. It's been an hour already since the last person was lynched."

"Last person? How many people were hanged?"

"Three."

Maria felt herself go weak all over. She cowered over her bike as she tried to take in a deep breath.

"*Signorina,* are you all right?" the old man asked her.

She nodded, closing her eyes tightly, trying to concentrate on keeping back the wave of nausea that threatened to surface.

"*Andate via!*" A soldier shouted to the crowds to leave.

The bystanders quickly dispersed. But Maria remained rooted in place. She noticed one of the officers looking at her. Lowering her gaze, she began walking her bike toward the entrance to the courtyard of the Palazzo Medici. She remembered her parents taking her to the courtyard when she was a little girl and her Papà telling her about the powerful Medici family who ruled Florence for much of the Renaissance era. The courtyard was beautiful with its enclosed space that was surrounded by marble columns and classical statues. A fountain stood in the space as well as large planters with small trees.

"How dare they," she whispered to herself. "How dare they turn one of Florence's beloved landmarks into a killing field."

As she reached the entrance to the courtyard, she slowed her steps. Two young German soldiers were exiting, laughing between themselves. Maria bent down, pretending she was inspecting the chain on her bike. Once they passed, she stood up and made her way to the courtyard. No one was there now. She perched her bike against the wall of the palace before stepping inside the courtyard.

Maria could make out the figures hanging from three of the marble columns. The ladder that had been used to hoist the bodies near the top of the columns still remained in place over one of the columns, indicating which victim had been the last to be hanged.

From a distance, she could see they were three men. She was relieved, but only for a moment. Though Enza was not among the dead, her father and brother could still be among the victims. She walked closer. The first man looked to be no more than twenty years old. His eyes were open, and his head lolled to the side. The second man was close in age to the first one. His eyes looked upward to the sky. She turned to look at the third man. Maria didn't realize she'd been holding her breath the entire time until she saw the face of the last victim and gasped. He looked to be in his early thirties, the same age as Michele. But it was not Michele. She dropped to her knees and began sobbing. Relief immediately washed over her along with guilt. Though she was happy none of the dead were her family, she felt horrible to be elated when three men had been killed so brutally.

When she finally regained her composure, she stood up. Making the sign of the cross, she said a prayer for each of the souls and then left. Once outside the courtyard, she retrieved her bicycle and walked it along. Her legs and arms shook terribly, and she didn't know if she would be able to keep the bike steady, let alone have the energy to pedal.

The police station was another five blocks away. She walked slowly. Few people remained on the streets. As she entered the Piazza del Duomo, Maria couldn't help but remember how the square used to be filled with people laughing, going about their daily errands, enjoying the sights that their gorgeous city afforded them. Of course that was before the Germans came. Now no one smiled or even exchanged greetings. Everyone kept his or her gaze lowered, despair and fear etched across their faces.

Maria suddenly felt embarrassed. Until she'd joined the Resistance, she had still been living as if nothing had changed in the world, let alone in Florence. True, she and her family had been forced to be more careful, especially with the rations that had been put in place. Though they only had one course for dinner instead of two courses like they'd had before, and their portions were smaller, they had not gone hungry yet. While she had known that Michele and Enza were involved in the Resistance and had been worried when she'd first realized they were participating, she had never actually envisioned their being imprisoned or killed. It was as if nothing could touch her and her family. Perhaps that was why she'd had the courage to take more risks in the

Resistance. Naturally, she was always nervous and afraid whenever she completed a task, but she always felt as if no harm could truly come to her family. How naïve she'd been.

The police station finally came into view. The station no longer housed *carabinieri*. Since October, the Germans had disbanded the *carabinieri* wherever the Axis powers were in control. The Germans no longer trusted their loyalty to the Fascist cause since the *carabinieri* had arrested and imprisoned Mussolini after his fall last July.

Two German soldiers stood guard in front of the station. Her heart stopped for a moment as she recognized the soldier whom she'd spoken to the day she was delivering FAF's newspapers. But maybe if he remembered her, he might be able to help her — that is, if her family was being held here.

Smoothing a hand over her hair, she took a deep breath as she walked over to the soldiers.

"Guten Tag," Maria said in as cheerful a voice as she could muster.

The first soldier merely nodded in her direction, but the one she had encountered during her delivery of the newspapers looked startled for a moment before saying, *"Buongiorno, signorina.* How good it is to see you again. I am surprised our paths have not crossed again sooner. I have even walked along that route where we first met to see if I would bump into you delivering your newspapers." He smiled warmly.

"*Si,* I am sorry we have not seen each other sooner. I am no longer delivering newspapers."

"Forgive me, *Fräulein,* but I stupidly forgot to ask for your name that day. I am Wilhelm Becker."

Maria paused for a moment. Should she give him her real name? Since she was inquiring about her family, she would have to give her surname, so what did it matter if he knew her first name as well? And then she realized that if he or any of the other soldiers asked for her identity papers, they would see if she were lying. She mentally slapped herself for the grave error she almost made.

"Maria Rossi."

"Beautiful name."

"*Grazie,* Herr Becker."

"Please, Wilhelm." He smiled for a moment before his face grew somber. "I must say, Maria — I may call you, Maria?"

Maria forced a smile. "You may."

"I must say you look a bit pale. Are you all right, Maria?"

"I'm afraid I am not. You see, I am looking for my family. My neighbor told me they were escorted out of our house, and I came to see if they are here."

Wilhelm frowned. Maria's heart skipped a beat. Would he think she were an enemy too and imprison her?

"Do you have any idea why they would've been picked up?"

"None at all. My father is an old man who rarely leaves the house, and my brother and his wife are good, hardworking citizens. I am baffled." She opened her eyes wide, doing her best to look innocent as she shrugged her shoulders. "But I do not wish to disturb you while you are working. I will go inside and make my inquiries. *Buongiorno*, Wilhelm. It was nice to see you again." She began to climb up the steps that led to the police station's entrance, but Wilhelm placed a hand on her arm.

"Please, let me come with you and see if I can be of assistance."

He shouted to a soldier who was standing with a German shepherd in the square in front of the police station. The soldier quickly hurried over and took Wilhelm's place alongside the other soldier standing guard.

"Come, Maria." Wilhelm placed his hand

on her elbow.

She wanted to pull her arm away, but didn't. As they stepped inside, her pulse raced. They climbed a long set of stairs, and, once they reached the top, he walked over to an office at the end of the corridor. The door was shut, but Wilhelm knocked, announcing himself. A voice from behind the door told him to enter.

Maria waited a few steps behind Wilhelm. She heard him talking in German. After a moment, he motioned for Maria to join him.

"Signorina Rossi, this is Kommandant Schmidt." She walked over and nodded her head to the soldier behind the desk. He was much older than Wilhelm, and she assumed he had a much higher rank. *"Guten Tag, Kommandant."* Her voice sounded incredibly nervous. The soldier scanned her from head to toe, his eyes resting for a moment on her legs.

"Sit down, *Fräulein.*"

She looked at Wilhelm, who slightly nodded, before sitting down.

"You are looking for your family? May I see your identity papers first?"

Maria took the papers out of her purse. Her hands were shaking terribly. She needed to appear calmer.

"I am sorry to disturb you, *Kommandant.*

387

I am sure you must be very busy."

Kommandant Schmidt ignored her. Once he inspected her papers and handed them back, he perused a very large ledger.

"No one by your surname has been brought in today. Are you sure they were picked up this morning?"

"That is what my neighbor told me."

"Would he have any reason to lie?"

"I don't see why he would. Also, my family would not suddenly leave without letting me know in a note."

Kommandant Schmidt nodded his head, before adding, "Well, they are not here so I cannot do anything for you. If they are brought in, I can have Wilhelm come pick you up. He tells me you have no idea why they would've been picked up. Is that true, *Fräulein?*" The *Kommandant*'s eyes bore into Maria's.

She looked directly into his eyes as she said, "No, none at all, *Kommandant.* This has all been a shock to me. What would they want with an old man? And my brother and sister-in-law are loyal to our new regime. We are not people who break the law. I can assure you of that."

"Your father's advanced age means nothing. Every day we pick up old men and women. Perhaps your brother was involved in some Resistance activity? You do know what the penalty is for such crimes?"

"Of course, I do. But there is no way my brother would be involved in anything like that." She gave a soft laugh, looking over at Wilhelm, who was staring at the wall behind Kommandant Schmidt. If she wasn't mistaken, she would have sworn he looked afraid. Returning her gaze to Kommandant Schmidt, she said, "You see, my brother has always been afraid of his own shadow. He startles easily and has avoided any conflict his whole life. He is a bit of a coward. I know he is my brother, but that is the truth. No, it would be absurd for him to be so bold as to be a partisan."

The commander looked at her for a moment, before his face broke into a wide grin just as she was beginning to think he never cracked. "You seem to have a lot of spunk, *signorina*. Perhaps you can join us for an espresso. It is just about time for my break." He glanced at the clock on his desk.

Maria's mouth felt very dry as she remained silent. She needed to find her family, not entertain two bored soldiers, and from the way Kommandant Schmidt kept staring at her legs and now her lips, she knew he would expect more than just friendly conversation over an espresso.

Though she knew Wilhelm was also attracted to her, he seemed to exhibit more manners. But she knew very well appearances could be deceiving.

There was a rap on the open door.

"Excuse me, *Kommandant,* but we have an urgent matter that needs your attention right away."

"Scheisse!" Kommandant Schmidt cursed at the top of his voice, nearly making Maria jump out of her seat. "Just as I was about to relax. All right. I am coming. Excuse me, Signorina Rossi." He stood up and followed the soldier who had interrupted them out of the office.

Wilhelm escorted Maria out of the station.

"I am sorry, Maria. Perhaps when you go home, they will have returned and can explain the misunderstanding as to why the officers picked them up if they are truly innocent as you say."

In that moment, Maria knew Wilhelm had not believed that her family had no reason to be picked up.

"*Grazie* for your help, Herr Becker." She ignored his earlier wish to be called by his first name as she kept her voice cool. "I must return home. *Arrivederci.*"

Wilhelm looked as if he were about to say

something, but then he merely nodded his head and said, "*Arrivederci,* Signorina Rossi."

Maria wanted to run down the steps of the police station and get far away from him and the other soldiers who were standing guard. But she willed herself to walk very slowly to her bike. Once she got on, she pedaled at a leisurely pace until she was out of their sight. Tears streamed down her face as her mind ran through possible scenarios of what could have happened to her family. She began to take the route that would lead her back home, but then she changed direction and headed to the FAF office.

Once she reached her destination, she got off her bike, letting it fall to the sidewalk. She began to run up the alleyway leading to the back entrance of the office, but then she heard someone from the street shout her name. She froze and slowly turned around. Franco was standing still and smiling at her, but when he saw her face, his smile quickly vanished as he ran over to her.

"Maria, what is it?"

She collapsed against him, her shoulders shuddering with each sob she took. Franco grabbed her by the shoulders, pushing her back and forcing her to look at him.

"Please, Maria. You're scaring me."

"My family. The Germans came by my house this morning and took them."

"Oh God!" Franco pulled her to him, holding her so tightly she couldn't catch her breath. But after a moment, he sharply pulled away.

"But wait. Why aren't you with them? Why didn't they take you?"

"I wasn't home." Maria's face flushed for a moment when she remembered she had been delivering ammunitions to the partisans in the hills. "When I returned, dinner wasn't on the table. The refrigerator door had been left ajar, and cans of preserved fruit lay shattered on the floor. I then realized how quiet the house was and that no one was answering my calls. I grabbed the largest knife I could find and walked through the house. My brother and Enza's room was ransacked, as was mine. But my father's was left intact. And there was blood in Michele and Enza's room." Her eyes filled with tears. Franco squeezed her hand, giving her the strength to continue. "I went back downstairs. I noticed a shadow behind one of the windows of the house next door to mine. I saw my neighbor, Felice Salamone, peering from behind his curtains. So I went to ask him if he'd seen anything. He was reluctant to let me in at first until I started shouting. He confirmed for me that he saw a few German soldiers escorting my family out. He said my father's forehead was bleeding, and Michele's eye was swollen shut and his nose was bleeding. And poor Enza. Her dress was torn." Maria shut her eyes, trying to regain the strength to continue.

"Her dress being torn doesn't necessarily mean they touched her, Maria," Franco said softly as he wrapped his arm around her shoulders.

Maria took a deep breath before continuing. "Signore Salamone said he'd heard shouts and that it sounded as if Michele was putting up a fight."

"You said they left your father's room undisturbed and just ransacked your room and your brother and sister-in-law's room?"

"*Sì.*"

Franco paled.

"What is it?" But as soon as she'd uttered the question, realization washed over her. "Wait. I already know what you're thinking because naturally the thought occurred to me as well. You believe that they found out somehow of Michele's and Enza's involvement with the Resistance and possibly my involvement."

"That is what I was thinking. It is suspicious that they didn't ransack your father's room, which is odd even if they got wind of your and your brother's involvement with the Resistance. I would think they would have searched every room in the house to cover their bases unless . . ."

"Unless they found evidence in one of the other rooms."

"Perhaps."

"They didn't find FAF's newspapers and the articles I was drafting, which I keep hidden under the floorboards of my bedroom. I checked. But if they did find evidence in my brother and sister-in-law's room, then why didn't they just take Michele and Enza? Why take my father, an innocent old man?"

"Maria, you know the Nazis don't care whether someone is truly innocent, and you know they have made it clear that all will suffer for the efforts of the partisans. We have been getting reports of innocent men, women, and children being killed in the villages in retaliation whenever the partisans succeed in a mission."

Maria thought about the poor souls she'd seen hanging earlier.

"They hanged three people today in the Palazzo Medici courtyard."

"You witnessed it?"

"I arrived after they'd been killed, but I

saw the bodies. I had to make sure they weren't my family." She closed her eyes, remembering the terror she'd felt before she saw the victims.

"Why did you go there after discovering your family was missing?"

"I went to the police station to see if they'd been taken there for questioning."

"Maria!" Franco's voice rose. "They could've imprisoned you, especially after you told them your family had already been arrested. You should've called me first."

Tears spilled from Maria's eyes. "You're right, but I wasn't thinking clearly. All I was thinking in that moment was that I had to find my family. I know I took a chance."

"So I take it they weren't at the station? What did the Germans tell you?"

"Nothing. Just that no one by my surname had been brought in, and that if they were brought in, they'd notify me."

"That sounds too courteous for the Germans."

"Well . . ." Maria's voice trailed off.

"What?" Franco lowered his face so his gaze met Maria's.

"I knew one of the soldiers, so I think he put in a good word for me with the commanding officer."

Franco's eyebrows knit furiously. "And

how do you know this soldier?"

"It was that soldier I ran into that day when I was delivering the newspapers. I never saw him again until today, and he remembered me. I told him I was there to inquire about my family. He offered to go inside with me and see what he could find out. That's all."

"I'm sorry I raised my voice, Maria. Just hearing that you knew one of the soldiers made me go nuts, thinking that perhaps you have put yourself in risky situations without telling me."

Guilt washed over Maria as she remembered what she'd been doing this morning. Perhaps she should come clean with him now and tell him about her delivering the ammunitions? No, now was not the time. She'd already wasted so much time. She had to find her family.

"As soon as I left the station, I rode here to see if you could help me find my family."

"Of course." Franco thought for a moment. "Did your neighbor say if your family got into a vehicle with the soldiers?"

"I don't know. He didn't mention that, and I didn't think to ask. But I assume the soldiers would've arrived by vehicle."

"All right. Let's go back to your house first. Who knows? Maybe your family was released and is home worrying about where you are."

"That sounds like a fantasy right now." Maria's voice sounded very sad as she said this.

Franco lifted her chin. "Always hold hope. You hear me?"

She nodded as she silently prayed he was right.

Franco recruited Nino, Gaetano, and Vito — three FAF members who were in the office — to help them search for her family. They set out in Nino's car. No one spoke throughout the drive. Franco sat next to Maria in the back, holding her hand. She rested her head against his shoulder. Nino, Gaetano, and Vito were not among the FAF members who knew that Franco and Maria were dating. In this moment, neither of them cared about their secret being found out. It seemed silly now to Maria that they had kept their romantic relationship a secret, even if Franco had good reason to do so as a means of trying to keep her safe. But none of them were safe. If her family could be taken from their home without warning, anything was possible.

As they approached Maria's street, she began to smell a pungent odor. Her eyes soon stung.

"It smells like there's a fire," Gaetano said.

"Look!" Vito reached his hand out the passenger window and pointed off to the distance. Billows of black smoke were mushrooming up into the air.

Nino pressed down harder on the gas pedal. When they reached Maria's home, she was relieved to see her house was still standing. They stepped out of the car. The smoke seemed to be coming from around the block.

Maria walked to her front door and quickly unlocked it. Her heart sank when she saw the house was as she'd left it — empty. She still called out to Papà, Michele, and Enza and made her way to each room, just in case. Hearing their names said aloud sent a shiver down her spine. Images began flooding her mind as she remembered the moments they'd shared in the house — Michele and Enza's wedding celebration, each of their birthdays, the beautiful meals Maria and Enza had prepared for the holidays, their heated political debates and laughter over jokes. Franco came up behind Maria as she stood in the dining room. She jumped.

"You scared me." She placed a hand on her chest. The smell of the fire was quickly filling up the interior of her house.

"I'm sorry. Maria, I just spoke to Felice Salamone. He said the Germans walked away with your family. In fact, he said the soldiers arrived on foot. He was positive there was no vehicle."

"That's strange."

"They could've been parked somewhere else. Maybe they had picked up other people at other houses down the road and just left their car parked there."

Maria looked behind Franco's shoulder. "Where are the others?"

"They've gone to see where the fire is coming from. I told them we'd meet up with them there."

Maria and Franco left the house. As they rounded the corner of her street, they could see where the flames were shooting from.

"It's the abandoned leather warehouse," Maria said.

Franco grabbed Maria's hand and ran toward the warehouse. She didn't know why he was rushing. From the looks of the fire, nothing could be done. As she ran, she noticed most of the doors of the neighboring houses were open. But no one was outside. She looked toward the burning warehouse and could make out Gaetano and Vito standing across the street from the inferno. No one else stood with them, which was odd. Whenever there had been a fire before, people always came out of their houses to watch and get help.

"Where is Nino?" Franco asked Gaetano and Vito when they reached them.

"He's searching the houses," Gaetano said.

"Maria, we should go back to your house. It's not safe here. It's only a matter of time before the fire jumps to the neighboring buildings. Unfortunately, there isn't anything we can do here."

As Franco and Maria began walking away, they finally heard sirens. Maria stopped and glanced over her shoulder. Firemen descended from the trucks and began pulling out their hoses.

"Why aren't Gaetano and Vito coming back with us?"

"They're waiting for Nino."

As they passed the houses, she saw once again that the doors were open. Laundry that was hanging on clotheslines was strewn across several front lawns. A few of the houses had toys scattered on the front steps and sidewalks. Maria looked at the house to her left. She was able to see inside, all the way to the dining room. The table had been set for dinner. But it looked like no one was present. Then Maria saw a trail of splattered blood leading from the front door all the way down the steps and onto the sidewalk. She stopped.

Your father was holding his forehead. Blood was running down his face and clothes. Felice Salamone's words came back to her.

"Maria, are you all right?" Franco asked, but his voice sounded far off, even though he was standing beside her. She then remembered what Gaetano had said about Nino searching the houses. She looked at the houses again; they all looked as if their occupants had been interrupted and had suddenly left. She turned around and ran in the direction of the burning warehouse.

"Maria, come back!" Franco shouted as he ran after her.

As she got closer to the warehouse, she saw that a few of the firemen were carrying bodies out and lining them up on the street. Nino ran to her, trying to block her path, but she ducked beneath his outstretched arms and ran to the corpses on the ground. Their faces were burned beyond recognition.

Franco caught up to her. Grabbing her arm, he pulled her away.

"Leave me! I need to see if they were in there!" Maria shouted.

Franco looked at her. Sympathy filled his eyes.

She shook her head frantically. "Maybe they were brought to the police station after I left. They could still be alive."

"Of course. Please, Maria. Don't drive yourself crazy until we know for certain."

"But you know already, don't you?"

"No, Maria. I don't."

"You believe they're in there. That is why you suggested we return to my house."

"I won't lie to you, Maria. I am worried your family was brought here along with the other villagers. When Felice Salamone said the Germans left with your family on foot, I wondered if they had been brought somewhere nearby. But we don't absolutely know. There's still hope."

"I know. They're gone. I can feel it. And the feeling only grew stronger once I returned to my house and called out to each of them to see if they had come back."

Franco took Maria in his arms and wept softly as he whispered over and over, "I'm sorry."

Maria stood still as Franco held her. She felt so, so numb. She wasn't even crying. How she wished she could feel Franco's strong arms around her and his breath on her neck. How she wanted to take comfort in his arms, but she wasn't able to. If only she could feel something. But instead she felt dead, and, in that moment, she wished she were. For then at least she would be with her family — all of them together again. Nothing and no one, not even Franco, could make her feel better.

Days later, Maria received confirmation that her family had indeed been among the victims of the leather warehouse fire. Not all of the townspeople had been taken. A few had been spared so they could warn the others that the Germans were retaliating for the acts of the partisans. Corpses of entire families had been found, bound to one another with rope. Children as young as two were also among the dead.

After the fire, Maria went to stay with Franco in his apartment. She could not bear to return to her house with only the ghosts of her loved ones echoing through the halls. For weeks, she did nothing, letting Franco bathe her, clothe her, and feed her. While she slept, he held her throughout the night. And when she woke up screaming from the nightmares in which she could smell the acrid smoke from the warehouse and hear her family's screams, he rocked her until she calmed down. But once she fell back asleep, the nightmares that would plague her for the rest of her life returned.

CHAPTER 28
SIGNORA FERRARO

Pienza, 1971

It was an extremely windy March day in Pienza. Though spring was only a few weeks away, to Signora Ferraro it still felt like an eternity. She had never liked the winter, and, ever since she'd moved here and had grown her rose garden, she especially detested winter. For she could not be outside watching her roses bloom to life. As she walked through the rows of roses that grew in her greenhouse, her spirits refused to lift. While the greenhouse ensured she could continue selling flowers in the colder months, these roses never felt the same to her as the ones that grew outdoors. Her special garden would remain barren until June when most of the roses would start to bloom. That was still three long months away. This is what saddened her the most about autumn and winter. And Anabella's absence had made the season all the more

405

unbearable.

While Anabella had continued being a loyal, dutiful child, writing to Signora Ferraro regularly, Signora Ferraro could not bring herself to send even a short note to her daughter. It was cruel for a mother to behave this way. But she still felt Anabella's betrayal just as painfully as on that day she'd left. There were times she had picked up a pen and begun to write to her, but she never made it past the greeting. Signora Ferraro knew deep down the real reason why she refused to stay in touch with her daughter. She simply did not want to be hurt again. How much could a woman her age take? She had turned fifty-six this year. While that wasn't necessarily old, the hard work she did on the farm and the immense pain she'd suffered since she was a young woman and had lost all of those who were once dear to her had taken their toll, causing her to look and feel much older. No, it was better this way — better that she and Anabella lead separate lives. Besides, Anabella seemed to be doing fine without her and had even wed the artist, even though she'd told her she wanted to have the wedding at the rose farm and wanted her to be present. Words. That was all they had been. Her heart broke every time she thought about how her daughter had not returned soon as Anabella had told her she would. Instead, seven months had gone by. What especially hurt was that Anabella hadn't even attempted to gain her mother's forgiveness, nor had she insisted on not getting married until Signora Ferraro gave her blessing. But then again, could she blame Anabella after the way she'd turned her back on her that day in the garden, refusing to say good-bye?

The tears returned once more along with the heavy sobs that always followed soon afterward. After Anabella's departure, she'd had these severe crying episodes every day for the first two weeks. But then they'd subsided to just a few times a week. She walked over to the yellow roses — Anabella's favorite. Plucking one from the stem, she held it tightly, indifferent to the sharp thorns that stabbed her. She pressed the rose to her nose, inhaling deeply and remembering how Anabella would always offer each rose to her mother to smell first before she took in its scent. Even as a child, she'd been utterly selfless.

Soon, the tears stopped, and Signora Ferraro felt herself able to breathe normally. Her beautiful roses. They'd always been able to calm her and make her happy. But that feeling of elation had been disappearing. She told herself it was just because she missed the roses that grew in the gardens, and that nothing compared to watching new life spring from the earth. It had nothing to do with losing her daughter. The roses were a constant. Even when disease attacked the roses and they were killed, she could always grow more to take their place.

Ever since Signora Ferraro had overheard her neighbors that day at the market discussing how they thought she was crazy with her obsession over her roses, she had realized that probably most people who knew her felt this way. But none of them had any idea just how much these roses meant to her. Now that Anabella was gone, they were all she had. And as she grew older and contemplated her mortality, she knew her days with the roses were numbered — just as her days with her family, Franco, and Anabella had been numbered.

Yes, her roses had been a lifeline to her when she'd been ready to completely give up. Signora Ferraro had never shared the secret of them with anyone, not even Anabella. She could tell that even her employees thought she was obsessed with the roses, and that was why she was so demanding, expecting nothing but perfection from her workers. She'd eavesdropped on the conversation of two of the teenage boys she'd hired recently.

"These roses are her lovers! Who knows? Maybe she takes a bunch of them into bed with her at night!"

"You're terrible!" The other boy had scolded the first one, but he still laughed.

"This is what happens to old maids. They become miserable and have to obsess over the lack of a lover in their lives. Some people collect pets. As for Signora Ferraro, she can't stop expanding her rose gardens. But her property is almost used up. I wonder what she will do then."

"She's not an old maid. I've heard the older workers talking about her daughter. They had some falling out."

"She probably got tired of the roses."

They had laughed so hard that she saw one of the boys wiping his eyes. Signora Ferraro had been tempted to show herself and berate them. She knew she should've fired them. But the thought of exerting so much energy had been draining. So she'd ignored them and had walked away before she could hear more of their ugly words.

From the greenhouse's skylight, she could see dusk quickly taking over. Glancing at her watch, she saw it was ten minutes before five. She was starting to feel light-headed and remembered she had not eaten her midday meal, which wasn't uncommon these days. What once was a lavish meal shared with Anabella as they laughed and discussed topics that interested them had now become a cold, lonely experience. And even when she did eat in the middle of the day, she merely had a piece of bread with a sun-dried tomato on top, drizzled with olive oil, or a piece of fruit. Her dresses had begun hanging off her, but she didn't care. Little mattered to her anymore — except for the roses of course.

As she locked the door to the greenhouse, she heard a car pull up onto the property. She frowned; it was late at this time of year to be receiving customers. In late autumn and winter, she closed the nursery at two o'clock. Maybe one of the workers had forgotten something.

She wrapped her coat around herself and walked over to the car. But she stopped after just a few steps. Surely, she was seeing things. It could not be.

Anabella stepped out of the driver's seat of the car. But she looked far different from the daughter who had abandoned her seven months prior. She had gained a lot of weight, and her face . . . It had lost the innocent look she'd managed to hold on to even into her twenties. As soon as Anabella looked up and locked eyes with her mother, Anabella ran to her.

Signora Ferraro let out a gasp. She had come back! Walking quickly toward her daughter, she began to cry as Anabella caught up to her and embraced her tightly.

"Mamma!" Anabella said through choked sobs. "I've missed you so much."

Signora Ferraro wanted to tell her how much she, too, had missed her, but she was still overcome by shock.

Anabella pulled away. She stroked back the graying wisps of frizzy hair that had blown into her mother's face.

"Are you all right? I'm sorry. I should have called to let you know I was coming. I gave you a shock. But I was worried . . ."

She didn't have to finish the sentence for Signora Ferraro to know Anabella had been going to say she was afraid her mother wouldn't pick up the phone. For Anabella had tried calling a few times, but Signora Ferraro had always let the answering machine pick up and had ignored the calls.

She struggled to find the right words. But what was she to say after all these months? So instead she merely said, "I was about to go in to have a *panino*. Come."

Anabella locked her arm with her mother's and walked slowly with her. Whimpering could be heard from behind the front door.

"Bruno!" Anabella cried out, leaving her mother's side to let the dog out.

Bruno licked Anabella's face, making her giggle as she told him over and over again, "I missed you, Bruno. I'm sorry I couldn't take you with me."

"He missed you terribly. For months, he slept in your room every night and whimpered." Signora Ferraro couldn't help thinking how Bruno's behavior had been similar to her own those first weeks after Anabella had left. For Signora Ferraro had often lain awake at night in bed, crying and asking God what she'd done to lose the most precious person in her life. She should tell her daughter how much she had missed her — and loved her — but she simply couldn't.

Once Bruno calmed down, they went inside. Signora Ferraro got to work right away preparing sandwiches. She noticed out of her peripheral vision that Anabella looked lost in thought as she sat at the kitchen table.

"It is so good to see you, Mamma — and the farm and the house."

"Even though it's winter and the gardens are empty?"

Anabella frowned for a moment but then added, "*Si.* It is good to see nothing has changed. But you look as if you've lost weight. Are you feeling all right? I've asked Chiara, and she's told me you have been fine, but maybe she didn't want to worry me."

"I didn't realize you were in touch with Chiara." Signora Ferraro didn't know why this surprised her. They had always been close since Anabella was a little girl. Jealousy began to seep through her.

"Since you weren't answering my phone calls or writing back to me, I needed to know that you were all right." Anabella looked at her mother, but Signora Ferraro glanced away.

Signora Ferraro joined Anabella at the table. She took a small bite out of her eggplant and sweet pepper *panino,* chewing slowly. Her appetite had disappeared. Again, she felt at a loss for words, so she pretended to eat and drink. She could feel Anabella's eyes on her as she watched and waited patiently. But Signora Ferraro remained silent. Anabella finally began eating her *panino.* She chewed ravenously. It pleased Signora Ferraro to see her daughter eating here again. Finally, she broke her silence. "I'll make you another one." Signora Ferraro stood up, but Anabella placed her hand on her mother's arm.

"No, please. Sit down. I am fine. My appetite is out of control these days." She smiled and blushed slightly.

"I have noticed you've gained weight. And your face. You look very different."

"I know I do not look my best."

"No, no. You still look beautiful. *Mi dispiaccio.* I'm sorry. I didn't mean to say you looked bad." Signora Ferraro managed a small smile.

"You cannot tell."

"Tell what?"

"Mamma, I am with child. Well, with children." Anabella giggled softly. "I am having twins!"

Signora Ferraro was stunned. Of course, why hadn't she noticed the telltale signs that Anabella was pregnant? How could she not realize something so important with her own flesh and blood? Besides Anabella's obvious weight gain, she had a glow in her face, much like Signora Ferraro had had when she was pregnant with Anabella. She looked at Anabella's stomach. Her stomach looked quite large and protruded quite a bit, even though she was wearing a rather large cardigan. It looked like a man's sweater. No doubt it was Dante's. Signora

Ferraro hadn't thought about him since she'd first laid eyes on Anabella stepping out of her car. Anger began to course through her. He was still in the picture. And now Anabella was having his children. She couldn't help laughing silently in her head as she chided herself. *You fool! What did you think, that she had left her husband to return to you?*

Signora Ferraro softly asked, "How far along are you?"

"Five months. I got pregnant right after we were married in October. I look bigger since I'm carrying two babies."

Signora Ferraro remained silent for a moment before she stood up and prepared a pot of espresso. Neither spoke until she sat down again at the table as they waited for the coffee to percolate.

"Mamma, I know I hurt you terribly by leaving with Dante. I'm sorry."

Signora Ferraro wrapped her wool shawl around her, keeping her arms crossed. She pursed her lips together. She could feel the well of tears forming inside her, but she refused to let her daughter see just how much she had hurt her.

"Dante and I want you to be a part of our lives — a part of the babies' lives. As I mentioned to you before we left, we want to

415

live in Pienza."

"How will the starving artist make a living?" Signora Ferraro said in a snide voice. She couldn't help herself.

"I guess you don't remember what I told you in my letters about Dante's exhibiting his work in several galleries in Florence. He made quite a bit of money. That was why we stayed there so long. He wanted to save enough money so we could come back to Pienza and buy a small house."

"So he plans on continuing to be an artist, even here?"

"He will go to Florence and Siena whenever he lands an exhibit. His name is spreading among the art world and serious art buyers. We will be fine financially if that's what you are worried about."

"So he is going to leave you alone with two children? Is that why you are here? You want me to help you raise your children?"

Anabella narrowed her eyes as if something had stung her. Tears filled her eyes, and soon they dropped onto her cheeks. She whispered, "How can you think that, Mamma?"

"How can I not? You assured me you would be back soon and that your trip would be short, but you were gone for seven months, and in such a short time you married a man you hardly knew — a man whom your mother did not approve of — and now you return saying you want me to be a part of your life again. Your husband will be too busy following a boy's dream of painting instead of being a man and taking care of his family. Now that you need me, you have come back."

Anabella shook her head and stood up, grabbing her coat from behind the chair. "I should've known you would act this way. How can you turn me away, Mamma? How can you turn your grandchildren away?" She gestured to her stomach. "My entire life, when you were sheltering me, teaching me lessons at home instead of letting me go to a real school, not letting me play with other children my age, you told me it was for my own good. That I had everything I needed here, and I was the lucky one to be living on this beautiful farm with nothing to want. But that is where you were wrong, Mamma! I had everything to want — friends . . . interactions with others besides you, the farm workers, and my dog . . . experiences that would help me grow up. But instead you wanted me to remain your little girl forever so that I would never leave you. You have only thought about yourself and your fears of being left alone!"

"That is not true!" Signora Ferraro's voice rose to match Anabella's.

"It is true! Stop lying to me and to yourself! You are selfish. A mother always puts her children's needs before hers. I pray I am not the mother you were to me!"

Anabella shoved the chair hard against the kitchen table, causing the vase of flowers on it to topple over. She stormed out of the house with Bruno at her heels.

"Come, Bruno. We are not wanted here." She held the door for Bruno, who was only too happy to leave with her.

This stung Signora Ferraro. Even the dog didn't want her. She shouldn't care. After all, he'd been Anabella's pet, but Signora Ferraro had taken comfort in his steady presence after her daughter had gone to Florence. Sometimes, she'd found herself talking to him just to hear the sound of a voice in her house again, even if it was just her own.

She didn't know how long she sat at the kitchen table. Her body felt paralyzed as she kept her hand pressed over her heart. How it hurt. Anabella had been right with her harsh words. It had always been more about her and trying to control everything so that she would be spared the anguish again — so that Anabella would remain safe and protected. In the end though, Signora Ferraro had hurt her daughter worse than anyone else could have. And now it was too late.

Go to her, a voice whispered in her head. She thought about it for a moment. Surely, Anabella would forgive her. And Signora Ferraro could tell that Anabella was also looking for forgiveness when she'd come here. She had noticed how Anabella had waited after she'd told her mother that she missed her and after she'd apologized for leaving her. But Signora Ferraro's stubborn pride had refused to allow her to make her daughter feel better.

I pray I am not the mother you were to me! Anabella's words came back to her, sending another sharp stab of pain into her chest. No, she would not go to her and ask for forgiveness. She would not make the same mistakes with her grandchildren that she had made with Anabella. They would all be better off without her.

Slowly she got up from the table and made her way upstairs. Once she entered her room, she took the small framed photo of Franco and herself on their wedding day, which she kept on her night table, and held it to her as she got into bed. How she wished he were here to comfort her and tell her he would protect her — much the way he had every night for weeks after her family was killed in the fire. Soon, she fell fast asleep as she dreamed about the man who had made her so happy — but who had been taken from her too quickly.

CHAPTER 29
MARIA FERRARO

Florence, 1944

The beautiful bells were ringing from the nearby Santa Maria Maggiore church. Anabella cried out as she did every morning when the bells rang. But as soon as Maria picked her up from her crib, Anabella stopped crying. Maria loved this time of the day the most; the streets were at their quietest, and the sun was rising higher in the sky. She didn't mind that Anabella cried every morning. For the feeling of her baby needing her, and only her mother being able to soothe her, was the most gratifying experience she'd ever had. Franco was good with their daughter, too, but he was either at FAF's offices before Maria or Anabella woke up, or he was out on a mission.

As Maria rocked Anabella, she went over to the window and looked outside. The soldiers who had been stationed out front last night were no longer present. With one

421

hand, she held Anabella, and, with the other, she picked up the birdcage she kept on a nearby small table and placed it in the window. The lovely pale-blue parakeet that sat in the cage had been a wedding gift from Franco to Maria. But for the past few months, the birdcage had served another purpose. When Franco was out, Maria would place the birdcage in the window, letting him know no soldiers were inquiring at their home or standing guard outside. Weekly interrogations and searches of homes had become a regular occurrence, and, with the partisans gaining ground, the Nazis were determined to root every one of them out.

Franco had been gone for more than a week. Although his mission was supposed to be over five days ago, the soldiers had been guarding their street for each of those days. This morning was the first that Maria was able to place the birdcage in the window.

"God, please keep Franco safe. His daughter and I need him."

A month after Maria's family had been killed, she had wed Franco in an intimate ceremony at Santa Maria Maggiore. The pastor had agreed to wed them in secret. The only people present were their witnesses — Giuliana, the young woman who had been distributing FAF's leaflets at the outdoor market the day Maria had run into Franco after their first meeting, and Gaetano. Maria had to do her best not to let her mind wander to the day of the leather warehouse fire whenever she looked at him. Every time she saw Gaetano, Vito, or Nino, her thoughts would inevitably return to that day when they watched the flames overtake the warehouse.

Maria had only been to her house once after the fire — to retrieve her mother's wedding dress. The thought of returning to the home she once shared with her family was almost too much to bear, and she had even considered not wearing her mother's dress on her wedding day. But she wanted to have some connection to her family on her special day — to feel as if a part of them would be with her. So she'd mustered the emotional strength to go back.

The warehouse fire had been the catalyst that set off a chain of events in which more and more people Maria knew were either killed or imprisoned. They had lost a few of FAF's members, which only increased Maria's anxiety that Franco could be killed too. Then there were a few of Franco's neighbors whom she never saw again — their whereabouts unknown. Even a few strangers whom she and Franco had temporarily given a safe haven in their apartment had met with a grim fate.

While her wedding hadn't been a typical ceremony with lots of people in attendance, she hadn't minded. After all, it wasn't too long ago when she had thought she would never marry. Her only regret was that her family could not be present. She smiled as she remembered how Franco had surprised her with a small bouquet of white roses.

"Remember at our first dance, you were wearing that white silk rose in your gown, and then you placed it in your hair?" he had asked.

Of course Maria remembered, and she'd been immensely moved that he had also remembered what she'd been wearing the night of the dance.

"I wanted you to have white roses again to remember that day. When the war is over, I will buy you white roses all the time."

Maria had taken one of the roses and placed it in her hair, above her ear, just as she'd done at the dance. And she'd held the bouquet during their wedding ceremony.

After their vows, they had a small celebration at FAF's office. Later that night in bed, Maria had whispered to Franco, "You are my family now."

"And you are mine."

As Maria's thoughts returned to the present, she wondered if she would ever feel ready to go back to her father's house and possibly make it a home for herself, Franco, and Anabella. Could she ever erase the images of her house being vandalized — knowing her family members had been terrorized there — and the trail of blood that led outside, reminding her that those were the last steps her family had taken before being led to their deaths inside the warehouse? Franco had hired a woman to clean the house before Maria went to pick up her mother's wedding dress. But the house no longer felt like her loving childhood home that she'd shared with Papà, Michele, and Enza. The Nazis had managed to tarnish a place that had once represented nothing but innocence and love to her.

Maria and Franco had conceived their daughter on that beautiful August day when they'd made love for the first time in the sunflower garden. But Maria hadn't realized she was pregnant until November, shortly after her family was killed. Even during her pregnancy she had remained involved with her work for the Resistance, much to Franco's disapproval. But the deaths of her family members had made her want revenge on the Nazis. She no longer feared for her own safety, and, while she didn't want to jeopardize the life of her baby, she knew she would give up on her own life again as she had during those first few weeks after the fire if she wasn't doing something to bring about justice for Papà, Michele, and Enza. In addition to writing the newspaper, she continued delivering food, ammunitions, and other supplies to the partisans, many of whom had gone to live in the mountains as they carried out their ambushes against the Germans. She had finally confessed to Franco about how she'd been delivering supplies to the partisans and had told him nothing he said could stop her from carrying out this work. She had been forced to stop during the last month of her pregnancy when she was too uncomfortable to get on her bicycle and ride for long stretches. And, of course, once Anabella was born, the baby needed her undivided attention. At least she was able to continue writing the paper. She no longer delivered it herself, but had other FAF members do so.

Anabella. How precious her baby was. She still couldn't believe she was hers. When Maria broke the news that she was pregnant to Franco, he had picked her up and spun her around, only to realize he might be hurting her and quickly put her down, asking her to sit down. He was so excited, as was she. He began making plans for them and the baby. Franco and she couldn't wait to know the sex of the baby, but not because either of them had a certain preference. They just couldn't wait to meet the boy or girl who would be part of their family soon. Unlike most men she knew, Franco wasn't adamant about having a boy to carry on his name and legacy. He just wanted the baby to be healthy and to be able to grow up in an Italy that was free of German occupation. When Anabella was born, Franco and Maria agreed that hers was the most beautiful face they had ever laid eyes on. They decided to name her Anabella: Ana in honor of Maria's late mother, and Bella to acknowledge her beauty.

Maria was so lost in her thoughts that she almost didn't hear the footsteps coming up the stairs of the apartment. Quickly, she placed Anabella back in her crib and grabbed the revolver Franco kept in the top drawer of his desk. Tiptoeing over to the door, she pressed her back against the wall and held her breath as she waited for whomever was about to cross the threshold. When she saw Franco step inside, she exhaled deeply.

"Thank God. You're finally home." Maria lowered the revolver to her side.

Franco walked over to her and took the revolver. He put it back in the desk drawer and then returned to Maria's side, taking her in his arms.

"I'm sorry I haven't been here. It was driving me nuts when I didn't spot the birdcage in the window each of the days I wanted to return home."

"Where have you been sleeping?"

"What little sleep I got was either at the office or . . ." He stopped himself.

"Or where?"

"In the streets or deserted alleyways."

"How could you stay out in the open?"

Franco shrugged his shoulders. He looked worried.

"What is it, Franco? Don't keep anything from me. You promised not to."

"I just haven't felt as safe anymore at FAF's office, not that I ever thought any place was truly safe." His eyes met Maria's, and they both knew they were thinking about her family home.

"It has to be safer than staying out on the street."

"We've been talking about moving the office from the abandoned church. The Germans are getting more enraged after the recent successes the partisans have been having. Just look at how they keep searching homes in our neighborhood. It is a matter of time before they start searching abandoned places like the church. I'm even beginning to think it's time we go live somewhere else."

"Where? Who will take a couple and an infant?" Maria glanced over at Anabella, who was sleeping peacefully in her crib. Fear suddenly gripped her. What had she been thinking, being careless and letting herself get pregnant during wartime and with no guarantee about what the future would hold for them?

"Before you say no, Maria, please just listen to me." Franco paused.

Maria noticed how tired he looked. He'd also lost weight. Then again, everyone was losing weight these days with the food rations that were diminishing each week.

"Go on." She gently prodded him, placing her hand on his arm.

"I was thinking we should go stay at your house."

Maria dropped her hand. She was about to adamantly refuse, but then remembered Franco's request to hear him out.

"I know it's difficult for you to go back

there without your family, but Maria, the soldiers seem to not be searching the homes in your old neighborhood as much as they've been doing here."

"You said yourself a moment ago that no place is truly safe. And, as we know, my family and most of the townspeople were not safe in their homes."

"But that is the reason why homes aren't being searched there as much anymore; the Germans know they wiped out most of the residents."

Maria grimaced.

"I'm sorry." Franco took her in his arms. He stroked her back and kissed her temple before pulling away from her. He looked into her eyes.

"I am going crazy every day thinking about you alone here with the baby. And these past few days were the worst when I didn't see that damn birdcage in the window."

"Don't say that. I love Lula."

Franco laughed. "I love the parakeet too, but you know what I mean."

Maria laughed, before growing somber once more. "Do you really think Anabella and I will be safer there?"

"I do. And this way, I can return home when I'm done with a mission rather than trawl the streets like a stray dog. But we must still use our trick of putting the birdcage in the window when I am away. We cannot be too careful."

The thought of having Franco be able to return home as soon as he was done with his partisan work removed all hesitation from her mind about going to the house. And maybe the presence of a baby was what the house needed to rid Maria's mind of the horrible images of what had transpired there. It would be nice to raise Anabella where Maria had been raised and with her family's belongings so she could begin to teach her daughter about her ancestors. In time, the house would feel warm again with a child to bring laughter and cheer into it. Mamma and Papà would want Anabella to be there. Maria felt that in her heart.

"All right. We will go. I suppose we should leave as soon as possible."

"*Grazie,* Maria. This already eases some of the load off my mind."

Maria smiled and hugged him, but on the inside, she felt worried. She had never seen Franco look as anxious as he did today. Lately, he'd been assuring her that the Resistance would succeed and that an end was near. He'd felt confident with the recent strides the partisans had made. But naturally, no one would rest easy until the war was indeed truly over and the Germans were gone for good.

"Let me go say hello to my beautiful daughter." Franco kissed Maria softly on the lips before walking over to Anabella's crib. "Ah, she is awake." He picked her up and rocked her gently as he spoke to her. "I've missed you so much. Today, we are going somewhere much bigger than this tiny apartment. And you will have a beautiful yard to play in." But as soon as Franco uttered these last words, he looked at Maria, fear evident in his eyes, and said, "You can take her out for a little fresh air, but don't stay out for too long."

"Don't worry. I'll be very careful when you're not with us."

Maria thought back to that first day when she'd found Franco crouched low in her father's sunflower garden and how he had warned her to not go out there alone. No, for the time being, she would not take Anabella outside, even just for a few minutes. There would be time for Anabella to enjoy the outdoors — once this war was over.

Once they moved into her family's house, Maria had been busy, which helped keep her mind off the ugly events that had transpired there last year. She had taken whatever fabric she could find from clothes that had belonged to Papà, Michele, and Enza and made new curtains for the house. She even made slipcovers for the couch and chairs in the living room and rearranged the furniture. Franco had not asked her what she was doing, for it was obvious she was attempting to make the house look and feel different from when she and her family had lived there.

Thankfully, Anabella was a good sleeper, allowing Maria to get much work done. Anabella was still too young to take on the bicycle, and, of course, it was unsafe. Franco also didn't want any members of FAF going to his and Maria's house in case they were followed. As he reminded Maria, they had made this move to be safer.

Maria was finishing up sewing the last of her curtains on her machine when Franco came home. She tried to keep the tension she'd been feeling all day out of her voice as he greeted her. For he would be leaving before dawn tomorrow for a mission that would prevent him from returning home for at least several nights or more. Maria had asked him not to tell her what it was. Although she had made him promise never to keep anything from her, she had decided once they moved that she didn't want to know any longer about the missions. It would just make her more fraught with worry while he was away. She needed to keep her wits about her, especially now that she had a baby to protect.

"*Ciao,* Franco! I've prepared a special dinner for you." She stood up and went over to Franco, and they embraced.

They had fallen into the routine of hugging each other every day, before he left home and when he returned. Each day, the embrace seemed to last longer. Some days, Maria wanted to beg him not to leave them. She had even been tempted to plead with him to give up the Resistance work. But just as she'd refused to give up her partisan work months ago, she knew he would not turn his back on the organization. And, as he'd told her after Anabella was born, he was now also fighting to ensure Anabella's freedom and future.

"Hmmm . . . I can smell your wonderful cooking. What did you make?"

"It's just pasta with cannellini beans." Maria could not hide the sadness in her voice. She wished she could've made a more elaborate dish for Franco tonight. But she had to do the best she could with whatever food rations were doled out. The food she and Enza had preserved was just about gone. If the Germans hadn't broken the jars of preserved food in the refrigerator, Maria would've been able to stretch it longer.

"I cannot wait." He smiled.

Later that night, Franco and Maria lay in bed with baby Anabella nestled in the middle of them. It had been Maria's idea to keep Anabella with them throughout the night. Surely, they would be together again in a few days or weeks at the most. But for tonight, she wanted to feel the presence of her family with her. Sleep eluded Maria, and, from Franco's deep sighs every few minutes, she could tell he was also having a hard time falling asleep.

"You should try to sleep. Who knows when you will be able to sleep once you're out in the field."

"I know, but I just can't. It's all right. I like being fully present in this moment, feeling the warmth of my wife and my baby lying next to me."

"If only we weren't at war . . ." Maria left her thoughts unexpressed. It was too painful to voice aloud her fantasies of their living during peacetime, without the dark cloud of war hanging over them. True, the war couldn't last forever. But would they be victorious at the end? Or would they continue to live under occupation with no dreams for the future?

"You must not lose hope, Maria, whatever happens. You must not lose hope for Anabella's sake. Promise me that." Franco looked into Maria's eyes.

Though she tried to fight her tears back, she couldn't. With each day that the war dragged on, it was becoming increasingly difficult to be stoic and show a strong front to Franco. Terror had filled her heart ever since her family was killed and ever since Franco had become more involved in the dangerous aspects of the Resistance.

"I promise," Maria said in a choked voice.

Franco whispered, "Don't cry, Maria. I will always be with you. Right here. Just as you and Anabella will always be with me right here." He pressed one hand to her heart and the other to his heart.

"I just can't bear the thought of you sleeping in some trench alone."

"I won't be alone. The other partisans will be with me as well as Sacco."

"Who's that?"

"He's a stray dog we found. Well, he actually found us. He came over to us whimpering and has not left our sides. He curls up next to the partisans in the dugouts. So you have nothing to worry about."

Maria couldn't help giggling softly. The thought of a sweet dog keeping her husband company made her feel a bit better.

Franco leaned over and kissed Maria. She broke the kiss and sat up in bed, picking Anabella up carefully. She placed her back in her crib and returned to bed. She and Franco resumed their kiss and soon made love. It felt very similar to the first time they had made love in the sunflower garden behind the house, fraught with immense energy. Afterward, they rested in each other's arms, finally falling asleep. But in the middle of the night, Franco woke Maria up and made love to her again. She ingrained in her mind every nuance of their lovemaking — the feel of each of Franco's kisses . . . the warmth emanating from his hands as they traveled the length of her body . . . the pleasant sensations that reverberated throughout her . . . the all-encompassing love she felt for her husband and the father of her child.

When they were done, Maria glanced at the clock on her night table. In less than two hours, Franco would need to wake up and leave. She went over to Anabella's crib and brought her back to bed. Maria nestled the baby between them once more. Franco kept his arm wrapped over his child and wife. He soon fell asleep. Though Maria was tired, she fought off sleep so she could watch the faces of the two people she loved most in the world.

Maria woke up with a start. A sound had awakened her. The sun was shining brightly through the gap in her window where she hadn't fully drawn the shade down. She looked to her side and saw Franco was gone. She frowned. Maybe it had been too painful for him to wake her up and say good-bye. She had noticed lately it seemed harder for him to take his leave of them.

Anabella was no longer in the bed. Franco must've returned her to her crib. Maria could hear her cooing. Maria got out of bed and walked over to the crib and picked Anabella up. She then made her way to the kitchen. But when she reached the bottom of the steps, her heart stopped as she noticed the front door was wide-open. She then saw Franco's eyeglasses on the floor. The lenses were shattered. Suddenly, she remembered the strange noise that had awakened her. She realized now it had been the front door being opened. Her heart pounded.

Maria ran back upstairs and grabbed an old picnic basket from the linen closet outside the bathroom. She placed the baby inside, grateful that Anabella wasn't crying. She placed a few rolled up towels on either side of Anabella to ensure that she remained nestled snugly in the basket. She then placed it at the back of a shelf in the armoire in her father's bedroom.

"Don't worry. I'll be back. Just go to sleep," Maria whispered to Anabella before placing a pacifier in her mouth and kissing her on the forehead.

She hurried over to her bedroom and retrieved the revolver she kept under her pillow every night. Before Maria left the room, she went over to the window and crouched down. Lifting slightly one of the blinds with her index finger, she peered through. Sweat beads immediately dotted her forehead as she saw the backs of two German soldiers in the sunflower garden. Their assault rifles were pointed in front of them. One was talking in Italian, but she could not hear precisely what he was saying.

Maria ran down the stairs and stepped outside, closing the door quietly behind her. Her eyes immediately squinted, not accustomed to the bright light after the dim interior of her house. She crouched down and moved along the side of the house to the sunflower garden where the soldiers and no doubt Franco were. How had the soldiers known to come looking for Franco here? Or was it just a lucky coincidence that they had stumbled upon him as he was leaving the house? But no, they had entered the house. She remembered Franco's shattered eyeglasses on the floor in the foyer and the open door. He would never be so careless as to leave the door open and unlocked with Maria and Anabella sleeping upstairs. The soldiers had entered her house — once again. Anger began to course through her as she thought about how they'd violated her home a second time.

When she reached the back of the house, she almost passed out when she saw the sight before her. Franco, Gaetano, and Vito were standing with their arms raised above their heads. A deep gash oozed blood from Franco's forehead, and both of his eyes were bruised and swollen almost completely shut. Gaetano's and Vito's faces had also been roughed up. Gaetano's shirt was ripped open, and a crude Jewish star had been carved out on his chest. She then remembered Gaetano was Jewish.

Now both of the soldiers were taking turns speaking to the men in Italian. Maria strained to hear what they were saying, but she was still too far away. From their harsh tone, it sounded as if they were rebuking the men.

Maria aimed her revolver. Her hand was shaking so badly. She steadied it with her other hand, but just as she was about to pull the trigger, the two soldiers opened fire with their machine guns.

An anguished moan escaped from Maria's lips, but the gunfire muffled it. Her heart felt as if it was being torn from her chest as she watched Franco's body being riddled with bullets. Blood splattered everywhere and on the petals of the sunflowers that surrounded the men.

For a moment, it looked as if Franco's eyes met hers, but she knew there was no way he'd seen her, especially since his eyes had been almost completely shut from the beatings he had suffered at the soldiers' hands. Even after Franco's body and those of Gaetano and Vito fell to the ground, the soldiers continued shooting.

Maria stood up, slowly making her way to the soldiers. She was merely five feet away from them when she shot one soldier in the back of his head. The second soldier was still firing his machine gun, but when he saw his comrade collapse, he quickly turned around. There wasn't enough time for him to dodge the bullet from Maria's gun. The bullet hit him in the arm, causing him to drop his rifle. She walked up closer and shot him again, this time in the chest. Then she shot one final bullet in his head. She was tempted to continue firing her gun at them, just the way they had done to Franco and the others, but sense took hold, making her realize there might be other soldiers coming soon and she'd need the ammunition.

Going over to Franco, Maria knelt by his side. His body was heavy as she pulled him into her lap and wrapped her arms around him.

"I'm here, Franco. I'm here." She placed her hand against his heart as he'd done to her during the night. "I'll always be here, and you'll always be here in my heart and in Anabella's heart." She picked up his limp hand and pressed it to her heart.

She then let out the scream that had wanted to escape when she'd seen the bullets ripping open the body of her husband. If any of the few neighbors who had managed to not perish in the warehouse fire heard her, no one came out. How Maria wanted to take the revolver and end her life right there. And there was no question in her mind that she would have if it weren't for Anabella. Maria suddenly remembered that she'd hidden Anabella in the armoire.

Fear seized her once more. They needed to leave before the soldiers' bodies were discovered and the Germans began searching homes to find out who had killed them. But she couldn't leave Franco's body in the open like this.

She stood up and placed her hands under Franco's shoulders, dragging him back to the other side of the house. Laying him gently on the ground, she went over to the small shed her father had built, where his gardening tools were kept. She took out a shovel and began digging a hole.

As she dug, she prayed Anabella had fallen asleep and was still all right in the armoire. She had to work quickly. Every so often, she whispered to Franco.

"I love you so much, my dear, sweet husband. You brought so much happiness to me. You will always be my husband and the only man I will ever love. Do not worry about Anabella. I promise you, Franco, I will keep her safe, and I know you will be looking out for us in heaven now."

Before placing him in the hole she had dug, she wanted to cover his body. Running into the house, she pulled the linen cloth from the dining room table, knocking over the vase of silk white roses Franco had once bought for her.

This way you'll always have white roses even when they're not in season.

She winced as she remembered his words. Draping the tablecloth over her arm, she went to the kitchen sink and wet a dish towel. Hurrying back outside, she knelt down beside Franco and placed her arm beneath his head as she wiped the blood from his face. She then smoothed his hair back. It was now time to wrap him in the tablecloth. She struggled to shift the table-cloth beneath Franco. Once she did, she carefully rolled his body in the fabric until he was completely shrouded in it. Before lowering him into the ground, she pulled down just enough of the tablecloth to reveal his face.

"*Ti voglio bene, mio amore.* I love you, my love."

Maria kissed his lips and then took one last look at her husband's face before covering it once more. As she lowered his body into the ground, sobs escaped her throat. Working as quickly as she could, she covered the hole with dirt. Her muscles ached, but she dared not rest for even a second.

As soon as she was done, she ran over to the wagon Papà used in his gardening and wheeled it over Franco's resting place, hoping it would be enough to conceal that the ground had been dug up recently.

Picking up the revolver from the ground, she kept it in her hand as she made her way back into her house, constantly glancing over her shoulder to make sure no other soldiers were coming.

Maria closed the door behind her, but when she went to lock it, she noticed the lock had been broken. She'd almost forgotten the soldiers had entered the home. How had she not heard them breaking in while she slept? She pushed the dining room table up against the door and then ran upstairs to her father's bedroom.

Opening the armoire, she pulled out the picnic basket holding Anabella. Maria breathed a sigh of relief when she saw Anabella was sleeping.

"*Grazie,* Dio." She thanked God repeatedly as she quickly packed a few clothes for her and Anabella in a suitcase. The last items she packed were framed photographs — one of her and Franco on their wedding day and one of Franco holding Anabella.

Once outside, Maria went to the back of the house. She looked over to Franco's resting place. It did not seem real that her husband, who had made love to her only hours before and slept beside her in their bed, was now in the ground. She ripped her gaze away, pushing aside the tears that threatened to consume her again, and walked over to her father's Fiat. The car hadn't been used in months. She didn't know yet where she was going. All she knew was that she needed to leave Florence. It was truly no longer safe for her and Anabella.

Driving away from the property, Maria tried not to look at the garden, but her eyes inevitably traveled to the sunflowers. Images of Franco, Gaetano, and Vito being executed flashed through her mind. Gaetano and Vito. Their bodies still lay out in the open.

"I'm sorry I couldn't bury you, Gaetano and Vito. Please forgive me."

Except for the blood that had been sprayed on the sunflowers, they looked like they did every day, standing tall as they reached for the sun and swaying to and fro in the gentle breeze. But for Maria, they no longer appeared the same — even the ones that had managed not to be splattered with blood. Gone was the idyllic sunflower garden of her childhood when she and Michele would run through the field and hide behind the tall stems. Gone was the haven she had run to when she was a teenager and a woman in her twenties, seeking to be alone. Even the memories of first discovering Franco hidden in the garden and making love to him for the first time among the sunflowers were erased. Where once she had seen beauty in the flowers, now all she saw was death. As she drove through the Tuscan countryside, the numerous sunflower fields she passed only served to further torment Maria and remind her that where beauty lay, evil could also reside.

CHAPTER 30
SIGNORA FERRARO

Pienza, 1974

Signora Ferraro was sitting on the ground in the rose field, making small wreaths of roses. It was mid-June, and the rose gardens were all in bloom. She worked quickly, intertwining the stems of the roses with one another. One wreath contained yellow roses and the other peach roses. She made sure to keep Valeria and Mariella in her sight at all times. But the girls were too absorbed in their game of smelling a rose and then plucking it from its stem and offering it to the other to wander very far. Every so often one of them would come up to Signora Ferraro and offer a flower to her and say, *"Rosa."* Or sometimes, they would say, "Nonna, smell."

She couldn't believe the girls were now three years old. They seemed to be growing faster than Anabella had. Signora Ferraro picked up the wreath containing the yellow roses and stood up, walking over to Valeria.

"*Stai ferma,* Valeria." Signora Ferraro knew it was useless asking the toddler to remain still for more than a few seconds, not that it really mattered. She had removed the thorns from the roses' stems so she didn't have to worry they would prick the girls. When Valeria saw the wreath, she smiled and reached up for it.

"Isn't it pretty, Valeria? I will place it on your head so you can be a princess. Nonna's princess."

Valeria gave a little hop of excitement as Signora Ferraro placed the wreath on her head. She had chosen the yellow flowers to complement Valeria's chocolate-brown hair, which matched Anabella's hair. Like Anabella, Valeria had soft curls flowing throughout her mane. There were times Signora Ferraro mistakenly called her "Anabella." Valeria looked very much like Signora Ferraro's daughter when she was her age, but she also looked like Franco. Sometimes, Signora Ferraro swore it was Franco's eyes staring back at her instead of Valeria's. It gave her comfort to feel as if Franco and Anabella were still with her.

"Mariella!" Valeria pointed to her twin sister.

"*Si.* Here is Mariella's wreath."

Mariella looked as if she was about to cry when she saw Valeria had been crowned with a wreath and she hadn't. But as soon as Signora Ferraro brought over Mariella's wreath, her eyes lit up. The peach flowers in Mariella's wreath stood out beautifully against her honey-golden-brown hair. She took after Signora Ferraro, and it hadn't escaped Signora Ferraro's notice that Anabella and Dante had given her the name Mariella, which was a derivative of Maria. Dante had never admitted they had named Mariella after her, but she knew from the way he'd made a point of introducing her as a baby to her.

"Valeria was born first," he had said when he first visited Signora Ferraro with the newborns. "And this is Mariella. She has your hair color." He had smiled as he handed the babies, one at a time, to Signora Ferraro to hold.

She'd been so shocked that he had come to her house, and with the babies no less, that she'd remained speechless. When he had handed Valeria over, she'd immediately reached for the baby. Tears had sprung from her eyes as she was brought back to the day she'd first held Anabella in her arms, and a proud Franco had stood by her side. How strange — and wonderful at the same time

450

— that she was holding a baby again. And there were two babies! When she had given Valeria back to Dante and had held Mariella, she had felt a sharp stab of guilt. Though she'd been touched that they had named Mariella after her, Signora Ferraro had also felt she didn't deserve such an honor. Not after the way she'd treated both Anabella and Dante. And still, her son-in-law had brought his children to meet their grandmother and with no apparent animosity.

When Signora Ferraro had opened her door and had seen Dante standing there with the babies, her face had flushed profusely as she remembered the last time she'd seen him, when she had turned him and Anabella away after they'd announced they were going to Florence together. And she hadn't spoken to Anabella since the day Anabella had returned and shared her news that she was expecting — the same day they'd had that horrible argument.

Now three years had gone by, and neither Signora Ferraro nor Anabella had reached out to the other. Yes, Anabella had inherited her stubbornness — the same stubborn pride Signora Ferraro had exhibited as a young woman when she refused to give up her work in the Resistance. But Signora Ferraro's stubborn refusal to reach out to her daughter was no longer due to anger. She had stopped being angry a long time ago that Anabella had abandoned her and chosen Dante over her. No, it was shame that kept her from reaching out to her daughter as she replayed over and over in her mind the horrible words both she and Anabella had said to each other the last time they were together. Besides, she knew Anabella wanted nothing more to do with her. There had been times over the course of the past three years when Dante had left the twins with Signora Ferraro, and she'd seen Anabella was in the car. Dante always parked the car at the farm's entrance. On these occasions, Anabella wore a large straw hat that concealed her features. If it hadn't been for her beautiful, long curls that hung over her shoulders, Signora Ferraro would have had no idea that it was her daughter hiding from her in the car.

While their estrangement pained Signora Ferraro considerably and she'd thought of picking up the phone and ending it, she felt paralyzed whenever she thought about following through. She didn't know why. So instead, she'd poured her love and energy into her granddaughters. Though she'd wanted to push them away out of fear of losing them one day, too, she simply couldn't. That day when Dante first handed them to her, it was as if her body were separate from her mind as she reached forward to hold her grandchildren. And she couldn't get enough of them. Dante brought them once a week. In the beginning, he stayed, but when he saw Signora Ferraro was more than capable of handling the twins on her own, he began to leave them unattended.

"Papà!" Valeria squealed as she pointed to the driveway that led to the farm. Soon she and Mariella were running toward their father.

Dante parked the car and got out. He waved to Signora Ferraro and then bent down, taking the girls into his arms as they crashed into him. Every time he came to pick up the girls, Signora Ferraro felt a pang of disappointment that her time with them would soon be over. A few months ago, she had begun asking Dante to have his midday meal with her. Sometimes he did, but other times he didn't, saying that Anabella had cooked and was waiting for them. She hoped he could stay today.

"How were my girls today, Signora Ferraro?"

"Perfect angels as always." She walked

over and patted the curls on both of their heads. They looked at her, smiles beaming on their faces. Oh, how they made her happy. "Can you stay today to eat?"

Dante's face clouded over for a moment before he said, "I'm sorry. I can't. I need to go home and pack for my trip to Florence tomorrow. I've been so busy painting this week that I haven't gotten anything ready. I'm going to be gone for two weeks this time since I'll have two exhibits back-to-back."

"That long?" Signora Ferraro sounded concerned.

"I'm afraid so. I hate leaving Anabella alone with the girls for that long. Lord knows they can be a handful, can't you?" He squatted down and tickled the girls, much to their delight.

He stood up once more. "I wanted to ask you, Signora Ferraro, if you would consider checking in on Anabella while I'm gone?"

"Me?" She couldn't keep the incredulous tone from her voice. "I don't think that's a good idea, Dante. Have you spoken to Anabella about this?"

He shook his head. "I wanted to see how you felt about it first." Dante paused, looking off to the sprawling fields of roses behind Signora Ferraro. "This might not be my place, Signora Ferraro, but I must say

454

something. This needs to stop — you and Anabella not speaking to each other. It's crazy! We are all family and should be together, especially when Anabella and I live only ten minutes away. You know she wanted to be near you when we decided we were moving back to Pienza."

Signora Ferraro lowered her head as she looked at the ground. "I never asked her to come live near me," she said in a very soft voice.

"I'm sorry. I didn't mean to sound accusatory. I was just trying to let you know that she wanted you in her life, and I know she still does."

"Has she said that?" Signora Ferraro kept her gaze on the ground.

"No, but I know my wife. She misses you. Anabella always asks me how you are whenever the girls and I return home. And I know you miss her too just by the way you cook her favorite dishes whenever I eat here and always make sure to make enough for me to take back to Anabella."

Signora Ferraro blushed. So he'd figured out her ruse. But if he knew that the dishes she'd prepared for him were Anabella's favorite, then Anabella must've told him so. For a moment, she felt joy that Anabella had expressed to him that she'd loved the food her mother had cooked for her all those years. Perhaps Anabella hadn't completely closed herself off to her mother.

"So will you go visit your daughter?"

"I think you should make sure first that your wife is all right with that. After all, it is her home, and I don't want to go where I'm not wanted."

"She wouldn't turn you away, Signora Ferraro, if that's what you're afraid of."

This young man was too perceptive. She turned her back to him, crossing her arms over her chest, pretending she was watching one of her workers as he harvested roses. Shortly after the last time she'd seen Anabella, Signora Ferraro had decided to hire more workers to run the farm. She couldn't handle it any longer. It was too much for her, and, with Anabella gone, Signora Ferraro's physical stamina had seemed to dissipate almost overnight. She'd even contemplated selling a portion of the land, but couldn't bring herself to do that just yet, although she knew there would come a time when she'd be forced to. Sighing deeply, her thoughts turned to when Anabella was a child, and she'd envisioned Anabella taking over the rose farm one day and then passing it along to her children so that the nursery would remain a family legacy. But

Anabella had her own life now — one that didn't involve Signora Ferraro or the farm.

"Let me go inside and get you some food. This way Anabella won't have to cook as much, especially after you leave for your trip and she'll be busy with the girls." Signora Ferraro walked toward the house, even though she could see Dante was about to say something.

He followed her into the house and sat down at the kitchen table as Signora Ferraro poured bowls of minestrone into glass storage containers.

"Why don't you come back to the house with us now? This way you can eat with us. I could help break the ice between you and Anabella."

"*Grazie,* Dante. But your wife will be upset with you for not giving her any notice." She resumed pouring the minestrone into the containers. Then she used a wet dish towel to wipe any soup that had spilled on the edges of the containers before placing the lids on. She walked over to the kitchen counter where an almond hazelnut cake she had baked that morning stood on a porcelain pedestal. She cut half the cake and wrapped it in foil.

"I used to make this cake for Anabella once a week. She couldn't get enough of it, and now her girls can't seem to get enough of it either." Signora Ferraro laughed softly.

Valeria and Mariella looked up and both said in unison, *"Torta! Torta!"*

Signora Ferraro bent down so that she was at eye level with the twins. "After you go home and eat your lunch with Papà and Mamma, then you will get to eat your cake."

"You come?" Mariella asked her *nonna.* Lately, the girls would play this game of continually asking her if she would go back home with them whenever Dante picked them up.

"No, my little angels. Not this time," was always her response.

Dante stood up, shaking his head. "I've never met two more stubborn women than you and my wife. What I would give to have my mother here. All I know is that if she were still alive and we had had an argument, I would do whatever it took to make amends. The two of you make me so mad." Dante pushed his chair roughly up against the kitchen table, startling Mariella and Valeria, who began to cry.

"I'm sorry, Dante. I didn't mean to upset you." Signora Ferraro patted the cheeks of the twins with her aprons, drying their tears.

"Just think about what I said. Will you promise me that?" He looked into her eyes.

She looked down. "I will."

Dante picked up the girls and headed outside.

"Oh, the food, Dante. I'll carry it to the car for you."

Once they reached Dante's car and he had placed the twins inside, he took the food from Signora Ferraro. He leaned over and kissed her on both cheeks, stunning her. He had never kissed her before.

"We care about you very much. Remember that. Thank you for the food." He smiled and turned around, but Signora Ferraro placed a hand on his arm.

"Dante, I have never thanked you for bringing the girls here, and I have never apologized to you for the horrible way I acted toward you when you first came here, asking for my permission to see Anabella. You are a good man, and I am very happy my daughter is with you. I don't deserve your kindness."

"You were just trying to protect your daughter. Thank you, Signora Ferraro. I accept your apology. As for bringing the girls here, I could not live with myself if they didn't know their grandmother, and, while Anabella doesn't say so, I know it also makes her happy that Mariella and Valeria get to spend time at the farm with their

459

grandmother. *Arrivederci.*"

"*Arrivederci.* Drive safely even though it's a short trip." She smiled as she waved to Dante and the girls, waiting until they drove down the road.

Signora Ferraro walked slowly to her special white rose garden. When she reached it, she sat on the small white bench and looked at her perfect roses. The air was filled with their fragrance, and she inhaled deeply.

Everything Dante had said was true. She had never seen it from another perspective until he brought up how he couldn't understand her continued estrangement from Anabella. No wonder he had become so angry. She felt shame once again. For Dante had lost his mother and wished she were still here so he could see and talk to her, whereas Signora Ferraro was still alive, yet she and Anabella chose to remain apart.

Perhaps Signora Ferraro should go to her instead of waiting for Anabella to make the first move? She had been worried when Dante mentioned he would be away in Florence for two weeks. Anabella needed help. Signora Ferraro knew Chiara went to visit Anabella. They had remained friends, and even Chiara had tried to talk sense into Signora Ferraro, asking her to go to her daughter. But Chiara was now married and

460

had her own family to look after. She couldn't go and stay with Anabella for two weeks and help her with twin toddlers.

"What should I do, Franco?" Signora Ferraro looked up to the sky as she said this aloud.

But she didn't need to ask Franco — for she knew what his answer would be. Without a shred of doubt, she was certain that he must be ashamed and angry with her that she had turned away their child.

"I was just so tired of being hurt, Franco. So tired of losing those I loved. And yes, I was angry with her too for choosing Dante over me. I know. I was a selfish fool, thinking she would never grow up and leave my side." She laughed. "Can you believe what has become of me, Franco? Do you recognize this woman? I am a far cry from the assertive, confident, and independent young woman you met and fell in love with. Losing you, and Papà, Michele, and Enza, turned me into this shell of a woman who became so needy that she smothered her only child. No wonder she left me."

Tears slid down her face as she whispered, "Forgive me, Franco. Forgive me."

CHAPTER 31
ANABELLA

Pienza, 1974

The stitches lined up neatly on the sundress Anabella was sewing on her machine for Valeria. She had made an identical one for Mariella and was now finishing up Valeria's. It was midnight, and she worked quickly so she would finish soon and be able to go to bed. She was exhausted and, with Dante in Florence, her fatigue had only intensified since she didn't have him to help her. Although he was always busy with his paintings, whatever help he could give was better than nothing.

She smiled as she did her work, thinking about how Dante had surprised her with the sewing machine as a gift after she'd had the twins. Mamma had taught her how to sew when she was a child. Anabella had missed not having a sewing machine, especially now that she had Valeria and Mariella, and longed to make their clothes as her mother had done for her. Suddenly, a memory flashed before her eyes of when she was five years old and she and her mother had worn matching pale yellow dresses, which her mother had sewn for them. From the yellow roses Anabella loved to the lemon chiffon dress she had worn as a teenager on Easter Sunday, yellow had always been her favorite color. Maybe that was why she also had grown to love sunflowers so much. Anabella remembered clearly that day when she was little and had been walking hand in hand with her mother to church in their new dresses; she had glanced up at her mother every few seconds and couldn't stop giggling over the fact that they were wearing matching dresses. After that, Signora Ferraro had made a few other matching outfits for them. Perhaps Anabella should make matching dresses for herself and the twins. That way the three of them could wear them together to church one day just as she had done with Mamma. The thought made her giggle softly to herself. But as always, whenever she thought about her mother a sadness soon enveloped her.

How many times had Dante tried to convince her to go talk to her mother or pick up the phone? She had thought she would be able to get out of the car and at least exchange a simple greeting with her the few times she had accompanied Dante to drop off the girls at the rose farm. But Anabella had felt paralyzed and could not step out of the car. She couldn't even look at her mother and had used the wide brim of her straw hat to shield her face.

Whenever she thought about the ugly words her mother had uttered to her that day when she'd visited her to tell her she was pregnant, a knife went through her. She couldn't bear feeling that way again. What if Mamma spoke to her like that again if she called her or went to the farm? True, she had said horrible things back to Mamma, which she regretted, but she'd been so angry that her own mother was turning her away and at a time when she needed her. How could she forgive that?

Anabella finished up the last stitching on the dress and examined it. Content with her work, she laid it on top of the pile of clothes that needed to be ironed. Mariella and Valeria would love the dresses. Anabella rubbed her eyes and looked around her. Dante had provided a good life for them just as he'd promised he would. He was now a much sought-after artist in both Florence and Siena. And next month, he would have an exhibit in Milan as well. They had bought this house soon after they returned from Florence. Dante and her daughters had made her very happy. If only she could have all the people she loved in her life.

Anabella stood up, and suddenly the room spun before her. She stumbled over to the nearest wall, bracing herself against it as she tried to fight off the sharp wave of vertigo that had hit her. Lately, she'd been having dizzy spells, which she attributed to either being dehydrated or not eating enough or sleeping enough. She needed to start taking better care of herself, but often she forgot to eat or drink or even sometimes bathe with all the demands of her children.

Pressing her forehead to the wall, she waited for the vertigo to pass. It usually just took a few seconds. She waited, but it seemed to intensify. Making her way to the kitchen slowly, she went over to the sink and splashed water on her face. But when she was done, she felt herself beginning to lose consciousness as her body felt weaker. *The girls!* she thought to herself. Using whatever little strength she had left, she did her best to stay conscious as she went over to the phone that hung on the wall, next to the refrigerator. She waited as the phone on the other end of the line seemed to ring forever. Her body felt cold as she began to

465

sweat profusely.

"Pronto."

"Mamma! Please come quickly. I'm not feeling well. I think I'm about to faint. The girls are alone."

"Anabella?"

"Hurry, Mamma. I can't hold on any longer." Anabella let the phone hang from the receiver as she slumped down to the ground and lost consciousness.

CHAPTER 32
DANTE

Pienza, 1975

Dante painted a few last strokes on his canvas before stepping away from it and examining it. The painting was the first he'd ever done of Signora Ferraro's rose garden. He couldn't believe he hadn't thought to capture the roses in any of his paintings before. But now that he'd been living here for the past year, he'd found inspiration in the gorgeous flowers.

Signora Ferraro and the girls waved to him as they made their way slowly over to him. His mother-in-law had been out picking roses with Valeria and Mariella, who never tired of collecting the flowers and setting them up in small vases in the room they shared in Signora Ferraro's house. Sometimes they made a mess as they pulled the petals off their stems and scattered them all over the house, but their grandmother never scolded them. If anything, she spoiled them too much. The girls loved it here and had stopped asking months ago when they would be going back home.

"It's hot out there." Signora Ferraro tugged at the collar of her shirtwaist dress as she fanned herself with her straw hat.

"Let's go inside and have something to drink."

He began to head back to the house, but noticed Signora Ferraro remained rooted in place. Dante glanced over his shoulder. "Are you coming, Signora Ferraro?"

She was staring at the painting he'd completed.

"Ah! That was supposed to be a surprise for you."

Signora Ferraro looked up, stunned. Her hand was over her mouth as tears filled her eyes.

"You don't like it?" Dante held out his hands as if he were hurt.

Signora Ferraro playfully swatted his arm. "I love it! It's just strange to see myself in it. You've captured the rose garden perfectly, and the children look gorgeous!"

"You can hang it up on that bare wall you have over the dining room table."

The painting depicted Signora Ferraro picking roses with Valeria and Mariella in the garden. She held a rose out to the girls as they leaned forward to smell the flower. Signora Ferraro's face glowed as she looked at her granddaughters. There was no doubt of the love that was evident in her features.

"*Grazie,* Dante." She walked over and embraced him. He hugged her back.

They had grown close in the past year, and not just because he was living here. For they both now stood to lose the love of their life — Anabella.

Signora Ferraro and Dante had bonded over their shared goal of helping Anabella fight her battle with leukemia. Ever since that night when Signora Ferraro had rushed over to their house after Anabella had fainted, she hadn't left her daughter's side. Chiara had met Signora Ferraro at their house, and she had stayed behind with the twins as Signora Ferraro rode with Anabella in the ambulance on the way over to the hospital.

Dante had driven as fast as possible from Florence, and when he arrived at the hospital, he'd found Signora Ferraro and Anabella talking. They were laughing and reminiscing about when she was a child. When he stepped into the room and saw Anabella, he knew immediately she was seriously ill, even though they were still waiting for the test results. He just sensed it. Dante had barely been able to keep his voice from shaking as he spoke to her, and Signora Ferraro, noticing immediately that he was about to lose his composure, had quickly filled in the gaps with conversation, giving him time to regain his strength.

After the doctor had told them Anabella had leukemia, he had walked over to the patient waiting area and had broken down crying. Thankfully, no one besides him and Signora Ferraro had been present. His mother-in-law had taken him into her arms and comforted him, much the way he knew his own mother would have if she were still alive. Signora Ferraro had cried too, but she had been more in control than he was, at least at that moment. He was certain when she was alone, she must've been beside herself.

So Anabella had begun her chemo treatments right away. And when she was able to return home, Signora Ferraro had asked them if they wanted to stay at the rose farm. This way, Dante could continue to work, and she could help out with the twins as well as care for Anabella. Dante had been worried that it would be too much for Signora Ferraro, but when he'd spoken to Anabella about it, she had wasted no time in saying she wanted to return to her childhood home and make up for all the time she'd lost these past few years being estranged from her mother. He knew Anabella was thinking what both he and Signora Ferraro had thought about every day since they learned of her illness — that she might not have more time. True, the doctors had said the cancer was at an intermediate stage, and she had a good chance of beating it, but Dante knew he had to prepare for the worst in case that happened.

During the day, he told Anabella jokes and played with the girls, making sure the atmosphere was as positive as possible. But at night, he lay awake, imagining what his days would be like if he lost the love of his life. He should've known it was too good to be true — meeting the woman he had dreamed about night after night, and then discovering she was this incredibly sweet, wonderful person.

"I was beginning to think you all had gone off to some party." Anabella made her way over to them with the help of a cane. Some days when the chemo treatments had left her feeling especially weak, she resorted to getting around in a wheelchair, which the twins loved since they would sit in her lap and ask her to take them for a ride. But Dante had had to limit these "rides," for

Anabella never complained in front of the children or mentioned if they were hurting her while in her lap.

"Anabella, it's too hot here. We should go back inside." Signora Ferraro rushed to her daughter's side.

"I'm fine, Mamma. Please. It's good for me to get fresh air. Dr. Biaggi said so as well."

"Well, let me go get a pitcher of rose water so we can at least have something to drink." Signora Ferraro smiled and patted Anabella's arm before she walked toward the house.

"Mamma, look at my roses." Mariella held out her small basket of roses to Anabella.

"*Belli.* Do you like living here more than our house, Mariella?"

"Sometimes!" Mariella giggled.

"And what about you, Valeria?"

"I like it here, but I miss the sunflowers. Why doesn't Nonna have sunflowers, too?"

Signora Ferraro walked out just in time to hear Valeria's question. She stopped and paled considerably. Anabella quickly changed the topic.

"Ah! Let us have some rose water, and then we can go inside and have Nonna's special biscotti that she made." Anabella busied herself with pouring rose water into

472

glasses for the girls. Dante noticed how her hand shook, but he didn't offer to help. She had rebuked him every time he'd done so for the first few months of her illness. Though she had made considerable strides, she still had a ways to go to regain her former strength.

Signora Ferraro put down the pitcher of rose water and excused herself.

"I will go get the plate of biscotti. I'll be right back."

Anabella and Dante looked at each other.

"You know how weird she gets about sunflowers. I've just learned to ignore it." Anabella shrugged her shoulders.

Dante frowned. He had noticed that Signora Ferraro never ventured into the basement where he'd been working and storing his paintings. He had tried to show her once a few of the portraits he'd made of Anabella standing in their sunflower garden. After they'd purchased their house in Pienza, Anabella had started gardening. She had planted an assortment of flowers, from lavender to hydrangeas and even roses. But she had wanted most of the garden to have sunflowers. For she said they reminded her of when she and Dante first fell in love and of course of Dante's dreams of her running through the sunflower field and later his painting her among the flowers.

"*Biscotti e* Nutella . . . *biscotti e* Nutella!" Signora Ferraro sang this little chant whenever she brought out two of the twins' favorite desserts. Soon Anabella, Mariella, and Valeria were singing along with her as well.

Dante laughed. He watched as Signora Ferraro and Anabella spread generous dollops of Nutella on the biscotti, which were huge. Naturally, the girls would never finish the biscotti.

"I'm going to head down to the basement and get some more work done." Dante kissed Anabella on the forehead before he took his leave.

"You work too much, Dante," Signora Ferraro said. Concern filled her eyes. He was touched that she worried about him.

"Painting isn't work for me. It's my passion, and I can't live without it." *Just like Anabella,* he couldn't help thinking, but fortunately, he'd had the sense not to utter it aloud.

An hour later, Signora Ferraro made her way down the creaking stairs of her basement. Dante was so absorbed in his work that he didn't hear her until he saw a shadow over his canvas.

"Ah! Signora Ferraro, you startled me.

What are you doing down here? You never come down here."

Signora Ferraro didn't answer. Her eyes traveled from painting to painting that lined the walls of the basement and even covered much of the floor. In a few of the corners, rows of easels stood with more completed work. Though he had begun painting other subjects besides Anabella after they were married, in the past year he had returned to painting his favorite subject. He'd even pleaded with Anabella to pose for a few when she'd begun feeling stronger, but he was always certain to have her sitting comfortably or even lying in bed.

"I'm not beautiful anymore," Anabella had told him.

She had lost much of her hair after her chemo treatments and kept her head covered in vividly colored silk scarves.

"You are still as beautiful as the first time I saw you in my dreams, if not more so. Every day I notice something new and radiant about you. That is why I've returned to making you my sole subject in my work."

Dante's cheeks flushed a bit as he remembered the small lie he had told his wife. While it was true that he did notice another beautiful aspect of Anabella on a daily basis, it wasn't the only reason why he'd returned

475

to creating so many paintings of her.

"These are breathtaking," Signora Ferraro said.

Dante watched her as she walked slowly around the room looking at each of the canvases.

"You are so talented, Dante. No wonder my daughter fell in love with you, and look at how beautiful you've made my daughter appear even now that she is . . ." Her voice caught as her eyes filled with tears.

"Well, I have Anabella to thank just as much for my success. She has been the perfect muse." He began wiping the paint from his hands as he went to stand by Signora Ferraro.

"Dante, may I be frank with you?"

"Of course. I would think after all we've been through, especially the past year, you would feel comfortable always speaking freely with me."

"I am worried about you."

Once again, Signora Ferraro's eyes filled with concern as she looked at him. He put his arm around her shoulders.

"I am fine. How can I not be? I have my wife, my daughters, and a wonderful mother-in-law, all living under one roof. We are finally a real family. And I know Anabella will be fine." Dante's voice shook a little as he spoke this last sentence.

"Please, Dante. You don't need to pretend or be strong in front of me. I see how terrified you are of losing Anabella, and, after seeing your studio here, I know it for certain."

Dante knitted his brows. "What do you mean?"

"You have been painting almost nonstop except for when you go to Siena to sell your work. Although I haven't seen these paintings until now, Anabella had mentioned to me that you had resumed using her as your main subject. And she, too, expressed worry to me that you were working too hard. She's afraid you're trying to bury yourself in your work so you won't be faced with the possibility that she might not make it. But now that I see just how many paintings you have created, I see this has become an obsession for you."

"That is absurd! This is my livelihood, and, with Anabella's medical bills, I cannot afford to start taking it easy!" He turned his back on Signora Ferraro and busied himself with adding a few more strokes to the painting he was working on.

"Please, Dante, don't be offended. I know you are painting at a frenzied pace and only painting Anabella because you are trying to ensure she stays alive if she does not make it. And don't tell me I'm wrong. Anabella told me how, when you first met her, you admitted to her that initially it was difficult for you to part with your paintings of her. And she's noticed you are not taking as many paintings as you normally do for your exhibits. But the real reason I know this has become an obsession for you is that it reminds me of my obsession."

Dante had stopped painting as he listened to Signora Ferraro's words, which were all true. He'd known deep down this was why he'd returned to making Anabella his sole subject in all his works and why he'd created so many. He needed to still have her with him if she died. He needed to remember every nuance of her expressions, every curve of her body, every detail of her beauty. He couldn't forget, but more important, he didn't want Valeria and Mariella to forget their mother. He was doing this as much for them as for himself.

He let out a deep sigh and went over to sit on the lower steps leading down to the basement. Signora Ferraro had returned her attention to the paintings. She was staring at one in particular. It featured Anabella, seen from the back, walking through a row of sunflower fields. Off in the distance, a hazy shadow of elaborate buildings stood.

"Is this supposed to represent Anabella leaving? Leaving our world?" Signora Ferraro looked up at Dante.

He paused for a moment before nodding. He then added, "You are quite good at analyzing art."

She smiled. "I've lived more than half a century. It doesn't take a master's degree in art history to understand life."

"That is true."

Signora Ferraro stared at the painting once more, but her attention seemed elsewhere as her eyes took on a faraway look.

"Is it true that you detest sunflowers?"

She looked up, slightly startled by the question. "How did you —" She stopped for a moment. "Ah. Anabella told you."

"She remembered you having very strong reactions to them when she was a child, and you forbid her from having them in the house."

Signora Ferraro looked incredibly sad. Dante instantly regretted asking her about the sunflowers.

"That is true, I am afraid. I scared her as a child and went into a rage when I saw she had sunflowers in her room. And whenever we drove by a sunflower field, I would scold her if she pointed them out to me. I didn't mean to frighten her or make her hate them too."

"May I ask why you started this rose farm, Signora Ferraro, especially since you didn't come from a family of farmers? It seems like such a huge undertaking for a single mother."

"It all began when I was a young woman, not long after the Germans had occupied Florence, where I lived with my family."

"Anabella told me when we were in Florence that you were originally from there. Why did you leave?"

"I had to. I had no one there any longer, and it wasn't safe — for me or for Anabella."

Dante waited for her to continue.

"You see, Dante, Anabella's father and I were part of the Resistance."

"You?" Dante could not hide the shock in his voice.

Signora Ferraro laughed as she lowered herself onto the step next to Dante.

"*Si.* This bitter old woman who overprotected her daughter and kept her secluded on this immense rose nursery worked for the Italian Resistance."

"I'm sorry. I'm just so shocked."

"It is all right. Sometimes when I think back to that time, I am still amazed that I became a part of it. But, you see, it is so true when they say that love can make you do the craziest things, not that working to rid Florence and Italy of the Germans was crazy. Besides Anabella, I've never been more proud of anything I have done — even more than starting this rose farm."

"Please go on, Signora Ferraro."

"I didn't always hate sunflowers. In fact, I used to love them. My father had a sunflower garden behind our house. He wanted to replicate in a small way the vast fields of sunflowers he'd see whenever he drove through the Tuscan countryside. Michele, my brother, and I used to love playing in the sunflower garden. And when I became a teenager and into my twenties, the sunflower garden was my haven where I could be alone and daydream. It was in my father's sunflower garden where I met Franco, Anabella's father. He immediately intrigued me. . . ."

As Dante listened to Signora Ferraro narrate the story of how she had met and fallen in love with Franco and how he had convinced her to work for the Resistance, Dante finally began to understand her and what had led to her fierce protection of Anabella. But he wasn't prepared for the details toward the end of her story as she related how her family had been taken from their home and burned in a leather warehouse with most of their other neighbors while she watched the flames engulf the building, knowing her loved ones were dying a torturous death . . . how she had witnessed Franco and two of the other members of the Resistance being executed in her father's sunflower garden . . . how she had walked up to the soldiers afterward and shot them.

"So you see I had to get Anabella out of there right away. We drove to Siena, where I rented a room from an old widow. I didn't know how long I would be able to stay there since I only had so much money on me. And then, just two weeks after Franco was killed, Florence was liberated. Can you believe that? Just two weeks." Signora Ferraro shook her head. "For months, I kept asking God why He couldn't have let Franco live. We were so near to the end. But it wasn't to be. The retreating Germans destroyed what they could of the city. They blew up all of its bridges except for the Ponte Vecchio, and they murdered many of the partisans out in public — in the streets and piazzas. Many of the people whom Franco and I had worked with in the Resistance were among those partisans who were murdered.

"After the Germans left, I returned to Florence. I packed up whatever valuables were left in my father's house and put the house up for sale. We went back to Siena. It took a little more than a year to sell my father's house. Once I had the money from the proceeds, we headed for Pienza.

"I bought this house and land quite cheaply. After I acquired the property, I tended the fields to rid them of their weeds and I discovered, the more I worked the land, the better I felt. It was easy for me to lose myself in the work and not think about the war and all I had lost. One day while I was out on the property, I began thinking about the white roses Franco gave me. He loved it when I wore one in my hair or attached it to my dress. So I decided to plant a small white rose garden. And then the other gardens followed soon afterward. Naturally, I had to wait until the following year for the roses to bloom in order to be able to start selling them, and I knew it would take a few years until I had enough roses to sustain a profitable business. So, until then, I lived off the savings my father had left behind, and I baked goods and sold them to the bakery in the village. I also took in whatever seamstress work I could get from the townspeople. Money was very tight, but we made it through, and then God blessed me with these roses. Once my gardens were in full bloom and word spread that I was not only selling the flowers but that they were among the most exquisite roses one could find for miles, Anabella and I never struggled again financially."

"So that is what you meant when you said you had your own obsession? You became obsessed with growing more roses and expanding the farm out of fear that you and Anabella would not have enough money to live off of?"

"No. I didn't get the idea for turning the rose garden into a business right away. Initially, when I planted the seeds for the rose garden, I was just going to have my one special white rose garden."

"Anabella told me about your special garden and how she was forbidden to take roses from it or to play in that garden. She also told me how terrible she felt that she had destroyed it when she was angry with you after you told her we could no longer see each other."

Signora Ferraro nodded. "Although it's taken me a long time, I have grown to realize she never meant to hurt me when she left with you. When I started that rose garden, it was in tribute to Franco's memory as well as to the memory of my family. I then started remembering other people I had known who had lost their lives in the war. So I decided to plant more roses in honor of them. And then I couldn't stop. The more people I discovered who had been killed in Florence, the more I wanted to honor them in this small way."

"So these roses represent all the lives that were lost in Florence during the war?" Dante thought about the vast rose farm. As he pictured all the roses, it became easier for him to envision just how many people had been killed. He suddenly felt moved in a way he had never felt before.

Signora Ferraro nodded in answer to his question. "As long as Anabella and I were alive to tend to the gardens and ensure there would be new roses every year, the memories of those who had died during the war would be kept alive in this small way. I suppose that is why I also took it so hard when she went off to Florence with you and started a new life. I thought there would be no one left to keep the garden going."

"But you have all of these workers."

"True, but even if the farm was bought by someone else and it continued to exist as a rose nursery, it wouldn't be the same. There wouldn't be one of my descendants to watch over my special white rose garden. My legacy — my family's legacy — would be lost. After Anabella and I were no longer talking, I imagined she would sell the farm once I died, especially since she was angry with me and probably wanted nothing more to do with the farm."

"You are so wrong, Signora Ferraro. She has missed the roses. I was hesitant about taking you up on your offer to come live here while Anabella recovered. I was afraid it would be too much of a burden for you to care for her and the twins, especially when I would be away. But as soon as I mentioned your invitation, she immediately said she wanted to be here. There was a light in her eyes that I hadn't seen since before that day we left for Florence. She loves you very much. And the rose farm will always be her home."

Signora Ferraro remained silent for a moment before resuming her story. "One night, Franco came to me in a dream and told me I had to start selling the flowers. He said they would be my salvation. I didn't realize it then that he wasn't just talking about my financial salvation, but also my emotional salvation. After he died, I cried myself to sleep every night. And even sometimes during the day when I was with Anabella, I

486

would sob uncontrollably. Poor Anabella would come over to me and plant little kisses on my face to make me stop. If it weren't for her and my rose farm, I would have had a complete nervous breakdown. I am sure of that."

"Franco came to you in your dreams just as Anabella came to me in mine." Dante looked pensive as he said this.

"*Si*. So now you know why I have this immense rose nursery and my obsession behind it. Now you know why the crazy rose lady became the way she did." Signora Ferraro wiped her brow with the back of her hand as she took a deep breath. "I've never told anyone this story before. And no one knows that I killed two men to avenge my husband's death and to protect my child."

Dante placed his hand over hers. "You did the right thing. I can't even imagine how frightened you were. Signora Ferraro, you are a very strong woman — a survivor. Never forget that or what you did for your daughter."

Signora Ferraro pursed her lips, closing her eyes tightly for a moment as if she were trying to close the chest of memories she had opened.

"Have you ever thought about telling Anabella? She knows so little about her father, and she doesn't even know the truth of how he died. She thinks he was a soldier."

"I thought I was protecting her by not telling her the truth about the horrific way that Franco and my family died. After all, how do you tell a child something like that? And then when she became an adult, I still couldn't bring myself to tell her — or rather I couldn't bring myself to relive those awful days. The pain . . ." Signora Ferraro took a deep breath before continuing. "The pain was unbearable. I'd never felt pain like that. I didn't want to feel such enormous grief again. Most of all, I wanted to shield Anabella from that ugliness, just like I wanted to guard her from the outside world so that no one could hurt her the way I had been hurt. Everyone is right. I am crazy. Who in life can escape being hurt? It was absurd that I thought I could control her fate. I see that now. I also acted out of fear of losing another loved one. After I lost my entire family and the love of my life, I couldn't bear ever being apart from Anabella. The irony is that I tried so hard to prevent Anabella from getting hurt, then instead I ended up being the one who hurt her terribly, and I pushed her away. I don't know how she has forgiven me. To think I've wasted these past few years by my stubborn refusal to go to her, and now I might lose her forever." Signora Ferraro placed her hands over her face as she wept into them.

Dante draped his arm around her shoulders. Signora Ferraro leaned into him, letting him comfort her.

"I don't know what Anabella and I would have done without you, Dante. You have been such a blessing. I think Franco sent you to us, knowing we would need you."

"And you and Anabella saved me. I, too, was lost after I lost my mother and grandmother. I know how difficult it was for you to share all of this with me, Signora Ferraro. Thank you. I hope you will consider telling Anabella. It would answer so many questions for her and even help her to see why you were so overprotective."

"Every time I see sunflowers, it just brings me back to that day when I watched my husband's execution. So now you know why I detest those flowers so much. But I must say your paintings of them are extraordinary, and seeing Anabella among them takes me back to when I was an innocent, young woman. Ah!" She sighed. "I will give more thought to sharing all of this with Anabella. So much guilt has plagued me over the years, especially the guilt that I have spoken so little about Franco to Anabella."

"Well, maybe it is time she gets to know how brave both of her parents were. Someday, I will share the story with Valeria and Mariella, so that they will know what amazing grandparents they had and the risks their grandparents took to ensure Italy would be free again. We all have so much to thank the partisans for."

"I never thought of it that way. Dante, I have lived with so much guilt — guilt that I lived when my family, husband, and so many others died. That is probably why I also never told anyone about my work with the Resistance. I didn't work with the Resistance for a sense of recognition or to receive any honors. I don't want people to commend me. But I promise I will think about telling Anabella."

"You've been an excellent mother, Signora Ferraro. Don't be so hard on yourself. We've all made mistakes." He glanced at his watch. "I think we should check on Anabella and the twins."

Dante stood and made his way up the basement stairs. When he reached the top of the stairs, he saw Signora Ferraro remained seated. She was staring at the painting of Anabella walking among the sunflower fields. He reflected on what she'd said about how Franco had appeared to her

490

in a dream, telling her the roses would be her salvation. And he thought about how Anabella had first come to him in his dreams, walking through a sunflower field. Was Franco trying to give them all a message? Was he possibly trying to tell Signora Ferraro that it was time for her to finally put the horrors of the past behind her?

CHAPTER 33
ANABELLA

Pienza, 1975

Anabella kept the window of the car rolled down as her mother drove through the Tuscan countryside. These days, she wanted to feel everything life had to offer, even the pain she felt on her bad days — for it reminded her she was still alive.

Mamma had suggested they go for a drive and leave the twins at home with Dante. Though she missed the girls whenever they weren't with her, it was nice to have some quiet time when she could reflect. Anabella also enjoyed the moments she and Mamma were alone and could catch up on all the conversations they had missed during the years they'd been estranged from each other.

What a fool she had been. Hadn't Dante pleaded with her on several occasions to forgive her mother and end the long feud they'd had? But she and her mother had been so alike in their stubbornness — and fear. She realized now that Mamma had been just as afraid as she'd been of being rejected. But what was important was that they were together again and living as a family. That gave Anabella comfort, especially if she didn't make it. Valeria, Mariella, and Dante would have her mother, and Mamma would have them. No, she could not think that. She *would* overcome this illness.

But just as soon as she was optimistic, the dark thoughts followed. Though there were times when she was incredibly angry that she might not live to see her daughters grow up and that she wouldn't have more time with Dante and Mamma, she had learned to make her peace with the possibility that she might die. God had given her so many blessings the past few years — discovering what it was like to fall in love, having a devoted husband and two precious children, and having her mother back in her life. Even her childhood had been special. True, Mamma had sheltered her too much, but Anabella couldn't deny how wonderful it had been to grow up in such a special, beautiful place as the rose farm. How she had missed it the years she wasn't talking to Mamma. Though she had planted a small rose garden on the property she shared with Dante, it hadn't felt the same. There was something about Mamma's rose garden — an ethereal essence she had always felt whenever she walked among the rows of rose bushes. She had previously felt it the most when she was a child, but lately, the sensation seemed the strongest.

Anabella was so lost in her thoughts that she hadn't noticed her mother had stopped the car until she heard Mamma say, "Let's get out and take a walk."

Anabella searched in her tote bag for her sunglasses and straw hat. When she looked up, she froze. They were parked alongside a vast field of sunflowers. She turned to look at Mamma, but she was already outside walking farther into the dense rows of sunflowers. Was she feeling all right?

Anabella got out of the car and shouted, "Mamma, why did you stop here? Are you not feeling well?"

Signora Ferraro stopped and waited for Anabella to catch up to her.

"I'm fine, Anabella. I thought this would be a good place to stop and take a walk."

"But you hate —"

"Sunflowers." Signora Ferraro finished Anabella's sentence. "It's all right. I'm fine. Come. Let's walk." She linked her arm through her daughter's.

Bees were buzzing everywhere, and there was a light summer breeze. It was early August. Anabella hadn't seen the sunflowers in the countryside all summer since she had been too busy with the girls and hadn't felt well enough to take car drives. The chemo treatments had given her horrible bouts of nausea. But she had finished her last treatment a little over four weeks ago. Her hair was growing back, and, since she hadn't lost all of it, she was able to have a cute bob. She couldn't wait until her hair grew long again. For she missed it and had looked longingly at Dante's portraits of her when they'd first met and her hair was down to her waist. Did Dante miss her long hair, too? If he did, he never let on. He still looked at her and made her feel as if she were the most beautiful woman in the world — the only woman for him. Tears filled her eyes as she thought about how much she loved him. Had Mamma loved her father this way?

"Mamma, I don't think I've thanked you for all that you've done for me and the girls — and even Dante — since I've become sick. It means the world to me."

"*È niente!* It's my pleasure having you all with me. And of course I would do anything for you, just as I know you would do anything for me." Signora Ferraro looked at Anabella and gave her arm a squeeze.

"We are lucky to live in such a beautiful place," Anabella said as she took in the vast horizon of sunflowers before her.

"*Si, i girasoli sono bellissimi.* They along with our verdant green hills make Tuscany so enchanting."

Anabella looked at her mother, surprise etched across her features. "You think the sunflowers are beautiful? When did you have a change of heart?"

Signora Ferraro laughed. "I didn't always detest them, Anabella. In fact, I used to love them very much. And my father loved them even more. That is why I chose for us to live in Pienza when I left Florence, after your father died."

"Really? But I don't understand. Why did you tell me when I was a child and we drove by the sunflower fields not to look at them? Why did you get so upset that day when you found the sunflowers Chiara had given me in my room?"

Signora Ferraro stopped walking and released Anabella's arm. She took a few steps forward, shielding her eyes from the sun as she looked off into the distance.

"I'm so sorry I acted that way, Anabella.

Please believe me, I wasn't upset with you that day when I exploded in your room. I should have explained to you then, but I didn't know how. And I was afraid to share too much with you. You were so young, and there were questions I'm sure you would have had that I wouldn't have been sure how to answer."

She glanced over her shoulder at Anabella. Her eyes suddenly clouded over, and she turned her gaze away once more as she resumed talking.

"My father had a sunflower garden behind our house in Florence, and he always said he wanted to have sunflowers as beautiful as the ones in the countryside. He also always said he wanted to live out his old years in Pienza. But that never happened." Signora Ferraro's voice sounded very sad as she said this.

"My father, brother, and sister-in-law were taken by the German soldiers from our house one afternoon while I was out. They took them along with many of our neighbors to an abandoned leather warehouse and bound their legs and hands. Then they set fire to the warehouse. No one survived."

Anabella gasped.

"When I returned home and saw they

were missing and that there had been foul play, I tried to find them. I rode my bicycle to the police headquarters to see if they had been brought in for questioning. Then I went to where your father worked. He came back with me to my house. When we arrived, we saw the plumes of smoke coming from around the block where the warehouse was. I didn't suspect anything at first. But as I approached the fire, I noticed that many of the front doors of the houses on the streets were wide-open. Children's toys, articles of clothing, and other belongings from the households were strewn on the steps and in front of the property, as if people had left in a hurry. When I realized that they had probably been taken to the warehouse and were in there dying as I watched the flames flicker, I ran toward the building, still thinking there was a chance maybe they could get out alive. But your father knew it was impossible. He kept me from getting any closer."

"Why didn't you ever tell me? I just thought my grandfather died from old age, and I seem to remember you once told me that Zio Michele and Zia Enza died in a car crash."

"As I said before, you were so young. I didn't want to frighten you by telling you

498

they had been kidnapped and died an agonizing death."

"Why did the Nazis take them?"

"At first, your father suspected they had found out that Zio Michele and Zia Enza were working for the Resistance, but that didn't explain why they took the other neighbors, many of whom were innocent of any partisan activity, especially the old people and children. What crimes could the children have committed?" Signora Ferraro shook her head, and a look of disgust passed over her face. "When I saw they were missing from home, at first I thought it might've also been my fault."

"Your fault, Mamma? How?"

"Your father and I also worked for the Resistance." Signora Ferraro turned and looked at Anabella as she said this.

"Papà didn't die fighting in the war like you told me?"

"No."

"So you lied."

"*Si.* I thought I was protecting you."

"But you always told me when I was a little girl that we were not to keep secrets from each other or lie." Anabella was hurt.

"I know. I'm so sorry, Anabella. I didn't do it out of malice, please believe that. It is just that I always wanted to shield you from anything ugly or evil. And I couldn't bear to relive the excruciating pain I endured after my family and your father died. How could I expect you as a young child to hear about such horrors and to see your mother fall apart?"

"I remember now when I was maybe three or four, you would cry so hard sometimes, and I would kiss you to make you stop."

Signora Ferraro smiled. "*Si,* you did make me feel better, my sweet daughter."

"But you could've told me when I was older."

"I know, but at that point I had become so accustomed to trying to repress the memories, and, again, part of me thought it was best that you never knew what really happened to them."

"What did you and Papà do for the Resistance?"

"Your father had started an anti-Fascist newspaper, long before the war began and the Germans occupied Florence. Because his articles ranted against Mussolini and the Fascist regime, he had been arrested. I met him after he had managed to escape from jail; he was hiding in my father's sunflower garden." Signora Ferraro smiled as she remembered the first time she had laid eyes on Franco. "That was just a few months before the Germans came to Florence. I saw him again at the outdoor market a couple of weeks later, and that was when he asked me to join the Resistance. Naturally, I was reluctant at first, afraid of the danger I would be putting myself as well as my family in. I had suspected that my brother and his wife were also working with the Resistance, but it was a different group from the one Franco was affiliated with. So Franco, your father, told me I could write articles for his newspaper. He intrigued me, and I was also moved by the work they were doing. I began to want to do something as well. So at first I was just writing for the newspaper, but then I began delivering the newspapers, and then, behind your father's back, I delivered food, supplies, and even ammunitions to a few of the partisans who were staked out in the hills and elsewhere, waiting to attack the Germans."

"You did all of that?" Anabella's eyes widened as she looked at her mother, not knowing who this other woman she was describing was.

"*Si*, your mother who rarely leaves Pienza except to sell her flowers in Siena was this crazy young woman who refused to listen when someone told her that she couldn't do something. Believe me, your father began

501

to have second thoughts about having me involved. We fell in love almost immediately after meeting. He was afraid of losing me, and I was afraid of losing him, too. But how could I stop risking my life when I knew he wouldn't because he believed so much in what he was doing? And I began to realize how important it was that we follow through to the end and do all we could to restore freedom to Italy. So that was why I thought that possibly I was to blame for my family's being taken away and killed. I wondered if the Nazis had found out that I was also part of the Resistance. But then, after the fire, we found out that not all of my neighbors had been rounded up and killed. The German soldiers spared a few of them so that they could tell everyone in the village that they burned our loved ones in retaliation for the partisan attacks. As the partisans began having more victories, the Germans made it more of a habit to kill as many villagers as they could in retaliation. They hoped it would deter the partisans and stop the Resistance, but they were wrong."

"What about Papà?"

"He kept fighting and became involved in the more dangerous aspects of the work."

"No, Mamma. I meant how did Papà die?" Signora Ferraro took a deep breath and crossed her arms in front of her chest. Her lips quivered as tears slid down her face. Anabella walked toward her.

"You can tell me, Mamma. I'm here." Anabella wrapped her arms around her mother, holding her tightly.

"He died in my father's sunflower garden. You were only three months old and were sleeping in your crib. Something woke me up. Your father had planned to leave that morning for a dangerous mission. I don't know what the operation entailed. We had decided the less I knew the better, for I would've gone absolutely mad with worry. So I got out of bed and went downstairs. The front door had been left open, and your father's eyeglasses were lying on the floor, shattered. I ran back upstairs. I placed you in a picnic basket and hid you in the back of my father's bedroom armoire. Then, I grabbed the revolver we kept in the house and made my way outside. When I reached the back of the house, I saw your father and two other partisans he worked with standing in the garden with their arms raised over their heads. Two German soldiers aimed their rifles and shot them — over and over again."

"Oh, Mamma!" Anabella cried out.

Signora Ferraro leaned fully into her

daughter as she hugged her back. They both sobbed uncontrollably. Anabella could feel her mother's chest heaving against hers, and as she held her, she couldn't help but notice the sunflowers. No wonder Mamma had despised the sight of them. And now she had chosen to tell Anabella how her father had died in, of all places, a sunflower field. Was Mamma seeing Papà standing before her once again as bullets riddled his body? Why had she tortured herself by coming here?

Once Signora Ferraro composed herself, she continued. "Within seconds of your father's being shot, my thoughts raced furiously through my head, and I realized there was only one course of action I could take. Slowly, I walked up to the soldiers and shot both of them."

Signora Ferraro waited for Anabella's reaction, but Anabella only nodded for her to continue as she pushed back a few loose, wet strands of hair that were clinging to her mother's cheek.

"I had no other choice. If I had let them live, there was a chance they would've killed me and then gone to search the house. If they had found you —"

"It is all right, Mamma. You were protecting me."

"That's not the only reason I killed them. I admit that I also wanted to avenge your father's death. In that moment, when I saw them shoot him, a rage took over me, and I was determined they weren't going to kill any other of my loved ones. I had no family left but you, Anabella."

"Mamma, you have been through so much. I wish you had told me all of this a long time ago. I wouldn't have ever gotten angry with you for trying to protect me so much throughout my life. And now that I am a mother, I find myself wanting to shelter the twins. So I understand better why you behaved the way you did."

"Please, take it from me that you must allow your daughters the freedom to grow up. Let them get hurt. For none of us can ever truly escape that. I'm sorry, Anabella, that I sheltered you so much, both when you were growing up and even as a young woman. These past few years I have finally realized how many mistakes I made with you and how selfish I've been."

"No, no, don't say that, Mamma! I am the one who has been selfish. I should've come to you a second time, and, even if you turned me away again, I should not have given up so easily. How many times did Dante plead with me to go to you, but I

505

stubbornly refused."

"I suppose we are alike that way." Signora Ferraro smiled.

"That's what Dante says. Two stubborn mules." Anabella laughed.

"I didn't want you to be hurt the way I had been, Anabella. I never wanted you to experience the pain I had felt. In an absurd way, I didn't want you to fall in love and get married and possibly know the heartache I suffered after losing my husband."

Anabella noticed her mother's cheeks redden suddenly before she continued.

"And I was terrified of being alone." She shook her head. "I've been nothing more than a stupid, foolish woman who pushed her own sweet child away."

"It's all behind us now, Mamma. Let us not talk about these past few years anymore. What matters now is that we are all together. You have a growing family and God willing . . ." Anabella let her voice trail off.

Signora Ferraro gripped Anabella's hand and gave it a tug. "You will beat this illness. Do not give up hope."

"That's not what I was going to say, Mamma. Yes, there is always the thought that I might not make it at the back of my mind. As soon as it surfaces, I do my best to quickly push it out. My children and husband still need me, and you still need me. But I suppose a moment ago when I didn't finish my sentence, I was starting to give in to the dark thoughts once more. For I was about to say, God willing, perhaps I will have another child — a son to continue Dante's legacy."

"You must still dream, my daughter. That is what will get you through this."

"I'm so lucky to have you, Mamma. You have been a tremendous help to all of us since I've become sick. And it's been so wonderful to be back on the rose farm. I grew a few roses and sunflowers in my own garden, but I don't know, it's just not the same. Not only because it's a small garden, but also because you weren't there. And there's something about the rose farm. I don't know how to describe it, but ever since I was a child, it was as if there was a certain magical feeling to it, especially when I was in your special white rose garden, Mamma."

"You felt that way in my special garden?"

Anabella nodded. "I can't believe I destroyed it that day when I was angry with you, but I wasn't thinking. Not a day went by in the years we were estranged that I didn't feel guilty about vandalizing your garden. I know I apologized to you back

507

then, but again, Mamma, I'm so sorry."

Signora Ferraro held up her hand. "As you've seen, there was no permanent damage done. The roses grew back the following year."

They resumed walking through the sunflowers as they remained silent for a few minutes.

"You know, Anabella, I'm not entirely surprised about the feeling you have whenever you are in my white rose garden. I am moved so much to hear that. It *is* special, and not just because white roses are my favorite." Signora Ferraro stopped walking as she faced Anabella. "You see, your father is buried there."

"He is?" Anabella's eyes widened.

"I wasn't lying to you when you were a child and I said Papà was always with you." Signora Ferraro smiled.

"But he died in Florence."

"*Si.* But before I left, I buried him in the yard behind my father's house. And then once the war was over, when I had to go back to sell the house, I dug up his remains and brought them back here with me. That was how it all started — the rose farm. I just wanted to have your father near us, and, in addition to the garden's being his resting place, I also wanted it to be a tribute to his memory. Then I thought about the other people I had lost — my father, Michele, and Enza — so I planted another small rose garden for them. And then I thought about the other people I knew who had lost their lives during the war, so I planted more roses. And the gardens just grew and grew. Your father came to me in a dream and told me that the roses would be my salvation. We were struggling financially, so I considered his words and realized I could sell the roses and turn the huge property I owned into a nursery. But the roses didn't just save me financially. They also saved me emotionally. I wanted to die after losing your father. What kept me going was you. But still, I was so close to succumbing to a nervous breakdown. Instead, I poured all of my energy into the roses. So now you know why they have been so important to me."

"And everyone thought you were crazy," Anabella said in a sad voice before she realized what she had said. "I'm sorry, Mamma, I didn't mean —"

Signora Ferraro smiled. "That is okay. I know what everyone has thought about me. I've overheard the villagers gossiping about me and even a few of the workers. I don't blame them."

"It's so unfair, Mamma. You didn't deserve to be spoken of that way. If they only knew the sacrifices you made during the war."

"It's all right, Anabella. Now, you know everything, and I must say I finally feel a huge load has been lifted off my shoulders."

"Mamma, I must ask you. Why did you decide to tell me about Papà's death here among the sunflowers? It must be so painful for you."

"It's time I let go of the past. I've been its prisoner for too long. And seeing your husband's gorgeous paintings of the sunflowers and you in them reminded me of how beautiful they are and how much I used to love them. After all, it was in my father's sunflower garden that I first laid eyes on your papà. We even made love there for the first time. In fact, that was when you were conceived."

Anabella saw something she'd never seen in her mother's face before — a glow of happiness. She stared at the sunflowers as she no doubt was remembering that day she'd shared with Anabella's father.

"I should have remembered all of that instead of only seeing the evil that had happened in the sunflower garden that day."

"It's kind of strange, Mamma — my meeting Dante, who first saw me in his dreams walking in a sunflower field, and your past association with them."

"I know. It is a bit odd." Signora Ferraro glanced at her watch. "It's almost time for our midday meal. How about we clip a few sunflowers to give to the girls? I brought a pair of pruning shears with me. I'll clip extra to put in vases throughout the house."

Anabella's eyes met her mother's. She smiled before saying, "That would be lovely, Mamma."

CHAPTER 34
SIGNORA FERRARO

Fourteen years later . . .
Pienza, 1989

Signora Ferraro was enjoying the perfect afternoon in late May. No clouds were visible in the sky. And the roses had begun blooming. She sat in her wheelchair by the wooden table that stood on the porch in front of the house. As she sipped her rose water through a straw, she watched Mariella and Valeria, who were setting the table with the contents of a picnic basket. They were arguing, but Signora Ferraro wasn't close enough to hear. The girls were now eighteen and were as beautiful as their mother had been at that age.

Though she was now seventy-four years old and had suffered a stroke last year that had left her partially paralyzed on the left side of her body, Signora Ferraro still managed to get around the farm in her wheelchair as she continued to oversee the workers cultivating her roses. While she hadn't done the physical labor on her farm in quite some time now, she still wanted to participate in whatever small way she could. About ten years ago, Dante had decided he wanted to learn all about growing roses and take a step back from his painting. While he still painted and sold his work, he no longer traveled to Florence or Siena to have exhibits. After Anabella's illness, he had decided he wanted to be with his family more. Since he'd made so much money those first years with his paintings, he was able to cut back on the number of pieces he created. The rose business had made the most money it ever had since her son-in-law had come on board. It had surprised — but greatly pleased — Signora Ferraro when she learned Dante wanted to manage the nursery.

"Mamma! I was looking for you. I thought you were still in the greenhouse." Dante came over to her, holding a gardening hoe in one hand and a bottle of Peroni beer in the other. He bent over to kiss his mother-in-law on the cheek before taking a long swig of his beer. He'd begun calling her "Mamma" about fourteen years ago, and she hadn't objected when he first asked her if he could do so. She'd been honored that he thought of her as a second mother. And in turn, he came to feel like the son she'd never had. Franco would've adored Dante had he been alive to meet him. She was sure of that.

"It was beginning to get too warm in there. Besides, I wanted to see how the girls were coming along with the picnic."

Dante glanced over at his daughters. "Whoa! What are you arguing about? Enough! All you ever do lately is quibble between yourselves."

"Don't worry, Papà, we still love each other!" Valeria called out as she exchanged glances with Mariella, who broke out laughing.

Signora Ferraro shook her head. They had a lot of spunk. Is that what the young generation called it now? But what Valeria had said was true. While Valeria and Mariella did argue more as teenagers, they were still as close as ever, and she hoped it would always be that way.

"I'm afraid to see what the two of you cooked for our picnic today," Dante ribbed them, frowning, but then when they weren't looking, he winked at Signora Ferraro.

"Our cooking has gotten better, Papà! Nonna has been helping us with it, so I'm sure you'll see how much it has improved."

"You'll be wonderful cooks in no time, girls. I'm sure of it. Don't listen to your father," Signora Ferraro said.

"*Grazie,* Nonna. We love you!" the girls sang out in unison.

"*Ti voglio bene!*" Signora Ferraro replied. She grabbed her sunglasses, which she kept in the pocket of her skirt, and quickly pulled them on, not wanting the twins to notice her eyes were filling up with tears. It was silly that she would come close to crying every time they told her they loved her, but she couldn't help it. She noticed Dante was looking at her and smiling, but he didn't comment that he'd seen her tears.

"Mamma, you looked deep in thought when I was walking toward you before. I hope nothing is wrong?"

"Can't an old woman have some privacy, especially where her thoughts are concerned?" She made a face, but a soft smile escaped, letting him know she was only teasing him.

"Fine. Fine. You women are all the same." Dante shook his head.

Signora Ferraro hesitated before saying, "Well, if you must know, I was thinking about how lucky I am to have you for a son, and, if Franco were alive, he would've felt the same way."

515

Dante looked at Signora Ferraro. His eyes glistened as they filled with tears. He took a sip of beer before saying, "*Grazie,* Mamma. That means the world to me."

Normally, Signora Ferraro didn't express her emotions readily. That was why she'd paused before telling him what she'd been thinking about. But something deep inside of her had urged her to tell him, and now she was glad she had. It made her feel good to know she'd made Dante happy, especially after all of the happiness he'd brought to Anabella, her grandchildren, and even herself.

The door to the house swung open as Francesco came running toward them.

"Papà, Italy just scored against Brazil. You have to come watch the rest of the soccer game. I just know Italy is going to beat them!"

"All right, I'm coming, but it will be time soon for our picnic."

"But we're going to miss the end of the game!"

"Enough, Francesco! Your sisters have been working hard all morning cooking, and we cannot let their efforts go to waste. We'll record the game and watch it after we eat. Besides, if they go into overtime, we might still catch the end of it live."

"That's right, Francesco! You're not going to ruin our picnic!" Mariella called out to her brother.

"If it were a real picnic, we'd be having it on the ground or at a park somewhere, not on a porch table!" Francesco shot back.

Signora Ferraro glanced down, feeling guilty. For it was because of her that they could not have a real picnic. She'd tried to tell them they could lay out the picnic on the ground, and she could just eat her food in her wheelchair, but the girls had refused. She was touched at what thoughtful young women they'd become.

"Francesco!" Dante bellowed, lowering his face so his eyes met his son's.

"It is all right, Dante. Please, don't be upset with him. He didn't mean it," Signora Ferraro pleaded with him.

Francesco was beet red now. He looked down at his feet. Signora Ferraro noticed he had inherited the same trait his mother had had of staring at her feet whenever she was embarrassed — or in Francesco's case whenever he was in trouble, which seemed to happen a lot. With a rebellious streak, he reminded her a little of herself when she was young and had stood up to her father and brother. And he was a dead ringer for Franco. Dante and Anabella had named him "Francesco" in honor of Franco.

"I'm sorry, Nonna. You're right. I didn't mean it. I just forgot. You know I love you." He gave his grandmother the most charming smile she'd ever seen. Like his grandfather, he knew how to win over hearts.

"Come here." Signora Ferraro waved to him with her arm that was still good.

He walked over, glancing at his feet the entire way. When he reached her, he finally looked up and leaned forward, placing a kiss on both of her cheeks.

"I love you, too, Francesco. You're a good boy. Don't forget that. But you need to respect your father and even your sisters. I know that's not fair, but they are older than you. Someday, you will understand."

"What is all this yelling out here?" Anabella stepped out onto the porch, her hands on her hips.

"It's nothing," Signora Ferraro quickly said before Mariella and Valeria could rat their younger brother out. She whispered in Francesco's ear, "Now, go inside with your father and watch the game."

Francesco walked toward the house, avoiding his mother's gaze. Dante followed him, but stopped as he passed Anabella and gave her a light kiss on the lips. Signora Ferraro was amazed at how he never failed to shower affection on his wife throughout the day. And she noticed they still looked at each other as they had that first day all those years ago when they'd come to her, asking for her blessing. To think she had almost put an end to their union. She shuddered now to think of the grave mistake she had made. Thankfully, Anabella had rebelled and not listened to her.

As Anabella walked toward her, Signora Ferraro admired the burnt-orange sundress her daughter was wearing — a dress Anabella had made herself. Though she was now forty-five, she looked as beautiful, if not more beautiful, than when she was younger. Just as Signora Ferraro had told her she would that day when Signora Ferraro had taken Anabella out to the sunflower field, Anabella had successfully won her battle with leukemia. And two years later, she'd given birth to Francesco. Signora Ferraro had thanked God every day since then that He'd answered her prayers. For once, He had not taken someone she loved from her.

"Dinner is ready, girls. Why don't you start carrying it out, and I'll be in to help you in a moment," Anabella called out to her daughters.

"Wait until you see what we cooked for

you, Nonna!" Mariella said as she and Valeria walked by. Signora Ferraro could hear them giggling as they hurried inside.

"How are you feeling, Mamma?" Anabella placed her hand on her mother's shoulder.

"Fine. Before you know it, I will have my full mobility back, and I'll be in your hair and the children's hair again." She patted Anabella's hand.

"You are never in our hair, Mamma."

After Anabella had recovered from her illness, she and Dante had asked Signora Ferraro if they could permanently stay on the farm. Signora Ferraro had been stunned. She'd always thought they would return to their own home once Anabella was better. But Anabella had told her she didn't want to be apart from her again. And the girls had loved having their grandmother with them every day. So they'd sold their house and moved in. Once Francesco came along, Dante had added an extension to the house, which gave them an additional two rooms.

"When you get old and become more reliant on others, you begin to feel like a burden."

"Mamma! Don't ever feel that way! You know how much we love you."

Signora Ferraro wiped the tears from her eyes with the back of her hand. "I'm sorry. I don't know what's gotten into me. I just feel more emotional today." Signora Ferraro thought about how she'd felt the overwhelming need to tell Dante earlier how much he meant to her.

"Ah! We all have our days like that. And I can relate to what you said about feeling like a burden when you become more reliant on others. Remember I felt that way when I was sick? And you chided me back then for feeling that way, just as I'm scolding you now."

"True. I must say we have been blessed these past fourteen years, ever since you recovered. Anabella, these have been the happiest years of my life — well, apart from when your father was in my life." Once again, Signora Ferraro managed to surprise herself with her candid sentiment.

"And these have been my happiest years — apart from when I was a child running among the roses." Anabella laughed. Signora Ferraro joined her.

They sat quietly for a few moments as they looked out over the rose gardens.

"You know, Mamma, ever since you told me how you planted the roses in honor of all those who died in Florence during the war, I have thought about them every day — the lost souls. I know I don't know their names with the exception of Papà, Nonno, Zio Michele, and Zia Enza, but I still think about them and the families they left behind."

"I always think about them too. Though it's painful to remember, it is also good to remember. I made the mistake of trying to repress those memories for so long."

"Allora!" Mariella stepped outside, carrying a ceramic baking dish.

"Ti voglio bene, Mamma," Anabella whispered.

"Ti voglio bene, mia figlia." Signora Ferraro smiled as she told her daughter she loved her. Anabella gave her a hug. Her hair had grown back to her waist, the way she'd worn it before she lost it during her chemo treatments. Signora Ferraro reached out and stroked it before letting her daughter go.

"Close your eyes, Nonna! Can you guess what's in the baking dish?" Valeria called out as she placed a pitcher of red wine on the table.

Signora Ferraro obeyed and closed her eyes. She could tell they had made manicotti, but she pretended not to know.

"I think I smell sauce, but I'm just not sure."

"Open your eyes now!" Mariella called out. Once Signora Ferraro had opened her

522

eyes, Mariella lifted the foil from the baking dish.

"Ah! *Manicotti!* My favorite! *Grazie,* Mariella and Valeria!"

Dante and Francesco joined them as they began eating. Signora Ferraro looked at her family and froze the moment in her mind. She wanted to remember this happy day forever.

After they had cleaned up, Signora Ferraro excused herself to go take her siesta. She wheeled her chair to her room and waited until Anabella came in to help her onto the bed.

"It's going to take two of us today," Dante said as he walked into her room with Anabella.

"I'm exhausted. Sorry, Mamma, but I'll tuck you in."

"Now I'm a baby!" Signora Ferraro said, pretending to be mad, but when her gaze met her son-in-law's and daughter's, the three broke out laughing.

Dante helped her onto her bed, and Anabella took her mother's shoes off.

"I don't know what I would do without you all. I have to be the luckiest mother and grandmother in the world."

"And we are the luckiest children and grandchildren to have you."

Anabella and Dante leaned over and kissed her on either cheek before they left to take their own siestas.

Soon, Signora Ferraro was fast asleep and dreaming. She was in her wheelchair, making the rounds of the rose garden. The roses always looked even more vivid in her dreams. Suddenly, her body felt light, and, when she looked down, she saw she was no longer in her wheelchair, but instead on a bicycle — the same bicycle she had ridden when she lived in Florence. How good it felt to pedal, and she then realized she was no longer paralyzed on the left side of her body. She giggled and pedaled faster.

As she traveled down the street of her childhood home, she recognized the route she was taking — it was the same route she'd taken when she had delivered the newspapers for the Resistance. Fear gripped her as she wondered if she was going to run into any German soldiers, but when she reached the Piazza del Duomo, she stopped her bike. People were on the steps of the famed Cathedral of Saint Mary of the Flowers, dancing and cheering. Cars sped by on the side streets as their drivers honked their horns. People were waving Italian flags and singing the national anthem. She resumed pedaling and made her way to the center of the piazza. People were holding signs that read "Victory!" And other signs proclaimed "The Germans are gone!"

Her heart leapt when she realized it had finally happened. Florence was free! She was free at last. Franco would be so happy. But then she remembered he was gone.

As she continued pedaling, she noticed the crowds were moving off to the side and waving to her. She nodded her head and smiled in acknowledgment. People raised their fists in the air and began chanting something in unison. It wasn't until the chanting became louder that she realized what they were saying: *"Grazie! Grazie!"*

Instinct made her glance over her shoulder. She was the only one riding down the path. She turned her attention back to the road, and it seemed as if everyone was looking right at her. Why wasn't there anyone else on his or her bike or walking behind her?

The street narrowed as she approached the Ponte Vecchio. The sun was setting over the Arno River, and she gasped softly — for it was the most breathtaking sunset she'd ever witnessed. She got off her bike and made her way toward the bridge. Throngs of people closed in on her, and for a moment she became frightened, until, one by one, each of them walked up to her and handed her a white rose.

"*Grazie,* Maria," they each said.

She looked at them, confused. Soon her arms were filled with long-stemmed white roses. Their white petals gleamed so bright. She'd never seen such a radiant white. When she looked up, she saw a trio of people standing a couple of feet before her. An old man and a couple. They were smiling and holding their hands out. They, too, held white roses. As she approached, she was able to make out their faces. Tears slid down her face. She opened her mouth to talk, but nothing came out.

First, the old man approached her. As he gave her his rose, he leaned forward and kissed her. "Maria! My brave, beautiful daughter."

"Papà," she said.

Then the couple approached her. They threw their roses into the large pile she was carrying and embraced her.

"Michele. Enza," she said through choked sobs.

"We are with you, Maria. We've always been with you," Michele said.

Enza took her by the arm and led her forward. "Come."

They walked to the wall of the Ponte Vecchio. The sun was even lower now in the sky, casting deep copper and bronze hues over the water. A man was staring at the sunset. When Enza and Maria were about a foot away from the bridge, Enza let go of her arm. The man turned around and smiled the most beautiful smile Maria had ever seen.

"Oh!" she cried out, falling to her knees. The roses spilled all around her. She could smell their sweet fragrance. Even her roses had never smelled this intense.

"You've finally come, Maria." Franco stepped forward and held a hand out to her.

She took his hand and let him help her to her feet. "Is it really you?"

Franco leaned forward and kissed her. And with that kiss, she knew without a doubt her husband was standing before her.

When they finally broke their kiss, Franco said, "I've been waiting so long, but now that you're here, it feels like you were never gone." He kept his arm around her waist, holding her to him while his other arm remained behind his back.

She leaned into him and breathed deeply, remembering his scent, and then ran her hand through his thick, wavy hair. Her mind raced back to the last night they had shared together as they made love again and again.

He was finally back in her arms.

"These are for you." Franco brought the arm he'd been keeping behind his back forward and held out a large bouquet of sunflowers.

She took them. Their bright petals, like those of the roses, seemed to be glowing.

"I don't understand, Franco. Why are all these people giving me flowers? Why are they saying thank you?"

"Think about it, Maria."

She looked into his eyes, and suddenly, she was taken back to her rose farm. Working so hard, always working so hard to plant more roses — the roses that would pay tribute to those poor souls who were lost during the war. Once more, she took in the crowds before her. They were still staring at her and smiling.

"You paid honor to them, Maria. Now they are paying tribute to you."

A strange sensation came over her, and then she knew.

"I'm not dreaming, am I?"

"No, my love. You've come home to me."

"But what about Anabella? She needs me . . . and the twins and Francesco need me, too."

"They're fine, Maria. You protected our baby after I was killed. You've done a wonderful job with her. I'm so proud of you."

She bowed her head as tears slid down her face. She thought back to earlier in the day when she had been surrounded by her family. A feeling of contentment had spread through her — a feeling that everything was as it should be. And she had told them all she loved them. It was true. They no longer needed her. Now, it was time for her to be reunited with the love of her life.

"I'm ready, Franco."

Linking their arms, Maria and Franco walked along the length of the Ponte Vecchio. Maria was still holding the sunflowers he'd given to her. As she admired their beauty, she couldn't believe she had ever despised them.

ABOUT THE AUTHOR

Rosanna Chiofalo is also the author of *Bella Fortuna, Carissima, Stella Mia,* and *Rosalia's Bittersweet Pastry Shop,* and *The Sunflower Girl.* An avid traveler, she enjoys setting her novels in the countries she's visited. Her novels also draw on her rich cultural background as an Italian American. When she isn't traveling or daydreaming about her characters, Rosanna keeps busy testing out new recipes in her kitchen and tending to her ever-growing collection of houseplants. She lives in New York City with her husband.

The employees of Thorndike Press hope you have enjoyed this Large Print book. All our Thorndike, Wheeler, and Kennebec Large Print titles are designed for easy reading, and all our books are made to last. Other Thorndike Press Large Print books are available at your library, through selected bookstores, or directly from us.

For information about titles, please call:
(800) 223-1244

or visit our website at:
gale.com/thorndike

To share your comments, please write:
Publisher
Thorndike Press
10 Water St., Suite 310
Waterville, ME 04901